# CY WHITTAKER'S PLACE

"'Isn't it a truly bell? Didn't it ought to ring?'"

[Page 91]

# CY WHITTAKER'S PLACE

By

## JOSEPH C. LINCOLN

Author of
"Cap'n Eri," "Mr. Pratt," etc.

WITH ILLUSTRATIONS BY
WALLACE MORGAN

**WILDSIDE PRESS**

TO

F. S. L.

# CONTENTS

vii

# CONTENTS

# LIST OF ILLUSTRATIONS

ix

# LIST OF ILLUSTRATIONS

# CY WHITTAKER'S PLACE

## CHAPTER I

### THE PERFECT BOARDING HOUSE

IT is queer, but Captain Cy himself doesn't remember whether the day was Tuesday or Wednesday. Asaph Tiddit's records ought to settle it, for there was a meeting of the board of selectmen that day, and Asaph has been town clerk in Bayport since the summer before the Baptist meeting house burned. But on the record the date, in Asaph's handwriting, stands "Tuesday, May 10, 189–" and, as it happens, May 10 of that year fell on Wednesday, not Tuesday at all.

Keturah Bangs, who keeps "the perfect boarding house," says it was Tuesday, because she remembers they had fried cod cheeks and cabbage that day—as they have every Tuesday—and neither Mr. Tiddit nor Bailey Bangs, Keturah's husband, was on hand when the dinner bell rang. Keturah says she is certain it was Tuesday, because she remembers smelling the boiled cabbage as she stood at the side door, looking up the road to see if either Asaph or Bailey was coming. As for Bailey, he says he remembers being

I

late to dinner and his wife's "startin' to heave a broadsides into him" because of it, but he doesn't remember what day it was. This isn't surprising; Keturah's verbal cannonades are likely to make one forgetful of trifles.

At any rate, whether Tuesday or Wednesday, it is certain that it was quarter past twelve, according to the clock presented to the Methodist Society by the Honorable Heman Atkins, when Asaph Tidditt came down the steps of the townhall, after the selectmen's meeting, and saw Bailey Bangs waiting for him on the opposite side of the road.

"Hello, Ase!" hailed Mr. Bangs. "You'll be late to dinner, if you don't hurry. I was headin' for home, all sail sot, when I see you. What kept you?"

"Town business, of course," replied Mr. Tidditt, with the importance pertaining to his official position. "What kept *you*, for the land sakes? Won't Ketury be in your wool?"

Bailey hasn't any "wool" worth mentioning now, and he had very little more then, but he mopped his forehead, or the extension above it, taking off his cap to do so.

"I cal'late she will," he said, uneasily. "Tell you the truth, Ase, I was up to the store, and Cap'n Josiah Dimick and some more of 'em drifted in and we got talkin' about the chances of the harbor appropriation, and one thing or 'nother, and 'twas later'n I thought 'twas 'fore I knew it."

2

# THE PERFECT BOARDING HOUSE

The appropriation from the government, which was to deepen and widen our harbor here at Bayport, was a very vital topic among us just then. Heman Atkins, the congressman from our district, had promised to do his best for the appropriation, and had for a time been very sanguine of securing it. Recently, however, he had not been quite as hopeful.

"What's Cap'n Josiah think about the chances?" asked Asaph eagerly.

"Well, sometimes he thinks 'Yes' and then again he thinks 'No,'" replied Bailey. "He says, of course, if Heman is able to get it he will, but if he ain't able to, he—he——"

"He won't, I s'pose. Well, I can think that myself, and I don't set up to be no inspired know-it-all, like Joe Dimick. He ain't heard from Heman lately, has he?"

"No, he ain't. Neither's anybody else, so fur as I can find out."

"Oh, yes, they have. I have, for one."

Mr. Bangs stopped short in his double-quick march for home and dinner, and looked his companion in the face.

"Ase Tidditt!" he cried. "Do you mean to tell me you've had a letter from Heman Atkins, from Washin'ton?"

Asaph nodded portentously.

"Yes, sir," he declared. "A letter from the Honorable Heman G. Atkins, of Washin'ton,

3

D. C., come to me last night. I read it afore I turned in."

"You did! And never said nothin' about it?"

"Why should I say anything about it? 'Twas addressed to me as town clerk, and was concernin' a matter to be took up with the board of s'lectmen. I ain't in the habit of hollerin' town affairs through a speakin' trumpet. Folks that vote for me town-meetin' day know that, I guess. Angie Phinney says to me only yesterday, 'Mr. Tidditt,' says she, 'there's one thing I'll say for you—you don't talk.'"

Miss Phinney boarded with the Bangses, and Bailey was acquainted with her personal peculiarities; for that matter so were most of Bayport's permanent residents.

"Humph!" he snorted indignantly. "She thought 'twas a good thing not to talk, hey? *She* did? Well, by mighty! you never get no *chance* to talk when she's around. Angie Phinney! Why, when that poll parrot of hers died, Alph'us Smalley declared up and down that what killed it was jealousy and disapp'inted ambition; he said it broke its heart tryin' to keep up with Angie. Her ma was the same breed of cats. I remember——"

The talking proclivities of females is the one topic upon which Keturah's husband is touchiest. Asaph knew this, but he delighted to stir up his chum occasionally. He chuckled as he interrupted the flow of reminiscence.

4

" There, there, Bailey! " he exclaimed. " I know as much about Angie's tribe as you do, I cal'late. Ain't we a little mite off the course? Seems to me we was talkin' about Heman's letter."

" Is that so? I judged from what you said we wa'n't goin' to talk about it. Aw, don't be so mean, Ase! Showin' off your importance like a young one! What did Heman say about the appropriation? Is he goin' to get it? "

Mr. Tidditt paused before replying. Then, bending over, he whispered in his chum's ear:

" He never said one word about the appropriation, Bailey; not one word. He wanted to know if we'd got this year's taxes on the Whittaker place. And, if we hadn't, what was we goin' to do about it? Bailey, between you and me and the mizzenmast, Heman Atkins wants to get ahold of that place the worst way."

" He does? He *does*? For the land sakes, ain't he got property enough already? Ain't a—a palace like that enough for one man, without wantin' to buy a rattletrap like *that*? "

The first " that " was emphasized by a brandished but reverent left hand; the second by a derisively pointing right. The two friends had reached the crest of the long slope leading up from the townhall. On one side of the road stretched the imposing frontage of the " Atkins estate," with its iron fence and stone posts; on the other slouched the weed-grown, tumble-down desolation of the "Cy Whittaker place." The contrast was that of opulent prosperity and poverty-stricken neglect.

If our village boasted one of those horseless juggernauts, such as are used to carry sightseers in Boston from the old North Church to the Public Library and other points of interest—that is, if there was a "seeing Bayport" car, it is from this hill that its occupants would be given their finest view of the village and its surroundings. As Captain Josiah Dimick always says: "Bayport is all north and south, like a codfish line. It puts me in mind of Seth Higgins's oldest boy. He was so tall and thin that when they bought a suit of clothes for him, they used to take reefs in the sides of the jacket and use the cloth to piece onto the bottoms of the trousers' legs." What Captain Joe means is that the houses in the village are all built beside three roads running longitudinally. There is the "main road" and the "upper road"—or "Woodchuck Lane," just as you prefer—and the "lower road," otherwise known as Bassett's Holler."

The "upper road" is sometimes called the "depot road," because the railroad station is conveniently located thereon—convenient for the railroad, that is—the station being a full mile from Simmons's "general store," which is considered the center of the town. The upper road enters the main road at the corner by the store, and there also are the Methodist meetinghouse and the schoolhouse. The townhall is in the hollow farther on. Then comes the big hill —" Whittaker's Hill "—and from the top of this hill you can, on a clear day, see for miles across the salt marshes and over the bay to the eastward, and west as far as the church steeple in Orham. If there happens to be a fog, with a strong easterly wind, you cannot see the marshes or the bay, but you can smell them, wet and salty and sweet. It is a smell that the born Bayporter never forgets, but carries with him in memory wherever he goes; and that, in the palmy days of the merchant marine, was likely to be far, for every male baby in the village was born with web feet, so people said, and was predestined to be a sailor.

When Heman Atkins came back from the South Seas early in the '60's, " rich as dock mud," though still a young man, he promptly tore down his father's old house, which stood on the crest of Whittaker's Hill, and built in its place a big imposing residence. It was by far the finest house in Bayport, and Heman made it finer as the years passed. There were imitation brownstone pillars supporting its front porch, iron dogs and scroll work iron benches bordering its front walk, and a pair of stone urns, in summer filled with flowers, beside its big iron front gate.

Heman was our leading citizen, our representative in Washington, and the town's philanthropist. He gave the Atkins memorial window and the Atkins tower clock to the Methodist Church. The Atkins

7

town pump, also his gift, stood before the townhall. The Atkins portrait in the Bayport Ladies' Library was much admired; and the size of the Atkins fortune was the principal subject of conversation at sewing circle, at the table of " the perfect boarding house," around the stove in Simmons's store, or wherever Bayporters were used to gather. We never exactly worshipped Heman Atkins, perhaps, but we figuratively doffed our hats when his name was mentioned.

The " Cy Whittaker place " faced the Atkins estate from the opposite side of the main road, but it was the general opinion that it ought to be ashamed to face it. Almost everybody called it " the Cy Whittaker place," although some of the younger set spoke of it as the " Sea Sight House." It was a big, old-fashioned dwelling, gambrel-roofed and brown and dilapidated. Originally it had enjoyed the dignified seclusion afforded by a white picket fence with square gateposts, and the path to its seldom-used front door had been guarded by rigid lines of box hedge. This, however, was years ago, before the second Captain Cy Whittaker died, and before the Howes family turned it into the " Sea Sight House," a hotel for summer boarders.

The Howeses " improved " the house and grounds. They tore down the picket fence, uprooted the box hedges, hung a sign over the sacred front door, and built a wide veranda under the parlor windows.

# THE PERFECT BOARDING HOUSE

They took boarders for five consecutive summers; then they gave up the unprofitable undertaking, returned to Concord, New Hampshire, their native city, and left the Cy Whittaker place to bear the ravages of Bayport winters and Bayport small boys as best it might.

For years it stood empty. The weeds grew high about its foundations; the sparrows built nests behind such of its shutters as had not been ripped from their hinges by February no'theasters; its roof grew bald in spots as the shingles loosened and were blown away; the swallows flew in and out of its stone-broken windowpanes. Year by year it became more of a disgrace in the eyes of Bayport's neat and thrifty inhabitants—for neat and thrifty we are, if we do say it. The selectmen would have liked to tear it down, but they could not, because it was private property, having been purchased from the Howes heirs by the third Cy Whittaker, Captain Cy's only son, who ran away to sea when he was sixteen years old, and was disinherited and cast off by the proud old skipper in consequence. Each March, Asaph Tidditt, in his official capacity as town clerk, had been accustomed to receive an envelope with a South American postmark, and in that envelope was a draft on a Boston banking house for the sum due as taxes on the " Cy Whittaker place." The drafts were signed " Cyrus M. Whittaker."

But this particular year—the year in which this

chronicle begins—no draft had been received. Asaph waited a few weeks and then wrote to the address indicated by the postmark. His letter was unanswered. The taxes were due in March and it was now May. Mr. Tidditt wrote again; then he laid the case before the board of selectmen, and Captain Eben Salters, chairman of that august body, also wrote. But even Captain Eben's authoritative demand was ignored. Next to the harbor appropriation, the question of what should be done about the " Cy Whittaker place " filled Bayport's thoughts that spring. No one, however, had supposed that the Honorable Heman might wish to buy it. Bailey Bangs's surprise was excusable.

" What in the world," repeated Bailey, " does Heman want of a shebang like that? Ain't he got enough already? "

His friend shook his head.

" 'Pears not," he said. " I judge it's this way, Bailey: Heman, he's a proud man——"

" Well, ain't he got a right to be proud? " broke in Mr. Bangs, hastening to resent any criticism of the popular idol. " Cal'late you and me'd be proud if we was able to carry as much sail as he does, wouldn't we? "

" Yes, I guess like we would. But you needn't get red in the face and strain your biler just because I said that. I ain't finding fault with Heman; I'm only tellin' you. He's proud, as I said, and his wife——"

" She's dead this four year. What are you resurrectin' her for? "

" Land! you're peppery as a West Injy omelet this mornin'. Let me alone till I've finished. His wife, when she was alive, she was proud, too. And his daughter, Alicia, she's eight year old now, and by and by she'll be grown up into a high-toned young woman. Well, Heman is fur-sighted, and I s'pose likely he's thinkin' of the days when there'll be young rich fellers—senators and—and—well, counts and lords, maybe—cruisin' down here courtin' her. By that time the Whittaker place'll be a worse disgrace than 'tis now. I presume he don't want those swells to sit on his front piazza and see the crows buildin' nests in the ruins acrost the road. So——"

" Crows! Did you ever see a crow build a nest in a house? I never did! "

" Oh, belay! Crows or canary birds, what difference does it make? *Somethin'* 'll nest there, if it's only A'nt Sophrony Hallett's hens. So Heman he writes to the board, askin' if the taxes is paid, if we've heard any reason why they ain't paid, and what we're goin' to do about it. If there's a sale for taxes he wants to be fust bidder. Then, when the place is his, he can tear down or rebuild, just as he sees fit. See? "

" Yes, I see. Well, I feel about that the way Joe Dimick felt when he heard the doctor had told Elviry Pepper she must stop singin' in the choir or lose her voice altogether. ' Whichever happens 'll be an improvement,' says Cap'n Joe; and whatever Heman does 'll help the Whittaker place. What did you decide at the meetin'?"

"Nothin'. We can't decide yet. We ain't sure about the law and we want to wait a spell, anyhow. But I know how 'twill end: Atkins 'll get the place. He always gets what he wants, Heman does."

Bailey turned and looked back at the old house, forlorn amidst its huddle of blackberry briers and weeds, and with the ubiquitous "silver-leaf" saplings springing up in clusters everywhere about it and closing in on its defenseless walls like squads of victorious soldiery making the final charge upon a conquered fort.

"Well," sighed Mr. Bangs, "so that 'll be the end of the old Whittaker place, hey? Sho! things change in a feller's lifetime, don't they? You and me can remember, Ase, when Cap'n Cy Whittaker was one of the biggest men we had in this town. So was his dad afore him, the Cap'n Cy that built the house. I wonder the looks of things here now don't bring them two up out of their graves. Do you remember young Cy—'Whit' we used to call him—or 'Reddy Whit,' 'count of his red hair? I don't know's you do, though; guess you'd gone to sea when he run away from home."

Mr. Tidditt shook his head.

"No, no!" he said. "I was to home that year. Remember 'Whit'? Well, I should say I did. He

12

was a holy terror—yes, sir! Wan't no monkey shines
or didos cut up in this town that young Cy wan't into.
Fur's that goes, you and me was in 'em, too, Bailey.
We was all holy terrors then. Young ones nowadays
ain't got the spunk we used to have."

His friend chuckled.

" That's so," he declared. " That's so. Whit
was a good-hearted boy, too, but full of the Old
Scratch and as sot in his ways as his dad, and if Cap'n
Cy wan't sot, then there ain't no sotness. ' You'll go
to college and be a parson,' says the Cap'n. ' I'll go
to sea and be a sailor, same as you done,' says Whit.
And he did, too; run away one night, took the packet
to Boston, and shipped aboard an Australian clipper.
Cap'n Cy didn't go after him to fetch him home.
No, sir—ee! not a fetch. Sent him a letter plumb to
Melbourne and, says he: ' You've made your bed;
now lay in it. Don't you never dast to come back to
me or your ma,' he says. And Whit didn't, he wan't
that kind."

" Pretty nigh killed the old lady—Whit's ma—
that did," mused Asaph. " She died a little spell afterwards. And the old man pined away, too, but he
never give in or asked the boy to come back. Stubborn as all get-out to the end, he was, and willed the
place, all he had left, to them Howes folks. And a
nice mess *they* made of it. Young Cy, he——"

" Young Cy!" interrupted Bailey. " We're always callin' him ' young Cy,' and yet, when you come

"'We *was* a spunky, dare-devil lot in the old days,
wan't we, Ase?'"

to think of it, he must be pretty nigh fifty-five now;
'most as old as you and I be. Wonder if he'll ever
come back here."

"You bet he won't!" was the oracular reply.

" You bet he won't! From what I hear he got to be a sea cap'n himself and settled down there in Buenos Ayres. He's made all kinds of money, they say, out of hides and such. What he ever bought his dad's old place for, *I* can't see. He'll never come back to these common, one-horse latitudes, now you mark my word on that! "

It was a prophecy Mr. Tidditt was accustomed to make each year to the crowd at the post office, when the receipt for the draft for taxes caused him to wax reminiscent. The younger generation here in Bayport regard their town clerk as something of an oracle, and this regard has made Asaph a trifle vain and positive.

Bailey chuckled again.

" We *was* a spunky, dare-devil lot in the old days, wan't we, Ase? " he said. " Spunk was kind of born in us, as you might say. And even now we're——"

The Atkins tower clock boomed once—a solemn, dignified stroke. Mr. Tidditt and his companion started and looked at each other.

" Godfrey scissors! " gasped Asaph. " Is that half past twelve? "

Mr. Bangs pulled a big worn silver watch from his pocket and glanced at the dial.

" It is! " he moaned. " As sure's you're born, it is! We've kept Ketury's dinner waitin' twenty minutes. You and me are in for it now, Ase Tidditt! Twenty minutes late! She'll skin us alive."

15

Mr. Tidditt did not pause to answer, but plunged headlong down the hill at a race-horse gait, Bailey pounding at his heels. For " born dare-devils," self-confessed, they were a nervous and apprehensive pair.

The " perfect boarding house " is situated a quarter of a mile beyond " Whittaker's Hill," nearly opposite the Salters homestead. The sign, hung on the pole by the front gate, reads, " Bayport Hotel. Bailey Bangs, Proprietor," but no one except the stranger in Bayport accepts that sign seriously. When, owing to an unexpected change in the administration at Washington, Mr. Bangs was obliged to relinquish his position as our village postmaster, his wife came to the rescue with the proposal that they open a boarding house. " ' Whatsoe'er you find to do,' quoted Keturah at sewing-circle meeting, ' do it then with all your might ! ' That's a good Sabbath-school hymn tune and it's good sense besides. I intend to make it my life work to run just as complete a—a eatin' and lodgin' establishment as I can. If, when I'm laid to rest, they can put onto my gravestone, ' She run the perfect boardin' house,' *I'll* be satisfied."

This remark, and subsequent similar declarations, were widely quoted, and, therefore, though casual visitors may refer to the " Bayport Hotel," to us natives the Bangs residence is always " Keturah's perfect boarding house." As for the sign's affirmation of Mr. Bangs proprietorship, that is considered the cream of the joke. The idea of meek, bald-headed little Bailey posing as proprietor of anything while his wife is on deck, tickles Bayport's sense of humor.

The perspiring delinquents panted into the yard of the perfect boarding house and tremblingly opened the door leading to the dining room. Dinner was well under way, and Mrs. Bangs, enthroned at the end of the long table, behind the silver-plated teapot, was waiting to receive them. The silence was appalling.

"Sorry to be a little behindhand, Ketury," stammered Asaph hurriedly. "Town affairs are important, of course, and can't be neglected. I——"

"Yes, yes; that's so, Ketury," cut in Mr. Bangs. "You see——"

"Hum! Yes, I see." Keturah's tone was several degrees below freezing. "Hum! I s'pose 'twas town affairs kept you, too, hey?"

"Well, well—er—not exactly, as you might say, but—" Bailey squeezed himself into the armchair at the end of the table opposite his wife, the end which, with sarcasm not the less keen for being unintentional, was called the "head." "Not exactly town affairs, 'twan't that kept me, Ketury, but—My! don't them cod cheeks smell good? You always could cook cod cheeks, if I do say it."

The compliment was wasted. Mrs. Bangs had a sermon to deliver, and its text was not "cod cheeks."

"Bailey Bangs," she began, "when I was brought

to realize that my husband, although apparently an able-bodied man, couldn't support me as I'd been used to be supported, and when I was forced to support *him* by keepin' boarders, I says, ' If there's one thing that my house shall stand for it's punctual promptness at meal times. I say nothing,' I says ' about the inconvenience of gettin' on with only one hired help when we ought to have three. If Providence, in its unscrutable wisdom,' I says, ' has seen fit to lay this burden onto me, the burden of a household of boarders and a husband whom——' "

And just then the power referred to by Mrs. Bangs intervened to spare her husband the remainder of the preachment. From the driveway of the yard, beside the dining-room windows, came the rattle of wheels and the tramp of a horse's feet. Mrs. Matilda Tripp, who sat nearest the windows, on that side, rose and peered out.

" It's the depot wagon, Ketury," she said. " There's somebody inside it. I wonder if they're comin' here."

" Transients " were almost unknown quantities at the Bayport Hotel in May. Consequently, all the boarders and the landlady herself crowded to the windows. The " depot wagon " had drawn up by the steps, and Gabe Lumley, the driver, had descended from his seat and was doing his best to open the door of the ancient vehicle. It stuck, of course; the doors of all depot wagons stick.

# THE PERFECT BOARDING HOUSE

" Hold on a shake! " commanded some one inside the carriage. " Wait till I get a purchase on her. Now, then! All hands to the ropes! Heave—*ho*! *There* she comes! "

The door flew back with a bang. A man sprang out upon the lower step of the porch. The eye of every inmate of the perfect boarding house was on him. Even the " hired help " peered from the kitchen door.

" He's a stranger," whispered Mrs. Tripp. " I never see him before, did you, Mr. Tidditt? "

The town clerk did not answer. He was staring at the depot wagon's passenger, staring with a face the interested expression of which was changing to that of surprise and amazed incredulity. Mrs. Tripp turned to Mr. Bangs; he also was staring, open-mouthed.

" Godfrey scissors! " gasped Asaph, under his breath. " Godfrey—*scissors*! Bailey, I—I believe —I swan to man, I believe——"

" Ase Tidditt! " exclaimed Mr. Bangs, " am I goin' looney, or is that—is that——"

Neither finished his sentence. There are times when language seems so pitifully inadequate.

## CHAPTER II

### THE WANDERER'S RETURN

HERE in Bayport, nowadays, the collecting of " antiques " is a favorite amusement of our summer visitors. Those of us who were fortunate enough to possess a set of nicked blue dishes, a warming pan, or a tall clock with wooden wheels, have long ago parted with these treasures for considerable sums. Oddly enough Sylvanus Cahoon has profited most by this craze. Sylvanus used to be judged the unluckiest man in town; of late this judgment has been revised.

It was Sylvanus who, confined to the house by an illness brought on by eating too much " sugar cake " at a free sociable given by the Methodist Society, arose in the night and drank copiously of what he supposed to be the medicine left by the doctor. It happened to be water-bug poison, and Sylvanus was nearly killed by the dose. He is reported as having admitted that he " didn't mind dyin' so much, but hated to die such a dum mean death."

While convalescent he took to smoking in bed and was burned out of house and home in consequence.

Then it was that his kind-hearted fellow citizens donated, for the furnishing of his new residence, all the cast-off bits of furniture and odds and ends from their garrets. "Charity," observed Captain Josiah Dimick at the time, "begins at home with us Bayporters, and it generally begins up attic, that bein' nighest to heaven."

Later Sylvanus sold most of the donations as " antiques " and made money enough therefrom to buy a new plush parlor set. Miss Angeline Phinney never called on the Cahoons after that without making her appearance at the front door. " I'll get some good out of that plush sofy I helped to pay for," declared Angeline, "if it's only to wear it out by settin' on it."

There are two " antiques " in Bayport which have not yet been sold or even bid for. One is Gabe Lumley's " depot wagon," and the other is " Dan'l Webster," the horse which draws it. Both are very ancient, sadly in need of upholstery, and jerky of locomotion.

Gabe was, as usual, waiting at the station when the down train arrived, on the Tuesday—or Wednesday —of the selectmen's meeting. The train was due, according to the time-table, at eleven forty-five. This time-table, and the signboard of the " Bayport Hotel " are the only bits of humorous literature peculiar to our village, unless we add the political editorials of the *Bayport Breeze*.

So, at eleven forty-five, Mr. Lumley was serenely dozing on the baggage truck, which he had wheeled to the sunny side of the platform. At five minutes past twelve, he yawned, stretched, and looked at his watch. Then, rolling off the truck, he strolled to the edge of the platform and spoke authoritatively to " Dan'l Webster."

" Hi there ! stand still ! " commanded Mr. Lumley. Standing still being Dan'l's long suit, the order was obeyed. Gabe then loafed to the door of the station and accosted the depot master, who was nodding in his chair beside the telegraph instrument.

"Where is she now, Ed ? " asked Mr. Lumley, referring to the train.

" Just left South Harniss. Be here pretty soon. What's your hurry ? Expectin' anybody ? "

" Naw ; nobody that I know of, special. Sophrony Hallett's gone to Ostable, but she won't be back till to-morrow I cal'late. Hello ! there she whistles now."

Needless to say it was the train, not the widow Hallett, that had whistled. The depot master rose from his chair. A yellow dog, his property, scrambled from beneath it, and rushing out of the door and to the farther end of the platform, barked furiously. Cephas Baker, who lives across the road from the depot, slouched down to his front gate. His wife opened the door of her kitchen and stood there, her

22

wet arms wrapped in her apron. The five Baker children tore round the corner of the house, over the back fence, and lined up, whooping joyously, on the platform. A cloud of white smoke billowed above the clump of cedars at the bend of the track. Then the locomotive rounded the curve and bore down upon the station.

"Stand still, I tell you!" shouted Gabe, addressing the horse.

Dan'l Webster opened one eye, closed it and relapsed into slumber.

The train, a combination baggage car and smoker, two freight cars and a passenger coach, rolled ponderously alongside the platform. From the open door of the baggage car were tossed the mail sack and two express packages. The conductor stepped from the passenger coach. Following him came briskly a short, thickset man with a reddish-gray beard and grayish-red hair.

"Goin' down to the village, Mister?" inquired Mr. Lumley. "Carriage right here."

The stranger inspected the driver of the depot wagon, inspected him deliberately from top to toe. Then he said:

"Down to the village? Why, yes, I wouldn't wonder. Say! you're a Lumley, ain't you?"

"Why! why—yes, I be! How'd you know that? Ain't ever seen you afore, have I?"

"Guess not," with a quiet chuckle. "I've never

seen you, either, but I've seen your nose. I'd know a Lumley nose if I run across it in China."

The possessor of the "Lumley nose" rubbed that organ in a bewildered fashion. Recovering in a measure he laughed, rather half-heartedly, and begged to know if the trunk, then being unloaded from the baggage car, belonged to his prospective passenger. As the answer was an affirmative nod, he secured the trunk check and departed, still rubbing his nose.

When he returned, with the trunk on the truck, he found the stranger, with his hands in his pockets, standing before Dan'l Webster and gazing at that animal with an expression of acute interest.

"Is this your—horse?" demanded the newcomer, pausing before the final word of his question.

"It's so cal'lated to be," replied Gabe, with dignity.

"Hum! Does he work nights?"

"Work nights? No, course he don't!"

"Oh, all right! Then you can wake him up with a clear conscience. I didn't know but he needed the sleep. What's his record?"

"Record?"

"Yup; his trottin' record. Anybody can see he's built for speed, narrow in the beam and sharp fore and aft. Shall I get aboard the barouche?"

The depot master, who was on hand to help with the trunk, grinned broadly. Mr. Lumley sulkily

" ' Is this your—horse ? ' demanded the newcomer."

made answer that his passenger might get aboard if he wanted to. Apparently he wanted to, for he sprang into the depot wagon with a bounce that made the old vehicle rock on its springs.

"Jerushy!" he exclaimed, "she rolls some, don't she? Never mind, *my* ballast 'll keep her on an even keel. Trunk made fast astern? All right! Say! you might furl some of this spare canvas so's I can take an observation as we go along. Don't go so fast that the scenery gets blurred, will you? It's been some time since I made this cruise, and I'd rather like to keep a lookout."

The driver "furled the canvas"—that is, he rolled up the curtains at the sides of the carryall. Then he climbed to the front seat and took up the reins.

"Git up!" he shouted savagely. Dan'l Webster did not move.

The passenger offered a suggestion. "Why don't you try hangin' an alarm clock in his fore-riggin'?" he asked.

"Haw! haw!" roared the depot master.

"Git up, you—you lump!" bellowed the harassed Mr. Lumley. Dan'l pricked up one ear, then a hoof, and slowly got under way. As the equipage passed the Baker homestead, the whole family was clustered about the gate, staring at the occupant of the wagon. The stare was returned.

"Who lives in there?" demanded the stranger. "Who are those folks?"

"Ceph Baker's tribe," was the sullen answer.

"Baker, hey? Humph! new folks, I presume likely. Used to be Seth Snow's house, that did. Where'd Seth go to?"

Gabe grunted that he did not know. He believed Mr. Snow was dead, had died years before.

"Humph! dead, hey? Then I know where he went. Do you ever smoke—or does drivin' this horse make you too nervous?"

Mr. Lumley thawed a bit at the sight of the proffered cigar. He admitted that he smoked occasionally and that he guessed " 'twouldn't interfere with the drivin' none."

"Good enough! then we'll light up. I can talk better if I'm under a head of steam. There's a new house; who built that?"

The " new " house was fifteen years old, but Gabe gave the name of its builder. Then, thinking that the catechising had been altogether too one-sided, he ventured an observation of his own.

"This is a pretty good cigar, Mister," he said. "Smokes like a Snowflake."

"Like a what?"

"Like a Snowflake. That's about the best straight five center you can get around here. Simmons used to keep 'em, but the drummer's cart ain't called lately and he's all out."

"That's a shame. I told the train boy that these smoked like somethin', but I didn't know what to call

26

it. Much obliged to you. Here's another; put it in your pocket. Oh, no thanks; pleasure's all mine. Who's Simmons?"

Gabe described the Simmons general store and its proprietor. Then he added:

"I was noticin' that trunk of yours, Mister; it's all plastered over with labels, ain't it? Cal'late that trunk's done some travelin', hey?"

"Think so, do you?"

"Yup. Gee! I'd like to travel myself. But no! I got to stay all my life in this dead 'n' alive hole. I wanted to go to Boston and clerk in a store, but the old man put his foot down, and here I've stuck ever sence. Git up, Dan'l! What's the matter with you?"

The passenger smiled, but there was a dreamy look in his gray eyes.

"Don't find fault, son," he said. "There's worse places in the world than old Bayport, and worse judgment than mindin' your dad. Don't forget that or you may be sorry for it some day." He sniffed eagerly. "Ah!" he exclaimed, "just smell that, will you? Ain't that fine?"

"Humph! that's the flats. You can smell 'em any time when the tide's out and the wind's right. You see, the tide goes out pretty fur here and——"

"Don't I know it? Son, I've been waitin' thirty odd year for that smell and here 'tis at last. Drive slow and let me fill up on it. Just blow that—that

27

Snowstorm of yours the other way for a spell, won't
you? Thanks."

The request to be driven slow was so superfluous
that Mr. Lumley paid no attention to it. He puffed
industriously at the Snowflake and watched his companion, who, leaning forward on the seat, was gazing
out at the town and the bay beyond it. The "depot
hill" is not as high as Whittaker's Hill, but the view
is almost as extensive.

"Excuse me, Mister," observed Gabe, after an interval, "but you ain't said where you're goin'."

The passenger came out of his day dream with a
start.

"Why, that's right!" he exclaimed. "So I
haven't! Well, now, where would you go, if you
was me? Is there a hotel or tavern or somethin'?"

"Yup. There's the Bayport Hotel. 'Tain't exactly a hotel, neither. We call it the perfect boardin'
house 'round here. You see——"

He proceeded to tell the story of "the perfect
boarding house." His listener seemed greatly interested, and although he laughed, did not interrupt until the tale was ended.

"So!" he said, chuckling. "Bailey Bangs, hey?
Stub Bangs! Well, well! And he married Ketury
Payson! How in time did he ever find spunk enough
to propose? And Ketury runs the perfect boardin'
house! Well, that ought to be job enough for one
woman. She runs Bailey, too, on the side, I s'pose?"

"You bet you! He don't dast to say 'boo' to a chicken when she's 'round. I say, Mister! I don't know's I know your name, do I? I judge you've been here afore so——"

"Yes, I've been here before. Whose is that big place up there across our bows? The one with the cupola on the main truck?"

"That, sir," said Mr. Lumley, oratorically, "belongs to the Honorable Heman G. Atkins, and it's probably the finest in this county. Heman is our representative in Washin'ton, and—— Did you say anything?"

The passenger had said something, but he did not repeat it. He was leaning from the carriage and gazing steadily up the slope ahead. And his gaze, strange to say, was not directed at the imposing Atkins estate, but at its opposite neighbor, the old "Cy Whittaker place."

Slowly, laboriously, Dan'l Webster mounted the hill. At the crest he would have paused to take breath, but the driver would not let him.

"Git along, you!" he commanded, flapping the reins.

And then Mr. Lumley suffered the shock of a surprise. The hitherto cool and self-possessed occupant of the rear seat seemed very much excited. His big red hand clasped Mr. Lumley's over the reins, and Dan'l was brought to an abrupt standstill.

"Heave to!" he ordered, sharply, and the tone

was that of one who has given many orders and expects them to be obeyed. "Belay! Whoa, there! Great land of love! look at that! *look* at it! Who did that?"

The mate to the big red hand pointed to the front door of the Whittaker place. Gabe was alarmed.

"Done what? Done which?" he gasped. "What you talkin' about? There ain't nobody lives in there. That house has been empty for——"

"Where's the front fence?" demanded the excited passenger. "What's become of the hedge? And who put up that—that darned piazza?"

The piazza had been where it now was almost since Mr. Lumley could remember. He hastened to reply that he didn't know; he wasn't sure; he presumed likely 'twas "them New Hampshire Howeses," when they ran a summer boarding house.

The stranger drew a long breath. "Well, of all the——" he began. Then he choked, hesitated, and ordered his driver to heave ahead and run alongside the hotel as quick as the Almighty would let him. Gabe hastened to obey. He was now absolutely certain that his companion was an escaped lunatic, and the sooner another keeper was appointed the better. The remainder of the trip was made in silence.

Mrs. Bangs opened the door of the perfect boarding house and stood majestically waiting to receive the prospective guest. Over her shoulders peered the faces of the boarders.

" Good afternoon," began the landlady. " I presume likely you would like to——"

She was interrupted. The newcomer turned toward her and extended his hand.

" Hello, Ketury! " he said. " I ain't seen you
sence you wore your hair up, but you're just as good-
lookin' as ever. And ain't that Bailey? Yes, 'tis,
and Asaph, too! How are you, boys? Shake! "

Mr. Bangs and his chum, the town clerk, had
emerged from the doorway. Their mouths and eyes
were wide open and they seemed to be suffering from
a sort of paralysis.

" Well? What's the matter with you? " demanded the arrival. " Ain't too stuck up to shake
hands after all these years, are you? "

Bailey's mouth closed in order that it's possessor
might swallow. Then it slowly reopened.

" I swan to man! " he ejaculated. " *Well!* I swan
to man! I—I b'lieve you're Cy Whittaker! "

" Course I am. Have to dye my carrot top if I
want to play anybody else. But look here, boys, you
answer my question: who had the cheek to rig up that
blasted piazza on my house? It starts to come down
to-morrow mornin'! "

# CHAPTER III

## " FIXIN' OVER "

MISS ANGELINE PHINNEY made no less than nine calls that afternoon. Before bedtime it was known, from the last house in " Woodchuck Lane " to the fish shanties at West Bayport, that " young Cy " Whittaker had come back; that he had come back " for good "; that he was staying temporarily at the perfect boarding house; that he was " awful well off "—having made lots of money down in South America; that he intended to " fix over " the Whittaker place, and that it was to be fixed over, not in a modern manner, with plush parlor sets—*à la* Sylvanus Cahoon—nor with onyx tables and blue and gold chairs like those adorning the Atkins mansion. It was to be, as near as possible, a reproduction of what it had been in the time of the late " Cap'n Cy," young Cy's father.

" *I* think he's out of his head," declared Miss Phinney, in confidence, to each of the nine females whom she favored with her calls. " Not crazy, you understand, but sort of touched in the upper story. I says so to Matildy Tripp, said it right out, too:

32

" ' Matildy,' I says, ' he's got a screw loose up aloft just
as sure as you're a born woman! ' "

' Matildy,' I says, ' he's got a screw loose up aloft just
as sure as you're a born woman! ' ' What makes
you think so?' says she. ' Well,' says I, ' do you
s'pose anybody that wan't foolish would be for
spendin' good money on an old house to make it
*older*?' I says. Goin' to tear down the piazza the
fust thing! Perfectly good piazza that cost ninety-

eight dollars and sixty cents to build; I know, because I see the bill when the Howeses had it done. And he's goin' to set out box hedges, somethin' that ain't been the style in this town sence Congressman Atkins pulled up his. 'What in the world, Cap'n Whittaker,' says I to him, ' do you want of box hedges? Homely and stiff and funeral lookin'! I might have 'em around my grave in the buryin' ground,' I says, ' but nowheres else.' 'All right, Angie,' says he, ' you shall have 'em there; I'll cut some slips purpose for you. It'll be a pleasure,' he says. Now ain't that crazy talk for a grown man? "

Miss Phinney was not the only one in our village to question Captain Cy Whittaker's sanity during the next few months. The majority of our people didn't understand him at all. He was generally liked, for although he had money, he did not put on airs, but he had his own way of doing things, and they were not Bayport ways.

True to his promise, he had a squad of carpenters busy, on the day following his arrival, tearing down the loathed piazza. These carpenters, and more, were kept busy throughout that entire spring and well into the summer. Then came painters and gardeners. The piazza disappeared; a new picket fence, exactly like the old one torn down by the Howeses, was erected; new shutters were hung; new window-panes were set; the roof was newly shingled. Captain Cy, Senior, had, in his day, cherished a New

34

England fondness for white and green paint; therefore the new fence was white and the house was white and the blinds a brilliant green. Rows of box hedge, the plants brought from Boston, were set out on each side of the front walk. The Howes front-door bell—a clamorous gong—was removed, and a glass knob attached to a spring bell of the old-fashioned " jingle " variety took its place. An old-fashioned flower garden—Cap'n Cy's mother had loved posies—was laid out on the west lawn beyond the pear trees. All these changes the captain superintended; when they were complete he turned his attention to interior decoration.

And now Captain Cy proceeded to, literally, astonish the natives. Among the Howes " improvements " were gilt wall papers and modern furniture for the lower floor of the house. The furniture they had taken with them; the wall paper had perforce been left behind. And the captain had every scrap of that paper stripped from the walls, and the latter re-covered with quaint, ugly, old-fashioned patterns, stripes and roses and flowered sprays with impossible birds flitting among them. The Bassett decorators has pasted the gilt improvement over the old Whittaker paper, and it was the Whittaker paper that the captain did his best to match, sending samples here, there, and everywhere in the effort. Then, upon the walls he hung old-fashioned pictures, such as Bayport dwellers had long ago relegated to their attics,

pictures like " From Shore to Shore," " Christian
Viewing the City Beautiful," and " Signing the Declaration." To these he added, bringing them from
the crowded garret of the homestead, oil paintings
of ships commanded by his father and grandfather,
and family portraits, executed—which is a peculiarly
fitting word—by deceased local artists in oil and
crayon.

He boarded up the fireplace in the sitting room
and installed a base-burner stove, resurrected from
the tinsmith's barn. He purchased a full " haircloth
set " of parlor furniture from old Mrs. Penniman,
who never had been known to sell any of her hoarded
belongings before, even to the " antiquers," and
wouldn't have done so now, had it not been that the
captain's offer was too princely to be real, and the
old lady feared she might be dreaming and would
wake up before she received the money. And from
Trumet to Ostable he journeyed, buying a chair here
and a table there, braided rag mats from this one,
and corded bedsteads and " rising sun " quilts from
that. At least half of Bayport believed with Gabe
Lumley and Miss Phinney that, if Captain Cy had
not escaped from a home for the insane, he was a
likely candidate for such an institution.

At the table of the perfect boarding house the captain was not inclined to be communicative regarding
his reasons and his intentions. He was a prime favorite there, praising Keturah's cooking, joking with

36

Angeline concerning what he was pleased to call her
" giddy " manner of dressing and wearing " side
curls," and telling yarns of South American dress
and behavior, which would probably have shocked
Mrs. Tripp—she having recently left the Methodist
church to join the " Come-Outers," because the
Sunday services of the former were, with the organ
and a paid choir, altogether " too play-actin' "—if
they had not been so interesting, and if Captain Cy
had not always concluded them with the observation:
" But there! you can't expect nothin' more from ignorant critters denied the privileges of congregational
singin' and experience meetin's; hey, Matilda ? "

Mrs. Tripp would sigh and admit that she supposed not.

" Only I do wish Mr. Daniels, *our* minister, might
have a chance to preach over 'em, poor things! "

" So do I," with a covert wink at Mrs. Bangs, who
was a stanch adherent of the regular faith. " South
America 'd be just the place for him; ain't that so,
Keturah? "

He evaded all personal questions put to him by
the boarders, explaining that he was renovating the
old place just for fun—he always had had a gang
of men working for him, and it seemed natural somehow. But to the friends of his boyhood, Asaph Tidditt and Bailey Bangs, he told the real truth.

" I swan to man! " exclaimed Bailey, almost tear-
fully, as the trio wandered through the rooms of the

Cy Whittaker place, dodging paper hangers and plasterers; " I swan to man, Whit, if it don't almost seem as though I was a boy again. Why! it's your dad's house come back alive, it is so! Look at this settin' room! Seem's if I could see him now a-settin' by that ere stove, and Mrs. Whittaker, your ma, over there a-sewin', and old Cap'n Cy—your granddad —snoozin' in that big armchair— Why! why, Whit! it's the very image of the chair he always set in!"

Captain Cy laughed aloud.

" It's more n' that, Bailey," he said; " it's *the* chair. 'Twas up attic, all busted and crippled, but I had it made over like new. And there's granddad's picture, lookin' just as I remember him—only he wan't quite so much of a frozen wax image as he's painted there. I'm goin' to hang it where it always hung, over the mantelpiece, next to the lookin' glass.

" Great land of love, boys!" he went on, " you fellers don't know what this means to me. Many and many's the time I've had this old house and this old room in my mind. I've seen 'em aboard ship in a howlin' gale off the Horn. I've seen 'em down in Surinam of a hot night, when there wan't a breath scurcely and the Caribs went around dressed in a handkerchief and a paper cigar, and it made you wish you could. I've seen 'em—but there! every time I've seen 'em I've swore that some day I'd come back and *live* 'em, and now, by the big dipper! here I am. Oh,

I tell you, chummies, you want to be fired *out* of a home and out of a town to appreciate 'em! Not that I blame the old man; he and I was too much alike to cruise in company. But Bayport I was born in, and in the Bayport graveyard they can plant me when I'm ready for the scrap heap. It's in the blood and— Why, see here! Don't I *talk* like a Bayporter?"

"You sartin do!" replied Asaph emphatically. "A body 'd think you'd been diggin' clams and pickin' cranberries in Bassett's Holler all your life long, to hear you."

"You bet! Well, that's pride; that's what that is. I prided myself on hangin' to the Bayport twang through thick and thin. Among all the Spanish 'Carambas' and 'Madre de Dioses' it did me good to come out with a good old Yankee 'darn' once in a while. Kept me feelin' like a white man. Oh, I'm a Whittaker! *I* know it. And I've got all the Whittaker pig-headedness, I guess. And because the old man—bless his heart, I say now—told me I shouldn't *be* a Whittaker no more, nor live like a Whittaker, I simply swore up and down I would be one and come back here, when I'd made my pile, to heave anchor and stay one till I die. Maybe that's foolishness, but it's me."

He puffed vigorously at the pipe which had taken the place of the Snowflake cigar, and added:

"Take this old settin' room—why, here it is; see!

Here's dad in his chair and ma in hers, and, if you go back far enough, granddad in his, just as you say, Bailey. And here's me, a little shaver, squattin' on the floor by the stove, lookin' at the pictures in a heap of Godey's Lady's Book. And says dad, ' Bos'n,' he says—he used to call me ' Bos'n ' in those days—' Bos'n,' says dad, ' run down cellar and fetch me up a pitcher of cider, that's a good feller.' Yes, yes; that's this room as I've seen it in my mind ever since I tiptoed through it the night I run away, with my duds in a bundle under my arm. Do you wonder I was fightin' mad when I saw what that Howes tribe had done to it?"

Superintending the making over of the old home occupied most of Captain Cy's daylight time that summer. His evenings were spent at Simmons's store. We have no clubs in Bayport, strictly speaking, for the sewing circle and the Shakespeare Reading Society are exclusively feminine in membership; therefore Simmons's store is the gathering place of those males who are bachelors or widowers or who are sufficiently free from petticoat government to risk an occasional evening out. Asaph Tidditt was a regular sojourner at the store. Bailey Bangs, happening in to purchase fifty cents' worth of sugar or to have the molasses jug filled, lingered occasionally, but not often. Captain Cy explained Bailey's absence in characteristic fashion.

" Variety," observed the captain, " is the spice of

life. Bailey gets talk enough to home. What's the use of his comin' up here to get more?"

"Oh, I don't know," said Josiah Dimick, with a grin, "we let him do some of the talkin' himself up here. Down at the boardin' house Keturah and Angie Phinney do it all."

"Yes. Still, if a feller was condemned to live over a biler factory he wouldn't hanker to get a job *in* it, would he? When Bailey was a delegate to the Methodist Conference up in Boston, him and a crowd visited the deef and dumb asylum. When 'twas time to go, he was missin', and they found him in the female ward lookin' at the inmates. Said that the sight of all them women, every one of 'em not able to say a word, was the most wonderful thing ever he laid eyes on. Said it made him feel kind of reverent and holy, almost as if he was in Paradise. So Ase Tidditt says, anyway; it's his yarn."

"'Tain't nuther, Cy Whittaker!" declared the indignant Asaph. "If you expect I'm goin' to father all your lies, you're mistaken."

The crowd at Simmons's discuss politics, as a general thing; state and national politics in their seasons, but county politics and local affairs always. The question in Bayport that summer, aside from that of the harbor appropriation, was who should be hired as downstairs teacher. Our schoolhouse is a two-story building, with a schoolroom on each floor. The lower room, where the little tots begin with their

" C—A—T Cat," and progress until they have mastered the Fourth Reader, is called " downstairs." " Upstairs " is, of course, the second story, where the older children are taught. To handle some of the " big boys " upstairs is a task for a healthy man, and such a one usually fills the teacher's position there. Downstairs being, in theory, at least, less strenuous, is presided over by a woman.

Miss Seabury, who had been downstairs teacher for one lively term, had resigned that spring in tears and humiliation. Her scholars had enjoyed themselves and would have liked her to continue, but the committee and the townspeople thought otherwise. There was a general feeling that enjoyment was not the whole aim of education.

" Betty," said Captain Dimick, referring to his small granddaughter, " has done fust rate so fur's marksmanship and lung trainin' goes. I cal'late she can hit a nail head ten foot off with a spitball three times out of four, and she can whisper loud enough to be understood in Jericho. But, not wishing to be unreasonable, still I should like to have her spell ' door ' without an ' e.' I've always been used to seein' it spelled that way and—well, I'm kind of old-fashioned, anyway."

There was a difference of opinion concerning Miss Seabury's successor. A portion of the townspeople were for hiring a graduate of the State Normal School, a young woman with modern training.

## "FIXIN' OVER"

Others, remembering that Miss Seabury had graduated from that school, were for proved ability and less up-to-date methods. These latter had selected a candidate in the person of a Miss Phœbe Dawes, a resident of Wellmouth, and teacher of the Wellmouth " downstairs " for some years. The arguments at Simmons's were hot ones.

" What's the use of hirin' somebody from right next door to us, as you might say? " demanded Alpheus Smalley, clerk at the store. " Don't we want our teachin' to be abreast of the times, and is Wellmouth abreast of *any*thing? "

" It's abreast of the bay, that's about all, I will give in," replied Mr. Tidditt. " But, the way I look at it, we need dis*cip*line more 'n anything else, and Phœbe Dawes has had the best dis*cip*line in her school, that's been known in these latitudes. Order? Why, say! Eben Salters told me that when he visited her room over there 'twas so still that he didn't dast to rub one shoe against t'other, it sounded up so. He had to set still and bear his chilblains best he could. And *popular*! Why, when she hinted that she might leave in May, her scholars more 'n ha'f of 'em, bust out cryin'. Now you hear me, I——"

" It seems to me," put in Thaddeus Simpson, who ran the barber shop and was something of a politician, " it seems to me, fellers, that we'd better wait and hear what Mr. Atkins has to say in this matter.

43

I guess that's what the committee 'll do, anyhow. We wouldn't want to go contrary to Heman, none of us; hey?"

"Tad" Simpson was known to be deep in Congressman Atkins's confidence. The mention of the great man's name was received with reverence and nods of approval.

"That's right. We mustn't do nothin' to displease Heman," was the general opinion.

Captain Cy did not join the chorus. He refilled his pipe and crossed his legs.

"Humph!" he grunted. "Heman Atkins seems to be— Give me a match, Ase, won't you? Thanks. I understand there's a special prayer meetin' at the church to-morrow night, Alpheus. What's it for?"

"For?" Mr. Smalley seemed surprised. "It's to pray for rain, that's what. You know it, Cap'n, as well's I do. Ain't everybody's garden dryin' up and the ponds so low that we shan't be able to get water for the cranberry ditches pretty soon? There's need to pray, I should think!"

"Humph! Seems a roundabout way of gettin' a thing, don't it? Why don't you telegraph to Heman and ask him to fix it for you? Save time."

This remark was received in horrified silence. Tad Simpson was the first to recover.

"Cap'n," he said, "you ain't met Mr. Atkins yet. When you do, you'll feel same as the rest of us. He's comin' home next week; then you'll see."

44

# "FIXIN' OVER"

A part at least of Mr. Simpson's prophecy proved true. The Honorable Atkins did come to Bayport the following week, accompanied by his little daughter Alicia, the housekeeper, and the Atkins servants. The Honorable and his daughter had been, since the adjournment of Congress, on a pleasure trip to the Yosemite and Yellowstone Park, and now they were to remain in the mansion on the hill for some time. The big house was opened, the stone urns burst into refulgent bloom, the iron dogs were refreshed with a coat of black paint, and the big iron gate was swung wide. Bayport sat up and took notice. Angeline Phinney was in her glory.

The meeting between Captain Cy and Mr. Atkins took place the morning after the latter's return. The captain and his two chums had been inspecting the progress made by the carpenters and were leaning over the new fence, then just erected, but not yet painted. Down the gravel walk of the mansion across the road came strolling its owner, silk-hatted, side-whiskered, benignant.

"Godfrey!" exclaimed Asaph. "There's Heman. See him, Whit?"

"Yup, I see him. Seems to be headin' this way."

"I—I do believe he's comin' across," whispered Mr. Bangs. "Yes, he is. He's real everyday, Cy. *He* won't mind if you ain't dressed up."

"Won't he? That's comfortin'. Well, I'll do the best I can without stimulants, as the doctor says.

If you hear my knees rattle just nudge me, will you, Bailey?"

Mr. Tidditt removed his hat. Bailey touched his. Captain Cy looked provokingly indifferent; he even whistled.

"Good mornin', Mr. Atkins," hailed the town clerk, raising his voice because of the whistle. "I'm proud to see you back among us, sir. Hope you and Alicia had a nice time out West. How is she— pretty smart?"

Mr. Atkins smiled a bland, congressional smile. He approached the group by the fence and extended his hand.

"Ah, Asaph!" he said; "it is you then? I thought so. And Bailey, too. It is certainly delightful to see you both again. Yes, my daughter is well, I thank you. She, like her father, is glad to be back in the old home nest after the round of hotel life and gayety which we have—er—recently undergone. Yes."

"Mr. Atkins," said Bailey, glancing nervously at Captain Cy, who had stopped whistling and was regarding the Atkins hat and whiskers with an interested air, "I want to make you acquainted with your new neighbor. You used to know him when you was a boy, but—but—er—Mr. Atkins, this is Captain Cyrus Whittaker. Cy, this is Congressman Atkins. You've heard us speak of him."

The great man started.

46

"'How are you, Heman? Fatter'n you used to be, ain't you?'"

## "FIXIN' OVER"

"Is it possible!" he exclaimed. "Is it possible that this is really my old playmate Cyrus Whittaker?"

"Yup," replied the captain calmly. "How are you, Heman? Fatter'n you used to be, ain't you? Washin'ton must agree with you."

Bailey and Asaph were scandalized. Mr. Atkins himself seemed a trifle taken aback. Comments on his personal appearance were not usual in Bayport. But he rallied bravely.

"Well, well!" he cried. "Cyrus, I am delighted to welcome you back among us. I should scarcely have known you. You are older—yes, much older."

"Well, forty year more or less, added to what you started with, is apt to make a feller some older. Don't need any Normal School graduate to do that sum for us. I'm within seven or eight year of bein' as old as you are, Heman, and that's too antique to be sold for veal."

Mr. Atkins changed the subject.

"I had heard of your return, Cyrus," he said. "It gave me much pleasure to learn that you were rebuilding and—er—renovating the—er—the ancestral—er——"

"The old home nest? Yup, I'm puttin' back a few feathers. Old birds like to roost comf'table. You've got a fairly roomy coop yourself."

"Hum! Isn't it—er—I should suppose you

would find it rather expensive. Can you—do you——"

"Yes, I can afford it, thank you. Maybe there'll be enough left in the stockin' to buy a few knick-knacks for the yard. You can't tell."

The captain glanced at the iron dogs guarding the Atkins gate. His tone was rather sharp.

"Yes, yes, certainly; certainly; of course. It gives me much pleasure to have you as a neighbor. I have always felt a fondness for the old place, even when you allowed it—even when it was most—er—run down, if you'll excuse the term. I always felt a liking for it and——"

"Yes," was the significant interruption. "I judged you must have, from what I heard."

This was steering dangerously close to the select-men and the contemplated "sale for taxes." The town clerk broke in nervously.

"Mr. Atkins," he said, "there's been consider'ble talk in town about who's to be teacher downstairs this comin' year. We've sort of chawed it over among us, but naturally we wanted your opinion. What do you think? I'm kind of leanin' toward the Dawes woman, myself."

The Congressman cleared his throat.

"Far be it from me," he said, "to speak except as a mere member of our little community, an ordinary member, but, as such a member, with the welfare of my birthplace very near and dear to me, I confess

48

that I am inclined to favor a modern teacher, one educated and trained in the institution provided for the purpose by our great commonwealth. The Dawes —er—person is undoubtedly worthy and capable in her way, but—well—er—*we* know that Wellmouth is not Bayport."

The reference to " our great commonwealth " had been given in the voice and the manner wont to thrill us at our Fourth-of-July celebrations and October " rallies." Two of his hearers, at least, were visibly impressed. Asaph looked somewhat crestfallen, but he surrendered gracefully to superior wisdom.

" That's so," he said. " That's so, ain't it, Cy? I hadn't thought of that."

" What's so? " asked the captain.

" Why—why, that Wellmouth ain't Bayport."

" No doubt of it. They're twenty miles apart."

" Yes. Well, I'm glad to hear you put it so conclusive, Mr. Atkins. I can see now that Phœbe wouldn't do. Hum! Yes."

Mr. Atkins buttoned the frock coat and turned to go.

" Good day, gentlemen," he said. " Cyrus, permit me once more to welcome you heartily to our village. We—my daughter and myself—will probably remain at home until the fall. I trust you will be a frequent caller. Run in on us at any time. Pray do not stand upon ceremony."

" No," said Captain Cy shortly, " I won't."

"That's right. That's right. Good morning."

He walked briskly down the hill. The trio gazed after him.

"Well," sighed Mr. Tidditt. "That's settled. And it's a comfort to know 'tis settled. Still I did kind of want Phœbe Dawes; but of course Heman knows best."

"Course he knows best!" snapped Bailey. "Ain't he the biggest gun in this county, pretty nigh? I'd like to know who is if he ain't. The committee 'll call the Normal School girl now, and a good thing, too."

Captain Cy was still gazing at the dignified form of the "biggest gun in the county."

"Let's see," he asked. "Who's on the school committee? Eben Salters, of course, and——"

"Yes. Eben's chairman and he'll vote Phœbe, anyhow; he's that pig-headed that nobody—not even a United States Representative—could change him. But Darius Ellis 'll be for Heman's way and so 'll Lemuel Myrick.

"Lemuel Myrick? Lem Myrick, the painter?"

"Sartin. There ain't but one Myrick in town."

"Hum!" murmured the captain and was silent for some minutes.

The school committee met on the following Wednesday evening. On Thursday morning a startling rumor spread throughout Bayport. Phœbe Dawes had been called, by a vote of two to one, to teach the downstairs school. Asaph, aghast, rushed out of Simmons's store and up to the hill to the Cy Whittaker place. He found Captain Cy in the front yard. Mr. Myrick, school committeeman and house painter, was with him.

"Hello, Ase!" hailed the captain. "What's the matter? Hasn't the tide come in this mornin'?"

Asaph, somewhat embarrassed by the presence of Mr. Myrick, hesitated over his news. Lemuel came to his rescue.

"Ase has just heard that we called Phœbe," he said. "What of it? I voted for her, and I ain't ashamed of it."

"But—but Mr. Atkins, he——"

"Well, Heman ain't on the committee, is he? I vote the way I think right, and no one in this town can change me. Anyway," he added, "I'm going to resign next spring. Yes, Cap'n Whittaker, I think three coats of white 'll do on the sides here."

"Lem's goin' to do my paintin' jobs," explained Captain Cy. "His price was a little higher than some of the other fellers, but I like his work."

Mr. Tidditt pondered deeply until dinner time. Then he cornered the captain behind the Bangs barn and spoke with conviction.

"Whit," he said, "you're the one responsible for the committee's hirin' Phœbe Dawes. You offered Lem the paintin' job if he'd vote for her. What did you do it for? You don't know her, do you?"

" Never set eyes on her in my life."

" Then—then— You heard Heman say he wanted the other one. What made you do it? "

Captain Cy grinned.

" Ase," he said, " I've always been a great hand for tryin' experiments. Had one of my cooks aboard put raisins in the flapjacks once, just to see what they tasted like. I judged Heman had had his own way in this town for thirty odd year. I kind of wanted to see what would happen if he didn't have it."

# CHAPTER IV

## BAILEY BANGS'S EXPERIMENT

LEMUEL MYRICK'S painting jobs have the quality so prized by our village small boys in the species of candy called " jaw breakers," namely, that of " lasting long." But even Lem must finish sometime or other and, late in July, the Cy Whittaker place was ready for occupancy. The pictures were in their places on the walls, the old-fashioned furniture filled the rooms, there was even a pile of old magazines, back numbers of Godey's Lady's Book, on the shelf in the sitting room closet.

Then, when Captain Cy had notified Mrs. Bangs that the perfect boarding house would shelter him no longer than the coming week, a new problem arose.

"Whit," said Asaph earnestly, " you've sartin made the place rise up out of its tomb; you have so. It's a miracle, pretty nigh, and I cal'late it must have cost a heap, but you've done it—all but the old folks themselves. You can't raise them up, Cy; money won't do that. And you can't live in this great house all alone. Who's goin' to cook for you, and sweep and dust, and swab decks, and one thing a'nother?

You'll have to have a housekeeper, as I told you a spell ago. Have you done any thinkin' about that?"

And the captain, taking his pipe from his lips, stared blankly at his friend, and answered:

"By the big dipper, Ase, I ain't! I remember we did mention it, but I've been so busy gettin' this craft off the ways that I forgot all about it."

The discussion which followed Mr. Tidditt's reminder was long and serious. Asaph and Bailey Bangs racked their brains and offered numerous suggestions, but the majority of these were not favorably received.

"There's Matildy Tripp," said Bailey. "She'd like the job, I'm sartin. She's a widow, too, and she's had experience keepin' house along of Tobias, him that was her husband. But, if you do hire her, don't let Ketury know I hinted at it, 'cause we're goin' to lose one boarder when you quit, and that's too many, 'cordin' to the old lady's way of thinkin'."

"You can keep Matildy, for all me," replied the captain decidedly. "Come-Outer religion's all right, for those that have that kind of appetite, but havin' it passed to me three times a day, same as I've had it at your house, is enough; I don't hanker to have it warmed over between meals. If I shipped Matildy aboard here she and the Reverend Daniels would stand over me, watch and watch, till I was converted or crazy, one or the other."

# BAILEY BANGS'S EXPERIMENT

"Well, there's Angie. She——"

"Angie!" sniffed Mr. Tidditt. "Stop your jokin', Bailey. This is a serious matter."

"I wan't jokin'. What——"

"There! there! boys," interrupted the captain; "don't fight. Bailey didn't mean to joke, Ase; he's full of what the papers call ' unconscious humor.' I'll give in that Angie is about as serious a matter as I can think of without settin' down to rest. Humph! so fur we haven't gained any knots to speak of. Any more candidates on your mind?"

More possibilities were mentioned, but none of them seemed to fill the bill. The conference broke up without arriving at a decision. Mr. Bangs and the town clerk walked down the hill together.

"Do you know, Bailey," said Asaph, "the way I look at it, this pickin' out a housekeeper for Whit ain't any common job. It's somethin' to think over. Cy's a restless critter; been cruisin' hither and yon all his life. I'm sort of scared that he'll get tired of Bayport and quit if things here don't go to suit him. Now if a real good nice woman—a nice-*lookin'* woman, say—was to keep house for him it—it——"

"Well?"

"Well, I mean—that is, don't you s'pose if some such woman as that was to be found for the job he might in time come to like her and—and—er——"

"Ase Tidditt, what are you drivin' at?"

55

"Why, I mean he might come to marry her; there! Then he'd be contented to settle down to home and stay put. What do you think of the idea?"

"Think of it? I think it's the dumdest foolishness ever I heard. I declare if the very mention of a woman to some of you old baches don't make your heads soften up like a jellyfish in the sun! Ain't Cy Whittaker got money? Ain't he got a nice home? Ain't he happy?"

"Yes, he is now, I s'pose, but——"

"*Well*, then! And you want him to get married! What do you know about marryin'? Never tried it, have you?"

"Course I ain't! You know I ain't."

"All right. Then I'd keep quiet about such things, if I was you."

"You needn't fly up like a settin' hen. Everybody's wife ain't——"

He stopped in the middle of the sentence.

"What's that?" demanded his companion, sharply.

"Nothin'; nothin'. *I* don't care; I was only tryin' to fix things comf'table for Whit. Has Heman said anything about the harbor appropriation sence he's been home? I haven't heard of it if he has."

Mr. Bangs's answer was a grunt, signifying a negative. Congressman Atkins had been, since his return to Bayport, exceedingly noncommittal concerning the appropriation. To Tad Simpson and a very few chosen lieutenants and intimates he had said that he hoped to get it; that was all. This was a disquieting change of attitude, for, at the beginning of the term just passed, he had affirmed that he was *going* to get it. However, as Mr. Simpson reassuringly said: " The job's in as good hands as can be, so what's the use of *our* worryin'? "

Bailey Bangs certainly was not troubled on that score; but the town clerk's proposal that Captain Cy be provided with a suitable wife did worry him. Bailey was so very much married himself and had such decided, though unspoken, views concerning matrimony that such a proposal seemed to him lunacy, pure and simple. He had liked and admired his friend " Whit " in the old days, when the latter led them into all sorts of boyish scrapes; now he regarded him with a liking that was close to worship. The captain was so jolly and outspoken; so brave and independent—witness his crossing of the great Atkins in the matter of the downstairs teacher. That was a reckless piece of folly which would, doubtless, be rewarded after its kind, but Bailey, though he professed to condemn it, secretly wished he had the pluck to dare such things. As it was, he didn't dare contradict Keturah.

With the exception of one voyage as cabin boy to New Orleans, a voyage which convinced him that he was not meant for a seaman, Mr. Bangs had never been farther from his native village than Boston. Captain Cy had been almost everywhere and seen almost everything. He could spin yarns that beat the serial stories in the patent inside of the *Bayport Breeze* all hollow. Bailey had figured that, when the "fixin' over" was ended, the Cy Whittaker place would be for him a delightful haven of refuge, where he could put his boots on the furniture, smoke until dizzy without being pounced upon, be entertained and thrilled with tales of adventure afloat and ashore, and even express his own opinion, when he had any, with the voice and lung power of a free-born American citizen.

And now Asaph Tidditt, who should know better, even though he was a bachelor, wanted to bring a wife into this paradise; not a paid domestic who could be silenced, or discharged, if she became a nuisance, but a *wife*! Bailey guessed not; not if he could prevent it.

So he lay awake nights thinking of possible housekeepers for Captain Cy, and carefully rejecting all those possessing dangerous attractions of any kind. Each morning, after breakfast, he ran over the list with the captain, taking care that Asaph was not present. Captain Cy, who was very busy with the finishing touches at the new old house, wearied on the third morning.

"There, there, Bailey!" he said. "Don't bother me now. I've got other things on my mind. How do I know who all these women folks are you're stringing off to me? Let me alone, do."

"But you must have a housekeeper, Cy. You'll move in Monday and you won't have nobody to——"

"Oh, dry up! I want to think who I must see this morning. There's Lem and old lady Penniman, and——"

"But the housekeeper, Cy! Don't you see——"

"Hire one yourself, then. You know 'em; I don't."

"Hey? Hire one myself? Do you mean you'll leave it in my hands?"

"Yes, yes! I guess so. Run along, that's a good feller."

He departed hurriedly. Mr. Bangs scratched his head. A weighty responsibility had been laid upon him.

Monday morning after breakfast Captain Cy's trunk was put aboard the depot wagon, and Dan'l Webster drew it to its owner's home. The farewells at the perfect boarding house were affecting. Mrs. Tripp said that she had spoken to the Reverend Mr. Daniels, and he would be sure to call the very first thing. Keturah affirmed that the captain's stay had been a real pleasure.

"You never find fault, Cap'n Whittaker," she said. "You're such a manly man, if you'll excuse my sayin' so. I only wish there was more like you," with a significant glance at her husband. As for Miss

Phinney, she might have been saying good-by yet if the captain had not excused himself.

Asaph accompanied his friend to the house on the hill. The trunk was unloaded from the wagon and carried into the bedroom on the first floor, the room which had been Captain Cy's so long ago. Gabe shrieked at Dan'l Webster, and the depot wagon crawled away toward the upper road.

"Got to meet the up train," grumbled the driver. "Not that anybody ever comes on it, but I cal'late I'm s'posed to be there. Be more talk than a little if I wan't. Git dap, Dan'l! you're slower'n the moral law."

"So you're goin' to do your own cookin' for a spell, Cy?" observed Asaph, a half hour later. "Well, I guess that's a good idea, till you can find the right housekeeper. I ain't been able to think of one that would suit you yet."

"Nor I, either. Neither's Bailey, I judge, though for a while he was as full of suggestions as a pine grove is of woodticks. He started to say somethin' about it to me last night, but Ketury hove in sight and yanked him off to prayer meetin'."

"Yes, I know. She cal'lates to get him into heaven somehow."

"I guess 'twouldn't *be* heaven for her unless he was round to pick at. There he comes now. How'd he get out of wipin' dishes?"

Mr. Bangs strolled into the yard.

# BAILEY BANGS'S EXPERIMENT

"Hello!" he hailed. "I was on my way to Simmons's on an errand and I thought I'd stop in a minute. Got somethin' to tell you, Whit."

"All right. Overboard with it! It won't keep long this hot weather."

Bailey smiled knowingly. "Didn't I hear the up train whistle as I was comin' along?" he asked. "Seems to me I did. Yes; well, if I ain't mistaken somebody's comin' on that train. Somebody for you, Cy Whittaker."

"Somebody for *me*?"

"Um—hum! I can gen'rally be depended on, I cal'late, and when you says to me: 'Bailey, you get me a housekeeper,' I didn't lose much time. I got her."

Mr. Tidditt gasped.

"*Got* her?" he repeated. "Got who? Got what? Bailey Bangs, what in the world have——"

"Belay, Ase!" ordered Captain Cy. "Bailey, what are you givin' us?"

"Givin' you a housekeeper, and a good one, too, I shouldn't wonder. She may not be one of them ten-thousand-dollar prize museum beauties," with a scornful wink at Asaph, "but if what I hear's true she can keep house. Anyhow she's kept one for forty odd year. Her name's Deborah Beasley, she's a widow over to East Trumet, and if I don't miss my guess, she's in the depot wagon now headed in this direction."

Captain Cy whistled. Mr. Tidditt was too much surprised to do even that.

"I was speakin' to the feller that drives the candy cart," continued Bailey, "and I asked him if he'd run acrost anybody, durin' his trips 'round the country, who'd be likely to hire out for a housekeeper. He thought a spell and then named over some. Among 'em was this Beasley one. I asked some more questions and, the answers bein' satisfactory to *me*, though they might not be to some folks——" another derisive wink at Asaph——"I set down and wrote her, tellin' what you'd pay, Cy, what she'd have to do, and when she'd have to come. Saturday night I got a letter, sayin' terms was all right, and she'd be on hand by this mornin's train. Course she's only on trial for a month, but you had to have *somebody*, and the candy-cart feller said——"

The town clerk slapped his knee.

"Debby Beasley!" he cried. "I know who she is! I've got a cousin in Trumet. Debby Beasley! Aunt Debby, they call her. Why! she's old enough to be Methusalem's grandmarm, and——"

"If I recollect right," interrupted Bailey, with dignity, "Cy never said he wanted a *young* woman —a frivolous, giddy critter, always riggin' up and chasin' the fellers. He wanted a sot, sober housekeeper."

"Godfrey! Aunt Debby ain't frivolous! She couldn't chase a lame clam—and catch it. And *deef!*

62

Godfrey—scissors! she's deefer 'n one of them cast-iron Newfoundlands in Heman's yard! Do you mean to say, Bailey Bangs, that you went ahead, on your own hook, and hired that old relic to——"

"I did. And I had my authority, didn't I, Whit? You told me you'd leave it in my hands, now didn't you?"

The captain smiled somewhat ruefully, and scratched his head. "Why, to be honest, Bailey, I believe I did," he admitted. "Still, I hardly expected — Humph! is she deef, as Ase says?"

"I understand she's a little mite hard of hearin'," replied Mr. Bangs, with dignity; "but that ain't any drawback, the way I look at it. Fact is, I'd call it an advantage, but you folks seem to be hard to please. I ruther imagined you'd thank me for gettin' her, but I s'pose that was too much to expect. All right, pitch her out! Don't mind *my* feelin's! Poor homeless critter comin' to——"

"Homeless!" repeated Asaph. "What's that got to do with it? Cy ain't runnin' the Old Woman's Home."

"Well, well!" observed the captain resignedly. "There's no use in rowin' about what can't be helped. Bailey says he shipped her for a month's trial, and here comes the depot wagon now. That's her on the aft thwart, I judge. She *ain't* what you'd call a spring pullet, is she!"

She certainly was not. The occupant of the depot

wagon's rear seat was a thin, not to say scraggy, female, wearing a black, beflowered bonnet and a black gown. A black knit shawl was draped about her shoulders and she wore spectacles.

"Whoa!" commanded Mr. Lumley, piloting the depot wagon to the side door of the Whittaker house. Dan'l Webster came to anchor immediately. Gabe turned and addressed his passenger.

"Here we be!" he shouted.

"Hey?" observed the lady in black.

"Here—we—be!" repeated Gabe, raising his voice.

"See? See what?"

"Oh, heavens to Betsey! I'm gettin' the croup from howlin'. I—say—*here—we—be! Get out!*"

He accompanied the final bellow with an expressive pantomime indicating that the passenger was expected to alight. She seemed to understand, for she opened the door of the carriage and slowly descended. Mr. Bangs advanced to meet her.

"How d'ye do, Mrs. Beasley!" he said. "Glad to see you all safe and sound."

Mrs. Beasley shook his hand; hers were covered, as far as the knuckles, by black mitts.

"How d'ye do, Cap'n Whittaker?" she said, in a shrill voice. "You pretty smart?"

Bailey hastened to explain.

"I ain't Cap'n Whittaker," he roared. "I'm Bailey Bangs, the one that wrote to you."

"Hey?"

Mr. Lumley and Asaph chuckled. Bailey colored and tried again.

"I ain't the cap'n," he whooped. "Here he is— here!"

He led her over to her prospective employer and tapped the latter on the chest.

"How d'ye do, sir?" said the housekeeper. "I don't know's I just caught your name."

In five minutes or so the situation was made reasonably clear. Mrs. Beasley then demanded her trunk and carpet bag. The grinning Lumley bore them into the house. Then he drove away, still grinning. Bailey looked fearfully at Captain Cy.

"She *is* kind of hard of hearin', ain't she?" he said reluctantly. "You remember I said she was."

The captain nodded.

"Yes," he answered, "you're a truth-tellin' chap, Bailey, I'll say that for you. You don't exaggerate your statements."

"Hard of hearin'!" snapped Mr. Tiditt. "If the last trump ain't a steam whistle she'll miss Judgment Day. I'll stop into Simmons's on my way along and buy you a bottle of throat balsam, Cy; you're goin' to need it."

The captain needed more than throat balsam during the fortnight which followed. The widow Beasley's deafness was not her only failing. In fact she was altogether a failure, so far as her housekeeping

6     

was concerned. She could cook, after a fashion, but the fashion was so limited that even the bill of fare at the perfect boarding house looked tempting in retrospect.

"Baked beans again, Cy!" exclaimed Asaph, dropping in one evening after supper. "'Tain't Saturday night so soon, is it?"

"No," was the dismal rejoinder. "It's Tuesday, if my almanac ain't out of joint. But we had beans Saturday and they ain't all gone yet, so I presume we'll have 'em till the last one's swallowed. Aunt Debby's got what the piece in the Reader used to call a ' frugal mind.' She don't intend to waste anything. Last Thursday I spunked up courage enough to yell for salt fish and potatoes—fixed up with pork scraps, you know, same's we used to have when I was a boy. We had 'em all right, and if beans of a Saturday hadn't been part of her religion we'd be warmin' 'em up yet. I took in a cat for company 'tother day, but the critter's run away. To see it look at the beans in its saucer and then at me was pitiful; I felt like handin' myself over to the Cruelty to Animals' folks."

"Is she neat?" inquired Mr. Tidditt.

"I don't know. I guess so—on the installment plan. It takes her a week to scrub up the kitchen, and then one end of it is so dirty she has to begin again. Consequently the dust is so thick in the rest of the house that I can see my tracks. If 'twan't so late in

66

the season I'd plant garden stuff in the parlor—nice soil and lots of shade, with the curtains down."

From the rooms in the rear came the words of a gospel hymn sung in a tremulous soprano and at concert pitch.

"Music with my meals, just like a high-toned restaurant," commented Captain Cy.

"But what makes her sing so everlastin' *loud*?"

"Can't hear herself if she don't. I could stand her deefness, because that's an affliction and we may, all come to it; but——"

The housekeeper, still singing, entered the room and planted herself in a chair.

"Good evenin', Mr. Tidditt," she said, smiling genially. "Nice weather we've been havin'."

Asaph nodded.

"Sociable critter, ain't she!" observed the captain. "Always willin' to help entertain. Comes and sets up with me till bedtime. Tells about her family troubles. Preaches about her niece out West, and how set the niece and the rest of the Western relations are to have her make 'em a visit. I told her she better go—I thought 'twould do her good. I know 'twould help *me* consider'ble to see her start.

"She's got so now she finds fault with my neckties," he added, "says I must be careful and not get my feet wet. Picks out what I ought to wear so's I won't get cold. She'll adopt me pretty soon. Oh, it's all right! She can't hear what you say. Are your dishes done?" he shrieked, turning to the old lady.

"One? One what?" inquired Mrs. Beasley.

"They won't *be* done till you go, Ase," continued the master of the house. "She'll stay with us till the last gun fires. T'other day Angie Phinney called and I turned Debby loose on her. I didn't believe anything could wear out Angie's talkin' machinery, but she did it. Angeline stayed twenty minutes and then quit, hoarse as a crow."

Here the widow joined in the conversation, evidently under the impression that nothing had been said since she last spoke. Continuing her favorable comments on the weather she observed that she was glad there was so little fog, because fog was hard for folks with "neuralgy pains." Her brother's wife's cousin had "neuralgy" for years, and she described his sufferings with enthusiasm and infinite detail. Mr. Tidditt answered her questions verbally at first; later by nods and shakes of the head. Captain Cy fidgeted in his chair.

"Come on outdoor, Ase," he said at last. "No use to wait till she runs down, 'cause she's a self-winder, guaranteed to keep goin' for a year. Goodnight!" he shouted, addressing Mrs. Beasley, and heading for the door.

"Where you goin'?" asked the old lady.

"No. Yes. Who said so? Hooray! Three cheers for Gen'ral Scott! Come on, Ase!" And the captain, seizing his friend by the arm, dragged him into the open air, and slammed the door.

" Are you crazy? " demanded the astonished town clerk. " What makes you talk like that? "

" Might as well. She wouldn't understand it any better if 'twas Scripture, and it saves brain work. The only satisfaction I get is bein' able to give my opinion of her and the grub without hurtin' her feelin's. If I called her a wooden-headed jumpin' jack she'd only smile and say No, she didn't think 'twas goin' to rain, or somethin' just as brilliant."

" Well, why don't you give her her walkin' papers? "

" I shall, when her month's up."

" I wouldn't wait no month. I'd heave her overboard to-night. You hear *me*! "

Captain Cy shook his head.

" I can't, very well," he replied. " I hate to make her feel *too* bad. When the month's over I'll have some excuse ready, maybe. The joke of it is that she don't really need to work out. She's got some money of her own, owns cranberry swamps and I don't know what all. Says she took up Bailey's offer 'cause she cal'lated I'd be company for her. I had to laugh, even in the face of those beans, when she said that."

" Humph! if I don't tell Bailey what I think of him, then——"

" No, no! Don't you say a word to Bailey. It's principally on his account that I'm tryin' to stick it

out for the month. Bailey did his best; he thought
he was helpin'. And he feels dreadfully because she's
so deef. Only yesterday he asked me if I believed
there was anything made that would fix her up and
make it more comfortable for me. I could have prescribed a shotgun, but I didn't. You see, he thinks
her deefness is the only trouble; I haven't told him the
rest, and don't you do it, either. Bailey's a good-
hearted chap."

"Humph! his heart may be good, but his head's
goin' to seed. I'll keep quiet if 'twill please you,
though."

"Yes. And, see here, Ase! I don't care to be
the laughin' stock of Bayport. If any of the folks
ask you how I like my new housekeeper, you tell 'em
there's nothin' like her anywhere. That's no lie."

So Mrs. Beasley stayed on at the Whittaker place
and, thanks to Mr. Tidditt, the general opinion of in-
quisitive Bayport was that the new housekeeper was
a grand success. Only Captain Cy and Asaph knew
the whole truth, and Mr. Bangs a part. That part,
Deborah's deafness, troubled him not a little and he
thought much concerning it. As a result of this
thinking he wrote a letter to a relative in Boston.
The answer to this letter pleased him and he wrote
again.

One afternoon, during the third week of Mrs.
Beasley's stay, Asaph called and found Captain Cy
in the sitting room, reading the *Breeze*. The captain

urged his friend to remain and have supper. "We've run out of beans, Ase," he explained, " and are just startin' in on a course of boiled cod. Do stay and eat a lot; then there won't be so much to warm over."

Mr. Tidditt accepted the invitation, also a section of the *Breeze*. While they were reading they heard the back door slam.

" It's the graven image," explained the captain. " She's been on a cruise down town somewheres. Be a lot of sore throats in that direction to-morrow mornin'."

The town clerk looked up.

" There now! " he exclaimed. " I believe 'twas her I saw walkin' with Bailey a spell ago. I thought so, but I didn't have my specs and I wan't sure."

" With Bailey, hey? Humph! this is serious. Hope Ketury didn't see 'em. We mustn't have any scandal."

The housekeeper entered the dining room. She was singing " Beulah Land," but her tone was more subdued than usual. They heard her setting the table.

" How's she gettin' along? " asked Asaph.

" Progressin' backwards, same as ever. She's no better, thank you, and the doctor's given up hopes."

" When you goin' to tell her she can clear out? "

" What? " Captain Cy had returned to his paper and did not hear the question.

" I say when is she goin' to be bounced? Deefness ain't catchin', is it? "

" I wouldn't wonder if it might be. If 'tis, mine ought to be developin' fast. What makes her so still all at once?"

" Gone to the kitchen, I guess. Wonder she hasn't sailed in and set down with us. Old chromo! You must be glad her month's most up?"

Asaph proceeded to give his opinion of the house-keeper, raising his voice almost to a howl, as his indignation grew. If Mrs. Beasley's ears had been ordinary ones she might have heard the unflattering description in the kitchen; as it was Mr. Tidditt felt no fear.

" Comin' here so's you could be company for her! The idea! Good to herself, ain't she! Godfrey scissors! And Bailey was fool enough to——"

" There, there! Don't let it worry you, Ase. I've about decided what to say when I let her go. I'll tell her she is gettin' too old to be slavin' herself to death. You see, I don't want to make the old critter cry, nor I don't want her to get mad. Judgin' by the way she used to coax the cat outdoors with the broom handle she's got somethin' of a temper when she gets started. I'll give her an extry month's wages, and——"

" You will, hey? You *will*?"

The interruption came from behind the partially closed dining-room door. Mr. Tidditt sank back in his chair. Captain Cy sprang from his and threw the door wide open. Behind it crouched Mrs. Deborah Beasley. Her eyes snapped behind her specta-

72

cles, her lean form was trembling all over, and in her right hand she held a mammoth trumpet, the smaller end of which was connected with her ear.

"'Well, I don't want none of your miser'ble money!'"

"You will, hey?" she screamed, brandishing her left fist, but still keeping the ear trumpet in place with her right. "You *will*? Well, I don't want none of your miser'ble money! Land knows how you made it, anyhow, and I wouldn't soil my hands with it. After all I've put up with, and the way I've done my work, and the things I've had to eat, and—and——"

She paused for breath. Captain Cy scratched his chin. Asaph, gazing open-mouthed at the trumpet, stirred in his chair. Mrs. Beasley swooped down upon him like a gull on a minnow.

"And you!" she shrieked. "You! a miserable little, good-for-nothin', lazy, ridiculous, dried-up— . . . Oo—oo—oh! You call yourself a town clerk! *You* do! I—I wouldn't have you clerk for a hen house! I'm an old chromo, be I? Yes! that's nice talk, ain't it, to a woman old enough to be— that is—er—er—'most as old as you be! You sneakin', story-tellin', little, fat *thing*, you! You— oh, I can't lay my tongue to words to tell you *what* you are."

"You're doin' pretty well, seems to me," observed Captain Cy dryly. "I wouldn't be discouraged if I was you."

The only effect of this remark was to turn the wordy torrent in his direction. The captain bore it for a while; then he rose to his feet and commanded silence.

"That's enough! Stop it!" he ordered, and, strange to say, Mrs. Beasley did stop. "I'm sorry, Debby," he went on, "but you had no business to be listenin' even if—" and he smiled grimly, "you have got a new fog horn to hear with. You can go and

74

pack your things as soon as you want to. I made up my mind the first day you come that you and me wouldn't cruise together long, and this only shortens the trip by a week or so. I'll pay you for this month and for the next, and I guess, when you come to think it over, you'll be willin' to risk soilin' your hands with the money. It's your own fault if anybody knows that you didn't leave of your own accord. *I* shan't tell, and I'll see that Tidditt doesn't. Now trot! Ase and I'll get supper ourselves."

It was evident that the ex-housekeeper had much more which she would have liked to say. But there was that in her late employer's manner which caused her to forbear. She slammed out of the room, and they heard her banging things about on the floor above.

" But where—*where*," repeated Mr. Tidditt, over and over, " did she get that trumpet? "

The puzzle was solved soon after, when Bailey Bangs entered the house in a high state of excitement.

" Well," he demanded, expectantly. " Did they help her? Has anything happened? "

" *Happened!* " began Asaph, but Captain Cy silenced him by a wink.

" Yes," answered the captain; " something's happened. Why? "

" Hurrah! I thought 'twould. She can hear better, can't she? "

" Yes, I guess it's safe to say she can."

75

"Good! You can thank me for it. When I see how dreadful deef she was I wrote my cousin Eddie T, who's an optician up to Boston—you know him, Ase—and I says: 'Ed, you know what's good for folks who can't see? Ain't there nothin',' says I, 'that'll help them who can't hear? How about ear trumpets?' And Ed wrote that an ear trumpet would probably help some, but why didn't I try a pair of them patent fixin's that are made to put inside deef people's ears? He'd known of cases where they helped a lot. So I sent for a pair, and the biggest ear trumpet made, besides. And when I met Debby to-day I give 'em to her and told her to put the patent things *in* her ears and couple on the trumpet outside 'em. And not to say nothin' **to** you, but just surprise you. And it did surprise you, didn't it?"

The wrathful Mr. Tidditt could wait no longer. He burst into a vivid description of the "surprise." Bailey was aghast. Captain Cy laughed until his face was purple.

"I declare, Cy!" exclaimed the dejected purchaser of the "ear fixin's" and the trumpet. "I do declare I'm awful sorry! if you'd only told me she was no good I'd have let her alone; but I thought 'twas just the deefness. I—I——"

"I know, Bailey; you meant well, like the layin'-on-of-hands doctor who rubbed the rheumatic man's wooden leg. All right; *I* forgive you. 'Twas worth

76

# BAILEY BANGS'S EXPERIMENT

it all to see Asaph's face when Marm Beasley was complimentin' him. Ha! ha! Oh, dear me! I've laughed till I'm sore. But there's one thing I *should* like to do, if you don't mind: I should like to pick out my next housekeeper myself."

## CHAPTER V.

### A FRONT-DOOR CALLER

MRS. BEASLEY departed next morning, taking with her the extra month's wages, in spite of fervid avowals that she wouldn't touch a cent of it. On the way to the depot she favored Mr. Lumley with sundry hints concerning the reasons for her departure. She " couldn't stand it no longer "; if folks only knew what she'd had to put up with she cal'lated they'd be some surprised; she could " tell a few things " if she wanted to, and so on. Incidentally she was kind of glad she didn't like the place, because now she cal'lated she should go West and visit her niece; they'd been wanting her to come for so long.

Gabe was much interested and repeated the monologue, with imaginative additions, to the depot master, who, in turn, repeated it to his wife when he went home to dinner. That lady attended sewing circle in the afternoon. Next day a large share of Bayport's conversation dealt with the housekeeper's leaving and her reasons therefor. The reasons differed widely, according to the portion of the town

78

in which they were discussed, but it was the general opinion that the whole affair was not creditable to Captain Whittaker.

Only at the perfect boarding house was the captain upheld. Miss Phinney declared that she knew he had made a mistake as soon as she heard the Beasley woman talk; nobody else, so Angeline declared, could " get a word in edgeways." Mrs. Tripp sighed and affirmed that going out of town for a woman to do housework was ridiculous on the face of it; there were plenty of Bayport ladies, women of capability and sound in their religious views, who might be hired if they were approached in the right way. Keturah gave, as her opinion, that if the captain knew when he was well off, he would " take his meals out." Asaph snorted and intimated that that Debby Beasley wasn't fit to " keep house in a pigsty, and anybody but a born gump would have known it." Bailey, the " born gump," said nothing, but looked appealingly at his chum.

As for Captain Cy, he did not take the trouble to affirm or deny the rumors. Peace and quiet dominated the Whittaker house for the first time in three weeks and its owner was happier. He cooked his own food and washed his own dishes. The runaway cat ventured to return, found other viands than beans in its saucer, and decided to remain, purring thankful contentment. The captain made his own bed, after a fashion, when he was ready to occupy it, but he was

79

conscious that it might be better made. He refused, however, to spend his time in sweeping and dusting, and the dust continued to accumulate on the carpets and furniture. This condition of affairs troubled him, but he kept his own counsel. Asaph and Bailey called often, but they offered no more suggestions as to hiring a housekeeper. Mr. Tidditt might have done so, but the captain gave him no encouragement. Mr. Bangs, recent humiliation fresh in his mind, would as soon have suggested setting the house on fire.

One evening Asaph happened in, on his way to Simmons's. He desired the captain to accompany him to that gathering place of the wise and talkative. Captain Cy was in the sitting room, a sheet of note paper in his hand. The town clerk entered without ceremony and tossed his hat on the sofa.

"Evenin', Ase," observed the captain, folding the sheet of paper and putting it into his pocket. "Glad you come. Sit down. I wanted to ask you somethin'."

"All right! Here I be. Heave ahead and ask."

Captain Cy puffed at his pipe. He seemed about to speak and then to think better of it, for he crossed his legs and smoked on in silence, gazing at the nickel work of the "base-burner" stove. It was badly in need of polishing.

"Well?" inquired Asaph, with impatient sarcasm. "Thinkin' of askin' me to build a fire for you, was you? Nobody else but you would have set up a stove in summer time, anyhow."

"Hey? No, you needn't start a fire yet awhile. That necktie of yours 'll keep us warm till fall, I shouldn't wonder. New one, ain't it? Where'd you get it?"

Mr. Tidditt was wearing a crocheted scarf of a brilliant crimson hue, particularly becoming to his complexion. The complexion now brightened until it was almost a match for the tie.

"Oh!" he said, with elaborate indifference. "That? Yes, it's new. Yesterday was my birthday, and Matildy Tripp she knew I needed a necktie, so she give me this one."

"Oh! One she knit purpose for you, then? Dear me! Look out, Ase. Widow women are dangerous, they say; presents are one of the first baits they heave out."

"Don't be foolish, now! I couldn't chuck it back at her, could I? That would be pretty manners. You needn't talk about widders—not after Debby! Ho! ho!"

Captain Cy chuckled. Then he suddenly became serious.

"Ase," he said, "you remember the time when the Howes folks had this house? Course you do. Yes; well, was there any of their relations here with 'em? A—a cousin, or somethin'?"

"No, not as I recollect. Yes, there was, too, come

to think. A third cousin, Mary Thayer her name
was. I *think* she was a third cousin of Betsy Howes,
Seth Howes's second wife. Betsy's name was Ginn
afore she married, and the Ginns was related on their
ma's side to a Richards—Emily Richards, I think
'twas—and Emily married a Thayer. Would that
make this Mary a third cousin? Now let's see; Sarah
Jane Ginn, she had an aunt who kept a boardin' house
in Harniss. I remember that, 'count of her sellin'
my Uncle Bije a pig. Seems to me 'twas a pig, but I
ain't sure that it mightn't have been a settin' of Ply-
mouth Rock hens' eggs. Anyhow, Uncle Bije *kept*
hens, because I remember one time——"

"There! there! we'll be out of sight of land in a
minute. This Mary Thayer—old, was she?"

"No, no! Just a young girl, eighteen or twenty
or so. Pretty and nice and quiet as ever I see. By
Godfrey, she *was* pretty! I wan't as old as I be now,
and——"

"Ase, don't tell your heart secrets, even to me. I
might get absent-minded and mention 'em to Matildy.
And then—whew!"

"If you don't stop tryin' to play smarty I'll go
home. What's Matildy Tripp to me, I'd like to
know? And even when Mary Thayer was here I
was old enough to be her dad. But I remember what
a nice girl she was and how the boarders liked her.
They used to say she done more than all the Howes
tribe put together to make the Sea Sight House a

good hotel. Young as she was she done most of the housekeepin' and done it well. If the rest of 'em had been like her you mightn't have had the place yet, Whit. But what set you to thinkin' about her?"

"Oh, I don't know! Nothin' much; that is—well, I'll tell you some other time. What became of her?"

"She went up to New Hampshire along with the Howes folks and I ain't seen her since. Seems to me I did hear she was married. See here, Whit, what is it about her? Tell a feller; come!"

But Captain Cy refused to gratify his chum's lively curiosity. Also he refused to go to Simmons's that evening, saying that he was tired and guessed he'd stay at home and "turn in early." Mr. Tidditt departed grumbling. After he had gone the captain drew his chair nearer the center table, took from his pocket a sheet of notepaper, and proceeded to read what was written on its pages. It was a letter which he had received nearly a month before and had not yet answered. During the past week he had read it many times. The writing was cramped and blotted and the paper cheap and dingy. The envelope bore the postmark of a small town in Indiana, and the inclosure was worded as follows:

CAPTAIN CYRUS WHITTAKER.

DEAR SIR: I suppose you will be a good deal surprised to hear from me, especially from way out West here. When you bought the old house of Seth, he and I was living in Concord, N. H. He couldn't make a go of his business there, so we came West and he has been sick most of the time since. We ain't well off like you, and times are hard with us. What I wanted to write you about was this. My cousin Mary Thomas, Mary Thayer that was, is still living in Concord and she is poor and needs help, though I don't suppose she would ask for it, being too proud. False pride I call it. Me and Seth would like to do something for her, but we have a hard enough job to keep going ourselves. Mary married a man by the name of Henry Thomas, and he turned out to be a miserable good-for-nothing, as I always said he would. She wouldn't listen to me though. He run off and left her seven year ago last April, and I understand was killed or drowned somewheres up in Montana. Mary and [several words scratched out here] got along somehow since, but I don't know how. While we lived in Concord Seth sort of kept an eye on her, but now he can't of course. She's a good girl, or woman rather, being most forty, and would make a good housekeeper if you should need one as I suppose likely you will. If you could help her it would be an act of charity and you will be rewarded Above. Seth says why not write to her and tell her to come and see you? He feels bad about her, because he is so sick I suppose. And he knows you are rich and could do good if you felt like it. Her father's name was John Thayer. I wouldn't wonder if you used to know her mother. She was Emily Richards afore she married and they used to live in Orham. Yours truly,

ELIZABETH HOWES.

P. S.—Mary's address is Mrs. Mary Thomas, care Mrs. Oliver, 128 Blank Street, Concord, N. H.

N. B.—Seth won't say so, but I will: we are very hard up ourselves and if you could help him and me with the loan of a little money it would be thankfully received.

Captain Cy read the letter, folded it, and replaced it in his pocket. He knew the Howes family by reputation, and the reputation was that of general sharpness in trade and stinginess in money matters. Betsy's personal appeal did not, therefore, touch his heart to any great extent. He surmised also that for Seth Howes and his wife to ask help for some person other than themselves premised a darky in the woodpile somewhere. But for the daughter of Emily Richards to be suggested as a possible housekeeper at the Cy Whittaker place—that was interesting, certainly.

When the captain was not a captain—when he was merely " young Cy," a boy, living with his parents, a dancing school was organized in Bayport. It was an innovation for our village, and frowned upon by many of the older and stricter inhabitants. However, most of the captain's boy friends were permitted to attend; young Cy was not. His father considered dancing a waste of time and, if not wicked, certainly frivolous and nonsensical. So the boy remained at home, but, in spite of the parental order, he practiced some of the figures of the quadrilles and the contra dances in his comrades' barns, learning them at second hand, so to speak.

One winter there was to be a party in Orham, given by the Nickersons, wealthy people with a fifteen-year-old daughter. It was to be a grand affair, and most of the boys and girls in the neighboring towns were invited. Cy received an invitation, and, for a wonder, was permitted to attend. The

Bayport contingent went over in a big hayrick on runners and the moonlight ride was jolly enough. The Nickerson mansion was crowded and there were music and dancing.

Young Cy was miserable during the dancing. He didn't dare attempt it, in spite of his lessons in the barn. So, while the rest of his boy friends sought partners for the " Portland Fancy " and " Hull's Victory " he sat forlorn in a corner.

As he sat there he was approached by a young lady, radiant in muslin and ribbons. She was three or four years older than he was, and he had worshipped her from afar as she whirled up and down the line in the Virginia Reel. She never lacked partners and seemed to be a great favorite with the young men, especially one good-looking chap with a sunburned face, who looked like a sailor.

They were forming sets for " Money Musk "; it was " ladies' choice," and there was a demand for more couples. The young lady came over to Cy's corner and laughingly dropped him a courtesy.

"If you please," she said, " I want a partner. Will you do me the honor? "

Cy blushingly avowed that he couldn't dance any to speak of.

"Oh, yes, you can! I'm sure you can. You're the Whittaker boy, aren't you? I've heard about your barn lessons. And I want you to try this with

86

me. Please do. No, John," she added, turning to
the sunburned young fellow who had followed her
across the room; "this is my choice and here is my
partner. Susie Taylor is after you and you mustn't
run away. Come, Mr. Whittaker."

So Cy took her arm and they danced "Money
Musk" together. He made but a few mistakes, and
these she helped him to correct so easily that none
noticed. His success gave him courage and he es-
sayed other dances; in fact, he had a very good time
at the party after all.

On the way home he thought a great deal about
the pretty young lady, whose name he discovered was
Emily Richards. He decided that if she would only
wait for him, he might like to marry her when he
grew up. But he was thirteen and she was seventeen,
and the very next year she married John Thayer, the
sailor in the blue suit. And two years after that
young Cy ran away to be a sailor himself.

In spite of his age and his lifetime of battering
about the world, Captain Cy had a sentimental streak
in his makeup; his rejuvenation of the old home
proved that. Betsy's letter interested him. He had
made guarded inquiries concerning Mary Thayer,
now Mary Thomas, of others besides Asaph, and the
answers had been satisfactory so far as they went;
those who remembered her had liked her very much.
The captain had even begun a letter to Mrs. Thomas,
but laid it aside unfinished, having, since Bailey's un-

fortunate experience with the widow Beasley, a prejudice against experiments.

But this evening, before Mr. Tidditt called, he had been thinking that something would have to be done and done soon. The generally shiftless condition of his domestic surroundings was getting to be unbearable. Dust and dirt did not fit into his mental picture of the old home as it used to be and as he had tried to restore it. There had been neither dust nor dirt in his mother's day.

He meditated and smoked for another hour. Then, his mind being made up, he pulled down the desk lid of the old-fashioned secretary, resurrected from a pile of papers the note he had begun to Mrs. Thomas, dipped a sputtering pen into the ink bottle and proceeded to write.

His letter was a short one and rather noncommittal. As Mrs. Thomas no doubt knew he had come back to live in his father's house at Bayport. He might possibly need some one to keep house for him. He understood that she, Mary Thayer that was, was a good housekeeper and that she was open to an engagement if everything was mutually satisfactory. He had known her mother slightly when the latter lived in Orham. He thought an interview might be pleasant, for they could talk over old times if nothing more. Perhaps, on the whole, she might care to risk a trip to Bayport, therefore he inclosed money for her railroad fare. " You understand, of course,"

88

so he wrote in conclusion, " that nothing may come of our meeting at all. So please don't say a word to anybody when you strike town. You've lived here yourself, and you know that three words hove overboard in Bayport will dredge up gab enough to sink a dictionary. So just keep mum till the business is settled one way or the other."

He put on his hat and went down to the post office, where he dropped his letter in the slot of the box fastened to the front door. Then he returned home and retired at exactly eleven o'clock. In spite of his remarks to Asaph, he had not " turned in " so early after all.

If the captain expected a prompt reply to his note he was disappointed. A week passed and he heard nothing. Then three more days and still no word from the New Hampshire widow. Meanwhile fresh layers of dust spread themselves over the Whittaker furniture, and the gaudy patterns of the carpets blushed dimly beneath a grimy fog. The situation was desperate; even Matilda Tripp, Come-Outer sermons and all, began to be thinkable as a possibility.

The eleventh day began with a pouring rain that changed, later on, to a dismal drizzle. The silverleaf tree in the front yard dripped, and the overflowing gutters gurgled and splashed. The bay was gray and lonely, and the fish weirs along the outer bar were lost in the mist. The flowers in the Atkins urns were draggled and beaten down. Only the iron dogs glistened undaunted as the wet ran off their newly painted backs. The air was heavy, and the salty flavor of the flats might almost be tasted in it.

Captain Cy was in the sitting room, as usual. His spirits were as gray as the weather. He was actually lonesome for the first time since his return home. He had kindled a wood fire in the stove, just for the sociability of it, and the crackle and glow behind the isinglass panes only served to remind him of other days and other fires. The sitting room had not been lonesome then.

He heard the depot wagon rattle by and, peering from the window, saw that, except for Mr. Lumley, it was empty. Not even a summer boarder had come to brighten our ways and lawns with reckless raiment and the newest slang. Summer boarding season was almost over now. Bayport would soon be as dull as dish water. And the captain admitted to himself that it *was* dull. He had half a mind to take a flying trip to Boston, make the round of the wharves, and see if any of the old shipowners and ship captains whom he had once known were still alive and in harness.

"JINGLE! Jingle! *Jingle!* Jingle! Jingle! Jing! Jing! Jing!"

Captain Cy bounced in his chair. That was the front-door bell. The *front*-door bell! Who on earth, or, rather, who in Bayport, would come to the *front* door?

He hurried through the dim grandeur of the best parlor and entered the little dark front hall. The bell was still swinging at the end of its coil of wire. The dust shaken from it still hung in the air. The captain unbolted and unlocked the big front door.

A girl was standing on the steps between the lines of box hedge—a little girl under a big " grown-up " umbrella. The wet dripped from the umbrella top and from the hem of the little girl's dress.

Captain Cy stared hard at his visitor; he knew most of the children in Bayport, but he didn't know this one. Obviously she was a stranger. Portuguese children from " up Harniss way " sometimes called to peddle huckleberries, but this child was no " Portugee."

" Hello! " exclaimed the captain wonderingly. " Did you ring the bell? "

" Yes, sir," replied the girl.

" Humph! Did, hey? Why? "

" Why? Why, I thought— Isn't it a truly bell? Didn't it ought to ring? Is anybody sick or dead? There isn't any crape."

" Dead? Crape? " Captain Cy gasped. " What in the world put that in your head? "

" Well, I didn't know but maybe that was why you thought I hadn't ought to have rung it. When mamma was sick they didn't let people ring our bell. And when she died they tied it up with crape."

"Did, hey? Hum!" The captain scratched his chin and gazed at the small figure before him. It was a self-poised, matter-of-fact figure for such a little one, and, out there in the rain under the tent roof of the umbrella, it was rather pitiful.

"Please, sir," said the child, "are you Captain Cyrus Whittaker?"

"Yup! That's me. You've guessed it the first time."

"Yes, sir. I've got a letter for you. It's pinned inside my dress. If you could hold this umbrella maybe I could get it out."

She extended the big umbrella at arm's length, holding it with both hands. Captain Cy woke up.

"Good land!" he exclaimed, "what am I thinkin' of? You're soakin' wet through, ain't you?"

"I guess I'm pretty wet. It's a long ways from the depot, and I tried to come across the fields, because a boy said it was nearer, and the bushes were so——"

"Across the *fields*? Have you walked all the way from the depot?"

"Yes, sir. The man said it was a quarter to ride, and auntie said I must be careful of my money because——"

"By the big dipper! Come in! Come in out of that this minute!"

92

He sprang down the steps, furled the umbrella, seized her by the arm and led her into the house, through the parlor and into the sitting room, where the fire crackled invitingly. He could feel that the dress sleeve under his hand was wet through, and the worn boots and darned stockings he could see were soaked likewise.

"There!" he cried. "Set down in that chair. Put your feet up on that h'ath. Sakes alive! Your folks ought to know better than to let you stir out this weather, let alone walkin' a mile—and no rubbers! Them shoes ought to come off this minute, I s'pose. Take 'em off. You can dry your stockings better that way. Off with 'em!"

"Yes, sir," said the child, stooping to unbutton the shoes. Her wet fingers were blue. It can be cold in our village, even in early September, when there is an easterly storm. Unbuttoning the shoes was slow work.

"Here, let me help you!" commanded the captain, getting down on one knee and taking a foot in his lap. "Tut! tut! tut! you're wet! Been some time sence I fussed with button boots; lace or long-legged cowhides come handier. Never wore cowhides, did you?"

"No, sir."

"I s'pose not. I used to when I was little. Remember the first pair I had. Copper toes on 'em—whew! The copper was blacked over when they come

93

out of the store and that wouldn't do, so we used to kick a stone wall till they brightened up. There! there she comes. Humph! stockin's soaked, too. Wish I had some dry ones to lend you. Might give you a pair of mine, but they'd be too scant fore and aft and too broad in the beam, I cal'late. Humph! and your top-riggin's as wet as your hull. Been on your beam ends, have you? "

"I don't know, sir. I fell down in the bushes coming across. There were vines and they tripped me up. And the umbrella was so heavy that——"

"Yes, I could see right off you was carryin' too much canvas. Now take off your bunnit and I'll get a coat of mine to wrap you up in."

He went into his bedroom and returned with a heavy " reefer " jacket. Ordering his caller to stand up he slipped her arms into the sleeves and turned the collar up about her neck. Her braided " pigtail " of yellow hair stuck out over the collar and hung down her back in a funny way. The coat sleeves reached almost to her knees and the coat itself enveloped her like a bed quilt.

"There! " said Captain Cy approvingly. " Now you look more as if you was under a storm rig. Set down and toast your toes. Where's that letter you said you had? "

" It's inside here. I don't know's I can get at it; these sleeves are so long."

" Reef 'em. Turn 'em up. Let me show you.

94

That's better! Hum! So you come from the depot, hey? Live up that way?"

" No, sir! I used to live in Concord, but——"

" Concord? *Concord?* Concord where?"

" Concord, New Hampshire. I came on the cars. Auntie knew a man who was going to Boston, and he said he'd take care of me as far as that and then put me on the train to come down here. I stopped at his folks' house in Charlestown last night, and this morning we got up early and he bought me a ticket and started me for here. I had a box with my things in it, but it was so heavy I couldn't carry it, so I left it up at the depot. The man there said it would be all right and you could send for it when——"

" I could *send* for it? *I* could? What in the world—— Say, child, you've made a mistake in your bearin's. 'Taint me you want to see, it's some of your folks, relations, most likely. Tell me who they are; maybe I know 'em."

The girl sat upright in the big chair. Her dark eyes opened wide and her chin quivered.

" Ain't you Captain Cyrus Whittaker?" she demanded. " You said you was."

" Yes, yes, I am. I'm Cy Whittaker, but what——"

" Well, auntie told me——"

" Auntie! Auntie who?"

" Auntie Oliver. She isn't really my auntie, but

mamma and me lived in her house for ever so long
and so——"

"Wait! wait! wait! I'm hull down in the fog.
This is gettin' too thick for *me*. Your auntie's name's
Oliver and you lived in Concord, New Hampshire.
For—for thunder sakes, what's *your* name?"

"Emily Richards Thomas."

"Em—Emily—Richards—*Thomas*!"

"Yes, sir."

"Emily Richards Thomas! What was your ma's
name?"

"Mamma was Mrs. Thomas. Her front name
was Mary. She's dead. Don't you want to see your
letter? I've got it now."

She lifted one of the flapping coat sleeves and extended a crumpled, damp envelope. Captain Cy took
it in a dazed fashion and drew a long breath. Then
he tore open the envelope and read the following:

DEAR CAPTAIN WHITTAKER:

The bearer of this is Emily Richards Thomas. She is seven,
going on eight, but old for her years. Her mother was Mary
Thomas that used to be Mary Thayer. It was her you wrote to
about keeping house for you, but she had been dead a fortnight
before your letter come. She had bronchial pneumonia and it
carried her off, having always been delicate and with more troubles
to bear than she could stand, poor thing. Since her husband, who
I say was a scamp even if he is dead, left her and the baby, she has
took rooms with me and done sewing and such. When she passed
away I wrote to Seth Howes, a relation of hers out West, and, so
far as I know, the only one she had. I told the Howes man that

96

# A FRONT-DOOR CALLER

Mary had gone and Emmie was left. Would they take her? I wrote. And Seth's wife wrote they couldn't, being poorer than poverty themselves. I was afraid she would have to go to a Home, but when your letter came I wrote the Howeses again. And Mrs. Howes wrote back that you was rich, and a sort of far-off relation of Mary's, and probably you would be glad to take the child to bring up. Said that she had some correspondence with you about Mary before. So I send Emmie to you. Somebody's got to take care of her and I can't afford it, though I would if I could, for she's a real nice child and some like her mother. I do hope she can stay with you. It seems a shame to send her to the orphan asylum. I send along what clothes she's got, which ain't many.

Respectfully yours,

Sarah Oliver.

Captain Cy read the letter through. Then he wiped his forehead.

"Well!" he muttered. "*Well!* I never in my life! I—I never did! Of all——"

Emily Richards Thomas looked up from the depths of the coat collar.

"Don't you think," she said, "that you had better send to the depot for my box? I can get dry *some* this way, but mamma always made me change my clothes as soon as I could. She used to be afraid I'd get cold."

## CHAPTER VI

### ICICLES AND DUST

CAPTAIN CY did not reply to the request
for the box. It is doubtful if he even heard
it. Mrs. Oliver's astonishing letter had, as
he afterwards said, left him "high and dry with no
tug in sight." Mary Thomas was dead, and her
daughter, her *daughter*! of whose very existence he
had been ignorant, had suddenly appeared from nowhere and been dropped at his door, like an out-of-
season May basket, accompanied by the modest suggestion that he assume responsibility for her thereafter. No wonder the captain wiped his forehead in
utter bewilderment.

"Don't you think you'd better send for the box?"
repeated the child, shivering a little under the big
coat.

"Hey? What say? Never mind, though. Just
keep quiet for a spell, won't you. I want to let this
soak in. By the big dipper! Of all the solid brass
cheek that ever I run across, this beats the whole
cargo! And Betsy Howes never hinted! 'Probably
you would be glad to take—' Be *glad*! Why, blast

98

their miserable, stingy— What do they take me for?
*I'll* show 'em! Indiana ain't so fur that I can't—
Hey? Did you say anything, sis? "

The girl had shivered again. " No, sir," she replied. " It was my teeth, I guess. They kind of
rattled."

" What? You ain't cold, are you? With all that
round you and in front of that fire? "

" No, sir, I guess not. Only my back feels
sort of funny, as if somebody kept dropping icicles
down it. Those bushes and vines were so wet that
when I tumbled down 'twas most like being in a
pond."

" Sho! sho! That won't do. Can't have you laid
up on my hands. That would be worse than—
Humph! Tut, tut! Somethin' ought to be done,
and I'm blessed if I know what. And not a woman
round the place—not even that Debby. Say, look
here, what's your name—er—Emmie, hadn't I better
get the doctor? "

The child looked frightened.

" Why? " she cried, her big eyes opening. " I'm
not sick, am I? "

" Sick? No, no! Course not, course not. What
would you want to be sick for? But you ought to
get warm and dry right off, I s'pose, and your duds
are all up to the depot. Say, what does—what did
your ma used to do when you felt—er—them icicles
and things? "

99

"She changed my clothes and rubbed me. And, if I was *very* wet she put me to bed sometimes."

"Bed? Sure! why, yes, indeed. Bed's a good place to keep off icicles. There's my bedroom right in there. You could turn in just as well as not. Bunk ain't made yet, but I can shake it up in no time. Say —er—er—you can undress yourself, can't you?"

"Oh, yes, sir! Course I can! I'm most eight."

"Sure you are! Don't act a mite babyish. All right, you set still till I shake up that bunk."

He entered the chamber, his own, opening from the sitting room, and proceeded, literally, to "shake up" the bed. It was not a lengthy process and, when it was completed, he returned to find his visitor already divested of the coat and standing before the stove.

"I guess perhaps you'll have to help undo me behind," observed the young lady. "This is my best dress and I can't reach the buttons in the middle of the back."

Captain Cy scratched his head. Then he clumsily unbuttoned the wet waist, glancing rather sheepishly at the window to see if anyone was coming.

"So this is your best dress, hey?" he asked, to cover his confusion. It was obviously not very new, for it was neatly mended in one or two places.

"Yes, sir."

"So. Where'd you buy it—up to Concord?"

"No, sir. Mamma made it, a year ago."

There was a little choke in the child's voice. The captain was mightily taken back.

"Hum! Yes, yes," he muttered hurriedly. "Well, there you are. Now you can get along, can't you?"

"Yes, sir. Shall I go in that room?"

"Trot right in. You might—er—maybe you might sing out when you're tucked up. I—I'll want to know if you're got bedclothes enough."

Emily disappeared in the bedroom. The door closed. Captain Cy, his hands in his pockets, walked up and down the length of the sitting room. The expression on his face was a queer one.

"I haven't got any nightgown," called a voice from the other room. The captain gasped.

"Good land! so you ain't," he exclaimed. "What in the world— Humph! I wonder——"

He went to the lower drawer of a tall "highboy" and, from the tumbled mass of apparel therein took one of his own night garments.

"Here's one," he said, coming back with it in his hand. "I guess you'll have to make this do for now. It'll fit you enough for three times to once, but it's all I've got."

A small hand reached round the edge of the door and the nightshirt disappeared. Captain Cy chuckled and resumed his pacing.

"I'm tucked up," called Miss Thomas. The captain entered and found her in bed, the patchwork points and diamonds of the " Rising Sun " quilt covering her to the chin and her head denting the uppermost of the two big pillows. Captain Cy liked to " sleep high."

" Got enough over you? " he asked.

" Yes, sir, thank you."

" That's good. I'll take your togs out and dry 'em in the kitchen. Don't be scared; I'll be right back."

In the kitchen he sorted the wet garments and hung them about the cook stove. It was a strange occupation for him and he shook his head whimsically as he completed it. Then he took a flat iron, one of Mrs. Beasley's purchases, from the shelf in the closet and put it in the oven to heat. Soon afterwards he returned to the bedroom, bearing the iron wrapped in a dish towel.

" My ma always used to put a hot flat to my feet when I was a young one and got chilled," he explained. " I ain't used one for some time, but I guess it's a good receipt. How do you feel now? Any more icicles? "

" No, sir. I'm ever so warm. Isn't this a nice bed? "

" Think so, do you? Glad of it. Well, now, I'm goin' to leave you in it while I step down street and see about havin' your box sent for. I'll be back in a shake. If anybody comes to the door while I'm gone don't you worry; let 'em go away again."

He put on his hat and left the house, walking rapidly, his head down and his hands in his pockets. At times he would pause in his walk, whistle, shake his head, and go on once more. Josiah Dimick met him, and his answers to Josiah's questions were so vague and irrelevant that Captain Dimick was puzzled, and later expressed the opinion that " Whit's cookin' must be pretty bad; acted to me as if he had dyspepsy of the brain."

Captain Cy stopped at Mr. Lumley's residence to leave an order for the delivery of the box. Then he drifted into Simmons's and accosted Alpheus Smalley.

" Al," he said, " what's good for a cold? "

" Why? " asked Mr. Smalley, in true Yankee fashion. " You got one? "

" Hey? Oh, yes! Yes, I've got one." By way of proof he coughed until the lamp chimneys rattled on the shelf.

" Judas! I should think you had! Well, there's ' Pine Bark Oil ' and ' Sassafras Elixir ' and two kinds of sass'p'rilla—that's good for most everything— and— Is your throat sore? "

" Hey? Yes, I guess so."

" Don't you *know*? If you've got sore throat there ain't nothin' better'n ' Arabian Balsam.' But what in time are you doin' out in this drizzle with a cold and no umbrella? Do you want to——"

" Never mind my umbrella. I left it in the church entry t'other Sunday and somebody got out afore I did. This ' Arabian Balsam '—seems to me I remember my ma's usin' that on me. Wet a rag with it, don't you, and tie it round your neck?"

"Yup. Be sure and use a flannel rag, and red flannel if you've got it; that acts quicker'n the other kinds. Fifteen cent bottle?"

"I guess so. Might's well give me some sass'-p'rilla, while you're about it; always handy to have in the house. And—er—say, is that canned soup you've got up on that shelf?"

The astonished clerk admitted that it was.

"Well, give me a can of the chicken kind."

Mr. Smalley, standing on a chair to reach the shelf where the soup was kept, shook his head.

"Now, that's too bad, Cap'n," he said, "but we're all out of chicken just now. Fact is, we ain't got nothin' but termatter and beef broth. Yes, and I declare if the termatter ain't all gone."

"Humph! then I guess I'll take the beef. Needn't mind wrappin' it up. So long."

He departed bearing his purchases. When Mr. Simmons, proprietor of the store, returned, Alpheus told him that he " cal'lated " Captain Cy Whittaker was preparing to " go into a decline, or somethin'."

"Anyhow," said Alpheus, "he bought sass'p'rilla and ' Arabian Balsam,' and I sold him a can of that beef soup you bought three year ago last summer, when Alicia Atkins had the chicken pox."

The captain entered the house quietly and tiptoed to the door of the bedroom. Emily was asleep, and the sight of the childish head upon the pillow gave him a start as he peeped in at it. It looked so natural, almost as if it belonged there. It had been in a bed like that and in that very room that he had slept when a boy.

Gabe, brimful of curiosity, brought the box a little later. His curiosity was ungratified, Captain Cyrus explaining that it was a package he had been expecting. The captain took the box to the bedroom, and, finding the child still asleep, deposited it on the floor and tiptoed out again. He went to the kitchen, poked up the fire, and set about getting dinner.

He was warming the beef broth in a saucepan on the stove when Emily appeared. She was dressed in dry clothes from the box and seemed to be feeling as good as new.

"Hello!" exclaimed Captain Cy. "You're on deck again, hey? How's icicles?"

"All gone," was the reply. "Do you do your own work? Can't I help? I can set the table. I used to for Mrs. Oliver."

The captain protested that he could do it himself just as well, but the girl persisting, he showed her where the dishes were kept. From the corner of his eye he watched her as she unfolded the tablecloth.

"Is this the only one you've got?" she inquired. "It's awful dirty."

"Hum! Yes, I ain't tended up to my washin'

and ironin' the way I'd ought to. I'll lose my job if I don't look out, hey?"

Before they sat down to the meal Captain Cy insisted that his guest take a tablespoonful of the sarsaparilla and decorate her throat with a section of red flannel soaked in the 'Arabian Balsam.' The perfume of the latter was penetrating and might have interfered with a less healthy appetite than that of Miss Thomas.

"Have some soup? Some I bought purpose for you. Best thing goin' for folks with icicles," remarked the captain, waving the iron spoon he had used to stir the contents of the saucepan.

"Yes, sir, thank you. But don't you ask a blessing?"

"Hey?"

"A blessing, you know. Saying that you're thankful for the food now set before us."

"Hum! Why, to tell you the truth I've kind of neglected that, I'm afraid. Bein' thankful for the grub I've had lately was most too much of a strain, I shouldn't wonder."

"I know the one mamma used to say. Shall I ask it for you?"

"Sho! I guess so, if you want to."

The girl bent her head and repeated a short grace. Captain Cy watched her curiously.

"Now, I'll have some soup, please," observed Emily. "I'm awful hungry. I had breakfast at five

"'Excuse me, . . . but don't you think that plate had better be done over?'"

o'clock this morning and we didn't have a chance to eat much."

A good many times that day the captain caught himself wondering if he wasn't dreaming. The whole affair seemed too ridiculous to be an actual experience. Dinner over, he and Emmie attended to the dishes, he washing and she wiping. And even at this early stage of their acquaintance her disposition to take charge of things was apparent. She found fault with the dish towels; they were almost as bad as the tablecloth, she said. Considering that the same set had been in use since Mrs. Beasley's departure, the criticism was not altogether baseless. But the young lady did not stop there—her companion's skill as a washer was questioned.

"Excuse me," she said, "but don't you think that plate had better be done over? I guess you didn't see that place in the corner. Perhaps you've forgot your specs. Auntie Oliver couldn't see well without her specs."

Captain Cy grinned and admitted that a second washing wouldn't hurt the plate.

"I guess your auntie was one of the particular kind," he said.

"No, sir, 'twas mamma. She couldn't bear dirty things. Auntie used to say that mamma hunted dust with a magnifying glass. She didn't, though; she only liked to be neat. I guess dust doesn't worry men so much as it does women."

"Why?"

"Oh, 'cause there's so much of it here; don't you think so? I'll help you clean up by and by, if you want to."

" *You* will?"

" Yes, sir. I used to dust sometimes when mamma was out sewing. And once I swept, but I did it so hard that auntie wouldn't let me any more. She said 'twas like trying to blow out a match with a tornado."

Later on he found her standing in the sitting room, critically inspecting the mats, the furniture, and the pictures on the walls. He stood watching her for a moment and then asked:

" Well, what are you lookin' for—more dust? 'Twon't be hard to find it. ' Dust thou art and unto dust thou shalt return.' Every time I go outdoor and come in again I realize how true that is."

Emily shook her head.

" No, sir," she said; " I was only looking at things and thinking."

" Thinkin', hey? What about? or is that a secret?"

" No, sir. I was thinking that this room was different from any I've ever seen."

" Humph! Yes, I presume likely 'tis. Don't like it very much, do you?"

" Yes, sir, I think I do. It's got a good many things in it that I never saw before, but I guess they're pretty—after you get used to 'em."

Captain Cy laughed aloud. " After you get used to 'em, hey?" he repeated.

" Yes, sir. That's what mamma said about Auntie

Oliver's new bonnet that she made herself. I—I was thinking that you must be peculiar."

" Peculiar? "

" Yes, sir. I like peculiar people. I'm peculiar myself. Auntie used to say I was the most peculiar child she ever saw. P'raps that's why I came to you. P'raps God meant for peculiar ones to live together. Don't you think maybe that was it? "

And the captain, having no answer ready, said nothing.

That evening when Asaph and Bailey, coming for their usual call, peeped in at the window, they were astounded by the tableau in the Whittaker sitting room. Captain Cy was seated in the rocking chair which had been his grandfather's. At his feet, on the walnut cricket with a haircloth top, sat a little girl turning over the leaves of a tattered magazine, a Godey's Lady's Book. A pile of these magazines was beside her on the floor. The captain was smiling and looking over her shoulder. The cat was curled up in another chair. The room looked more home-like than it had since its owner returned to it.

The friends entered without knocking. Captain Cy looked up, saw them, and appeared embarrassed.

" Hello, boys! " he said. " Glad to see you. Come right in. Clearin' off fine, ain't it? "

Mr. Tidditt replied absently that he wouldn't be surprised if it was. Bailey, his eyes fixed upon the occupant of the cricket, said nothing.

"'We—we didn't know you had company.'"

"We—we didn't know you had company, Whit,"
said Asaph. "We been up to Simmons's and Alpheus
said you was thin and peaked and looked sick. Said
you bought sass'p'rilla and all kind of truck. He
was afraid you had fever and was out of your head,
cruisin' round in the rain with no umbrella. The
gang weren't talkin' of nothin' else, so me and Bailey
thought we'd come right down."

"That's kind of you, I'm sure. Take your things
off and set down. No, I'm sorry to disappoint Smalley and the rest, but I'm able to be up and—er—
make my own bed, thank you. So Alpheus thought
I looked thin, hey? Well, if I had to live on
that soup he sold me, I'd be thinner'n I am now.
You tell him that canned hot water is all right
if you like it, but it seems a shame to put mud
in it. It only changes the color and don't help the
taste."

Mr. Bangs, who was still staring at Emily, now
ventured a remark.

"Is that a relation of yours, Cy?" he asked.

"That? Oh! Well, no, not exactly. And yet I
don't know but she is. Fellers, this is Emmie Thomas.
Can't you shake hands, Emmie?"

The child rose, laid down the magazine, which
was open at the colored picture of a group of ladies
in crinoline and chignons, and, going across the room,
extended a hand to Mr. Tiditt.

"How do you do, sir?" she said.

"Why—er—how d'ye do? I'm pretty smart, thank you. How's yourself?"

"I'm better now. I guess the sass'parilla was good for me."

"'Twan't the sass'p'rilla," observed the captain, with conviction. "'Twas the 'Arabian Balsam.' Ma always cured me with it and there's nothin' finer."

"But what in time—" began Bailey. Captain Cy glanced at the child and then at the clock.

"Don't you think you'd better turn in now, Emmie?" he said hastily, cutting off the remainder of the Bangs query. "It's after eight, and when I was little I was abed afore that."

Emily obediently turned, gathered up the Lady's Books and replaced them in the closet. Then she went to the dining room and came back with a hand lamp.

"Good night," she said, addressing the visitors. Then, coming close to the captain, she put her face up for a kiss.

"Good night," she said to him, adding, "I like it here ever so much. I'm awful glad you let me stay."

As Bailey told Asaph afterwards, Captain Cy blushed until the ends of the red lapped over at the nape of his neck. However, he bent and kissed the rosy lips and then quickly brushed his own with his hand.

"Yes, yes," he stammered. "Well—er—good

night. Pleasant dreams to you. See you in the mornin'."

The girl paused at the chamber door. "You won't have to unbutton my waist now," she said. "This is my other one and it ain't that kind."

The door closed. The captain, without looking at his friends, led the way to the dining room.

"Come on out here," he whispered. "We can talk better here."

Naturally, they wanted to know all about the girl, who she was and where she came from. Captain Cy told as much of the history of the affair as he thought necessary.

"Poor young one," he concluded, "she landed on to me in the rain, soppin' wet, and ha'f sick. I *couldn't* turn her out then—nobody could. Course it's an everlastin' outrage on me and the cheekiest thing ever I heard of, but what could I do? I was fixed a good deal like an English feller by the name of Gatenby that I used to know in South America. He woke up in the middle of the night and found a boa constrictor curled on the foot of his bed. Next day, when a crowd of us happened in, there was Gatenby, white as a sheet, starin' down at the snake, and it sound asleep. 'I didn't invite him,' he says, 'but he looked so bloomin' comf'table I 'adn't the 'eart to disturb 'im.' Same way with me; the child seemed so comf'table here I ain't had the heart to disturb her—yet."

" But she said she was goin' to stay," put in Bailey. " You ain't goin' to *keep* her, are you? "

The captain's indignation was intense.

" Who—me? " he snorted. " What do you think I am? I ain't runnin' an orphan asylum. No, sir! I'll keep the young one a day or so—or maybe a week —and then I'll pack her off to Betsy Howes. I ain't so soft as they think I am. *I'll* show 'em! "

Mr. Tidditt looked thoughtful.

" She's a kind of cute little girl, ain't she? " he observed.

Captain Cy's frown vanished and a smile took its place.

" That's so," he chuckled. " She is, now that's a fact! I don't know's I ever saw a cuter."

# CHAPTER VII

### CAPTAIN CY PROVES DELINQUENT

A WEEK isn't a very long time even in Bayport.
True, there was once a drummer for a Boston
"notion" house who sprained his ankle on
the icy sidewalk in front of Simmons's, and was therefore obliged to remain in the front bedroom of the
perfect boarding house for seven whole days. He is
quoted as saying that next time he hoped he might
break his neck.

"Brother," asked the shocked Rev. Mr. Daniels,
who was calling upon the stranger, "are you prepared to face eternity?"

"What?" was the energetic reply. "After a
week in this town, and in this bedroom? Look here,
Mister, if you want to scare me about the future you
just hint that they'll put me on a straw tick in an ice
chest. Anything hot and lively 'll only be tempting
after this."

But to us, who live here throughout the year, a
week soon passes. And the end of the week following Emily Thomas's arrival at the Cy Whittaker
place found the little girl still there and apparently

115

no nearer being shipped to Indiana than when she came. Not so near, if Mr. Tidditt's opinion counts for anything.

"Gone?" he repeated scoffingly in reply to Bailey Bangs's question. "Course she ain't gone! And, what's more, she ain't goin' to go. Whit's got so already that he wouldn't part with her no more'n he'd cut off his hand."

"But he keeps *sayin'* she's got to go. Only yesterday he was tellin' how Betsy'd feel when the girl landed on her with his letter in her pocket."

"Sayin' don't count for nothin'. Zoeth Cahoon keeps *sayin'* he's goin' to stop drinkin', but he only stops long enough to catch his breath. Cy's tellin' himself fairy yarns and he hopes he believes 'em. Man alive! can't you *see*? Ain't he gettin' more foolish over the young one every day? Don't she boss him round like the overseer on a cranberry swamp? Don't he look more contented than he has sence he got off the cars? I tell you, Bailey, that child fills a place in Whit's life that's been runnin' to seed and needed weedin'. Nothin' could fill it better— unless 'twas a nice wife."

"*Wife!* Oh, *do* be still! I believe you're woman-struck and at an age when it hadn't ought to be catchin' no more'n whoopin' cough."

Mr. Bangs and the town clerk were the only ones, except Captain Cy, who knew the whole truth concerning the little girl. Not that the child's arrival wasn't noted and vigorously discussed by a large portion of the townspeople. Emily had not been in the Whittaker house two days before Angeline Phinney called, hot on the trail of gossip and sensation. But, persistent as Angeline was, she departed knowing not quite as much as when she came. The interview between Miss Phinney and the captain must have been interesting, judging by the lady's account of it.

"I never see such a man in my born days," declared Angie disgustedly. "You couldn't get nothin' out of him. Not that he wan't pleasant and sociable; land sakes! he acted as glad to see me as if I was his rich aunt come on a visit. And he was willin' to talk, too. That's the trouble; he done *all* the talkin'. I happened to mention, just as a sort of starter, you know, somethin' about the cranb'ry crop this fall; and after that all he could say was ' cranb'ries, cranb'ries, cranb'ries!' 'Hear you've got comp'ny,' says I. 'Did you?' says he. 'Now ain't it strange how things'll get spread around? Only yesterday I heard that Joe Dimick's swamp was just loaded down with " early blacks." And yet when I went over to look at it there didn't seem to be so many. There ain't much better cranb'ries anywhere than our early blacks,' he says. 'You take 'em—' And so on, and so on, and so on. *I* didn't care nothin' about the dratted early blacks, but he didn't seem to care for nothin' else. He talked cranb'ries steady for an hour and a half and I left that house with my mouth all puckered up; it's tasted sour ever sence. I never see such a man!"

When Captain Cy was questioned by Asaph concerning the acid conversation, he grinned.

"I didn't know you was so interested in cranb'ries," observed Tidditt.

"I ain't," was the reply; "but I'm more interested in 'em than I am in Angie. I see she was sufferin' from a rush of curiosity to the head and I cured her by homeopath doses. Every time she opened her mouth I dropped an ' early black ' into it. It's a good receipt; you tell Bailey to try it on Ketury some time."

To his chums the captain was emphatic in his orders that secrecy be preserved. No one was to be told who the child was or where she came from. "What they don't know won't hurt 'em any," declared Captain Cy. And Emily's answer to inquiring souls who would fain have delved into her past was to the effect that " Uncle Cyrus " didn't like to have her talk about herself.

"I don't know's I'm ashamed of anything I've done so far," said the captain; "but I ain't braggin', either. Time enough to talk when I send her back to Betsy."

That time, apparently, was not in the near future. The girl stayed on at the Whittaker place and grew to be more and more a part of it. At the end of the second week Captain Cy began calling her " Bos'n."

"A bos'n's a mighty handy man aboard ship," he

118

explained, " and you're so handy here that it fits in first rate. And, besides, it sounds so natural. My dad called me ' Bos'n ' when I was little."

Emily accepted the title complacently. She was quite contented to be called almost anything, so long as she was permitted to stay with her new friend. Already the bos'n had taken charge of the deck and the rest of the ship's company; Captain Cy and " Lonesome," the cat, obeyed her orders.

On the second Sunday morning after her arrival " Bos'n " suggested that she and Captain Cy go to church.

" Mother and I always went at home," she said. " And Auntie Oliver used to say meeting was a good thing for those that needed it."

" Think I need it, do you? " asked the captain, who, in shirt sleeves and slippers, had prepared for a quiet forenoon with his pipe and the *Boston Transcript*.

" I don't know, sir. I heard what you said when Lonesome ate up the steak, and I thought maybe you hadn't been for a long time. I guess churches are different in South America."

So they went to church and sat in the old Whittaker pew. The captain had been there once before when he first returned to Bayport, but the sermon was more somnolent than edifying, and he hadn't repeated the experiment. The pair attracted much attention. Fragments of a conversation, heard by Captain Cy as they emerged into the vestibule, had momentous consequences.

"Kind of a pretty child, ain't she?" commented Mrs. Eben Salters, patting her false front into place under the eaves of her Sunday bonnet.

"Pretty enough in the face," sniffed Mrs. "Tad" Simpson, who was wearing her black silk for the first time since its third making-over. "Pretty enough that way, I s'pose. But, my land! look at the way she's rigged. Old dress, darned and patched up and all outgrown! If I had Cy Whittaker's money I'd be ashamed to have a relation of mine come to meetin' that way. Even if her folks was poorer'n Job's off ox I'd spend a little on my own account and trust to getting it back some time. I'd have more care for my own self-respect. Look at Alicia Atkins. See how nice she looks. Them feathers on her hat must have cost somethin', I bet you. Howdy do, 'Licia, dear? When's your pa comin' home?"

The Honorable Heman had left town on a business trip to the South. Alicia was accompanied by the Atkins housekeeper and, as usual, was garbed regardless of expense.

Mrs. Salters smiled sweetly upon the Atkins heir and then added, in a church whisper: "Don't she look sweet? I agree with you, Sarah; it is strange how Captain Whittaker lets his little niece go. And him rich!"

"Niece?" repeated Mrs. Simpson eagerly. "Who

said 'twas his niece? I heard 'twas a child he'd adopted out of a home. There's all sorts of queer yarns about. I— Oh, good mornin', Cap'n Cyrus! How *do* you do?"

The captain grunted an answer to the effect that he was bearing up pretty well, considering. There was a scowl on his face, and he spoke little as, holding Emily by the hand, he led the way home. That evening he dropped in at the perfect boarding house and begged to know if Mrs. Bangs had any " fashion books " around that she didn't want.

"I mean—er—er—magazines with pictures of women's duds in 'em," he stammered, in explanation. "Bos'n likes to look at 'em. She's great on fashion books, Bos'n is."

Keturah got together a half dozen numbers of the *Home Dressmaker* and other periodicals of a similar nature. The captain took them under his arm and departed, whispering to Mr. Tiditt, as he passed the latter in the hall:

"Come up by and by, Ase. I want to talk to you. Bring Bailey along, if you can do it without startin' divorce proceedings."

Later, when the trio gathered in the Whittaker sitting room, Captain Cy produced the "fashion books " and spoke concerning them.

"You see," he said, "I—I've been thinkin' that Bos'n—Emily, that is—wan't rigged exactly the way she ought to be. Have you fellers noticed it?"

His friends seemed surprised. Neither was ready with an immediate answer, so the captain went on.

" Course I don't mean she ain't got canvas enough to cover her spars," he explained; " but what she has got has seen consider'ble weather, and it seemed to me 'twas pretty nigh time to haul her into dry dock and refit. That's why I borrowed these magazines of Ketury. I've been lookin' them over and there seems to be plenty of riggin' for small craft; the only thing is I don't know what's the right cut for her build. Bailey, you're a married man; you ought to know somethin' about women's clothes. What do you think of this, now? "

He opened one of the magazines and pointed to the picture of a young girl, with a waspy waist and Lilliputian feet, who, arrayed in flounces and furbelows, was toddling gingerly down a flight of marble steps. She carried a parasol in one hand, and the other held the end of a chain to which a long-haired dog was attached.

The town clerk and his companion inspected the young lady with deliberation and interest.

" Well, what do you say? " demanded Captain Cy.

" I don't care much for them kind of dogs," observed Asaph thoughtfully.

" Good land! you don't s'pose they heave the dog in with the clothes, for good measure, do you? Bailey, what's your opinion? "

Mr. Bangs looked wise.

"'I should say that was a real stylish rig-out.'"

"I should say—" he said, "yes, sir, I should say that was a real stylish rig-out. Only thing is, that girl is consider'ble less fleshy than Emily. This one looks to me as if she was breakin' in two amidships. Still, I s'pose likely the duds don't come ready made, so they could be let out some, to fit. What's the price of a suit like that, Whit?"

123

The captain looked at the printed number beneath the fashion plate and then turned to the description in the text.

"'Afternoon gown for miss of sixteen,'" he read. "Humph! that settles that, first crack. Bos'n ain't but half of sixteen."

"Anyway," put in Asaph, "you need somethin' she could wear forenoons, if she wanted to. What's this one? She looks young enough."

The "one" referred to turned out to be a "coat for child of four." It was therefore scornfully rejected. One after another the different magazines were examined and the pictures discussed. At length a "costume for miss of eight years" was pronounced to be pretty nearly the thing.

"Godfrey scissors!" exclaimed the admiring Mr. Tidditt. "That's mighty swell, ain't it? What's the stuff goes into that, Cy?"

"'Material, batiste, trimmed with embroidered batiste.' What in time is batiste?"

"I don't know. Do you, Bailey?"

"No; never heard of it. Ketury never had nothin' like that, I'm sure. French, I shouldn't wonder. Well, Ketury's down on the French ever sence she read about Napoleon leavin' his fust wife to take up with another woman. Does it say any more?"

"Let's see. 'Makes a beautiful gown for evening or summer wear.' Summer! Why, by the big dip-

124

per, we're aground again! Bos'n don't want summer clothes. It's comin' on winter."

He threw the magazine on the floor, rubbed his forehead, and then burst into a laugh.

"For goodness sake, don't tell anybody about this business, boys!" he said. "I guess I must be havin' an early spring of second childhood. But when I heard those women at the meetin' house goin' on about how pretty 'Licia Atkins was got up and how mean and shabby Bos'n looked, it made me bile. And, by the big dipper, I *will* show 'em somethin' afore I get through, too! Only, dressin' little girls is some off my usual course. Bailey, does Ketury make her own duds?"

"Why, no! Course she helps and stands by for orders, but Effie Taylor comes and takes the wheel while the riggin's goin' on. Effie's a dressmaker and——"

"There! See, Ase? It *is* some good to have a married man aboard, after all. A dressmaker's what we want. I'll hunt up Effie to-morrow."

And hunt her up he did, with the result that Miss Taylor came to the Whittaker place each day during the following week and Emily was, as the captain said, "rigged out fresh from main truck to keelson." In this "rigging" Captain Cy and his two partners —Josiah Dimick had already christened the pair "The Board of Strategy"—took a marked interest. They were on hand when each new garment was tried on, and they approved or criticised as seemed to them best.

"Ain't that kind of sober lookin' for a young one like Bos'n?" asked the captain, referring to one of the new gowns. "I don't want her to look as if she was dressed cheap."

"Land sakes!" mumbled Miss Taylor, her mouth full of pins. "There ain't anything cheap about it, and you'll find it out when you get the bill. That's a nice, rich, sensible suit."

"I know, but it's so everlastin' quiet! Don't you think a little yellow and black or some red strung along the yards would sort of liven it up? Why! you ought to see them Greaser girls down in South America of a Sunday afternoon. Color! and go! Jerushy! they'd pretty nigh knock your eye out."

The dressmaker sniffed disdain.

"Cap'n Whittaker," she retorted, "if you want this child to look like an Indian squaw or a barber's pole you'll have to get somebody else to do it. I'm used to dressing Christians, not yeller and black heathen women. Red strung along a skirt like that! I never did!"

"There, there, Effie! Don't get the barometer fallin'. I was only suggestin', you know. What do you think, Bos'n?"

"Why, Uncle Cyrus, I don't believe I should like red very much; nor the other colors, either. I like this just as it is."

"So? Well, you're the doctor. Maybe you're right. I wouldn't want you to look like a barber's pole. Don't love Tad Simpson enough to want to advertise his business."

Miss Taylor's coming had other results besides the refitting of " Bos'n." She found much fault with the captain's housekeeping. It developed that her sister Georgiana, who had been working in a Brockton shoe shop, was now at home and might be engaged to attend to the household duties at the Whittaker establishment, provided she was allowed to " go home nights." Georgiana was engaged, on trial, and did well. So that problem was solved.

School in Bayport opens the first week in October. Of late there has been a movement, headed by some of the townspeople who think city ways are best, to have the term begin in September. But this idea has little chance of success as long as cranberry picking continues to be our leading industry. So many of the children help out the family means by picking cranberries in the fall that school, until the picking season was over, would be slimly attended.

The last week in September found us all discussing the coming of the new downstairs teacher, Miss Phœbe Dawes. Since it was definitely settled that she was to come, the opposition had died down and was less openly expressed; but it was there, all the same, beneath the surface. Congressman Atkins had accepted the surprising defiance of his wish with calm dignity and the philosophy of the truly great who are not troubled by trifles. His lieutenant, Tad Simpson, quoted him as saying that, of course, the will of the school committee was paramount, and he, as all good citizens should, bowed to their verdict. " Far be it from me," so the great man proclaimed, " to desire that my opinion should carry more weight than that of the humblest of my friends and neighbors. Speaking as one whose knowledge of the world was, perhaps—er—more extensive than—er—others, I favored the Normal School candidate. But the persons chosen to select thought—or appeared to think— otherwise. I therefore say nothing and await developments."

This attitude was considered by most of us to reflect credit upon Mr. Atkins. There were a few scoffers, however. When the proclamation was repeated to Captain Cy he smiled.

" Alpheus," he said to Mr. Smalley, his informant, " you didn't use to know Deacon Zeb Clark, who lived up by the salt works in my granddad's time, hey? No, course you didn't! Well, the deacon was a great believer in his own judgment. One time, it bein' Saturday, his wife wanted him to pump the washtub full and take a bath. He said, no; said the cistern was awful low and 'twould use up all the water. She said no such thing; there was water a-plenty. To prove she was wrong he went and pried the cistern cover off to look, and fell in. Mrs. Clark peeked down and saw him there, standin' up to his neck.

"'Tabby,' says he, 'you would have your way and I'm takin' the bath. But you can see for yourself that we'll have to cart water from now on. However, *I* ain't responsible; throw me down the soap and towel.'"

"Humph!" grunted Smalley, "I don't see what that's got to do with it. Heman ain't takin' no bath."

"I don't know's it's got anything to do with it. But he kind of made me think of Zeb, all the same."

The first day of school was, of course, a Monday. On Sunday afternoon Captain Cy and Bos'n went for a walk. These walks had become a regular part of the Sabbath programme, the weather, of course, permitting. After church the pair came home for dinner. The meal being eaten, the captain would light a cigar—a pipe was now hardly " dressed-up " enough for Sunday—and, taking his small partner by the hand, would lead the way across the fields, through the pines and down by the meadow " short cut " to the cemetery. The cemetery is a favorite Sabbath resort for the natives of Bayport, who usually speak of it as the graveyard. It is a pleasant, shady spot, and to visit it is considered quite respectable and in keeping with the day and a due regard for decorum. The ungodly, meaning the summer boarders and the village no-accounts, seem to prefer the beach and the fish houses, but the cemetery attracts the churchgoers.

One may gossip concerning the probable cost of a new tombstone and still remain faithful to the most rigid creed.

Captain Cy was not, strictly speaking, a religious man, according to Bayport standards. Between his attendance to churchly duties and that of the Honorable Heman Atkins there was a great gulf fixed. But he rather liked to visit the graveyard on Sunday afternoons. His mother had been used to stroll there with him, in his boyhood, and it pleased him to follow in her footsteps.

So he and Bos'n walked along the grass-covered paths, between the iron-fenced " lots " of the well-to-do and the humble mounds and simple slabs where the poor were sleeping; past the sumptuous granite shaft of the Atkins lot and the tilted mossy stone which told how " Edwin Simpson, our only son," had been " accidentally shot in the West Indies "; out through the back gate and up the hill to the pine grove overlooking the bay. Here, on a scented carpet of pine needles, they sat them down to rest and chat.

Emily, her small knees drawn up and encircled by her arms, looked out across the flats, now half covered with the rising tide. It was a mild day, more like August than October, and there was almost no wind. The sun was shining on the shallow water, and the sand beneath it showed yellow, checkered and marbled with dark green streaks and patches where the weed-bordered channels wound tortuously. On the horizon the sand hills of Wellmouth notched the blue sky. The girl drew a long breath.

"Oh!" she exclaimed. "Isn't this just lovely! I do like the sea an awful lot."

"That's natural enough," replied her companion. "There's a big streak of salt water in your blood on your ma's side. It pulls, that kind of a streak does. There's days when I feel uneasy every minute and hanker for a deck underneath me. The settin' room floor stays altogether too quiet on a day like that; I'd like to feel it heavin' over a ground swell.

"Say, Bos'n," he said a few minutes later; "I've been thinkin' about you. You've been to school, haven't you?"

"Course I have," was the rather indignant answer. "I went two years in Concord. Mamma used to help me nights, too. I can read almost all the little words. Don't I help you read your paper 'most every night?"

"Sartin you do! Yes, yes! Well, our school opens to-morrer and I've been thinkin' that maybe you'd better go. There's a new teacher comin', and I hear she's pretty good."

"Don't you *know*? Why, Mr. Tiditt said you was the one that got her to come here!"

"Yes; well, Asaph says 'most everything but his prayers. Still, he ain't fur off this time; I cal'late I was some responsible for her bein' voted in. Yet I don't really know anything about her. You see, I—

well, never mind. What do you think? Want to go?"

Bos'n looked troubled.

"I'd like to," she said. "Course I want to learn how to read the big words, too. But I like to stay at home with you more."

"You do, hey? Sho, sho! Well, I guess I can get along between times. Georgiana's there to keep me straight and she'll see to the dust and the dishes. I guess you'd better go to-morrer mornin' and see how you like it, anyhow."

The child thought for a moment.

"I think you're awful good," she said. "I like you next to mamma; even better than Auntie Oliver. I printed a letter to her the other day. I told her you were better than we expected and I had decided to live with you always."

Captain Cy was startled. Considering that, only the day before, he had repeated to Bailey the declaration that the arrangement was but temporary, and that Betsy Howes was escaping responsibility only for a month or so, he scarcely knew what to say.

"Humph!" he grunted. "You've decided it, have you? Well, we'll see. Now you trot around and have a good time. I'm goin' to have another smoke. I'll be here when you get back."

Bos'n wandered off in search of late golden rod. The captain smoked and meditated. By and by the puffs were less frequent and the cigar went out. It fell from his fingers. With his back against a pine tree Captain Cy dozed peacefully.

He awoke with a jump. Something had awakened him, but he did not know what. He blinked and gazed about him. Then he heard a faint scream.

"Uncle!" screamed Bos'n. "O—o—o—h! Uncle Cyrus, help me! Come quick!"

The next moment the captain was plunging through the scrub of huckleberry and bayberry bushes, bumping into pines and smashing the branches aside as he ran in the direction of the call.

Back of the pine grove was a big inclosed pasture nearly a quarter of a mile long. Its rear boundary was the iron fence of the cemetery. The other three sides were marked by rail fences and a stone wall. As the captain floundered from the grove and vaulted the rail fence he swore aloud.

" By the big dipper," he groaned, " it's that cussed heifer! I forgot her. Keep dodgin', Bos'n girl! I'm comin'."

The pasture was tenanted by a red and white cow belonging to Sylvanus Cahoon. Whether or not the animal had, during her calfhood days, been injured by a woman is not known; possibly her behavior was due merely to innate depravity. At any rate, she cherished a mortal hatred toward human beings of her own sex. With men and boys she was meek enough, but no person wearing skirts, and alone, might venture in that field without being chased by that cow. What would happen if the pursued one was caught could only be surmised, for, so far, no female had permitted herself to be caught. Few would come even so near as the other side of the pasture walls.

Bos'n had forgotten the cow. She had gone from one golden-rod clump to another until she had traversed nearly the length of the field. Then the vicious creature had appeared from behind a knoll in the pasture and, head down and bellowing wickedly, had rushed upon her. When the captain reached the far-off fence, the little girl was dodging from one dwarf pine to the next, with the cow in pursuit. The pines were few and Bos'n was nearly at the end of her defenses.

" Help! " she screamed. " Oh, uncle, where are you? What shall I do? "

Captain Cy roared in answer.

" Keep it up! " he yelled. " I'm a-comin'! Shoo! you everlastin' critter! I'll break your back for you! "

The cow didn't understand English it seemed, even such vigorous English as the captain was using. Emily dodged to the last pine. The animal was close upon her. Her rescuer was still far away.

And then the cemetery gate opened and another person entered the pasture. A small person—a woman. She said nothing, but picking up her skirts, ran straight toward the cow, heedless of the latter's repu-

"'Scat! Go home!' ordered the lady."

tation and vicious appearance. One hand clutched the gathered skirts. In the other she held a book.

"Don't be scared, dear," she called reassuringly. Then to the cow: "Stop it! Go away, you wicked thing!"

The animal heard the voice and turned. Seeing that the newcomer was only a woman, she lowered her head and pawed the ground.

"Run for the gate, little girl," commanded the rescuer. "Run quick!" Bos'n obeyed. She made a desperate dash from her pine across the open space, and in another moment was safe inside the cemetery fence.

"Scat! Go home!" ordered the lady, advancing toward the cow and shaking the book at her, as if the volume was some sort of deadly weapon. "Aren't you ashamed of yourself! Go away! You needn't growl at me! I'm not a bit afraid of you."

The "growling" was the muttered bellow with which the cow was wont to terrorize her feminine victims. But this victim refused to be terrorized. Instead of screaming and running she continued to advance, brandishing the book and repeating her orders that the creature "go home" at once. The cow did not know what to make of it. Before she could decide whether to charge or retreat, a good-sized stick descended upon her back with a "whack" that settled the question. Captain Cy had reached the scene of battle.

Then the rescuer's courage seemed to desert her, for she ran back to the cemetery even faster than she had run from it. When the indignant captain, having pursued and chastised the cow until the stick was but a splintered remnant, reached the haven behind the iron fence, he found her soothing the frightened Bos'n who was sobbing and hysterical.

Emily saw her " Uncle Cyrus " coming and rushed into his arms. He picked her up and, holding her with a grip which testified to the nerve strain he had been under, stepped forward to meet the stranger, whose coming had been so opportune.

And she *was* a stranger. The captain knew most of Bayport's inhabitants by this time, or thought he did, but he did not know her. She was a small woman, quietly dressed, and her hair, under a neat black and white hat, was brown. The hat was now a trifle to one side and the hair was the least bit disarranged, an effect not at all unbecoming. She was tucking in the stray wisps as the captain, with Bos'n in his arms, came up.

"Well, ma'am!" puffed Captain Cy. "*Well,* ma'am! I must say that was the slickest, pluckiest thing ever I saw anywheres. I don't know what would—I—I declare I don't know how to thank you."

The lady looked at him a moment before replying. Then she began to laugh, a jolly laugh that was pleasant to hear.

"Don't try, please," she said chokingly. "It wasn't anything. Oh, mercy me! I'm all out of breath. You see, I had been warned about that cow when I started to walk this afternoon. So when I saw her chasing your poor little girl here I knew right away what was the matter. It must have been foolish enough to look at. I'm used to dogs and cats, but I haven't had many pet cows. I told her to 'go home' and to 'scat' and all sorts of things. Wonder I didn't tell her to lie down! And the way I shook that ridiculous book at her was——"

She laughed again and the captain and Bos'n joined in the laugh, in spite of the fright they both had experienced.

"That book was dry enough to frighten almost anything," continued the lady. "It was one I took from the table before I left the place where I'm staying, and a duller collection of sermons I never saw. Oh, dear! . . . there! Is my hat any more respectable now?"

"Yes'm. It's about on an even keel, I should say. But I must tell you, ma'am, you done simply great and——"

"Seems to me the people who own that cow must be a poor set to let her make such a nuisance of herself. Did your daughter run away from you?"

"Well, you see, ma'am, she ain't really my daughter. Bos'n here—that's my nickname for her, ma'am—she and I was out walkin'. I set down in the pines and I guess I must have dozed off. Anyhow, when I woke up she was gone, and the first thing I knew of this scrape was hearin' her hail."

The little woman's manner changed. Her gray eyes flashed indignantly.

"You dozed off?" she repeated. "With a little girl in your charge, and in the very next lot to that cow? Didn't you know the creature chased women and girls?"

"Why, yes; I'd heard of it, but——"

"It wasn't Uncle Cyrus's fault," put in Bos'n eagerly. "It was mine. I went away by myself."

Beyond shifting her gaze to the child the lady paid no attention to this remark.

"What do you think her mother 'll say when she sees that dress?" she asked.

It was Emily's best gown, the finest of the new " rig out " prepared by Miss Taylor. The girl and Captain Cy gazed ruefully at the rents and pitch stains made by the vines and pine trees.

"Well, you see," replied the abashed captain, " the fact is, she ain't got any mother."

"Oh! I beg your pardon. And hers, too, poor dear. Well, if I were you I shouldn't go to sleep next time I took her walking. Good afternoon."

She turned and calmly walked down the path. At the bend she spoke again.

"I should be gentle with her, if I were you," she said. "Her nerves are pretty well upset. Besides, if you'll excuse my saying so, I don't think she is the one that needs scolding."

They thought she had gone, but she turned once more to add a final suggestion.

"I think that dress could be fixed," she said, "if you took it to some one who knew about such things."

She disappeared amidst the graveyard shrubbery. Captain Cy and Bos'n slowly followed her. From the pasture the red and white cow sent after them a broken-spirited "Moo!"

Bos'n was highly indignant. During the homeward walk she sputtered like a damp firecracker.

"The idea of her talking so to you, Uncle Cyrus!" she exclaimed. "It wasn't your fault at all."

The captain smiled one-sidedly.

"I don't know about that, shipmate," he said. "I wouldn't wonder if she was more than half right. But say! she was all business and no frills, wasn't she! Ha, ha! How she did spunk up to that heifer! Who in the dickens do you cal'late she is?"

# CHAPTER VIII

## THE "COW LADY"

THAT question was answered the very next day. Bos'n, carefully dressed by Georgianna under the captain's supervision, and weighted down with advice and counsel from the latter, started for the schoolhouse at a quarter to nine. Only a sense of shame kept Captain Cy from walking to school with her. He spent a miserable forenoon. They were quite the longest three hours in his varied experience. The house was dreadfully lonely. He wandered from kitchen to sitting room, worried Georgianna, woke up the cat, and made a complete nuisance of himself. Twelve o'clock found him leaning over the gate and looking eagerly in the direction of the schoolhouse.

Bos'n ran all the way home. She was in a high state of excitement.

"What do you think, Uncle Cyrus?" she cried. "What *do* you think? I've found out who the cow lady is!"

"The cow lady? Oh, yes, yes! Have you? Who is she?"

"She's teacher, that's who she is!"

The captain was astonished.

"No!" he exclaimed. "Phœbe Dawes? You
don't say so! Well, well!"

"Yes, sir. When I went into school and found
her sitting there I was so surprised I didn't know
what to do. She knew me, too, and said good morning, and was I all right again and was my dress really
as bad as it looked to be? I told her that Georgianna
thought she could fix it, and if she couldn't, her sister
could. She said that was nice, and then 'twas time
for school to begin."

"Did she say anything about me?" inquired Captain Cy when they were seated at the dinner table.

"Oh, yes! I forgot. She must have found out
who you are, 'cause she said she was surprised that a
man who had made his money out of hides should
have been so careless about the creatures that wore
'em."

"Humph! How'd she get along with the young
ones in school?"

It appeared that she had gotten along very well
with them. Some of the bigger boys in the back
seats, cherishing pleasant memories of the "fun"
they had under Miss Seabury's easy-going rule, at-
tempted to repeat their performances of the previous
term. But the very first "spitball" which spattered
upon the blackboard proved a disastrous missile for
its thrower.

"She made him clean the board," proclaimed Bos'n, big-eyed and awestruck, "and then he had to stand in the corner. He was Bennie Edwards, and he's most thirteen. Miss Seabury, they said, couldn't do anything with him, but teacher said 'Go,' as quiet as could be and just looked at him, and he went. And he's most as tall as she is. He did look so silly!"

The Edwards youth was not the only one who was made to "look silly" by little Miss Dawes during the first days of her stay in Bayport. She dealt with the unruly members of her classes as bravely as she had faced the Cahoon cow, and the results were just as satisfactory. She was strict, but she was impartial, and Alicia Atkins found, to her great surprise, that the daughter of a congressman was expected to study as faithfully and behave herself as well as freckled-faced Noah Hamlin, whose father peddled fish and whose everyday costume was a checkered "jumper" and patched overalls.

The school committee, that is, the majority of it, was delighted with the new teacher. Lemuel Myrick boasted loudly of his good judgment in voting for her. But Tad Simpson and Darius Ellis and others of the Atkins following still scoffed and hinted at trouble in the future.

"A new broom sweeps fine," quoted Mr. Simpson. "She's doin' all right now, maybe. Anyway, the young ones are behavin' themselves, but *discip-*

line ain't the whole thing. Heman told me that the teacher he wanted could talk French language and play music and all kinds of accomplishments. Phœbe —not findin' any fault with her, you understand— don't know no more about music than a hen; my wife says she don't even sing in church loud enough for anybody to hear her. And as for French! why everybody knows she uses the commonest sort of United States, just as easy to understand as what I'm sayin' now."

Miss Dawes boarded at the perfect boarding house. There opinion was divided concerning her. Bailey and Mr. Tidditt liked her, but the feminine boarders were not so favorably impressed.

"I think she's altogether too pert about what don't concern her," commented Angeline Phinney. "Sarah Emma Simpson dropped in t'other day to dinner, and we church folks got to talkin' about the minister's preachin' such 'advanced' sermons. And Sarah Emma told how she'd heard he said he'd known some real moral Universalists in his time, or some such unreligious foolishness. And I said I wondered he didn't get a new tail coat; the one he preached in Sundays was old as the hills and so outgrown it wouldn't scurcely button acrost him. 'A man bein' paid nine hundred a year,' I says, 'ought to dress decent, anyhow.' And that Phœbe Dawes speaks up, without bein' asked, and says for her part she'd ruther hear a broad man in a narrer coat than t'other way about. 'Twas a regular slap in the face for me, and Sarah Emma and I ain't got over it yet."

Captain Cy heard the gossip concerning the new teacher and it rather pleased him. She appeared to be independent, and he liked independence. He met her once or twice on the street, but she merely bowed and passed on. Once he tried to thank her again for her part in the cow episode, but she would not listen to him.

Bos'n was making good progress with her studies. She was naturally a bright child—not the marvel the captain and the "Board of Strategy" considered her, but quick to learn. She was not a saint, however, and occasionally misbehaved in school and was punished for it. One afternoon she did not return at her usual hour. Captain Cy was waiting at the gate when Asaph Tidditt happened along. Bailey, too, was with him.

"Waitin' for Bos'n, was you?" asked the town clerk. "Well, you'll have to wait quite a spell, I cal'late. She's been kept after school."

"Yes; and she's got to write fifty lines of copy," added Bailey.

Captain Cy was highly indignant.

"Get out!" he cried. "She ain't neither."

"Yes, she has, too. One of the Salters young ones told me. I knew you'd be mad, though I s'pose folks that didn't know her's well's we do would say she's no different from other children."

# THE "COW LADY"

This was close to heresy, according to the captain's opinion.

"She ain't!" he cried. "I'd like to know why not! If she ain't twice as smart as the run of young ones 'round here then— Humph! And she's kept after school! Well, now; I won't have it! There's enough time for studyin' without wearin' out her brains after hours. Oh, I guess you're mistaken."

"No, we ain't. I tell you, Whit, if I was you I'd make a fuss about this. She's a smart child, Bos'n is; I never see a smarter. And she ain't any too strong."

"That's so, she ain't." The idea that Emily's health was "delicate" had become a fixed fact in the minds of the captain and the "Board." It made a good excuse for the systematic process of "spoiling" the girl, which the indulgent three were doing their best to carry on.

"I wouldn't let her be kept, Cy," urged Bailey. "Why don't you go right off and see Phœbe and settle this thing? You've got a right to talk to her. She wouldn't be teacher if it wasn't for you."

Asaph added his arguments to those of Mr. Bangs. Captain Cy, carried away by his firm belief that Bos'n was a paragon of all that was brilliant and good, finally yielded.

"All right!" he exclaimed. "Come on! That poor little thing shan't be put upon by nobody."

The trio marched majestically down the hill. As

they neared the schoolhouse Bailey's courage began to fail. Miss Dawes was a boarder at his house, and he feared consequences should Keturah learn of his interference.

"I—I guess you don't need me," he stammered. "The three of us 'll scare that teacher woman most to death. And she's so little and meek, you know. If I should lose my temper and rare up I might say somethin' that would hurt her feelin's. I'll set on the fence and wait for you and Ase, Whit."

Mr. Tidditt's scornful comments concerning "white feathers" and "backsliders" had no effect. Mr. Bangs perched himself on the fence.

"Give it to her, fellers!" he called after them. "Talk Dutch to her! Let her know that there's one child she can't abuse."

At the foot of the steps Asaph paused.

"Say, Cy," he whispered, "don't you think I better not go in? It ain't really my business, you know, and—and— Well, I'm on the s'lectmen and she might be frightened if she see me pouncin' down on her. 'Tain't as if I was just a common man. I'll go and set along of Bailey and you go in and talk quiet to her. She'd feel so sort of ashamed if there was anyone else to hear the rakin' over—hey?"

"Now, see here, Ase," expostulated the captain, "I don't like to do this all by myself! Besides, 'twas you chaps put me up to it. You ain't goin' to pull out of the race and leave me to go over the course alone, are you? Come on! what are you afraid of?"

His companion hotly denied that he was "afraid" of anything. He had all sorts of arguments to back his decision. At last Captain Cy lost patience.

"Well, *be* a skulk, if you want to!" he declared. "I've set out to see this thing through, and I'm goin' to do it. Only," he muttered, as he entered the downstairs vestibule, "I wish I didn't feel quite so much as if I was stealin' hens' eggs."

Miss Dawes herself opened the door in response to his knock.

"Oh, it's you, Cap'n Whittaker," she said. "Come in, please."

Captain Cy entered the schoolroom. It was empty, save for the teacher and himself and one little girl, who, seated at a desk, was writing busily. She looked up and blushed a vivid red. The little girl was Bos'n.

"Sit down, Cap'n," said Miss Phœbe, indicating the visitor's chair. "What was it you wanted to see me about?"

The captain accepted the invitation to be seated, but he did not immediately reply to Miss Dawes's question. He dropped his hat on the floor, crossed his legs, uncrossed them, and then observed that it was pretty summery weather for so late in the fall. The teacher admitted the truth of his assertion and waited for him to continue.

147

" I—I s'pose school's pretty full, now that cran-b'ryin' 's over," said Captain Cy.

" Yes, pretty full."

" Gettin' along first rate with the scholars, I hear."

" Yes."

This was a most unpromising beginning, really no beginning at all. The captain cleared his throat, set his teeth, and, without looking at his companion, dove headlong into the business which had brought him there.

" Miss Dawes," he said, " I—I s'pose you know that Bos'n—I mean Emily there—is livin' at my house and that I'm taking care of her for—for the present."

The lady smiled.

" Yes," she said. " I gathered as much from what you said when we first met."

She herself had said one or two things on that occasion. Captain Cy remembered them distinctly.

" Yes, yes," he said hastily. " Well, my doin's that time wasn't exactly the best sample of the care, I will say. Wan't even a fair sample, maybe. I try to do my best with the child, long as she stays with me, and—er—and—er—I'm pretty particular about her health."

" I'm glad to hear it."

" Yes. Now, Miss Phœbe, I appreciate what you did for Bos'n and me that Sunday, and I'm thankful for it. I've tried to thank——"

"I know. Please don't say any more about it. I imagine there is something else you want to say, isn't there?"

"Why, yes, there is. I—I heard that Emmie had been kept after school. I didn't believe it, of course, but I thought I'd run up and see what——"

He hesitated. The teacher finished the sentence for him.

"To see if it was true?" she said. "It is. I told her to stay and write fifty lines."

"You did? Well, now that's what I wanted to speak to you about. Course I ain't interferin' in your affairs, you know, but I just wanted to explain about Bos'n—Emmie, I mean. She ain't a common child; she's got too much head for the rest of her. If you'd lived with her same as I have you'd appreciate it. Her health's delicate."

"Is it? She seems strong enough to me. I haven't noticed any symptoms."

"Course not, else you wouldn't have kept her in. But *I* know, and I think it's my duty to tell you. Never mind if she can't do quite so much writin'. I'd rather she wouldn't; she might bust a blood vessel or somethin'. Such things *have* happened, to extry smart young ones. You just let her trot along home with me now and——"

"Cap'n Whittaker," Miss Dawes had risen to her feet with a determined expression on her face.

"Yes, ma'am," said the captain, rising also.

149

"Cap'n Whittaker," repeated the teacher, "I'm very glad that you called. I've been rather expecting you might, because of certain things I have heard."

"You heard? What was it you heard—if you don't mind my askin'?"

"No, I don't, because I think we must have an understanding about Emily. I have heard that you allow her to do as she pleases at home; in other words, that you are spoiling her, and——"

"*Spoilin'* her! *I* spoilin' her? Who told you such an unlikely yarn as that? I ain't the kind to spoil anybody. Why, I'm so strict that I'm ashamed of myself sometimes."

He honestly believed he was. Miss Phœbe calmly continued.

"Of course, what you do at home is none of my business. I shouldn't mention it anyhow, if you hadn't called, because I pay very little attention to town talk, having lived in this county all my life and knowing what gossip amounts to. I like Emily; she's a pretty good little girl and well behaved, as children go. But this you must understand. She can't be spoiled here. She whispered this afternoon, twice. She has been warned often, and knows the rule. I kept her after school because she broke that rule, and if she breaks it again, she will be punished again. I kept the Edwards boy two hours yesterday and——"

"Edwards boy! Do you mean to compare that—

150

that young rip of a Ben Edwards with a girl like Bos'n? I never heard——"

"I'm not comparing anybody. I'm trying to be fair to every scholar in this room. And, so long as Emily behaves herself, she shall be treated accordingly. When she doesn't, she shall be punished. You must understand that."

"But Ben Edwards! Why, he's a wooden-head, same as his dad was afore him! And Emmie's the smartest scholar in this town."

"Oh, no, she isn't! She's a good scholar, but there are others just as good and even quicker to learn."

This was piling one insult upon another. Other children as brilliant as Bos'n! Captain Cy was bursting with righteous indignation.

"Well!" he exclaimed. "Well! for a teacher that we've called to——"

"And that's another thing," broke in Miss Dawes quickly. "I've been told that you, Cap'n Whittaker, are the one directly responsible for my being chosen for this place. I don't say that you are presuming on that, but——"

"I ain't! I never thought of such a thing!"

"But if you are you mustn't, that's all. I didn't ask for the position and, now that I've got it, I shall try to fill it without regard to one person more than another. Emily stays here until her lines are written. I don't think we need to say any more. Good day."

She opened the door. Captain Cy picked up his

hat, swallowed hard, and stepped across the threshold. Then Miss Phœbe added one more remark.

"Cap'n," she said, "when you were in command of a ship did you allow outsiders to tell you how to treat the sailors?"

The captain opened his mouth to reply. He wanted to reply very much, but somehow he couldn't find a satisfying answer to that question.

"Ma'am," he said, "all I can say is that if you'd been in South America, same as I have, and seen the way them half-breed young ones act, you'd——"

The teacher smiled, in spite of an apparent effort not to.

"Perhaps so," she said, "but this is Massachusetts. And—well, Emily isn't a half-breed."

Captain Cy strode through the vestibule. Just before the door closed behind him he heard a stifled sob from poor Bos'n.

The Board of Strategy was waiting at the end of the yard. Its members were filled with curiosity.

"Did you give it to her good?" demanded Asaph. "Did you let her understand we wouldn't put up with such cruelizin'?"

"Where's Bos'n?" asked Mr. Bangs.

Their friend's answers were brief and tantalizingly incomplete. He walked homeward at a gait which caused plump little Bailey to puff in his efforts to keep up, and he would say almost nothing about the interview in the schoolroom.

"'I don't think we need to say any more.  Good day.'"

# THE "COW LADY"

"Well," said Mr. Tidditt, when they reached the Whittaker gate, "I guess she knows her place now; hey, Cy? I cal'late she'll be careful who she keeps after school from now on."

"Didn't use no profane language, did you, Cy?" asked Bailey. "I hope not, 'cause she might have you took up just out of spite. Did she ask your pardon for her actions?"

"No!" roared the captain savagely. Then, banging the gate behind him, he strode up the yard and into the house.

Bos'n came home a half hour later. Captain Cy was alone in the sitting room, seated in his favorite rocker and moodily staring at nothing in particular. The girl gazed at him for a moment and then climbed into his lap.

"I wrote my fifty lines, Uncle Cyrus," she said. "Teacher said I'd done them very nicely, too."

The captain grunted.

"Uncle Cy," whispered Bos'n, putting her arms around his neck, "I'm awful sorry I was so bad."

"Bad? Who—you? You couldn't be bad if you wanted to. Don't talk that way or I'll say somethin' I hadn't ought to."

"Yes, I could be bad, too. I was bad. I whispered."

"Whispered! What of it? That ain't nothin'. When I was a young one in school I used to whis—

. . . Hum! Well, anyhow, don't you think any more about it. 'Tain't worth while."

They rocked quietly for a time. Then Bos'n said:

" Uncle Cyrus, don't you like teacher?"

" Hey? *Like* her? Well, if that ain't a question? Yes, I like her about as well as Lonesome likes Eben Salter's dog."

" I'm sorry. I like her ever so much."

" You *do*? Go 'long! After the way she treated you, poor little thing! "

" She didn't treat me any worse than she does the other girls and boys when they're naughty. And I did know the rule about whispering."

" Well, that's different. Comparin' you with that Bennie Edwards—the idea! And then makin' you cry! "

" She didn't make me cry."

" Did, too. I heard you."

The child looked up at him and then hid her face in his waistcoat.

" I wasn't crying about her," she whispered. " It was you."

" *Me!* " The captain gasped. " Good land! " he muttered. " It's just as I expected. She's studied too hard and it's touchin' her brain."

" No, sir, it isn't. It isn't truly. I did cry about you because I didn't like to hear you talk so. And I was so sorry to have you come there."

"You *was*!"

"Yes, sir. Other children's folks don't come when they're bad. And I kept feeling so sort of ashamed of you."

"Ashamed of *me*?"

Bos'n nodded vigorously.

"Yes, sir. Everything teacher said sounded so right, and what you said didn't. And I like to have you always right."

"Do, hey? Hum!" Captain Cy didn't speak again for some few minutes, but he held the little girl very tight in his arms. At length he drew a long breath.

"By the big dipper, Bos'n!" he exclaimed. "You're a wonder, you are. I wouldn't be surprised if you grew up to be a mind reader, like that feller in the show we went to at the townhall a spell ago. To tell you the honest Lord's truth, I've been ashamed of myself ever since I come out of that schoolhouse door. When that teacher woman sprung that on me about my fo'mast hands aboard ship I was set back about forty fathom. I never wanted to answer anybody so bad in *my* life, and I couldn't 'cause there wasn't anything to say. I cal'late I've made a fool of myself."

Bos'n nodded again.

"We won't do so any more, will we?" she said.

"You bet we won't! *I* won't, anyhow. You haven't done anything."

12          155

# CY WHITTAKER'S PLACE

"And you'll like teacher?"

The captain stamped his foot.

"No, *sir*!" he declared. "She may be all right in her way—I s'pose she is; but it's too Massachusettsy a way for me. No, sir! I don't like her and I *won't* like her. No, sir-ee, never! She—she ain't my kind of a woman," he added stubbornly. "That's what's the matter! She ain't my kind of a woman."

# CHAPTER IX

## POLITICS AND BIRTHDAYS

TOWN meeting " was called for the twenty-
first of November.

With the summer boarders gone, the
cranberry picking finished, state election over, school
begun and under way, and real winter not yet upon
us, Bayport, in the late fall, distinctly needs something to enliven it. The Shakespeare Reading Society
and the sewing circle continue, of course, to interest
the " women folks," there is the usual every evening
gathering at Simmons's, and the young people are
looking forward to the " Grand Ball " on Thanks-
giving eve. But for the men, on week days, there
is little to do except to " putter " about the house,
banking its foundations with dry seaweed as a pre-
caution against searching no'theasters, whitewashing
the barns and outbuildings, or fixing things in the
vegetable cellar where the sticks of smoked herring
hang in rows above the barrels of cabbages, potatoes,
and turnips. The fish weirs, most of them, are taken
up, lest the ice, which will be driven into the bay
later on, tear the nets to pieces. Even the hens grow

lazy and lay less frequently. Therefore, away back in the " airly days," some far-sighted board of select-men arranged that " town meeting " should be held during this lackadaisical season. A town meeting —and particularly a Bayport town meeting, where everything from personal affairs to religion is likely to be discussed—can stir up excitement when nothing else can.

This year there were several questions to be talked over and settled at town meeting. Two selectmen, whose terms expired, were candidates for reëlection. Lem Myrick had resigned from the school commit-tee, not waiting until spring, as he had announced that he should do. Then there was the usual senti-ment in favor of better roads and the usual opposi-tion to it. Also there was the ever-present hope of the government appropriation for harbor improvement.

Mr. Tidditt was one of the selectmen whose terms expired. In his dual capacity as selectman and town clerk Asaph felt himself to be a very important per-sonage. To elect some one else in his place would be, he was certain, a calamity which would stagger the township. Therefore he was a busy man and made many calls upon his fellow citizens, not to in-fluence their votes—he was careful to explain that— but just, as he said, " to see how they was gettin' along," and because he " thought consider'ble of 'em " and " took a real personal interest, you under-stand," in their affairs.

# POLITICS AND BIRTHDAYS

To Captain Cy he came, naturally, for encouragement and help, being—as was his habit at such times —in a state of gloom and hopeless despair.

"No use, Whit," he groaned. "'Tain't no use at all. I'm licked. I'm gettin' old and they don't want me no more. I guess I'd better get right up afore the votin' begins and tell 'em my health ain't strong enough to be town clerk no longer. It's better to do that than to be licked. Don't you think so?"

"Sure thing!" replied his friend, with sarcasm. "If I was you I'd be toted in on a bed so they can see you're all ready for the funeral. Might have the doctor walkin' ahead, wipin' his eyes, and the joyful undertaker trottin' along astern. What's the particular disease that's got you by the collar just now— facial paralysis?"

"No. What made you think of that?"

"Oh, nothin'! Only I heard you stopped in at ten houses up to the west end of the town yesterday, and talked three quarters of an hour steady at everyone. That would fit me for the scrap heap inside of a week, and you've been goin' it ever since September nearly. What does ail you—anything?"

"Why, no; nothin' special that way. Only there don't seem to be any enthusiasm for me, somehow. I just hint at my bein' a candidate and folks say, 'Yes, indeed. Looks like rain, don't it?' and that's about all."

"Well, that hadn't ought to surprise you. If any-body came to me and says, 'The sun's goin' to rise to-morrer mornin',' I shouldn't dance on my hat and crow hallelujahs. Enthusiasm! Why, Ase, you've been a candidate every two years since Noah got the ark off the ways, or along there. And there ain't been any opposition to you yet, except that time when Uncle 'Bial Stickney woke up in the wrong place and hollered 'No,' out of principle, thinkin' he was to home with his wife. If I was you I'd go and take a nap. You'll read the minutes at selectmen's meetings for another fifty year, more or less; take my word for it. As for the school committee, that's different. I ain't made up my mind about that."

There had been much discussion concerning the school committee. Who should be chosen to replace Mr. Myrick on the board was the gravest question to come before the meeting. Many names had been proposed at Simmons's and elsewhere, but some of those named had refused to run, and others had not, after further consideration, seemed the proper persons for the office. In the absence of Mr. Atkins, Tad Simpson was our leader in the political arena. But Tad so far had been mute.

"Wait a while," he said. "There's some weeks afore town meetin' day. This is a serious business. We can't have no more—I mean no unsuitable man to fill such an important place as that. The welfare of our posterity," he added, and we all recognized the quotation, "depends upon the choice that's to be made."

A choice was made, however, on the very next day but one after this declaration. A candidate announced himself. Asaph and Bailey hurried to the Cy Whittaker place with the news. Captain Cy was in the woodshed building a doll house for Bos'n. "Just for my own amusement," he hastily explained. "Somethin' for her to take along when she goes out West to Betsy."

Mr. Tidditt was all smiles.

"What do you think, Cy?" he cried. "The new school committee man's as good as elected. 'Lonzo Snow's goin' to take it."

The captain laid down his plane.

"'Lonzo Snow!" he repeated. "You don't say! Humph! Well, well!"

"Yes, sir!" exclaimed Bailey. "He's come forward and says it's his duty to do so. He——"

"Humph! His duty, hey? I wonder who pointed it out to him?"

"Well, I don't know. But even Tad Simpson's glad; he says that he knows Heman will be pleased with *that* kind of a candidate and so he won't have to do any more huntin'. He thinks 'Lonzo's comin' out by himself this way is a kind of special Providence."

"Yes, yes! I shouldn't wonder. Did you ever notice how dead sure Tad and his kind are that

161

Providence is workin' with 'em? Seems to me 'twould
be more satisfactory if we could get a sight of the
other partner's signature to the deed."

"What's the matter with you?" demanded Asaph.
"You ain't findin' fault with 'Lonzo, are you? Ain't
he a good man?"

"Good! Sure thing he's good! Nobody can say
he isn't and tell the truth."

No one could truthfully speak ill of Alonzo Snow,
that was a fact. He lived at the lower end of the
village, was well to do, a leading cranberry grower,
and very prominent in the church. A mild, easy-
going person was Mr. Snow, with an almost too keen
fear of doing the wrong thing and therefore prone
to be guided by the opinion of others. He was distinctly not a politician.

"Then what ails you?" asked Asaph hotly.

"Why, nothin', maybe. Only I'm always suspicious when Tad pats Providence on the back. I generally figure that I can see through a doughnut, when
there's a light behind the hole. Who is 'Lonzo's
best friend in this town? Who does he chum with
most of anybody?"

"Why, Darius Ellis, I guess. You know it."

"Um—hum. And Darius is on the committee—
why?"

"Well, I s'pose 'cause Heman Atkins thought he'd
be a good feller to have there. But——"

"Yes, and 'Lonzo's pew in church is right under

162

the Atkins memorial window. The light from it makes a kind of halo round his bald head every Sunday."

"Well, what of it? Heman, nor nobody else, could buy 'Lonzo Snow."

"Buy him? Indeed they couldn't. But there are some things you get without buyin'—the measles, for instance. And the one that's catchin' 'em don't know he's in danger till the speckles break out. Fellers, this committee voted in Phœbe Dawes by just two votes to one, and one of the two was Lem Myrick. Darius was against her. Now with Tad and his 'Providence' puttin' in 'Lonzo Snow, and Heman Atkins settin' behind the screen workin' his Normal School music box so's they can hear the tune—well, Phœbe *may* stay this term out, but how about next?"

"Hey? Why, I don't know. Anyhow, you're down on Phœbe as a thousand of brick. I don't see why you worry about *her*. After the way she treated poor Bos'n and all."

Captain Cy stirred uneasily and kicked a chip across the floor.

"Well," he said, "well, I—I don't know's that's— That is, right's right and wrong's wrong. I've seen bullfights down yonder—" jerking his thumb over his shoulder in the vague direction of Buenos Ayres, " and every time my sympathy's been with the bull. Not that I loved the critter for his own sake, but because all Greaserdom was out to down him. From what I hear, this Phœbe Dawes—for all her pesky down-East stubbornness—is teachin' pretty well, and

"'Look here, you two! how would I look on the school committee?'"

anyhow she's one little woman against Tad Simpson and Heman Atkins and—and Tad's special brand of Providence. She deserves a fair shake and, by the big dipper, she's goin' to have it! Look here, you two! how would I look on the school committee?"

"You?" repeated the pair in concert. "*You*?"

"Yes, me. I ain't a Solomon for wisdom, but I cal'late I'd be as near the top of the barrel as Darius Ellis, and only one or two layers under Eben Salters or 'Lonzo Snow. I'm a candidate—see?"

"But—but, Whit," gasped the town clerk, "are you popular enough? Could you get elected?"

"I don't know, but I can find out. You and Bailey 'll vote for me, won't you?"

"Course we will, but——"

"All right. There's two votes. A hundred and odd more'll put me in. Here goes for politics and popularity. I may be president yet; you can't tell. And say! this town meetin' won't be *dull*, whichever way the cat jumps."

This last was a safe prophecy. All dullness disappeared from Bayport the moment it became known that Captain Cyrus Whittaker was " out " for the school committee. The captain began his electioneering at once. That very afternoon he called upon three people—Eben Salters, Josiah Dimick, and Lemuel Myrick.

Captain Salters was chairman of selectmen as well as chairman of the committee. He was a hard-headed old salt, who had made money in the Australian packet service. He had common sense, independence, and considerable influence in the town. Next to

Congressman Atkins he was, perhaps, our leading citizen. And, more than all, he was not afraid, when he thought it necessary, to oppose the great Heman.

"Well," he said reflectively, after listening to Captain Cy's brief statement of his candidacy, " I cal'late I'll stand in with you, Cy. I ain't got anything against 'Lonzo, but—but—well, consarn it! maybe that's the trouble. Maybe he's so darned good it makes me jealous. Anyhow, I'll do what I can for you."

Joe Dimick laughed aloud. He was an iconoclast, seldom went to church, and was entirely lacking in reverence. Also he really liked the captain.

" Ho, ho! " he crowed. " Whit, do you realize that you're underminin' this town's constitution? Oh, sartin, I'm with you, if it's only to see the fur fly! I do love a scrap."

With Lem Myrick Captain Cy's policy was different. He gently reminded that gentleman of the painting contract, intimated that other favors might be forthcoming, and then, as a clincher, spoke of Tad Simpson's comment when Mr. Myrick voted for Phœbe Dawes.

" Of course," he added, " if you think Tad's got a right to boss all hands and the cook, why, I ain't complainin'. Only, if *I* was a painter doin' a good, high-class trade, and a one-hoss barber tried to dictate to me, I shouldn't bow down and tell him to kick

"'So get every vote you can. Never mind how; just get 'em.'"

easy as he could. Seems to me I'd kick first. But *I'm* no boss; I mustn't influence you."

Lemuel was indignant.

"No barber runs me," he declared. "You stand up for me when that townhall paintin's to be done and I'll work hard for you now, Cap'n Whittaker. 'Lonzo Snow's an elder and all that, but I can't help it. Anyway, his place was all fixed up a year ago and I didn't get the job. A feller has to look after himself these days."

With these division commanders to lead their forces into the enemy's country and with Asaph and Bailey doing what they could to help, Captain Cy's campaign soon became worthy of respectful consideration. For a while Tad Simpson scoffed at the opposition; then he began to work openly for Mr. Snow. Later he marshaled his trusted officers around the pool table in the back room of the barber shop and confided to them that it was anybody's fight and that he was worried.

"It's past bein' a joke," he said. "It's mighty serious. We've got to hustle, we have. Heman trusted me in this job, and if I fall down it 'll be bad for me and for you fellers, too. I wish he was home to run things himself, but he's got business down South there—some property he owns or somethin'—and says he can't leave. But we must win! By mighty! we've *got* to. So get every vote you can. Never mind how; just get 'em, that's all."

Captain Cy was thoroughly enjoying himself.
The struggle suited him to perfection. He was
young, in spite of his fifty-five years, and this tussle
against odds, reminding him of other tussles during
his first seasons in business, aroused his energies and,
as he expressed it, "stirred up his vitals and made
him hop round like a dose of 'pain killer.' "

He did not, however, forget Bos'n. He and she
had their walks and their pleasant evenings together
in spite of politics. He took the child into his confidence and told her of the daily gain, or loss, in
votes, as if she were his own age. She understood a
little of all this, and tried hard to understand the rest,
preaching between times to Georgianna how "the
bad men were trying to beat Uncle Cyrus because
he was gooder than they, but they couldn't, 'cause
everybody loved him so." Georgianna had some
doubts, but she kept them to herself.

Among the things in Bos'n's "box" was a long
envelope, sealed with wax and with a lawyer's name
printed in one corner. The captain opened it, at Emily's suggestion, and was astonished to find that the
inclosure was a will, dated some years back, in which
Mrs. Mary Thomas, the child's mother, left to her
daughter all her personal property and also the land
in Orham, Massachusetts, which had been willed to
her by her own mother. There was a note with the
will in which Mrs. Thomas stated that no one save
herself had known of this land, not even her husband.

She had not told him because she feared that, like everything else, it would be sold and the money wasted in dissipation. " He suspected something of the sort," she added, " but he did not find out the secret, although he—" She had evidently scratched out what followed, but Captain Cy mentally filled in the blank with details of abuse and cruelty. " If anything happens to me," concluded the widow, " I want the land sold and the money used for Emily's maintenance as long as it lasts."

The captain went over to Orham and looked up the land. It was a strip along the shore, almost worthless, and unsalable at present. The taxes had been regularly paid each year by Mary Thomas, who had sent money orders from Concord. The self-denial represented by these orders was not a little.

" Never mind, Bos'n," said Captain Cy, when he returned from the Orham trip. " Your ancestral estates ain't much now but a sand-flea menagerie. However, if this section ever does get to be the big summer resort folks are prophesying for it, you may sell out to some millionaire and you and me'll go to Europe. Meantime, we'll try to keep afloat, if the Harniss Bank don't spring a leak."

On the day following this conversation he took a flying trip to Ostable, the county seat, returning the same evening, and saying nothing to anyone about his reasons for going nor what he had done while there.

Bos'n's birthday was the eighteenth of November. The captain, in spite of the warmth of his struggle for committee honors, determined to have a small celebration on the afternoon and evening of that day. It was to be a surprise for Emily, and, after school was over, some of her particular friends among the scholars were to come in, there was to be a cake with eight candles on it, and a supper at which ice cream —lemon and vanilla, prepared by Mrs. Cahoon— was to be the principal feature. Also there would be games and all sorts of fun.

Captain Cy was tremendously interested in the party. He spent hours with Georgianna and the Board of Strategy, preparing the list of guests. His cunning in ascertaining from the unsuspecting child who, among her schoolmates, she would like to invite, was deep and guileful.

"Now, Bos'n," he would say, "suppose you was goin' to clear out and leave this town for a spell, who——"

"But, Uncle Cyrus—" Bos'n's eyes grew frightened and moist in a moment, "I ain't going, am I? I don't want to go."

"No, no! Course you ain't goin'—that is, not for a long while, anyhow," with a sidelong look at the members of the "Board," then present. "But just suppose you and me was startin' on that Europe trip. Who'd you want to say good-by to most of all?"

# POLITICS AND BIRTHDAYS

Each name given by the child was surreptitiously penciled by Bailey on a scrap of paper. The list was a long one and, when the great afternoon came, the Whittaker house was crowded.

The supper was a brilliant success. So was the cake, brought in with candles ablaze, by the grinning Georgianna. Beside the children there were some older people present, Bailey and Asaph, of course, and the " regulars " from the perfect boarding house, who had been invited because it was fairly certain that Mr. Bangs wouldn't be allowed to attend if his wife did not. Miss Dawes had also been asked, at Bos'n's well-understood partiality, but she had declined.

Toward the end of the meal, when the hilarity at the long table was at its height, an unexpected guest made his appearance. There was a knock at the dining-room door, and Georgianna, opening it, was petrified to behold, standing upon the step, no less a personage than the Honorable Heman Atkins, supposed by most of us to be then somewhere in that wide stretch of territory vaguely termed " the South."

" Good evening, all," said the illustrious one, removing his silk hat and stepping into the room. " What a charming scene! I trust I do not intrude."

Georgianna was still speechless, in which unwonted condition she was not alone, Messrs. Bangs and Tidditt being also stricken dumb. But Captain Cy rose to the occasion grandly.

" Intrude? " he repeated. " Not a mite of it!

171

Mighty glad to see you, Heman. Here, give us your hat. Pull up to the table. When did you get back? Thought you was in the orange groves somewheres."

"Ahem! I was. Yes, I was in that neighborhood. But it is hard to stay away from dear old Bayport. Home ties, you know, home ties. I came down on the morning train, but I stopped over at Harniss on business and drove across. Ahem! Yes. The housekeeper informed me that my daughter was here, and, seeing the lights and hearing the laughter, I couldn't resist making this impromptu call. I'm sure as an old friend and neighbor, Cyrus, you will pardon me. Alicia, darling, come and kiss papa."

Darling Alicia accepted the invitation with a rustle of silk and an ecstatic squeal of delight. During this affecting scene Asaph whispered to Bailey that he " cal'lated " Heman had had a hurry-up distress signal from Simpson; to which sage observation Mr. Bangs replied with a vigorous nod, showing that Captain Cy's example had had its effect, in that they no longer stood in such awe of their representative at Washington.

However true Asaph's calculation might have been, Mr. Atkins made no mention of politics. He was urbanity itself. He drew up to the table, partook of the ice cream and cake, and greeted his friends and neighbors with charming benignity.

"Wan't it sweet of him to come?" whispered

# POLITICS AND BIRTHDAYS

Miss Phinney to Keturah. "And him so nice and everyday and sociable. And when Cap'n Whittaker's runnin' against his friend, as you might say."

Keturah replied with a dubious shake of the head. "I think Captain Cyrus is goin' to get into trouble," she said. "I've preached to Bailey more 'n a little about keepin' clear, but he won't."

"Games in t'other room now," ordered Captain Cy. But Mr. Atkins held up his hand.

"Pardon me, just a moment, Cyrus, if you please," he said. "I feel that on this happy occasion, it is my duty and pleasure to propose a toast." He held his lemonade glass aloft. "Permit me," he proclaimed, "to wish many happy birthdays and long life to Miss— I beg pardon, Cyrus, but what is your little friend's name?"

"Emily Richards Thayer," replied the captain, carried away by enthusiasm and off his guard for once.

"To Em—" began Heman. Then he paused and for the first time in his public life seemed at a loss for words. "What?" he asked, and his hand shook. "I fear I didn't catch the name."

"No wonder," laughed Mr. Tidditt. "Cy's so crazy to-night he'd forget his own name. Know what you said, Cy? You said she was Emily Richards *Thayer!* Haw! haw! She ain't a Thayer, Heman; her last name's Thomas. She's Emily Richards Thayer's granddaughter though. Her granddad was

John Thayer, over to Orham. Good land! I forgot. Well, what of it, Cy? 'Twould have to be known some time."

Everyone looked at Captain Cy then. No one observed Mr. Atkins for the moment. When they did turn their gaze upon the great man he had sunk back in his chair, the glass of lemonade was upset upon the cloth before him, and he, with a very white face, was staring at Emily Richards Thomas.

" What's the matter, Heman? " asked the captain anxiously. " Ain't sick, are you? "

The congressman started.

" Oh, no! " he said hurriedly. " Oh, no! but I'm afraid I've soiled your cloth. It was awkward of me. I—I really, I apologize—I———"

He wiped his face with his handkerchief. Captain Cy laughed.

" Oh, never mind the tablecloth," he said. " I cal'late it's too soiled already to be hurt by a bath, even a lemon one. Well, you've all heard the toast. Full glasses, now. Here's *to* you, Bos'n! Drink hearty, all hands, and give the ship a good name."

If the heartiness with which they drank is a criterion, the good name of the ship was established. Then the assembly adjourned to the sitting room and —yes, even the front parlor. Not since the days when that sacred apartment had been desecrated by the irreverent city boarders, during the Howes *régime*, had its walls echoed to such whoops and shouts of laughter. The children played " Post Office " and " Copenhagen " and " Clap in, Clap out," while the grown folks looked on.

" Ain't they havin' a fine time, Cap? " gushed Miss Phinney. " Don't it make you wish you was young again? "

" Angie," replied Captain Cy solemnly, " don't tempt me; don't! If they keep on playin' that Copenhagen and you stand right alongside of me, there's no tellin' what 'll happen."

Angeline declared that he was " turrible," but she faced the threatened danger nevertheless, and bravely remained where she was.

Mr. Atkins went home early in the evening, taking Alicia with him. He explained that his long railroad journey had—er—somewhat fatigued him and, though he hated to leave such a—er—delightful gathering, he really felt that, under the circumstances, his departure would be forgiven. Captain Cy opened the door for him and stood watching as, holding his daughter by the hand, he marched majestically down the path.

" Hum! " mused the captain aloud. " I guess he has been travelin' nights. Thought he ought to be here quick, I shouldn't wonder. He does look tired, that's a fact, and kind of pale, seemed to me."

" Well, there, now! " exclaimed Mrs. Tripp, who was looking over his shoulder. " Did you see that? "

" No; what was it? "

175

# CY WHITTAKER'S PLACE

"Why, when he went to open his gate, one of them arbor vity bushes he set out this spring knocked his hat off. And he never seemed to notice, but went right on. If 'Licia hadn't picked it up, that nice new hat would have been layin' there yet. That's the most undignified thing ever I see Heman Atkins do. He *must* be tired out, poor man!"

## CHAPTER X

### A LETTER AND A VISITOR

"WHIT," asked Asaph next day, "wan't you surprised to see Heman last night?"

Captain Cy nodded. He was once more busy with the doll house, the construction of which had progressed slowly of late, owing to the demands which the party and politics made upon its builder's time.

"Yup," he said, "I sartinly was. Pretty good sign, I shouldn't wonder. Looks as if friend Tad had found the tide settin' too strong against him and had whistled for a tug. All right; the more scared the other side get, the better for us."

"But what in the world made Heman come over and have supper? He never so much as stepped foot in the house afore, did he? That's the biggest conundrum of all."

"Well, I guess I've got the answer. Strikes me that Heman's sociableness is the best sign yet. Heman's a slick article, and when he sees there's danger of losin' the frostin' on the cake he takes care to scrape the burnt part off the bottom. I may be

177

school committeeman after town meetin'. He'll move all creation to stop me, of course—in his quiet, round-the-corner way—but, if I do win out, he wants to be in a position to take me one side and tell me that he's glad of it; he felt all along I was the right feller for the job, and if there's anything he can do to make things easier for me just call on him. That's the way I size it up, anyhow."

"Cy, I never see anybody like you. You're dead set against Heman, and have been right along. And he's never done anything to you, fur's I see. He's given a lot to the town, and he's always been the most looked-up-to man we've got. Joe Dimick and two or three more chronic growls have been the only ones to sling out hints against him, till you come. Course I'm working for you, tooth and nail, and I will say that you seem to be gettin' the votes some way or other. But if Heman *should* step right out and say: 'Feller citizens, I'm behind Tad Simpson in this fight, and as a favor to me and 'cause I think it's right and best, I want 'Lonzo Snow elected'— well, *I* don't believe you'd have more'n one jack and a ten spot to count for game."

"Probably not, Ase; I presume likely not. But you take a day off some time and see if you can remember that Heman *ever* stepped right out and said things. Blame it! that's just it. As for *why* he riles me up and makes me stubborn as a balky mule, I don't know exactly. All I'm sure is that he does.

Maybe it's 'cause I don't like the way he wears his whiskers. Maybe it's because he's so top-lofty and condescendin'. A feller can whistle to me and say: 'Come on, Bill,' and I'll trot at his heels all day. But when he pats me on the head and says: 'There! there! nice doggie. Go under the bed and lay down,' my back bristles up and I commence to growl right off. There's consider'ble Whittaker in me, as I've told you before."

The town clerk pondered over this rather unsatisfactory line of reasoning for some minutes. His companion fitted a wooden chimney on the doll house, found it a trifle out of plumb, and proceeded to whittle a shaving off the lower edge. Then Asaph sighed, as one who gives up a perplexing riddle, put his hand in his pocket, and produced a bundle of papers.

"I made out a list of fellers down to the east'ard that I'm goin' to see this afternoon," he said. "Some of 'em I guess 'll vote for you, but most of 'em are pretty sartin' for 'Lonzo. However, I— Where is that list? I had it somewhere's. And— well, I swan! I come pretty near forgettin' it myself. I'm 'most as bad as Bailey."

From the bundle of papers he produced a crumpled envelope.

"That Bailey," he observed, "must be in love, I cal'late, though I don't know who with. Ketury, I s'pose, 'cordin' to law and order, but— Well, anyhow, he's gettin' more absent-minded all the time. Here's a letter for you, Cy, that he got at the post-office a week ago Monday. 'Twas the night of the church sociable, and he had on his Sunday cutaway, and he ain't worn it sence, till the party yesterday. When he took off the coat, goin' to bed, the letter fell out of it. I guess he was ashamed to fetch it round himself, so he asked me to do it. Better late than never, hey? Here's that list at last."

He produced the list and handed it to the captain for inspection. The latter looked it over, made a few comments and suggestions, and told his friend to heave ahead and land as many of the listed as possible. This Mr. Tidditt promised to do, and, replacing the papers in his pocket, started for the gate.

"Oh! Say, Ase!"

The town clerk, his hand on the gate latch, turned.

"Well, what is it?" he asked. "Don't keep me no longer'n you can help. I got work to do, I have."

"All right, I won't stop you. Only fallin' in love is kind of epidemic down at the boardin' house, I guess. Who is it that's got you in tow—Matildy?"

"What are you talkin' about? Didn't I tell you to quit namin' me with Matildy Tripp? I like a joke as well as most folks, but when it's wore into the ground I——"

"Sho, sho! Don't get mad. It's your own fault.

You said that absent-mindedness was a love symp-
tom, so I just got to thinkin', that's all. That letter that Bailey forgot—you haven't given it to me
yet."

Asaph turned red and hastily snatched the papers
from his pocket. He strode back to the door of the
woodshed, handed his friend the crumpled envelope,
and stalked off without another word. The captain chuckled, laid the letter on the bench beside
him and went on with his work. It was perhaps
ten minutes later when, happening to glance at the
postmark on the envelope, he saw that it was " Concord, N. H."

Asaph's vote-gathering trip "to the east'ard"
made a full day for him. He returned to the perfect boarding house just at supper time. During
the meal he realized that Mr. Bangs seemed to be
trying to attract his attention. Whenever he glanced
in that gentleman's direction his glance was met by
winks and mystifying shakes of the head. Losing
patience at last, he demanded to know what was the
matter.

"Want to say somethin' to me, do you?" he inquired briskly. "If you do, out with it! Don't
set there workin' your face as if 'twas wound up,
like a clockwork image."

This remark had the effect of turning all the
other faces toward Bailey's. He was very much
upset.

"No, no!" he stammered. "No, no! I don't want you for nothin'. Was I makin' my face go? I—I didn't know it. I've been washin' carriages and cleanin' up the barn all day and I cal'late I've overdone. I'm gettin' old, and hard work's likely to bring on shakin' palsy to old folks."

His wife tartly observed that, if *work* was the cause of it, she guessed he was safe from palsy for quite a spell yet. At any rate, a marked recovery set in and he signaled no more during the meal. But when it was over, and his task as dish-wiper completed, he hurried out of doors and found Mr. Tidditt, shivering in the November wind, on the front porch.

"Now what is it?" asked Asaph sharply. "I know there's somethin' and I've froze to death by sections waitin' to hear it."

"Have you seen Cy?" whispered Bailey, glancing fearfully over his shoulder at the lighted windows of the house.

"No, not sence mornin'. Why?"

"Well, there's somethin' the matter with him. Somethin' serious. I was swabbin' decks in the barn about eleven o'clock, when he come postin' in, white and shaky, and so nervous he couldn't stand still. Looked as if he had had a stroke almost. I——"

"Godfrey scissors! You don't s'pose Heman's comin' back has knocked out his chances for the committee, do you?"

"No, sir-ee! 'twan't that. Cy's anxious to be elected and all, but you know his politics are more of a joke with him than anything else. And any rap Heman or Tad could give him would only make him fight harder. And he wouldn't talk politics at all; didn't seem to give a durn about 'em, one way or t'other. No, 'twas somethin' about that letter, the one I forgot so long. He wanted to know why in time I hadn't given it to him when it fust come. He was real ugly about it, for him, and kept pacin' up and down the barn floor and layin' into me, till I begun to think he was crazy. I guess he see my feelin's were hurt, 'cause, just afore he left, he held out his hand and said I mustn't mind his talk; he'd been knocked on his beam ends, he said, and wan't really responsible."

"Wouldn't he say what had knocked him?"

"No, couldn't get nothin' out of him. And when he quit he went off toward home, slappin' his fists together and actin' as if he didn't see the road across his bows. Now, you know how cool and easy goin' Whit generally is. I swan to man, Ase! he made me so sorry for him I didn't know what to do."

"Ain't you been up to see him sence?"

"No, Ketury was sot on havin' the barn cleaned, and she stood over me with a rope's end, as you might say. I couldn't get away a minute, though I made up more'n a dozen errands at Simmons's and the like of that. You hold on till I sneak into the entry and get my cap and we'll put for there now. I won't be but a jiffy. I'm worried."

They entered the yard of the Cy Whittaker place together and approached the side door. As they stood on the steps Asaph touched his chum on the arm and pointed to the window beside them. The shade was half drawn and beneath it they had a clear view of the interior of the sitting room. Captain Cy was in the rocker before the stove, holding Bos'n in his arms. The child was sound asleep, her yellow braid hanging over the captain's broad shoulder. He was gazing down into her face with a look which was so full of yearning and love that it brought a choke into the throats of the pair who saw it.

They entered the dining room. The captain sprang from his chair and, still holding the little girl close against his breast, met them at the sitting-room door. When he saw who the visitors were, he caught his breath, almost with a sob, and seemed relieved.

"S-s-h-h!" he whispered warningly. "She's asleep."

The members of the Board of Strategy nodded understandingly and sat down upon the sofa. Captain Cy tiptoed to the bedroom, turned back the bedclothes with one hand and laid Bos'n down. They saw him tuck her carefully in and then stoop and kiss her. He returned to the sitting room and closed the door behind him.

"We see she was asleep afore we come in," explained Asaph. "We see you and her through the window."

The captain looked hurriedly at the window indicated. Then he stepped over and pulled the shade down to the sill, doing the same with the curtains of the other two windows.

"What's the matter?" inquired Bailey, trying to be facetious. "'Fraid of 'Lonzo's crowd spyin' on us?"

Captain Cy did not reply. He did not even sit down, but remained standing, his back to the stove.

"Well?" he asked shortly. "Did you fellers want to see me for anything 'special?"

"Wanted to see what had struck you all to once," replied Mr. Tidditt. "Bailey says you scared him half to death this forenoon. And you look now as if somebody's ghost had riz and hollered 'Boo!' at you. For the land sakes, Whit, what *is* it?"

The captain drew his hand across his forehead.

"Ghost?" he repeated absently. "No, I haven't *seen* a ghost. There! there! don't mind me. I ain't real well to-day, I guess." He smiled crookedly.

"Don't you want to hear about my vote-grabbin' cruise?" asked Tidditt. "I was flatterin' myself you'd be tickled to hear I'd done so well. Why, even Marcellus Parker says he may vote for you—if he makes up his mind that way."

Marcellus was a next-door neighbor of Alonzo Snow's. But Captain Cy didn't seem to care.

"Hey?" he murmured. "Yes. Well?"

"*Well!* Is that all you've got to say? Are you really sick, Cy? Or is Bos'n sick?"

"No!" was the answer, almost fierce in its utterance. "She isn't sick. Don't be a fool."

"What's foolish about that? I didn't know but she might be. There's mumps in town and——"

"She's all right; so shut up, will you! There, Ase!" he added. "I'm the fool myself. Don't mind my barkin'; I don't mean it. I am about sick, I cal'late. Be better to-morrer, maybe."

"What's got into you? Was that letter of Bailey's——"

"Hush!" The captain held up his hand. "I thought I heard a team."

"Depot wagon, most likely," said Bailey. "About time for it! Humph! seems to be stoppin', don't it? Was you expectin' anybody? Shall I go and——"

"No! Set still."

The pair on the sofa sat still. Captain Cy stood like a statue in the middle of the floor. He squared his shoulders and jammed his clenched fists into his pockets. Steps crunched the gravel of the walk. There came a knock at the door of the dining room.

Walking steadily, but with a face set as the figure-head on one of his own ships, the captain went to

answer the knock. They heard the door open, and
then a man's voice asked:

" Is this Cap'n Whittaker? "

" Yes," was the short answer.

"Well, Cap, I guess you don't know me, though
maybe you know some of my family. Ha, ha!
Don't understand that, hey? Well, you let me in
and I'll explain the joke."

The captain's reply was calm and deliberate.

" I shouldn't wonder if I understood it," he said.
" Come in. Don't—" The remainder of the sentence was whispered and the listeners on the sofa
could not hear it. A moment later Captain Cy entered the sitting room, followed by his caller.

The latter was a stranger. He was a broad-
shouldered man of medium height, with a yellowish
mustache and brown hair. He was dressed in rather
shabby clothes, without an overcoat, and he had a
soft felt hat in his hand. The most noticeable thing
about him was a slight hesitancy in his walk. He
was not lame, he did not limp, yet his left foot
seemed to halt for an instant as he brought it forward in the step. They learned afterwards that it
had been hurt in a mine cave-in. He carried himself
with a swagger, and, after his entrance, there was a
perceptible aroma of alcohol in the room.

He stared at the Board of Strategy and the stare
was returned in full measure. Bailey and Asaph
were wildly curious. They, of course, connected the

stranger's arrival with the mysterious letter and the captain's perturbation of the day.

But their curiosity was not to be satisfied, at least not then.

"How are you, gents?" hailed the newcomer cheerfully. "Like the looks of me, do you?"

Captain Cy cut off further conversation.

"Ase," he said, "this—er—gentleman and I have got some business to talk over. I know you're good enough friends of mine not to mind if I ask you to clear out. You'll understand. You *will* understand, boys, won't you?" he added, almost entreatingly.

"Sartin sure!" replied Mr. Tidditt, rising hurriedly. "Don't say another word, Whit." And the mystified Bangs concurred with a "Yes, yes! Why, of course! Didn't have nothin' that amounts to nothin' to stay for anyhow. See you to-morrer, Cy."

Outside and at the gate they stopped and looked at each other.

"Well!" exclaimed Asaph. "If that ain't the strangest thing! Who was that feller? Where'd he come from? Did you notice how Cy acted? Seemed to be holdin' himself in by main strength."

"Did you smell the rum on him?" returned Bailey. "On that t'other chap, I mean? Didn't he look like a reg'lar no-account to you? And say, Ase, didn't he remind you of somebody you'd seen somewheres—kind of, in a way?"

They walked home in a dazed state, asking un-

188

answerable questions and making profitless guesses. But Asaph's final remark seemed to sum up the situation.

" There's trouble comin' of this, Bailey," he declared. " And it's trouble for Cy Whittaker, I'm afraid. Poor old Cy! Well, *we'll* stand by him, anyhow. I don't believe he'll sleep much to-night. Didn't look as though he would, did he? Who *is* that feller?"

If he had seen Captain Cy, at two o'clock the next morning, sitting by Bos'n's bedside and gazing hopelessly at the child, he would have realized that, if his former predictions were wiped off the slate and he could be judged by the one concerning the captain's sleepless night, he might thereafter pose as a true prophet.

# CHAPTER XI

## A BARGAIN OFF

"MORNIN', Georgianna," said Captain Cy to his housekeeper as the latter unlocked the back door of the Whittaker house next morning. "I'm a little ahead of you this time."

Miss Taylor, being Bayport born and bred, was an early riser. She lodged with her sister, in Bassett's Hollow, a good half mile from the Cy Whittaker place, but she was always on hand at the latter establishment by six each morning, except Sundays. Now she glanced quickly at the clock. The time was ten minutes to six.

"Land sakes!" she exclaimed. "I should say you was! What in the world got you up so early? Ain't sick, are you?"

"No," replied the captain wearily. "I ain't sick. I didn't sleep very well last night, that's all."

Georgianna looked sharply at him. His face was haggard and his eyes had dark circles under them.

"Humph!" she grunted. "No, I guess you didn't. Looks to me as if you'd been up all night."

Then she added an anxious query: " 'Tain't Bos'n
—she ain't sick, I hope? "

" No. She's all right. I say, Georgianna, you
put on an extry plate this mornin'. Got company
for breakfast."

The housekeeper was surprised.

" For breakfast? " she repeated. " Land of goodness! who's comin' for breakfast? I never heard
of company droppin' in for breakfast. That's one
meal folks generally get to home. Who is it? Mr.
Tidditt? Has Ketury turned him out door because
he's too bad an example for her husband? "

" No, 'tain't Ase. It's a—a friend of mine. Well,
not exactly a friend, maybe, but an acquaintance
from out of town. He came last evenin'. · He's
up in the spare bedroom."

" Well, I never! Come unexpected, didn't he?
I wish I'd known he was comin'. That spare room
bed ain't been aired I don't know when."

" I guess he can stand it. I cal'late he's slept in
consider'ble worse—Hum! Yes, he did come kind
of sudden."

" What's his name? "

" What difference does that make? I don't know's
his name makes any odds about gettin' his breakfast for him."

Georgianna was hurt. Her easy-going employer
had never used this tone before when addressing
her.

"Oh!" she sniffed. "Is *that* the way you feel? All right! I can mind my own business, thank you. I only asked because it's convenient sometimes to know whether to call a person Bill Smith or Sol Jones. But I don't care if it's Nebuchadnezzar. I know when to keep my tongue still, I guess."

She flounced over to the range. Captain Cy looked ashamed of himself.

"I'm kind of out of sorts to-day," he said. "Got some headache. Why, his name is—is—yes, 'tis Smith, come to think of it—John Smith. Funny you should guess right, wan't it?"

"Humph!" was the ungracious answer. "Names don't interest me, I tell you."

The captain was in the dining room when Bos'n appeared.

"Good morning, Uncle Cyrus," she said. "You've been waiting, haven't you? Am I late? I didn't mean to be."

"No, no! you ain't late. Early, if anything. Breakfast ain't quite ready yet. Come here and set in my lap. I want to talk to you."

He took her on his knee. She looked up into his face.

"What's the matter, Uncle Cy?" she asked. "What makes you so sober?"

"Sober? If you ain't the oldest young one for eight years I ever saw! Why, I ain't sober. No,

no! Say, Bos'n, do you like your school as well as
ever?"

"Yes, sir. I like it better all the time."

"Do, hey? And that teacher woman—go on
likin' her?"

The child nodded emphatically. "Yes, sir," she
said. "And I haven't been kept after since that
once."

"Sho! sho! Course you ain't! So you think
Bayport's as nice as Concord, do you?"

"Oh! lots nicer! If mamma was only here I'd
never want to be anywhere else. And not then,
maybe, unless you was there, too."

"Hum! Want to know! Say, Bos'n, how would
you feel if you had to go somewheres else?"

"To live? Have we got to? I'd feel dreadful,
of course. But if you've got to go, Uncle Cyrus,
why——"

"Me? No; I ain't got to go anywheres. But
'twas you I was thinkin' of. Wouldn't want to leave
the old man, hey?"

"To leave *you*! Oh, Uncle Cyrus!"

She was staring at him now and her chin was
trembling.

"Uncle," she demanded, "you ain't going to send
me away? Haven't I been a good girl?"

The captain's lips shut tight. He waited a moment before replying. "'Deed you've been a good
girl!" he said brusquely. "I never saw a better

one. No, I ain't goin' to *send* you away. Don't you worry about that."

"But Alicia Atkins said one time you told somebody you was going to send me out West, after a while. I didn't believe it, then, she's so mean, but she said you said——"

"*Said!*" Captain Cy groaned. "The Lord knows what I ain't said! I've been a fool, dearie, and it's a judgment on me, I guess."

"But ain't you goin' to keep me? I—I——"

She sobbed. The captain stroked her hair.

"Keep you?" he muttered. "Yes, by the big dipper! I'm goin' to keep you, if I can—if I can."

"Hello!" said a voice. The pair looked up. The man who had arrived on the previous night stood in the sitting-room doorway. How long he had been standing there the captain did not know. What he did know was that Mr. John Smith by daylight was not more prepossessing than the same individual viewed by the aid of a lamp.

Emily saw the stranger and slid from Captain Cy's knees. The captain rose.

"Bos'n," he said, "this is Mr. — er — Smith, who's goin' to make us a little visit. I want you to shake hands with him."

The girl dutifully approached Mr. Smith and extended her hand. He took it and held it in his own.

"Is this the—" he began.

194

Captain Cy bowed assent.

"Yes," he said, his eyes fixed on the visitor's face. "Yes. Don't forget what you said last night."

Smith shook his head.

"No," he replied. "I ain't the kind that forgets, unless it pays pretty well. There's some things I've remembered for quite a few years."

He looked the child over from head to foot and his brows drew together in an ugly frown.

"So this is her, hey?" he muttered musingly. "Humph! Well, I don't know as I'd have guessed it. Favors the other side of the house more—the respectable side, I should say. Still, there's a little brand of the lost sheep, hey? Enough to prove property, huh? Mark of the beast, I s'pose the psalm-singin' relations would call it. D—n em! I——"

"Steady!" broke in the captain. Mr. Smith started, seemed to remember where he was, and his manner changed.

"Come and see me, honey," he coaxed, drawing the girl toward him by the hand he was holding. "Ain't you got a nice kiss for me this fine mornin'? Don't be scared. I won't bite."

Bos'n looked shrinkingly at Mr. Smith's unshaven cheeks and then at Captain Cy. The latter's face was absolutely devoid of expression. He merely nodded.

So Emily kissed one of the bristling cheeks. The kiss was returned full upon the mouth. She wiped her lips and darted away to her chair by the table.

"What's your hurry?" inquired the visitor. "Don't I do it right? Been some time since I kissed a girl—a little one, anyhow," he added, winking at his host. "Never mind, we'll know each other better by and by."

He looked on in wondering disgust as Bos'n said her "grace."

"What in blazes!" he burst out when the little blessing was finished. "Who put her up to that? A left-over from the psalm-singers, is it?"

"I don't know," answered the captain, speaking with deliberation. "I do know that I like to have her do it and that she shall do it as long's she's at this table."

"Oh! she shall, hey? Well, I reckon——"

"She shall—*as long as she's at this table*. Is that real plain and understandable, or shall I write it down?"

There was an icy clearness in the captain's tone which seemed to freeze further conversation on the part of Mr. Smith. He merely grunted and ate his breakfast in silence. He ate a great deal and ate it rapidly.

Bos'n departed for school when the meal was over. Captain Cy helped her on with her coat and hood. Then, as he always did of late, he kissed her good-by.

"Hi!" called Mr. Smith from the sitting room. "Ain't I in on that? If there's any kisses goin' I want to take a hand before the deal's over."

"Must I?" whispered Bos'n pleadingly. "Must I, Uncle Cy? I don't want to. I don't like him."

"Come on!" called Mr. Smith. "I'm gettin' over my bashfulness fast. Hurry up!"

"Must I kiss him, Uncle Cyrus?" whispered Bos'n. "*Must* I?"

"No!" snapped the captain sharply. "Trot right along now, dearie. Be a good girl. Good-by."

He entered the sitting room. His guest had found the Sunday box and was lighting one of his host's cigars.

"Well," he inquired easily, "what's next on the bill? Anything goin' on in this forsaken hole?"

"There's a barber shop down the road. You might go there first, I should say. Not that you need it, but just as a novelty like."

"Humph! I don't know. What's the matter with your razor?"

"Nothin'. At least I ain't found anything wrong with it yet."

"Oh! Say, look here! you're a queer guy, you are. I ain't got you right in my mind yet. One minute butter wouldn't melt in your mouth, and the next you're fresh as a new egg. What *is* your little game, anyway? You've got one, so don't tell me you ain't."

Captain Cy was plainly embarrassed. He gazed at the "Shore to Shore" picture on the wall as he answered.

"No game about it," he said. "Last night you and I agreed that nothin' was to be said for a few days. You was to stay here and I'd try to make you comfort'ble, that's all. Then we'd see about that other matter, settle on a fair price, and——"

"Yes, I know. That's all right. But you're too willin'. There's something else. Say!" The ugly scowl was in evidence again. "Say, look here, you! you ain't got somethin' up your sleeve, have you? There ain't somethin' more that I don't know about, is there? No more secrets than that——"

"No! You hear me? No! You'll get your rights, and maybe a little more than your rights, if you're decent. And it'll pay you to be decent."

"Humph!" Mr. Smith seemed to be thinking. Then he added, looking up keenly under his brows: "How about the—the incumbrance on the property? Of course, when I go I'll have to take that with me, and——"

Captain Cy interrupted.

"There! there!" he exclaimed, and there was a shake in his voice, "there! there! Don't let's talk about such things now. I—I— Let's wait a spell.

We'll have some more plans to make, maybe. If you want to use my razor it's right in that drawer. Just help yourself."

The visitor laughed aloud. He nodded as if satisfied. "Ho! ho!" he chuckled. "I see! Humph! yes—I see. The fools ain't all dead, and there's none to beat an old one. Well! well! All right, pard! I guess you and me'll get along fine. I've changed my mind; I *will* go to the barber shop, after all. Only I'm a little shy of dust just at present. So, to oblige a friend, maybe you'll hand over, huh?"

The captain reached into his pocket, extracted a two-dollar bill, and passed it to the speaker. Mr. Smith smiled and shook his head.

"You can't come in on that, pard," he said. "The limit's five."

Captain Cy took back the bill and exchanged it for one with a V in each corner. The visitor took it and turned toward the door.

"Ta! ta!" he said, taking his hat from the peg in the dining room. "I'm off for the clippers. When I come back I'll be the sweetest little Willie in the diggin's. So long."

Bos'n and the captain sat down to the dinner at noon alone. Mr. Smith had not returned from his trip to the barber's. He came in, however, just before the meal was over, still in an unshorn condition, somewhat flushed and very loquacious.

"Say!" he exclaimed genially. "That Simpson's the right sort, ain't he? Him and me took a shine to each other from the go-off. He's been West himself and he's got some width to him. He's no psalm singer."

"Humph!" commented the captain, with delicate sarcasm. "He don't seem to be much of a barber, either. What's the matter? Gone out of business, has he? Or was you so wild or woolly he got discouraged before he begun?"

"Great snakes!" exclaimed the visitor. "I forgot all about the clippers! Well, that's one on me, pard! I'll make a new try soon's grub's over. Don't be so tight-fisted with the steak; this is a plate I'm passin', not a contribution box."

He winked at Bos'n and would have chucked her under the chin if she had not dodged. She seemed to have taken a great aversion to Mr. Smith and was plainly afraid of him.

"Is he going to stay very long, Uncle Cyrus?" she whispered, when it was school time once more. "Do you think he's nice?"

Captain Cy did not answer. When she had gone and the guest had risen from the table and put on his hat, the captain said warningly:

"There's one little bit of advice I want to give you, Mister Man: A bargain's a bargain, but it takes two to keep it. Don't let your love for Tad Simpson lead you into talkin' too much. Talk's cheap, they say, but too much of it might be mighty dear for you. Understand?"

Smith patted him on the back. "Lord love you, pard!" he chuckled, "I'm no spring chicken. I'm as hard to open as a safe, I am. It takes a can opener to get anything out of me."

"Yes; well, you can get inside some folks easier with a corkscrew. I've been told that Tad's a kind of a medium sometimes. If he raises any spirits in that back room of his, I'd leave 'em alone, if I was you. So long as you're decent, I'll put up with——"

But Mr. Smith was on his way to the gate, whistling as if he hadn't a care in the world. Captain Cy watched him go down the road, and then, with the drawn, weary look on his face which had been there since the day before, he entered the sitting room and threw himself into a chair.

Miss Phœbe Dawes, the school teacher, worked late that evening. There were examination papers to be gone over, and experience had demonstrated that the only place where she could be free from interruptions was the schoolroom itself. At the perfect boarding house the shrill tones of Keturah's voice and those of Miss Phinney and Mrs. Tripp penetrated through shut doors. It is hard to figure percentages when the most intimate details of Bayport's family life are being recited and gloated over on the other side of a thin partition. And when Matilda undertook to defend the Come-Outer faith against

the assaults of the majority, the verbal riot was, as
Mr. Tidditt described it, "like feedin' time in a
parrot shop."

So Miss Phœbe came to the boarding house for
supper and then returned to the schoolroom, where,
with a lighted bracket lamp beside her on the desk,
she labored until nine o'clock. Then she put on her
coat and hat, extinguished the light, locked the door,
and started on her lonely walk home.

"The main road" in our village is dark after
nine o'clock. There is a street light—a kerosene
lamp—on a post in front of the Methodist meeting
house, but the sexton forgets it, generally speaking,
or, at any rate, neglects to fill it except at rare intervals. Simmons's front windows are ablaze, of
course, and so are the dingy panes of Simpson's
barber shop. But these two centers of sociability
are both at the depot road corner, and when they
are passed the only sources of illumination are the
scattered gleams from the back windows of dwellings. As most of us retire by half-past eight, the
glow along the main road is not dazzling, to say
the very least.

Miss Dawes was not afraid of the dark. She
had been her own escort for a good many years.
She walked briskly on, heard the laughter and loud
voices in the barber shop die away behind her,
passed the schoolhouse pond, now bleak and chill
with the raw November wind blowing across it, and

began to climb the slope of Whittaker's Hill. And here the wind, rushing in unimpeded over the flooded salt meadows from the tumbled bay outside, wound her skirts about her and made climbing difficult and breath-taking.

She was, perhaps, half way up the long slope, when she heard, in the intervals between the gusts, footsteps behind her. She knew most of the village people by this time and the thought of company was not unpleasant. So she paused and pantingly waited for whoever was coming. She could not see more than a few yards, but the footsteps sounded nearer and nearer, and, a moment later, a man's voice began singing "Annie Rooney," a melody then past its prime in the cities, but popularized in Bayport by some departed batch of summer boarders.

She did not recognize the voice and she did not particularly approve of singing in the streets, especially such loud singing. So she decided not to wait longer, and was turning to continue her climb, when the person behind stopped his vocalizing and called.

"Hi!" he shouted. "Hello, ahead there! Who is it? Hold on a minute, pard! I'm comin'."

She disobeyed the order to "hold on," and began to hurry. The hurry was of no avail, however, for the follower broke into a run and soon was by her side. He was a stranger to her.

"Whee! Wow!" he panted. "This is no race track, pard. Pull up, and let's take it easy. My off leg's got a kink in it, and I don't run so easy as I used to. Great snakes; what's your rush? Ain't you fond of company? Hello! I believe it's a woman!"

She did not answer. His manner and the smell of liquor about him were decidedly unpleasant. The idea that he might be a tramp occurred to her. Tramps are our bugaboos here in Bayport.

"A woman!" exclaimed the man hilariously. "Well, say! I didn't believe there was one loose in this tail-end of nowhere. Girlie, I'm glad to see you. Not that I can see you much, but never mind. All cats are gray in the dark, hey? You can't see me, neither, so we'll take each other on trust. 'She's my sweetheart, I'm her beau.' Say, Maud, may I see you home?"

She was frightened now. The Whittaker place on the hilltop was the nearest house, and that was some distance off.

"What's the matter, Carrie?" inquired the man. "Don't be scared. I wouldn't hurt you. I'm just lonesome, that's all, and I need society. Don't rush, you'll ruin your complexion. Here! come under my wing and let's toddle along together. How's mamma?"

He seized her arm and pulled her back beside him. She tried to free herself, but could not. Her unwelcome escort held her fast and she was obliged to move as slowly as he did. It was very dark.

"Say, what *is* your name?" coaxed the man. "Is is Maud, hey? Or Julia? I always liked Julia. Don't be peevish. Tell us, that's a good girl."

She gave a quick jerk and managed to pull her arm from his grasp, giving him a violent push as she did so. He, being unsteady on his feet, tumbled down the low bank which edged the sidewalk. Then she ran on up the hill as fast as she could. She heard him swear as he fell.

She had nearly reached the end of the Whittaker fence when he caught her. He was laughing, and that alarmed her almost as much as if he had been angry.

"Naughty! naughty!" he chuckled, holding her fast. "Tryin' to sneak, was you? Not much! Not this time! Did you ever play forfeits when you was little? Well, this is a forfeit game and you're It. You must bow to the prettiest, kneel to the wittiest, and kiss the one you love best. And I'll let you off on the first two. Come now! Pay up!"

Then she screamed. And her scream was answered at once. A gate swung back with a bang and she heard some one running along the walk toward her.

"O Cap'n Whittaker!" she called. "Come! Come quick, please!"

How she knew that the person running toward her was Captain Cy has not been satisfactorily ex-

plained even yet. She cannot explain it and neither
can the captain. And equally astonishing was the
latter's answer. He certainly had not heard her
voice often enough to recognize it under such circumstances.

"All right, teacher!" he shouted. "I'm comin'!
Let go of that woman, you— Oh, it's you, is it?"

He had seized Mr. Smith by the coat collar and
jerked him away from his victim. Miss Dawes took
refuge behind the captain's bulky form. The two
men looked at each other. Smith was recovering his
breath.

"It's you, is it?" repeated Captain Cy. Then,
turning to Miss Phœbe, he asked: "Did he hurt
you?"

"No! Not yet. But he frightened me dreadfully. Who is he? Do you know him?"

Her persecutor answered the question.

"You bet your life he knows me!" he snarled.
"He knows me mighty well! Pard, you keep your
nose out of this, d'you see! You mind your own
business. I wan't goin' to hurt her any."

The captain paid no attention to him.

"Yup, I know him," he said grimly. Then
he added, pointing toward the lighted window of
the house ahead: "You—Smith, you go in there
and stay there! Trot! Don't make me speak
twice."

But Mr. Smith was too far gone with anger and

the " spirits " raised by Tad Simpson to heed the menace in the words.

" Smith, hey? " he sneered. " Oh, yes, *Smith*! Well, Smith ain't goin', d'you see! He's goin' to do what he pleases. I reckon I'm on top of the roost here! I know what's what! You can't talk to me. I've got rights, I have, and——"

" Blast your rights! "

" What? *What?* Blast my rights, hey? Oh, yes! Think because you've got money you can cheat me out of 'em, do you? Well, you can't! And how about the other part of those rights? S'pose I walk right into that house and——"

" Stop it! Shut up! You'd better not——"

" And into that bedroom and just say: ' Emmie, here's your——' "

He didn't finish the sentence. Captain Cy's big fist struck him fairly between the eyes, and the back of his head struck the walk with a " smack! " Then, through the fireworks which were illuminating his muddled brain, he heard the captain's voice.

" You low - down, good - for - nothin' scamp! " growled Captain Cy. " All this day I've been hatin' myself for the way I've acted to you. I've hated myself and been tryin' to spunk up courage to say ' It's all off! ' But I was too much of a coward, I guess. And now the Lord A'mighty has *made* me say it. You want your rights, do you? So? Then get 'em if you can. It's you and me for it, and we'll

"'I'll kill you like a dog.'"

see who's the best man. Teacher, if you're ready I'll walk home with you now."

Mr. Smith was not entirely cowed.

"You go!" he yelled. "Go ahead! And I'll go to a lawyer's to-morrow. But to-night, and in-

side of five minutes, I'll walk into that house of
yours and get my——"

The captain dropped Miss Dawes's arm and
strode back to where his antagonist was sitting in
the dust of the walk. Stooping down, he shook a
big forefinger in the man's face.

"You've been out West, they tell me," he whispered sternly. "Yes! Well, out West they take
the law into their own hands, sometimes, I hear.
I've been in South America, and they do it there,
too. Just so sure as you go into my house to-night
and touch—well, you know what I mean—just so
sure I'll kill you like a dog, if I have to chase you
to Jericho. Now you can believe that or not. If
I was you I'd believe it."

Taking the frightened schoolmistress by the arm
once more he walked away. Mr. Smith said nothing till they had gone some distance. Then he
called after them.

"You wait till to-morrow!" he shouted. "You
just wait and see what'll happen to-morrow!"

Captain Cy was silent all the way to the gate of
the perfect boarding house. Miss Dawes was silent
likewise, but she thought a great deal. At the gate
she said:

"Captain Whittaker, I'm *ever* so much obliged
to you. I can't thank you enough."

"Don't try, then. That's what you said to me
about the cow."

" But I'm almost sorry you were the one to come.
I'm afraid that man will get you into trouble. Has
he—can he— What did he mean about to-morrow? Who *is* he?"

The captain pushed his cap back from his forehead.

"Teacher," he said, "there's a proverb, ain't
there, about lettin' to-morrow take care of itself?
As for trouble—well, I did think I'd had trouble
enough in my life to last me through, but I cal'late
I've got another guess. Anyhow, don't you fret.
I did just the right thing, and I'm glad I did it.
If it was only me I wouldn't fret, either. But
there's—" He stopped, groaned, and pulled the
cap forward again. "Good night," he added, and
turned to go.

Miss Dawes leaned forward and detained him.

"Just a minute, Cap'n Whittaker," she said. " I
was a little prejudiced against you when I came here.
I was told that you got me the teacher's position,
and there was more than a hint that you did it for
selfish reasons of your own. When you called that
afternoon at the school I was———"

"Don't say a word! I was the biggest fool in
town that time, and I've been ashamed to look
in the glass ever since. I ain't always such an
idiot."

"But I've had to judge people for myself in my
lifetime," continued the schoolmistress, " and I've

made up my mind that I was mistaken about you. I should like to apologize. Will you shake hands?"

She extended her hand. Captain Cy hesitated.

"Hadn't you better wait a spell?" he asked. "You've heard that swab call me partner. Hadn't——"

"No; I don't know what your trouble is, of course, and I certainly shan't mention it to anyone. But whatever it is I'm sure you are right and it's not your fault. Now will you shake hands?"

The captain did not answer. He merely took the proffered hand, shook it heartily, and strode off into the dark.

# CHAPTER XII

## "TOWN-MEETIN'"

**T**HIS is goin' to be a me*mo*riable town meetin'!" declared Sylvanus Cahoon, with unction, rising from the settee to gaze about him over the heads of the voters in the townhall. "I bet you every able-bodied man in Bayport 'll be here this forenoon. Yes, sir! that's what I call it, a me-*mo*-riable meetin'!"

"See anything of Cy?" inquired Josiah Dimick, who sat next to Sylvanus.

"No, he ain't come yet. And Heman ain't here, neither. Hello! there's Tad. Looks happy, seems to me."

Captain Dimick stood up to inspect Mr. Simpson.

"Humph!" he muttered. "Well, unless my count's wrong, he ain't got much to be happy about. 'Lonzo Snow's with him. Tad does look sort of joyful, don't he? Them that laughs last laughs best. When the vote for school committee's all in we'll see who does the grinnin'. But I can't understand— Hello! there's Tidditt. Asaph! Ase! S-s-t-t! Come here a minute."

Mr. Tidditt, trembling with excitement, and shaking hands effusively with everyone he met, pushed his way up the aisle and bent over his friend.

" Say, Ase," whispered Josiah, " where's Whit? Why ain't he on hand? Nothin's happened, has it? "

" No," replied the town clerk. " Everything seems to be all right. I stopped in on the way along and Cy said not to wait; he'd be here on time. He's been kind of off his feed for the last day or so, and I cal'late he didn't feel like hurryin'. Say, Joe, now honest, what do you think of my chances? "

Such a confirmed joker as Dimick couldn't lose an opportunity like this. With the aid of one trying to be cheerful under discouragement he answered that, so far, Asaph's chances looked fair, pretty fair, but of course you couldn't always sometimes tell. Mr. Tidditt rushed away to begin the handshaking all over again.

From this round of cordiality he was reluctantly torn and conducted to the platform. After thumping the desk with his fist he announced that the gathering would " come to order right off, as there was consider'ble business to be done and it ought to be goin' ahead." He then proceeded to read the call for the meeting. This ceremony was no sooner over than Abednego Small, " Uncle Bedny," was on his feet loudly demanding to be informed why the town " hadn't done nothin' " toward fixing up the Bassett's Hollow road. Uncle Bedny's speech had proceeded

no further than " Feller citizens, in the name of an
outrageous—I should say outraged portion of our
community I—" when he was choked off by a self-
appointed committee who knew Mr. Small of old and
had seated themselves near him to be ready for just
such emergencies. The next step, judged by meetings of other years, should have been to unani-
mously elect Eben Salters moderator; but as Captain Eben refused to serve, owing to his interest in
the Whittaker campaign, Alvin Knowles was, by a
small majority, chosen for that office. Mr. Knowles
was a devout admirer of the great Atkins, and his
election would have been considered a preliminary
victory for the opposition had it not been that many
of Captain Cy's adherents voted for Alvin from a
love of mischief, knowing from experience his ig-
norance of parliamentary law and his easy-going
rule. " Now there'll be fun ! " declared one delighted
individual. " Anything's in order when Alvin's
chairman."

The proceedings of the first half hour were dis-
appointingly tame. Most of us had come there to
witness a political wrestling match between Tad
Simpson and Cyrus Whittaker. Some even dared
hope that Congressman Atkins might direct his fight
in person. But neither the Honorable nor Captain
Cy was in the hall as yet. Solon Eldridge was re-
elected selectman and so also was Asaph Tidditt.
Nobody but Asaph seemed surprised at this result.

His speech of acceptance would undoubtedly have been a triumph of oratory had it not been interrupted by Uncle Bedny, who rose to emphatically protest against " settin' round and wastin' time " when the Bassett's Hollow road " had ruts deep enough to drown a cat in whenever there was a more'n average heavy dew."

The Bassett's Hollow delegate being again temporarily squelched, Moderator Knowles announced that nominations for the vacant place on the school committee were in order. There was a perceptible stir on the settees. This was what the meeting had been waiting for.

" No sign of Cy or Heman yet," observed Mr. Cahoon, craning his neck in the direction of the door. " It's the queerest thing ever I see."

" Queer enough about Cy, that's a fact," concurred Captain Dimick. " I ain't so surprised about Heman's not comin'. Looks as if Whit was right; he always said Atkins dodged a row where folks could watch it. Does most of his fightin' from round the corner. Hello! there's Tad. Now you'll see the crown of glory set on 'Lonzo Snow's head. Hope the crown's padded nice and soft. Anything with sharp edges would sink in."

But Mr. Simpson, it seemed, was not yet ready to proceed with the coronation. He had risen to ask permission of the meeting to defer the school committee matter for a short time. Persons, important persons, who should be present while the nominating was going on, had not yet arrived. He was sure that the gathering would wish to hear from these persons. He asked for only a slight delay. Matters such as this, affecting the welfare of our posterity, ought not to be hurried, etc., etc.

Mr. Simpson's request was unexpected. The meeting, apparently, didn't know how to take it. Uncle Bedny was firmly held in his seat by those about him. Lemuel Myrick took the floor to protest.

"I must say," he declared, "that I don't see any reason for waitin'. If folks ain't here, that's their own fault. Mr. Moderator, I demand that the nominatin' go ahead."

Tad was on his feet instantly.

"I'm goin' to appeal," he cried, "to the decency and gratitude of the citizens of the town of Bayport. One of the persons I'm—that is, we're waitin' for has done more for our beautiful village than all the rest of us put together. There ain't no need for me to name him. A right up-to-date town pump, a lovely memorial window, a——"

"How about that harbor appropriation?" cried a voice from the settees.

Mr. Simpson was taken aback. His face flushed and he angrily turned toward the interrupter.

"That's you, Joe Dimick!" he shouted, pointing an agitated forefinger. "You needn't scooch down. I know your tongue. The idea of you findin' fault

because a big man like Congressman Atkins don't
jump when you holler ' Git up ! '  What do *you* know
about doin's at Washington?  That harbor appropriation 'll go through if anybody on earth can get
it through.  There's other places besides Bayport to
be provided for and——"

" And their congressmen provide for 'em," called
another voice.  Tad whirled to face his new tor-
mentor.

" ' Huh ! ' he grunted with sarcasm.  " That's Lem
Myrick, *I* know.  Lem, the great painter, who votes
where he paints and gets paid accordin'."

" Order ! " cried several.

" Oh, all right, Mr. Moderator !  I'll keep order
all right.  But I say to you, Lem, and you, Joe Dimick, that I know who put these smart notions into
your heads.  We all know, unless we're born fools.
Who is it that's been sayin' the Honorable Heman
Atkins was shirkin' that appropriation?  Who was
it said if *he* was representative the thing would have
gone through afore this?  Who's been makin' his
brags that he could get it through if he had the
chance?  You know who !  So do I !  I wish he was
here.  I only wish he was here !  I'd say it to his
face."

" Well, he is.  Heave ahead and say it."

Everyone turned toward the door.  Captain Cy
had entered the hall.  He was standing in the aisle,
and with him was Bailey Bangs.  The captain looked

16        217

very tired, almost worn out, but he nodded coolly to
Mr. Simpson, who had retired to his seat with surprising quickness and apparent discomfiture.

"Here I am, Tad," continued the captain. "Say
your piece."

But Tad, it appeared, was not anxious to "say
his piece." He was whispering earnestly with a
group of his followers. Captain Cy held up his
hand.

"Mr. Moderator," he asked, "can I have the
floor a minute? All I want to say is that I cal'late
I'm the feller the last speaker had reference to. I
*have* said that I didn't see why that appropriation
was so hard to get. I say it again. Other appro-
priations are got, and why not ours? I *did* say if I
was a congressman I'd get it. Yes, and I'll say
more," he added, raising his voice, "I'll say that if
I was sent to Washin'ton by this town, congressman
or not, I'd move heaven and earth, and all creation
from the President down till I did get it. That's
all. So would any live man, I should think."

He sat down. There was some applause. Before
it had subsided Abel Leonard, one of the quickest-
witted of Mr. Simpson's workers, was on his feet,
gesticulating for attention.

"Mr. Moderator," he shouted, "I want to make
a motion. We've all heard the big talk that's been
made. All right, then! I move you, sir, that Captain Cyrus Whittaker be appointed a committee of

one to *go* to Washin'ton, if he wants to, or anywheres else, and see that we get the appropriation.
And if we don't get it the blame's his! There,
now! "

There was a roar of laughter. This was exactly
the sort of " tit-for-tat " humor that appeals to a
Yankee crowd. The motion was seconded half a
dozen times. Moderator Knowles grinned and
shook his head.

" A joke's a joke," he said, " and we all like a
good one. However, this meetin' is supposed to be
for business, not fun, so———"

" Question! Question! It's been seconded!
We've got to vote on it! " shouted a chorus.

" Don't you think—seems to me that ain't in
order," began the moderator, but Captain Cy rose
to his feet. The grim smile had returned to his face
and he looked at the joyous assemblage with almost
his old expression of appreciative alertness.

" Never mind the vote," he said. " I realize that
Brother Leonard has rather got one on me, so to
speak. All right, I won't dodge. I'll *be* a committee
of one on the harbor grab, and if nothin' comes of
it I'll take my share of kicks. Gentlemen, I appreciate your trustfulness in my ability."

This brief speech was a huge success. If, for a
moment, the pendulum of public favor had swung
toward Simpson, this trumping of the latter's leading card pushed it back again. The moderator had

some difficulty in restoring order to the hilarious meeting.

Then Mr. Myrick was accorded the privilege of the floor, in spite of Tad's protests, and proceeded to nominate Cyrus Whittaker for the school committee. Lem had devoted hours of toil and wearisome mental struggle to the preparation of his address, and it was lengthy and florid. Captain Cy was described as possessing all the virtues. Bailey, listening with a hand behind his ear, was moved to applause at frequent intervals, and even Asaph forgot the dignity of his exalted position on the platform and pounded the official desk in ecstasy. The only person to appear uninterested was the nominee himself. He sat listlessly in his seat, his eyes cast down, and his thoughts apparently far away.

Josiah Dimick seconded the captain's nomination. Then Mr. Simpson stepped to the front and, after a wistful glance at the door, began to speak.

" Feller citizens," he said, " it is my privilege to put in nomination for school committee a man whose name stands for all that's good and clean and progressive in this township. But afore I do it I'm goin' to ask you to let me say a word or two concernin' somethin' that bears right on this matter, and which, I believe, everyone of you ought to know. It's somethin' that most of you don't know, and it'll be a surprise, a big surprise. I'll be as quick as I can, and I cal'late you'll thank me when I'm done."

He paused. The meeting looked at each other in astonishment. There was whispering along the settees. Moderator Knowles was plainly puzzled. He looked inquiringly at the town clerk, but Asaph was evidently quite as much in the dark as he concerning the threatened disclosure.

" Feller Bayporters," went on Tad, " there's one thing we've all agreed on, no matter who we've meant to vote for. That is, that a member of our school committee should be an upright, honest man, one fit morally to look out for our dear children. Ain't that so? Well, then, I ask you this: Would you consider a man fit for that job who deliberately came between a father and his child, who pizened the mind of that child against his own parent, and when that parent come to claim that child, first tried to buy him off and then turned him out of the house? Yes, and offered violence to him. And done it— mark what I say—for reasons which—which—well, we can only guess 'em, but the guess may not be so awful bad. Is *that* the kind of man we want to honor or to look out for our own children's schoolin'? "

Mr. Simpson undoubtedly meant to cause a sensation by his opening remarks. He certainly did so. The stir and whispering redoubled. Asaph, his mouth open, stared wildly down at Captain Cy. The captain rose to his feet, then sank back again. His listlessness was gone and, paying no attention to those about him, he gazed fixedly at Tad.

"Gentlemen," continued the speaker, "last night I had an experience that I shan't forget as long as I live. I met a poor man, a poor, lame man who'd been away out West and got hurt bad. Folks thought he was dead. His wife thought so and died grievin' for him. She left a little baby girl, only seven or eight year old. When this man come back, well again but poor, to look up his family, he found his wife had passed away and the child had been sent off, just to get rid of her, to a stranger in another town. That stranger fully meant to send her off, too; he said so dozens of times. A good many of you folks right here heard him say it. But he never sent her—he kept her. Why? Well, that's the question. *I* shan't answer it. *I* ain't accusin' nobody. All I say is, what's easy enough for any of you to prove, and that is that it come to light the child had property belongin' to her. Property! land, wuth money!"

He paused once more and drew his sleeve across his forehead. Most of his hearers were silent now, on tiptoe of expectation. Dimick looked searchingly at Captain Cy. Then he sprang to his feet.

"Order!" he shouted. "What's all this got to do with nominatin' for school committee? Ain't he out of order, Alvin?"

The moderator hesitated. His habitual indecision was now complicated by the fact that he was as curious as the majority of those before him. There were shouts of, " Go ahead, Tad! " " Tell us the rest! " " Let him go on, Mr. Moderator! "

Cy Whittaker slowly rose.

" Alvin," he said earnestly, " don't stop him yet. As a favor to me, let him spin his yarn."

Simpson was ready and evidently eager to spin it.

" This man," he proclaimed, " this father, mournin' for his dead wife and longin' for his child, comes to the town where he was to find and take her. And when he meets the man that's got her, when he comes, poor and down on his luck, what does this man—this rich man—do? Why, fust of all, he's sweeter'n sirup to him, takes him in, keeps him overnight, and the next day he says to him: ' You just be quiet and say nothin' to nobody that she's your little girl. I'll make it wuth your while. Keep quiet till I'm ready for you to say it.' And he gives the father money—not much, but some. All right so fur, maybe; but wait! Then it turns out that the father knows about this land—this property. And *then* the kind, charitable man—this rich man with lots of money of his own—turns the poor father out, tellin' him to get the girl and the land if he can, knowin' —*knowin'*, mind you—that the father ain't got a cent to hire lawyers nor even to pay for his next meal. And when the father says he won't go, but

223

wants his dear one that belongs to him, the rich feller abuses him, knocks him down with his fist! Knocks down a poor, weak, lame invalid, just off a sick bed! Is *that* the kind of a man we want on our school committee?"

He asked the question with both hands outspread and the perspiration running down his cheeks. The meeting was in an uproar.

"No need for me to tell you who I mean," shouted Tad, waving his arms. "You know who, as well as I do. You've just heard him praised as bein' all that's good and great. But *I* say——"

"You've said enough! Now let me say a word!"

It was Captain Cy who interrupted. He had pushed his way through the crowd, down the aisle, and now stood before the gesticulating Mr. Simpson, who shrank back as if he feared that the treatment accorded the "poor weak invalid" might be continued with him.

"Knowles," said Captain Cy, turning to the moderator, "let me speak, will you? I won't be but a minute. Friends," he continued, facing the excited gathering—"for some of you are my friends, or I've come to think you are—a part of what this man says is so. The girl at my house is Emily Thomas; her mother was Mary Thomas, who some of you know, and her father's name is Henry Thomas. She came to me unexpected, bein' sent by a Mrs. Oliver up to Concord, because 'twas either me or an orphan

"' You've said enough! Now let me say a word!'"

asylum. I took her in meanin' to keep her a little while, and then send her away. But as time went on I kept puttin' off and puttin' off, and at last I realized I couldn't do it; I'd come to think too much of her.

"Fellers," he went on, slowly, "I—I hardly know how to tell you what that little girl's come to be to me. When I first struck Bayport, after forty years away from it, all I thought of was makin' over the old place and livin' in it. I cal'lated it would be a sort of Paradise, and *how* I was goin' to live or whether or not I'd be lonesome with everyone of my folks dead and gone, never crossed my mind. But the longer I lived there alone the less like Paradise it got to be; I realized more and more that it ain't furniture and fixin's that make a home; it's them you love that's in it. And just as I'd about reached the conclusion that 'twas a failure, the whole business, why, then, Bos'n—Emily, that is—dropped in, and inside of a week I knew I'd got what was missin' in my life.

"I never married and children never meant much to me till I got her. She's the best little— little . . . There! I mustn't talk this way. I bluffed a lot about not keepin' her permanent, bein' kind of ashamed, I guess, but down inside me I'd made up my mind to bring her up like a daughter. She and me was to live together till she grew up and got married and I . . . Well, what's the use? A few days ago come a letter from the Oliver woman in Concord sayin' that this Henry Thomas, Bos'n's father, wan't dead at all, but had turned up there, havin' learned somehow or 'nother that his wife was gone and that his child had been willed a little bit of land which belonged to her mother. He had found out that Emmie was with me, and the letter said he would likely come after her—and the land.

"That letter was like a flash of lightnin' to me. I

226

was dismasted and on my beam ends. I didn't know
what to do. I'd learned enough about this Henry
Thomas to know that he was no use, a drunken, good-
for-nothin' scamp who had cruelized his wife and
then run off and left her and the baby. But when
he come, the very night I got the letter, I gave him
a chance. I took him in; I was willin' to give him
a job on the place; I was willin' to pay for his keep,
and more. I *did* ask him to keep his mouth shut
and even to use another name. 'Twas weak of me,
maybe, but you want to remember this had come on
me sudden. And last night—the very second night,
mind you—he went out somewhere, perhaps we can
guess where, bought liquor with the money I gave
him, got drunk, and then insulted one of the best
women in this town. Yes, sir! I say it right here,
one of the best, pluckiest little women anywhere, although she and I ain't always agreed on certain matters. I *did* tell him to clear out, and I *did* knock
him down. Yes, and by the big dipper, I'd do it
again under the same circumstances!

"As for the property," he added fiercely, " why,
darn the property, I say! It ain't wuth much, anyhow, and, if 'twas anybody's else, he should have it
and welcome. But it's Bos'n's, and, bein' what he
is, he *shan't* have it. And he shan't have *her* to
cruelize, neither! By the Almighty! he shan't, so
long as I've got a dollar to fight him with. I say
that to you, Tad Simpson, and to the man—to who-

ever put you up to this. There! I've said my say. Now, gentlemen, you can choose your side."

He strode back to his seat. There was silence for a moment. Then Josiah Dimick sprang up and waved his hat.

"That's the way to talk!" he shouted. "That's a *man!* Three cheers for Cap'n Whittaker! Come on, everybody!"

But everybody did not "come on." The cheers were feeble. It was evident that the majority of those present did not know how to meet this unexpected contingency. It had taken them by surprise and they were undecided. The uproar of argument and question began again, louder than ever. The bewildered moderator thumped his desk and shouted feebly for order. Tad Simpson took the floor and, in a few words and at the top of his lungs, nominated Alonzo Snow. Abel Leonard seconded the nomination. There were yells of "Question! Question!" and "Vote! Vote!"

Eben Salters was recognized by the chair. Captain Salters made few speeches, and when he did make one it was because he had something to say.

"Mr. Moderator," he said, "I, for one, hate to vote just now. It isn't that the school committee is so important of itself. But I do think that the rights of a father with his child *is* pretty important, and our vote for Cap'n Whittaker—and most of you know I intended votin' for him and have been workin' for

228

him—might seem like an indorsement of his position. This whole thing is a big surprise to me. I
don't feel yet that we know enough of the inside facts
to give such an indorsement. I'd like to see this
Thomas man before I decide to give it—or not to
give it, either. It's a queer thing to come up at town
meetin', but it's up. Hadn't we better adjourn until
next week?"

He sat down. The meeting was demoralized.
Some were shouting for adjournment, others to
"Vote it out." A straw would turn the scale and the
straw was forthcoming. While Captain Cy was
speaking the door had silently opened and two men
entered the hall and sought seclusion in a corner.
Now one of these men came forward—the Honorable Heman Atkins.

Mr. Atkins walked solemnly to the front, amidst
a burst of recognition. Many of the voters rose to
receive him. It was customary, when the great man
condescended to attend such gatherings, to offer him
a seat on the platform. This the obsequious Knowles
proceeded to do. Asaph was too overcome by the
disclosure of "John Smith's" identity and by Mr.
Simpson's attack on his friend to remember even
his manners. He did not rise, but sat stonily
staring.

The moderator's gavel descended "Order!"
he roared. "Order, I say! Congressman Atkins
is goin' to talk to us."

The Honorable Heman faced the excited crowd. One hand was in the breast of his frock coat; the other was clenched upon his hip. He stood calm, benignant, dignified—the incarnation of wisdom and righteous worth. The attitude had its effect; the applause began and grew to an ovation. Men who had intended voting against his favored candidate forgot their intention, in the magnetism of his presence, and cheered. He bowed and bowed again.

"Fellow townsmen," he began, "far be it from me to influence your choice in the matter of the school committee. Still further be it from me to influence you against an old boyhood friend, a neighbor, one whom I believe—er—had believed to be all that was sincere and true. But, fellow townsmen, my esteemed friend, Captain Salters, has expressed a wish to see Mr. Thomas, the father whose story you have heard to-day. I happen to be in a position to gratify that wish. Mr. Thomas, will you kindly come forward?"

Then from the rear of the hall Mr. Thomas came. But the drunken rowdy of the night before had been transformed. Gone was the scrubby beard and the shabby suit. Shorn was the unkempt mop of hair and vanished the impudent swagger. He was dressed in clean linen and respectable black, and his manner was modest and subdued. Only a discoloration of one eye showed where Captain Cy's blow had left its mark.

"He stepped upon the platform beside the congressman."

He stepped upon the platform beside the congressman. The latter laid a hand upon his shoulder.

"Gentlemen and friends," said Heman, "my name has been brought into this controversy, by Mr. Simpson directly, and in insinuation by—er—another.

231

Therefore it is my right to make my position clear. Mr. Thomas came to me last evening in distress, both of mind and body. He told me his story—substantially the story which has just been told to you by Mr. Simpson—and, gentlemen, I believe it. But if I did not believe it, if I believed him to have been in the past all that his opponent has said; even if I believed that, only last evening, spurned, driven from his child, penniless and hopeless, he had yielded to the weakness which has been his curse all his life— even if I believed that, still I should demand that Henry Thomas, repentant and earnest as you see him now, should be given his rightful opportunity to become a man again. He is poor, but he is not— shall not be—friendless. No! a thousand times, no! You may say, some of you, that the affair is not my business. I affirm that it *is* my business. It is my business as a Christian, and that business should come before all others. I have not allowed sympathy to influence me. If that were the case, my regard for my neighbor and friend of former days would have held me firm. But, gentlemen, I have a child of my own. I know what a father's love is, as only a father can know it. And, after a sleepless night, I stand here before you to-day determined that this man shall have his own, if my money—which you will, I'm sure, forgive my mentioning—and my unflinching support can give it to him. That is my position, and I state it regardless of consequences." He paused, and with raised right hand, like the picture of Jove in the old academy mythology, launched his final thunderbolt. "Whom God hath joined," he proclaimed, "let no one put asunder!"

That settled it. The cheers shook the walls. Amidst the tumult Dimick and Bailey Bangs seized Captain Cy by the shoulders and endeavored to lift him from his seat.

"For the love of goodness, Whit!" groaned Josiah, desperately, "stand up and answer him. If you don't, we'll founder sure."

The captain smiled grimly and shook his head. He had not taken his eyes from the face of the great Atkins since the latter began speaking.

"What?" he replied. "After that 'put asunder' sockdolager? Man alive! do you want me to add Sabbath breakin' to my other crimes?"

The vote, by ballot, followed almost immediately. It was pitiful to see the erstwhile Whittaker majority melt away. Alonzo Snow was triumphantly elected. But a handful voted against him.

Captain Cy, still grimly smiling, rose and left the hall. As he closed the door, he heard the shrill voice of Uncle Bedny demanding justice for the Bassett's Hollow road.

It had, indeed, been a "memoriable" town meeting.

## CHAPTER XIII

### THE REPULSE

WHEN Deacon Zeb Clark—the same Deacon Zeb who fell into the cistern, as narrated by Captain Cy—made his first visit to the city, years and years ago, he stayed but two days. As he had proudly boasted that he should remain in the metropolis at least a week, our people were much surprised at his premature return. To the driver of the butcher cart who found him sitting contentedly before his dwelling, amidst his desolate acres, the nearest neighbor a half mile away, did Deacon Zeb disclose his reason for leaving the crowded thoroughfares. "There was so many folks there," he said, "that I felt lonesome."

And Captain Cy, returning from the town meeting to the Whittaker place, felt lonesome likewise. Not for the Deacon's reason—he met no one on the main road, save a group of school children and Miss Phinney, and, sighting the latter in the offing, he dodged behind the trees by the schoolhouse pond and waited until she passed. But the captain, his trouble now heavy upon him, did feel the need of

sympathy and congenial companionship. He knew
he might count upon Dimick and Asaph, and, whenever Keturah's supervision could be evaded, upon Mr.
Bangs. But they were not the advisers and com-
forters for this hour of need. All the rest of Bayport, he felt sure, would be against him. Had not
King Heman the Great from the steps of the throne,
banned him with the royal displeasure! "If Heman
ever *should* come right out and say—" began Asaph's
warning. Well, strange as it might seem, Heman
had "come right out."

As to why he had come out there was no question
in the mind of the captain. The latter had left Mr.
Thomas, the prodigal father, prostrate and blasphe-
mous in the road the previous evening. His next
view of him was when, transformed and sanctified,
he had been summoned to the platform by Mr. Atkins. No doubt he had returned to the barber shop
and, in his rage and under Mr. Simpson's cross examination, had revealed something of the truth.
Tad, the politician, recognizing opportunity when it
knocked at his door, had hurried him to the congressman's residence. The rest was plain enough, so Captain Cy thought.

However, war was already declared, and the reasons for it mattered little. The first skirmish might
occur at any moment. The situation was desperate.
The captain squared his shoulders, thrust forward
his chin, and walked briskly up the path to the door

of the dining room. It was nearly one o'clock, but Bos'n had not yet gone. She was waiting, to the very last minute, for her " Uncle Cyrus."

" Hello, shipmate," he hailed. " Not headed for school yet? Good! I cal'late you needn't go this afternoon. I'm thinkin' of hirin' a team and drivin' to Ostable, and I didn't know but you'd like to go with me. Think you could, without that teacher woman havin' you brought up aft for mutiny? "

Bos'n thought it over.

" Yes, sir," she said; " I guess so, if you wrote me an excuse. I don't like to be absent, 'cause I haven't been before, but there's only my reading lesson this afternoon and I know that ever so well. I'd love to go, Uncle Cy."

The captain removed his coat and hat and pulled a chair forward to the table.

" Hello! " he exclaimed. " What's this—the mail? "

Bos'n smiled delightedly.

" Yes, sir," she replied. " I knew you was at the meeting and so I brought it from the office. Ain't you glad? "

" Sure! Yes, indeed! Much obliged. Tryin' to keep house without you would be like steerin' without a rudder."

Even as he said it there came to him the realization that he might have to steer without that rudder

236

in the near future. His smile vanished. He smothered a groan and picked up the mail.

" Hum ! " he mused, " the *Breeze*, a circular, and one letter. Hello! it isn't possible that— Well! well! "

The letter was in a long envelope. He hastily tore it open. At the inclosure he glanced in evident excitement. Then his smile returned.

" Bos'n," he said, after a moment's reflection, " I guess you and me won't have to go to Ostable after all." Noticing the child's look of disappointment, he added: " But you needn't go to school. Maybe you'd better not. You and me'll take a tramp alongshore. What do you say? "

" Oh, yes, Uncle Cy! Let's—shall we? "

" Why, I don't see why not. We'll cruise in company as long as we can, hey, little girl? The squall's likely to strike afore night," he muttered half aloud. "We'll enjoy the fine weather till it's time to shorten sail."

They walked all that afternoon. Captain Cy was even more kind and gentle with his small companion than usual. He told her stories which made her laugh, pointed out spots in the pines where he had played Indian when a boy, carried her " pig back " when she grew tired, and kissed her tenderly when, at the back door of the Whittaker place, he set her on her feet again.

" Had a good time, dearie? " he asked.

237

"Oh, splendid! I think it's the best walk we ever had, don't you, Uncle Cy?"

"I shouldn't wonder. You won't forget our cruises together when you are a big girl and off somewheres else, will you?"

"I'll *never* forget 'em. And I'm never going any-where without you."

It was after five as they entered the kitchen.

"Anybody been here while I was out?" asked the captain of Georgianna. The housekeeper's eyes were red and swollen, and she hugged Bos'n as she helped her off with her jacket and hood.

"Yes, there has," was the decided answer. "First Ase Tidditt, and then Bailey Bangs, and then that—that Angie Phinney."

"Humph!" mused Captain Cy slowly. "So Angie was here, was she? Where the carcass is the vultures are on deck, or words similar. Humph! Did our Angelic friend have much to say?"

"*Did* she? And *I* had somethin' to say, too! I never in my life!"

"Humph!" Her employer eyed her sharply. "So? And so soon? Talk about the telegraph spreadin' news! I'd back most any half dozen tongues in Bayport to spread more news, and add more trimmin' to it, in a day than the telegraph could do in a week. Especially if all the telegraph operators was like the one up at the depot. Well, Georgianna, when you goin' to leave?"

"Leave? Leave where? What are you talkin' about?"

"Leave here. Of course you realize that this ship of ours," indicating the house by a comprehensive wave of his hand around the room, "is goin' to be a mighty unpopular craft from now on. We may be on a lee shore any minute. You've got your own well-bein' to think of."

"My own well-bein'! What do you s'pose I care for my well-bein' when there's— Cap'n Whittaker, you tell me now! Is it so?"

"Some of it is—yes. He's come back and he's who he says he is. You've seen him. He was here all day yesterday."

"So Angie said, but I couldn't scarcely believe it. That toughy! Cap'n Whittaker, do you intend to hand over that poor little innocent thing to—to such a man as *that*?"

"No. There'll be no handin' over about it. But the odds are against us, and there's no reason why you should be in the rumpus, Georgianna. You may not understand what we're facin'."

The housekeeper drew herself up. Her face was very red and her small eyes snapped.

"Cy Whittaker," she began, manners and deference to employer alike forgotten, "don't you say no more of that wicked foolishness to me. I'll leave the minute you're mean-spirited enough to let that child go and not afore. And when *that* happens I'll be

239

*glad* to leave. Land sakes! there's somebody at the door; and I expect I'm a perfect sight."

She rubbed her face with her apron, thereby making it redder than ever, and hurried into the dining room.

"Bos'n," said Captain Cy quickly, "you stay here in the kitchen."

Emmie looked at him in surprised bewilderment, but she suppressed her curiosity concerning the identity of the person who had knocked, and obeyed. The captain pulled the kitchen door almost shut and listened at the crack.

The first spoken words by the visitor appeared to relieve Captain Cy's anxiety; but they seemed to astonish him greatly.

"Why!" he exclaimed in a whisper. "Ain't that— It sounds like——"

"It's teacher," whispered Bos'n, who also had been listening. "She's come to find out why I wasn't at school. You tell her, Uncle Cy."

Georgianna returned to announce:

"It's Miss Dawes. She says she wants to see you, Cap'n. She's in the settin' room."

The captain drew a long breath. Then, repeating his command to Emmie to stay where she was, he left the room, closing the door behind him. The latter procedure roused Bos'n's indignation.

"What made him do that?" she demanded. "I haven't been bad. He *never* shut me up before!"

# THE REPULSE

The schoolmistress was standing by the center table in the sitting room when Captain Cy entered.

"Good evenin'," he said politely. "Won't you sit down?"

But Miss Dawes paid no attention to trivialities. She seemed much agitated.

"Cap'n Whittaker," she began, "I just heard something that——"

The captain interrupted her.

"Excuse me," he said, "but I think we'll pull down the curtains and have a little light on the subject. It gets dark early now, especially of a gray day like this one."

He drew the shades at the windows and lit the lamp on the table. The red glow behind the panes of the stove door faded into insignificance as the yellow radiance brightened. The ugly portraits and the stiff old engravings on the wall retired into a becoming dusk. The old-fashioned room became more homelike.

"Now won't you sit down?" repeated Captain Cy. "Take that rocker; it's the most comf'table one aboard—so Bos'n says, anyhow."

Miss Phœbe took the rocker, under protest. Her host remained standing.

"It's been a nice afternoon," he said. "Bos'n— Emmie, of course—and I have been for a walk. 'Twan't her fault, 'twas mine. I kept her out of school. I was—well, kind of lonesome."

241

# CY WHITTAKER'S PLACE

The teacher's gray eyes flashed in the lamp-light.

"Cap'n Whittaker," she cried, "please don't waste time. I didn't come here to talk about the weather nor Emily's reason for not attending school. I don't care why she was absent. But I have just heard of what happened at that meeting. Is it true that—" She hesitated.

"That Emmie's dad is alive and here? Yes, it's true."

"But—but that man last night? Was he *that* man?"

The captain nodded.

"That's the man," he said briefly.

Miss Dawes shuddered.

"Cap'n Whittaker," she asked earnestly, "are you sure he is really her father? Absolutely sure?"

"Sure and sartin."

"Then she belongs to him, doesn't she? Legally, I mean?"

"Maybe so."

"Are—are you going to give her up to him?"

"No."

"Then what I heard was true. You did say at the meeting that you were going to do your best to keep him from getting her."

"Um—hum! What I said amounts to just about that."

"Why?"

242

Captain Cy was surprised and a little disappointed apparently.

" Why? " he repeated.

" Yes. Why? "

" Well, for reasons I've got."

" Do you mind telling me the reasons? "

" I cal'late you don't want to hear 'em. If you don't understand now, then I can't make it much plainer, I'm afraid."

The little lady sprang to her feet.

" Oh, you are provoking! " she cried indignantly. " Can't you see that I want to hear the reasons from you yourself? Cap'n Whittaker, I shook hands with you last night."

" You remember I told you you'd better wait."

" I didn't want to wait. I believed I knew something of human nature, and I believed I had learned to understand you. I made up my mind to pay no more attention to what people said against you. I thought they were envious and disliked you because you did things in your own way. I wouldn't believe the stories I heard this afternoon. I wanted to hear you speak in your own defense and you refuse to do it. Don't you know what people are saying? They say you are trying to keep Emily because— Oh, I'm ashamed to ask it, but you make me: *Has* the child got valuable property of her own? "

Captain Cy had been, throughout this scene, standing quietly by the table. Now he took a step forward.

"Miss Dawes," he said sharply, "sit down."

"But I——"

"Sit down, please."

The schoolmistress didn't mean to obey the order, but for some reason she did. The captain went on speaking.

"It's pretty plain," he said, "that what you heard at the boardin' house—for I suppose that's where you did hear it—was what you might call a Phinney-ized story of the doin's at the meetin'. Well, there's another yarn, and it's mine; I'm goin' to spin it and I want you to listen."

He went on to spin his yarn. It was practically a repetition of his reply to Tad Simpson that morning. Its conclusion was also much the same.

"The land ain't worth fifty dollars," he declared, "but if it was fifty million he shouldn't have it. Why? Because it belongs to that little girl. And he shan't have her until he and those back of him have hammered me through the courts till I'm down forty fathom under water. And when they do get her—and, to be honest, I cal'late they will in the end—I hope to God I won't be alive to see it! There! I've answered you."

He was walking up and down the room, with the old quarter-deck stride, his hands jammed deep in his pockets and his face working with emotion.

"It's pretty nigh a single-handed fight for me," he continued, "but I've fought single-handed before. The other side's got almost all the powder and the men. Heman and Tad and that Thomas have got

"The teacher rose and laid a hand on his arm."

seven eighths of Bayport behind 'em, not to mention the 'Providence' they're so sure of. My crowd is a mighty forlorn hope: Dimick and Ase Tidditt, and Bailey, as much as his wife 'll let him. Oh, yes!" and he smiled whimsically, "there's another one. A new recruit's just joined; Georgianna's enlisted. That's my army. Sort of rag-jacketed cadets, we are, small potatoes, and few in a hill."

The teacher rose and laid a hand on his arm. He turned toward her. The lamplight shone upon her face, and he saw, to his astonishment, that there were tears in her eyes.

"Cap'n Whittaker," she said, "will you take another recruit? I should like to enlist, please."

"You? Oh, pshaw! I'm thick-headed to-night. I didn't see the joke of it at first."

"There isn't any joke. I want you to know that I admire you for the fight you're making. Law or no law, to let that dear little girl go away with that dreadful father of hers is a sin and a crime. I came here to tell you so. I did want to hear your story, and you made me ask that question; but I was certain of your answer before you made it. I don't suppose I can do anything to help, but I'm going to try. So, you see, your army is bigger than you thought it was —though the new soldier isn't good for much, I'm afraid," she added, with a little smile.

Captain Cy was greatly disturbed.

"Miss Phœbe," he said, "I—I won't say that it don't please me to have you talk so, for it does, more'n you can imagine. Sympathy means somethin' to the under dog, and it gives him spunk to keep on kickin'. But you mustn't take any part in the row; you simply mustn't. It won't do."

246

" Why not? Won't I be *any* help? "

" Help? You'd be more help than all the rest of us put together. You and me haven't seen a great deal of each other, and my part in the few talks we have had has been a mean one, but I knew the first time I met you that you had more brains and common sense than any woman in this county— though I was too pig-headed to own it. But that ain't it. I got you the job of teacher. It's no credit to me; 'twas just bull luck and for the fun of jarrin' Heman. But I did it. And, because I did it, the Atkins crowd—and that means most everybody now —haven't any love for you. My tryin' for school committee was really just to give you a fair chance in your position. I was licked, so the committee's two to one against you. Don't you see that you mustn't have anything to do with me? Don't you *see* it? "

She shook her head.

" I see that common gratitude alone should be reason enough for my trying to help you," she said. " But, beside that, I know you are right, and I *shall* help, no matter what you say. As for the teacher's position, let them discharge me. I——"

" Don't talk that way. The youngsters need you, and know it, no matter what their fool fathers and mothers say. And you mustn't wreck your chances. You're young——"

She laughed.

"Oh, no! I'm not," she said. "Young! Cap'n Whittaker, you shouldn't joke about a woman's age."

"I ain't jokin'. You *are* young." As she stood there before him he was realizing, with a curiously uncomfortable feeling, how much younger she was than he. He glanced up at the mirror, where his own gray hairs were reflected, and repeated his assertion. "You're young yet," he said, "and bein' discharged from a place might mean a whole lot to you. I'm glad you take such an interest in Bos'n, and your comin' here on her account——"

He paused. Miss Dawes colored slightly and said:

"Yes."

"Your comin' here on her account was mighty good of you. But you've got to keep out of this trouble. And you mustn't come here again. That's owner's orders. Why, I'm expectin' a boardin' party any minute," he added. "I thought when you knocked it was 'papa' comin' for his child. You'd better go."

But she stood still.

"I shan't go," she declared. "Or, at least, not until you promise to let me try to help you. If they come, so much the better. They'll learn where my sympathies are."

Captain Cy scratched his head.

"See here, Miss Phœbe," he said. "I ain't sure that you fully understand that Scripture and every-

thing else is against us. Did Angie turn loose on
you the 'Whom the Lord has joined' avalanche?"

The schoolmistress burst into a laugh. The captain laughed, too, but his gravity quickly returned.
For steps sounded on the walk, there was a whispering outside, and some one knocked on the dining-
room door.

The situation was similar to that of the evening
when the Board of Strategy called and "John
Smith" made his first appearance. But now, oddly
enough, Captain Cy seemed much less troubled. He
looked at Miss Dawes and there was a dancing twinkle in his eye.

"Is it—" began the lady, in an agitated whisper.

"The boardin' party? I presume likely."

"But what can you do?"

"Stand by the repel, I guess," was the calm reply. "I told you that they had most of the ammu-
nition, but ours ain't all blank cartridges. You stay
below and listen to the broadsides."

They heard Georgianna cross the dining room.
There was a murmur of voices at the door. The
captain nodded.

"It's them," he said. "Well, here goes. Now
don't you show yourself."

"Do you think I am afraid? Indeed, I shan't
stay ' below ' as you call it! I shall let them see——"

Captain Cy held up his hand.

"I'm commodore of this fleet," he said; "and

18          249

that bein' the case, I expect my crew to obey orders. There's nothin' you can do, and— Why, yes! there is, too. You can take care of Bos'n. Georgianna," to the housekeeper who, looking frightened and nervous, had appeared at the door, " send Bos'n in here quick."

"They're there," whispered Georgianna. "Mr. Atkins and Tad and that Thomas critter, and lots more. And they've come after her. What shall we do?"

" Jump when I speak to you, that's the first thing. Send Bos'n in here and you stay in your galley."

Emily came running. Miss Dawes put an arm about her. Captain Cy, the battle lanterns still twinkling under his brows, stepped forth to meet the " boarding party."

They were there, as Georgianna had said. Mr. Thomas on the top step, Heman and Simpson on the next lower, and behind them Abel Leonard and a group of interested volunteers, principally recruited from the back room of the barber shop.

"Evenin', gentlemen," said the captain, opening the door so briskly that Mr. Thomas started backward and came down heavily upon the toes of the devoted Tad. Mr. Simpson swore, Mr. Thomas clawed about him to gain equilibrium, and the dignity of the group was seriously impaired.

"Evenin'," repeated Captain Cy. "Quite a surprise party you're givin' me. Come in."

250

"'Evenin', gentlemen,' said the captain."

"Cyrus," began the Honorable Atkins, "we are here to claim——"

"Give me my daughter, you robber!" demanded Thomas, from his new position in the rear of the other two.

"Mr. Thomas," said Heman, "please remember that I am conducting this affair. I respect the natural indignation of an outraged father, but—ahem! Cyrus, we are here to claim——"

"Then do your claimin' inside. It's kind of chilly to-night, there's plenty of empty chairs, and we don't need to hold an overflow meetin'. Come ahead in."

The trio looked at each other in hesitation. Then Mr. Atkins majestically entered the dining room. Thomas and Simpson followed him.

"Abe," observed Captain Cy to Leonard, who was advancing toward the steps, "I'm sorry not to be hospitable, but there's too many of you to invite at once, and 'tain't polite to show partiality. You and the rest are welcome to sit on the terrace or stroll 'round the deer park. Good night."

He closed the door in the face of the disappointed Abel and turned to the three in the room.

"Well," he said, "out with it. You've come to claim somethin', I understand."

"I come for my rights," shouted Mr. Thomas.

"Yes? Well, this ain't State's prison or I'd give 'em to you with pleasure. Heman, you'd better do the talkin'. We'll probably get ahead faster."

The Honorable cleared his throat and waved his hand.

"Cyrus," he began, "you are my boyhood friend and my fellow townsman and neighbor. Under such circumstances it gives me pain——"

"Then don't let us discuss painful subjects. Let's get down to business. You've come to rescue Bos'n —Emily, that is,—from the ' robber '—I'm quotin' Deacon Thomas here—that's got her, so's to turn her over to her sorrowin' father. Is that it? Yes. Well, you can't have her—not yet."

"Cyrus," said Mr. Atkins, "I'm sorry to see that you take it this way. You haven't the shadow of a right. We have the law with us, and your conduct will lead us to invoke it. The constable is outside. Shall I call him in?"

"Uncle Bedny" was the town constable and had been since before the war. The purely honorary office was given him each year as a joke. Captain Cy grinned broadly, and even Tad was obliged to smile.

"Don't be inhuman, Heman," urged the captain. "You wouldn't turn me over to be man-handled by Uncle Bedny, would you?"

"This is not a humorous affair—" began the congressman, with dignity. But the "bereaved father" had been prospecting on his own hook, and now he peeped into the sitting room.

"Here she is!" he shouted. "I see her. Come on, Emmie! Your dad's come for you. Let go of

her, you woman! What do you mean by holdin' on
to her?"

The situation which was "not humorous" immediately became much less so. The next minute was
a lively one. It ended as Mr. Thomas was picked up
by Tad from the floor, where he had fallen, having
been pushed violently over a chair by Captain Cy.
Bos'n, frightened and sobbing, was clinging wildly
to Miss Dawes, who had clung just as firmly to her.
The captain's voice rang through the room.

"That's enough," he said. "That's enough and
some over. Atkins, take that feller out of this house
and off my premises. As for the girl, that's for us
to fight out in the courts. I'm her guardian, law-
fully appointed, and you nor nobody else can touch
her while that appointment's good. Here it is—
right here. Now look at it and clear out."

He held, for the congressman's inspection, the document which, inclosed in the long envelope, had been
received that morning. His visit to Ostable, made
some weeks before, had been for the purpose of ap-
plying to the probate court for the appointment as
Emily's guardian. He had applied before the news
of her father's coming to life reached him. The
appointment itself had arrived just in time.

Mr. Atkins studied the document with care. When
he spoke it was with considerable agitation and without his usual diplomacy.

"Humph!" he grunted. "Humph! I see. Well,

sir, I have some influence in this section and I shall
see how long your—your *trick* will prevent the
child's going where she belongs. I wish you to understand that I shall continue this fight to the very
last. I—I am not one to be easily beaten. Simpson,
you and Thomas come with me. This night's des-
picable chicanery is only the beginning. This is
bad business for you, Cy Whittaker," he snarled,
his self-control vanishing, " and "—with a vindictive
glance at the schoolmistress—" for those who are
with you in it. That appointment was obtained under false pretenses and I can prove it. Your tricks
don't scare me. I've had experience with *tricks* before."

"Yup. So I've heard. Well, Heman, I ain't as
well up in tricks as you claim to be, nor my stockin'
isn't as well padded as yours, maybe. But while
there's a ten-cent piece left in the toe of it I'll fight
you and the skunk whose ' rights ' you seem to have
taken such a shine to. And, after that, while there's
a lawyer that 'll trust me. And, meantime, that
little girl stays right here, and you touch her if you
dare, any of you! Anything more to say?"

But the Honorable's dignity had returned. Possibly he thought he had said too much already. A
moment later the door banged behind the discom-
forted boarding party.

Captain Cy pulled his beard and laughed.

"Well, we repelled 'em, didn't we?" he observed.

" But, as friend Heman says, the beginnin's only begun. I wish he hadn't seen you here, teacher."

Miss Dawes looked up from the task of stroking
poor Bos'n's hair.

" I don't," she said, " I'm glad of it." Then she
added, laughing nervously: " Cap'n Whittaker, how
could you be so cool? It was like a play. I declare, you were just splendid! "

# CHAPTER XIV

## A CLEW.

JOSIAH DIMICK has a unique faculty of grasping a situation and summing it up in an out-of-the-ordinary way.

"I think," observed Josiah to the excited group at Simmons's, "that this town owes Cy Whittaker a vote of thanks."

"Thanks!" gasped Alpheus Smalley, so shocked and horrified that he put the one-pound weight on the scales instead of the half pound. "*Thanks!* After what we've found out? Well, I must say!"

"Ya-as," drawled Captain Josiah, "thanks was what I said. If it wan't for him this gang and the sewin' circle wouldn't have nothin' to talk about but their neighbors. Our reputations would be as full of holes as a skimmer by this time. Now all hands are so busy jumpin' on Whit, that the rest of us can feel fairly safe. Ain't that so, Gabe?"

Mr. Lumley, who had stopped in for a half pound of tea, grinned feebly, but said nothing. If he noticed the clerk's mistake in weights he didn't mention it, but took his package and hurried out. After his

departure Mr. Smalley himself discovered the error
and charged the Lumley account with " 1 ¼ lbs.
Mixed Green and Black." Meanwhile the assemblage about the stove had put Captain Cy on the
anvil and was hammering him vigorously.

Bayport was boiling over with rumor and surmise.
Heman had appealed to the courts asking that Captain Cy's appointment as Bos'n's guardian be re-
scinded. Cy had hired Lawyer Peabody, of Ostable,
to look out for his interests. Mr. Atkins and the
captain had all but come to blows over the child.
Thomas, the poor father, had broken down and
wept, and had threatened to commit suicide. Mrs.
Salters had refused to speak to Captain Cy when she
met the latter after meeting on Sunday. The land in
Orham had been sold and the captain was using
the money. Phœbe Dawes had threatened to resign
if Bos'n came to school any longer. No, she had
threatened to resign if she didn't come to school.
She hadn't threatened to resign at all, but wanted
higher wages because of the effect the scandal might
have on her reputation as a teacher. These were
a few of the reports, contradicted and added to from
day to day.

To quote Josiah Dimick again: " Sortin' out the
truth from the lies is like tryin' to find a quart of
sardines in a schooner load of herrin'. And they
dump in more herrin' every half hour."

Angeline Phinney was having the time of her life.

257

The perfect boarding house hummed like a fly trap. Keturah and Mrs. Tripp had deserted to the enemy, and the minority, meaning Asaph and Bailey, had little opportunity to defend their friend's cause, even if they had dared. Heman Atkins, his Christian charity and high-mindedness, his devotion to duty, regardless of political consequences, and the magnificent speech at town meeting were lauded and exalted. The *Bayport Breeze* contained a full account of the meeting, and it was read aloud by Keturah, amidst hymns of praise from the elect.

"'Whom the Lord hath joined,'" read Mrs. Bangs, "'let no man put asunder.' Ain't that splendid? Ain't that *fine*? The paper says: 'When Congressman Atkins delivered this noble sentiment a hush fell upon the excited throng.' I should think 'twould. I remember when I was married the minister said pretty nigh the same thing, and I *couldn't* speak. I couldn't have opened my mouth to save me. Don't you remember I couldn't, Bailey?"

Mr. Bangs nodded gloomily. It is possible that he wished the effect of the minister's declaration might have been more lasting. Asaph stirred in his chair.

"I don't care," he said. "This puttin' asunder business is all right, but there's always two sides to everything. I see this Thomas critter when he fust come, and he didn't look like no saint then—nor

"'Ain't that *fine*? The paper says: "When Congressman Atkins delivered this noble sentiment a hush fell upon the excited throng."'"

smell like one, neither, unless 'twas a specimen pickled in alcohol."

Here was irreverence almost atheistic. Keturah's face showed her shocked disapproval. Matilda Tripp voiced the general sentiment.

"Humph!" she sniffed. "Well, all I can say is that I've met Mr. Thomas two or three times, and *I* didn't notice anything but politeness and good manners. Maybe my nose ain't so fine for smellin' liquor as some folks's—p'raps it ain't had the experience—but all *I* saw was a poor lame man with a black eye. I pitied him, and I don't care who hears me say it."

"Yes," concurred Miss Phinney, "and if he was a drinkin' man, do you suppose Mr. Atkins would have anything to do with him? Cyrus Whittaker made a whole lot of talk about his insultin' some woman or other, but nobody knows who the woman was. 'Bout time for her to speak up, I should think. Teacher," turning to Miss Dawes, "you was at the Whittaker place when Mr. Atkins and Emily's father come for her, I understand. I wish I'd have been there. It must have been wuth seein'."

"It was," replied Miss Dawes. She had kept silent throughout the various discussions of the week following the town meeting, but now, thus appealed to, she answered promptly.

Angeline's news created a sensation. The schoolmistress immediately became the center of interest.

"Is that so? Was you there, teacher? Well, I declare!" The questions and exclamations flew round the table.

"Tell us, teacher," pleaded Keturah. "Wasn't Heman grand? I should *so* like to have heard him. Didn't Cap'n Whittaker look ashamed of himself?"

"No, he did not. If anyone looked ashamed it was Mr. Atkins and his friends. Perhaps I ought to tell you that my sympathies are entirely with Captain Whittaker in this affair. To give that little girl up to a drunken scoundrel like her father would, in my opinion, be a crime."

The boarders and the landlady gasped. Asaph grinned and nudged Bailey under the table. Keturah was the first to recover.

"Well!" she exclaimed. "Everybody's got a right to their opinion, of course. But I can't see the crime, myself. And as for the drunkenness, I'd like to know who's seen Mr. Thomas drunk. Cyrus Whittaker *says* he has, but——"

She waved her hand scornfully. Phœbe rose from her chair.

"I have seen him in that condition," she said. "In fact, I am the person he insulted. I saw Captain Whittaker knock him down, and I honored the captain for it. I only wished I were a man and could have done it myself."

She left the room, and, a few moments later, the

house. Mr. Tidditt chuckled aloud. Even Bailey dared to look pleased.

"There!" sneered the widow Tripp. "Ain't that— Perhaps you remember that Cap'n Whittaker got her the teacher's place?"

"Yes," put in Miss Phinney, "and nobody knows why he got it for her. That is, nobody has known up to now. Maybe we can begin to guess a little after this."

"She was at his house, was she?" observed Keturah. "Humph! I wonder why? Seems to me if *I* was a young—that is, a single woman like her, I'd be kind of careful about callin' on bachelors. Humph! it looks funny to me."

Asaph rose and pushed back his chair.

"I cal'late she called to see Emily," he said sharply. "The child was her scholar, and I presume likely, knowin' the kind of father that has turned up for the poor young one, she felt sorry for her. Of course, nobody's hintin' anything against Phœbe Dawes's character. If you want a certificate of that, you've only got to go to Wellmouth. Folks over there are pretty keen on that subject. I guess the town would go to law about it rather'n hear a word against her. Libel suits are kind of uncomf'table things for them that ain't sure of their facts. *I'd* hate to get mixed up in one, myself. Bailey, I'm going up street. Come on, when you can, won't you?"

As if frightened at his own display of spirit, he hurried out. There was silence for a time; then Miss Phinney spoke concerning the weather.

Up at the Cy Whittaker place the days were full ones. There, also, legal questions were discussed, with Georgianna, the Board of Strategy, Josiah Dimick occasionally, and, more infrequently still, Miss Dawes, as participants with Captain Cy in the discussions. Rumors were true in so far as they related to Mr. Atkins's appeal to the courts, and the captain's retaining Lawyer Peabody, of Ostable. Mr. Peabody's opinion of the case was not encouraging.

"You see, captain," he said, when his client visited him at his office, "the odds are very much against us. The court appointed you as guardian with the understanding that this man Thomas was dead. Now he is alive and claims his child. More than that, he has the most influential politician in this county back of him. We wouldn't stand a fighting chance except for one thing—Thomas himself. He left his wife and the baby; deserted them, so she said; went to get work, *he* says. We can prove he was a drunken blackguard *before* he went, and that he has been drunk since he came back. But *they'll* say—Atkins and his lawyer—that the man was desperate and despairing because of your refusal to give him his child. They'll hold him up as a repentant sinner, anxious to reform, and needing the little girl's influence to help keep him straight. That's their game, and they'll play it, be sure of that. It sounds reasonable enough, too, for sinners have repented before now. And the long-lost father coming back to his child is the one sure thing to win applause from the gallery, you know that."

Captain Cy nodded.

" Yup," he said, " I know it. The other night, when Miss Ph—when a friend of mine was at the house, she said this business was like a play. I didn't say so to her, but all the same I realize it ain't like a play at all. In a play dad comes home, havin' been snaked bodily out of the jaws of the tomb by his coat collar, and the young one sings out ' Papa! Papa! ' and he sobs, ' Me child! Me child! ' and it's all lovely, and you put on your hat feelin' that the old man is goin' to be rich and righteous for the rest of his days. But here it's different; dad's a rascal, and anybody who's seen anything of the world knows he's bound to stay so; and as for the poor little girl, why—why——"

He stopped, rose, and, striding over to the window, stood looking out. After an interval, during which the good-natured attorney read a dull business letter through for the second time, he spoke again.

" I hope you understand, Peabody," he said. " It ain't just selfishness that makes me steer the course I'm runnin'. Course, Bos'n's got to be the world and all to me, and if she's taken away I don't know's I care a tinker's darn what happens afterwards. But, all the same, if her dad was a real man, sorry for what he's done and tryin' to make up for it—why, then, I cal'late I'm decent enough to take off my hat, hand her over, and say: 'God bless you and good luck.' But to think of him carryin' her off the Lord knows where, to neglect her and cruelize her, and to let her grow up among fellers like him, I—I—by the big dipper, I can't do it! That's all; I can't!"

"How does she feel about it, herself?" asked Peabody.

"Her? Bos'n? Why, that's the hardest of all. Some of the children at school pester her about her father. I don't know's you can blame 'em; young ones are made that way, I guess—but she comes home to me cryin', and it's 'O Uncle Cy, he *ain't* my truly father, is he?' and 'You won't let him take me away from you, will you?' till it seems as if I should fly out of the window. The poor little thing! And that puffed-up humbug Atkins blowin' about his Christianity and all! D—n such Christianity as that, I say! I've seen heathen Injuns, who never heard of Christ, with more of His spirit inside 'em. There! I've shocked you, I guess. Sometimes I think this place is too narrer and cramped for me. I've been around, you know, and my New England bringin' up has wore thin in spots. Seem's if I must get somewheres and spread out, or I'll bust."

He threw himself into a chair. The lawyer clapped him on the shoulder.

# A CLEW

"There, there, captain," he said. "Don't 'bust' yet awhile. Don't give up the ship. If we lose in one court, we can appeal to another, and so on up the line. And meantime we'll do a little investigating of friend Thomas's career since he left Concord. I've written to a legal acquaintance of mine in Butte, giving him the facts as we know them, and a description of Thomas. He will try to find out what the fellow did in his years out West. It's our best chance, as I told you. Keep your pluck up and wait and see."

The captain repeated this conversation to the Board of Strategy when he returned to Bayport. Miss Dawes had walked home from school with Bos'n, and had stopped at the house to hear the report. She listened, but it was evident that something else was on her mind.

"Captain Whittaker," she asked, "has it ever struck you as queer that Mr. Atkins should take such an interest in this matter? He is giving time and counsel and money to help this man Thomas, who is a perfect stranger to him. Why does he do it?"

Captain Cy smiled.

"Why?" he repeated. "Why, to down me, of course. I was gettin' too everlastin' prominent in politics to suit him. I'd got you in as teacher, and I had 'Lonzo Snow as good as licked for school committee. Goodness knows what I might have run for next, 'cordin' to Heman's reasonin', and I simply

had to be smashed. It worked all right. I'm so un-
healthy now in the sight of most folks in this town,
that I cal'late they go home and sulphur-smoke their
clothes after they meet me, so's not to catch my
wickedness."

But the teacher shook her head.

"That doesn't seem reason enough to me," she
declared. "Just see what Mr. Atkins has done. He
never openly advocated anything in town meeting before; you said so yourself. Even when he must have
realized that you had the votes for committeeman he
kept still. He might have taken many of them from
you by simply coming out and declaring for Mr.
Snow; but he didn't. And then, all at once, he takes
this astonishing stand. Captain Whittaker, Mr. Tidditt says that, the night of Emily's birthday party,
you and he told who she was, by accident, and that
Mr. Atkins seemed very much surprised and upset.
Is that so?"

Captain Cy laughed.

"His lemonade was upset; that's all I noticed
special. Oh! yes, and he lost his hat off, goin' home.
But what of it? What are you drivin' at?"

"I was wondering if—if it could be that, for some
reason, Mr. Atkins had a spite against Emily or her
people. Or if he had any reason to fear her."

"Fear? Fear Bos'n? Oh, my, that's funny!
You've been readin' novels, I'm 'fraid, teacher,
'though I didn't suspect it of you."

He laughed heartily. Miss Dawes smiled, too, but she still persisted.

"Well," she said, "I don't know. Perhaps it is because I'm a woman, and politics don't mean as much to me as to you men, but to me political reasons don't seem strong enough to account for such actions as those of Mr. Atkins. Emily's mother was a Thayer, wasn't she? and the Thayers once lived in Orham. I wish we could find out more about them while they lived there."

Asaph Tidditt pulled his beard thoughtfully.

"Well," he observed, "maybe we can, if we want to, though I don't think what we find out 'll amount to nothin'. I was kind of cal'latin' to go to Orham next week on a little visit. Seth Wingate over there —Barzilla Wingate's cousin, Whit—is a sort of relation of mine, and we visit back and forth every nine or ten year or so. The ten year's most up, and he's been pesterin' me to come over. Seth's been Orham town clerk about as long as I've been the Bayport one, and he|s lived there all his life. What he don't know about Orham folks ain't wuth knowin'. If you say so, I'll pump him about the Thayers and the Richards. 'Twon't do no harm, and the old fool likes to talk, anyhow. I don't know's I ought to speak that way about my relations," he added doubtfully, "but Seth *is* sort of stubborn and unlikely at odd times. We don't always agree as to which is the best town to live in, you understand."

So it was settled that Mr. Wingate should be subjected to the "pumping" process when Asaph visited him. He departed for this visit the following week, and remained away for ten days. Meanwhile several things happened in Bayport.

One of these things was the farewell of the Honorable Heman Atkins. Congress was to open at Washington, and the Honorable heeded the call of duty. Alicia and the housekeeper went with him, and the big house was closed for the winter. At the gate between the stone urns, and backed by the iron dogs, the great man bade a group of admiring constituents good-by. He thanked them for their trust in him, and promised that it should not be betrayed.

" I leave you, my fellow townsmen, er—ladies and friends," he said, " with regret, tempered by pride— a not inexcusable pride, I believe. In the trying experience which my self-respect and sympathy has so recently forced upon me, you have stood firm and cheered me on. The task I have undertaken, the task of restoring to a worthy man his own, shall be carried on to the bitterest extremity. I have put my hand to the plow, and it shall not be withdrawn. And, furthermore, I go to my work at Washington determined to secure for my native town the appropriation which it so sorely needs. I shall secure it if I can, even though—" and the sarcasm was hugely enjoyed by his listeners—" I am, as I seem likely to be, deprived of the help of the 'committee,' self-appointed at our recent town meeting. If I fail—and I do not conceal the fact that I may fail—I am certain you will not blame me. Now I should like to shake each one of you by the hand."

The hands were shaken, and the train bore the Atkins delegation away. And, on the day following, Mr. Thomas, the prodigal father, also left town. A position in Boston had been offered him, he said, and he felt that he must accept it. He would come back some of these days, with the warrant from the court, and get his little girl.

"Position offered him! Um—ya-as!" quoth Dimick the cynical, in conversation with Captain Cy. "Inspector of sidewalks, I shouldn't wonder. Well, please don't ask me if I think Heman sent him to Boston so's to have him out of the way, and 'cause he'd feel consider'ble safer than if he was loose down here. Don't ask me that, for, with my strict scruples against the truth I might say, No. As it is, I say nothin'—and wink my port eye."

The ten-day visit ended, Mr. Tidditt returned to Bayport. On the afternoon of his return he and Bailey called at the Whittaker place, and there they were joined by Miss Dawes, who had been summoned to the conclave by a note intrusted to Bos'n.

"Now, Ase," ordered Captain Cy, as the quartet gathered in the sitting room, "here we are, hangin' on your words, as the feller said. Don't keep us strung up too long. What did you find out?"

The town clerk cleared his throat. When he spoke, there was a trace of disappointment in his tone. To have been able to electrify his audience with the news of some startling discovery would have been pure joy for Asaph.

"Well," he began, "I don't know's I found out anything much. Yet I did find out somethin', too; but it don't really amount to nothin'. I hoped 'twould be somethin' more'n 'twas, but when nothin' come of it except the little somethin' it begun with, I——"

"For the land sakes!" snapped Bailey Bangs, who was a trifle envious of his friend's position in the center of the stage, "stop them 'nothin's' and 'somethin's,' won't you? You keep whirlin' 'em round and over and over till my head's *full* of 'nothin',' and——"

"That's what it's full of most of the time," interrupted Asaph tartly. Captain Cy hastened to act as peacemaker.

"Never mind, Bailey," he said; "you let Ase alone. Tell us what you did find out, Ase, and cut out the trimmin's."

"Well," continued Mr. Tidditt, with a glare at Bangs, "I asked Seth about the Thayers and the Richards folks the very fust night I struck Orham. He remembered 'em, of course; he can remember

"'I did find out somethin', too; but it don't really amount to nothin'.'"

Adam, if you let him tell it. He told me a whole mess about old man Thayer and old man Richards and their granddads and grandmarms, and what houses they lived in, and how many hens they kept, and what their dog's name was, and how they come to name him that, and enough more to fill a hogshead. 'Twas ten o'clock afore he got out of Genesis, and down so fur as John and Emily. He remembered their bein' married, and their baby—Mary Thayer, Bos'n's ma—bein' born.

"Folks used to call John Thayer a smart young feller, so Seth said. They used to cal'late that he'd rise high in the seafarin' and ship-ownin' line. May-be he would, only he died somewheres in Californy 'long in '54 or thereabouts. 'Twas the time of the gold craziness out there, and he left his ship and went gold huntin'. And the next thing they knew, he was dead and buried."

"When was that?" inquired the schoolmistress.

"In '54, I tell you. So Seth says."

"What ship was he on?" asked Bailey.

"Wan't on any ship. Why don't you listen, instead of settin' there moonin'? He was gold diggin', I tell you."

"He'd *been* on a ship, hadn't he? What was the name of her?"

"I didn't ask. What diff'rence does that make?"

"Wasn't Mr. Atkins at sea in those days?" put in the teacher. The captain answered her,

271

"Yes, he was," he said. "That is, I think he was. He was away from here when I skipped out, and he didn't get back till '61 or thereabouts."

"Well, anyhow," went on Asaph, "that's all I could find out. Seth and me went rummagin' through town records from way back to glory, him gassin' away and stringin' along about this old settler and that, till I 'most wished he'd choke himself with the dust he was raisin'. We found John's grandad's will, and Emily's dad's will, and John's own will, and that's all. John left everything he had and all he might become possessed of to his wife and baby and their heirs forever. He died poorer'n poverty. What's the use of a will when you ain't got nothin' to leave?"

"Why!" exclaimed Captain Cy. "The answer to that's easy. John was goin' to sea, and, more'n likely, intended to have a shy at the diggin's afore he got back. So, if he did make any money, he wanted his wife and baby to have it."

"Well, what they got wan't wuth havin'. Emily had to scrimp along and do dressmakin' till she died. She done fairly well at that, though, and saved somethin' and passed it over to Mary. And Mary married Henry Thomas, after she went with the Howes tribe to Concord, and he got rid of it for her in double quick time—all but the Orham land."

"So that was all you could find out, hey, Ase?" asked the captain. "Well, it's at least as much as I

expected. You see, teacher, these story-book notions
don't work out when it comes to real life."

Miss Dawes was plainly disappointed.

" I wish we knew more," she said. "Who was
on this ship with Mr. Thayer? And who sent the
news of his death home?"

"Oh, I can tell you that," said Asaph. "'Twas
some one-hoss doctor out there, gold minin' himself,
he was. John died of a quick fever. Got cold and
went off in no time. Seth remembered that much,
though he couldn't remember the doctor's name. He
said, if I wanted to learn more about the Thayers,
I might go see— Humph, well, never mind that.
'Twas just foolishness, anyhow."

But Phœbe persisted.

"To see whom?" she asked. "Some one you
knew? A friend of yours?"

Asaph turned red.

"Friend of mine!" he snarled. "No, *sir!* she
ain't no friend of mine, I'm thankful to say. More
a friend of Bailey's, here, if she's anybody's. One
of his pets, she was, for a spell. A patient of his,
you might say; anyhow, he prescribed for her. 'Twas
that deef idiot, Debby Beasley, Cy; that's who 'twas.
Her name was Briggs afore she married Beasley,
and she was hired help for Emily Thayer, when
Mary was born, and until John died."

Captain Cy burst into a roar of laughter. Bailey
sprang out of his chair.

"De—Debby Beasley!" he stammered. "Debby Beasley!"

"She was that deef housekeeper Bailey hired for me, teacher," explained the captain. "I've told you about her. Ho! ho! so that's the end of the mystery huntin'. We go gunnin' for Heman Atkins, and we bring down Debby! Well, Ase, goin' to see the old lady?"

Mr. Tidditt's retort was emphatic.

"Goin' to *see* her?" he repeated. "I guess not! Godfrey scissors! I told Seth, says I, 'I've had all the Debby Beasley *I* want, and I cal'late Cy Whittaker feels the same way.' Go to see her! I wouldn't go to see her if she was up in Paradise a-hollerin' for me."

"Nobody up there's goin' to holler for *you*, Ase Tidditt," remarked Bailey, with sarcasm; "so don't let that worry you none."

"Are *you* going to see her, Captain Whittaker?" asked Phœbe.

The captain shook his head.

"Why, no, I guess not," he said. "I don't take much stock in what she'd be likely to know; besides, I'm a good deal like Ase—I've had about all the Debby Beasley I want."

# CHAPTER XV

## DEBBY BEASLEY TO THE RESCUE

"MRS. BANGS," said the schoolmistress, as if it was the most casual thing in the world, "I want to borrow your husband to-morrow."

It was Friday evening, and supper at the perfect boarding house had advanced as far as the stewed prunes and fruit-cake stage. Keturah, who was carefully dealing out the prunes, exactly four to each saucer, stopped short, spoon in air, and gazed at Miss Dawes.

"You—you want to *what*?" she asked.

"I want to borrow your husband. I want him all day, too, because I'm thinking of driving over to Trumet, and I need a coachman. You'll go, won't you, Mr. Bangs?"

Bailey, who had been considering the advisability of asking for a second cup of tea, brightened up and looked pleased.

"Why, yes," he answered, "I'll go. I can go just as well as not. Fact is, I'd like to. Ain't been to Trumet I don't know when."

Miss Phinney and the widow Tripp looked at each other. Then they both looked at Keturah. That lady's mouth closed tightly, and she resumed her prune distribution.

"I'm sorry," she said crisply, "but I'm 'fraid he can't go. It's Saturday, and I'll need him round the house. Do you care for cake to-night, Elviry? I'm 'fraid it's pretty dry; I ain't had time to do much bakin' this week."

"Of course," continued the smiling Phœbe, "I shouldn't think of asking him to go for nothing. I didn't mean borrow him in just that way. I was thinking of hiring your horse and buggy, and, as I'm not used to driving, I thought perhaps I might engage Mr. Bangs to drive for me. I expected to pay for the privilege. But, as you need him, I suppose I must get my rig and driver somewhere else. I'm so sorry."

The landlady's expression changed. This was the dull season, and opportunities to " let " the family steed and buggy—" horse and team," we call it in Bayport—were few.

"Well," she observed, "I don't want to be unlikely and disobligin'. Far's he's concerned, he'd rather be traipsin' round the country than stay to home, any day; though it's been so long sence he took *me* to ride that I don't know's I'd know how to act."

"Why, Ketury!" protested her husband. "How

276

you talk! Didn't I drive you down to the graveyard only last Sunday—or the Sunday afore?"

"Graveyard! Yes, I notice our rides always fetch
up at the graveyard. You're always willin' to take
me *there*. Seems sometimes as if you enjoyed doin'
it."

"Now, Keturah! you know yourself that 'twas
you proposed goin' there. You said you wanted to
look at our lot, 'cause you was afraid 'twan't big
enough, and you didn't know but we'd ought to add
on another piece. You said that it kept you awake
nights worryin' for fear when I passed away you
wouldn't have room in that lot for me. Land sakes!
don't I remember? Didn't you give me the blue
creeps talkin' about it?"

Mrs. Bangs ignored this outburst. Turning to the
school teacher, she said with a sigh:

"Well, I guess he can go. I'll get along somehow.
I hope he'll be careful of the buggy; we had it
painted only last January."

Mrs. Tripp ventured a hinted question concerning
the teacher's errand at Trumet. The reply being
noncommittal, the widow cheerfully prophesied that
she guessed 'twas going to rain or snow next day.
"It's about time for the line storm," she added.

But it did not storm, although a brisk, cold gale
was blowing when, after breakfast next morning, the
"horse and team," with Bailey in his Sunday suit
and overcoat, and Miss Dawes on the buggy seat

beside him, turned out of the boarding-house yard
and started on the twelve-mile journey to Trumet.

It was a bleak ride. Denboro, the village adjoining Bayport on the bay side, is a pretty place,
with old elms and silverleafs shading the main street
in summer, and with substantial houses set each in
its trim yard. But beyond Denboro the Trumet road
winds out over rolling, bare hills, with cranberry
bogs, now flooded and skimmed with ice, in the hol-
lows between them, clumps of bayberry and beach-
plum bushes scattered over their rounded slopes, and
white scars in their sides showing where the cranberry growers have cut away the thin layer of coarse
grass and moss to reach the sand beneath, sand which
they use in preparing their bogs for the new vines.

And the wind! There is always a breeze along
the Trumet road, even in summer—when the mosquitoes lie in wait to leeward like buccaneers until,
sighting the luckless wayfarer in the offing, they
drive down before the wind in clouds, literally to eat
him alive. They are skilled navigators, those Trumet
road mosquitoes, and they know the advantage of
snug harbors under hat brims and behind spreading
ears. And each individual smashed by a frantic
palm leaves a thousand blood relatives to attend his
funeral and exact revenge after the Corsican fashion.

Now, in December, there were, of course, no mosquitoes, but the wind tore across those bare hilltops
in gusts that rocked the buggy on its springs. The

bayberry bushes huddled and crouched before it. The sky was covered with tumbling, flying clouds, which changed shape continually, and ripped into long, fleecy ravelings, that broke loose and pelted on until merged into the next billowy mass. The bay was gray and white, and in the spots where an occasional sunbeam broke through and struck it, flashed like a turned knife blade.

Bailey drove with one hand and held his hat on his head with the other. The road had been deeply rutted during the November rains, and now the ruts were frozen. The buggy wheels twisted and scraped as they turned in the furrows.

"What's the matter?" asked the schoolmistress, shouting so as to be heard above the flapping of the buggy curtains. "Why do you watch that wheel?"

"'Fraid of the axle," whooped Mr. Bangs in reply. "Nut's kind of loose, for one thing, and the way the wheel wobbles I'm scart she'll come off. Call this a road!" he snorted indignantly. "More like a plowed field a consider'ble sight. Jerushy, how she blows! No wonder they raise so many deef and dumb folks in Trumet. I'd talk sign language myself if I lived here. What's the use of wastin' strength pumpin' up words when they're blowed back down your throat fast enough to choke you? Git dap, Henry! Don't you see the meetin' house steeple? We're most there, thank the goodness."

In Trumet Center, which is not much of a center,

Miss Dawes alighted from the buggy and entered a building bearing a sign with the words "Metropolitan Variety Store, Joshua Atwood, Prop'r, Groceries, Coal, Dry Goods, Insurance, Boots and Shoes, Garden Seeds, etc." A smaller sign beneath this was lettered "Justice of the Peace," and one below that read "Post Office."

She emerged a moment later, followed by an elderly person in a red cardigan jacket and overalls.

"Take the fust turnin' to the left, marm," he said pointing. "It's pretty nigh to East Trumet townhall. Fust house this side of the blacksmith shop. About two mile, I'd say. Windy day for drivin', ain't it? That horse of yours belongs in Bayport, I cal'late. Looks to me like— Hello, Bailey!"

"Hello, Josh!" grunted Mr. Bangs, adding an explanatory aside to the effect that he knew Josh Atwood, the latter having once lived in Bayport.

"But say," he asked as they moved on once more, "have we got to go to *East* Trumet? Jerushy! that's the place where the wind *comes* from. They raise it over there; anyhow, they don't raise much else. Whose house you goin' to?"

He had asked the same question at least ten times since leaving home, and each time Miss Dawes had evaded it. She did so now, saying that she was sure she should know the house when they got to it.

The two miles to East Trumet were worse than

the twelve which they had come. The wind fairly shrieked here, for the road paralleled the edge of high sand bluffs close by the shore, and the ruts and "thank-you-marms" were trying to the temper. Bailey's was completely wrecked.

"Teacher," he snapped as they reached the crest of a long hill, and a quick grab at his hat alone prevented its starting on a balloon ascension, " get out a spell, will you? I've got to swear or bust, and 'long's you're aboard I can't swear. What you standin' still for, you?" he bellowed at poor Henry, the horse, who had stopped to rest. " I cal'late the critter thinks that last cyclone must have blowed me sky high, and he's waitin' to see where I light. Git dap!"

"I guess I shall get out very soon now," panted Phœbe. "There's the blacksmith shop over there near the next hill, and this house in the hollow must be the one I'm looking for."

They pulled up beside the house in the hollow. A little, story-and-a-half house it was, and, judging by the neglected appearance of the weeds and bushes in the yard, it had been unoccupied for some time. However, the blinds were now open, and a few fowls about the back door seemed to promise that some one was living there. The wooden letter box by the gate had a name stenciled upon it. Miss Dawes sprang from the buggy and looked at the box.

"Yes," she said. "This is the place. Will you

come in, Mr. Bangs? You can put your horse in that barn, I'm sure, if you want to."

But Bailey declined to come in. He declared he was going on to the blacksmith's shop to have that wheel fixed. He would not feel safe to start for home with it as it was. He drove off, and Miss Dawes, knowing from lifelong experience that front doors are merely for show, passed around the main body of the house and rapped on the door in the ell. The rap was not answered, though she could hear some one moving about within, and a shrill voice singing " The Sweet By and By." So she rapped again and again, but still no one came to the door. At last she ventured to open it.

A thin woman, with her head tied up in a colored cotton handkerchief, was in the room, vigorously wielding a broom. She was singing in a high cracked voice. The opening of the door let in a gust of cold wind which struck the singer in the back of the neck, and caused her to turn around hastily.

" Hey? " she exclaimed. " Land sakes! you scare a body to death! Shut that door quick! I ain't hankering for influenzy. Who are you? What do you want? Why didn't you knock? Where's my specs? "

She took a pair of spectacles from the mantel shelf, rubbed them with her apron, and set them on the bridge of her thin nose. Then she inspected the schoolmistress from head to foot.

"I beg pardon for coming in," shouted Phœbe. "I knocked, but you didn't hear. You are Mrs. Beasley, aren't you?"

"I don't want none," replied Debby, with emphasis. "So there's no use your wastin' your breath."

"Don't want—" repeated the astonished teacher. "Don't want what?"

"Hey? I say I don't want none."

"Don't want *what*?"

"Whatever 'tis you're peddlin'. Books or soap or tea, or whatever 'tis. I don't want nothin'."

After some strenuous minutes, the visitor managed to make it clear to Mrs. Beasley's mind that she was not a peddler. She tried to add a word of further explanation, but it was effort wasted.

"'Tain't no use," snapped Debby, "I can't hear you, you speak so faint. Wait till I get my horn; it's in the settin' room."

Phœbe's wonder as to what the "horn" might be was relieved by the widow's appearance, a moment later, with the biggest ear trumpet her caller had ever seen.

"There, now!" she said, adjusting the instrument and thrusting the bell-shaped end under the teacher's nose. "Talk into that. If you ain't a peddler, what be you—sewin' machine agent?"

Phœbe explained that she had come some distance on purpose to see Mrs. Beasley. She was interested in the Thayers, who used to live in Orham, particularly in Mr. John Thayer, who died in 1854. She had been told that Debby formerly lived with the Thayers, and could, no doubt, remember a great deal about them. Would she mind answering a few questions, and so on?

Mrs. Beasley, her hearing now within forty-five degrees of the normal, grew interested. She ushered her visitor into the adjoining room, and proffered her a chair. That sitting room was a wonder of its kind, even to the teacher's accustomed eyes. A gilt-framed crayon enlargement of the late Mr. Beasley hung in the center of the broadest wall space, and was not the ugliest thing in the apartment. Having said this, further description is unnecessary—particularly to those who remember Mr. Beasley's personal appearance.

"What you so interested in the Thayers for?" inquired Debby. "One of the heirs, be you? They didn't leave nothin'."

No, the schoolmistress was not an heir. Was not even a relative of the family. But she was—was interested, just the same. A friend of hers was a relative, and——

"What is your friend?" inquired the inquisitor. "A man?"

There was no reason why Miss Dawes should have changed color, but, according to Debby's subsequent testimony, she did; she blushed, so the widow declares.

284

"No," she protested. "Oh, no! it's a—she's a child, that's all—a little girl. But——"

"Maybe you're gettin' up one of them geographical trees," suggested Mrs. Beasley. "I've seen 'em, fust settlers down in the trunk, and children and grandchildren spreadin' out in the branches. Is that it?"

Here was an avenue of escape. Phœbe stretched the truth a trifle, and admitted that that, or something of the sort, was what she was engaged in. The explanation seemed to be satisfactory. Debby asked her visitor's name, and, misunderstanding it, addressed her as "Miss Dorcas" thereafter. Then she proceeded to give her reminiscences of the Thayers, and it did not take long for the disappointed teacher to discover that, for all practical purposes, these reminiscences were valueless. Mrs. Beasley remembered many things, but nothing at all concerning John Thayer's life in the West, nor the name of the ship he sailed in, nor who his ship-mates were.

"He never wrote home but once or twice afore he died," she said. "And when he did Emily, his wife, never told me what was in his letters. She always burnt 'em, I guess. I used to hunt around for 'em when she was out, but she burnt 'em to spite me, I cal'late. Her and me didn't get along any too well. She said I talked too much to other folks about what was none of their business. Now, anybody

that knows me knows *that* ain't one of my failin's.
I told her so; says I——"

And so on for ten minutes. Then Phœbe ventured to repeat the words " out West," and her companion went off on a new tack. She had just been West
nerself. She had been on a visit to her husband's
niece, who lived in Arizona. In Blazeton, Arizona.
" It's the nicest town ever you see," she continued.
" And the smartest, most up-to-date place. Talk
about the West bein' oncivilized! My land! you
ought to see that town! Electric lights, and tele-
phones, and——and——I don't know what all! Why,
Miss What's-your-name——Miss Dorcas, marm, you
just ought to see the photygraphs I've got that was
took out there. My niece, she took 'em with one of
them little mites of cameras. You wouldn't believe
such a little box of a thing could take such photygraphs. I'm goin' to get 'em and show 'em to you.
No, sir! you ain't got to go, neither. Set right still
and let me fetch them photygraphs. 'Twon't be a
mite of trouble. I'd love to do it."

Protests were unavailing. The photographs, at
least fifty of them, were produced, and the suffering
caller was shown the Blazeton City Hall, and the
Blazeton " Palace Hotel," and the home of the Beasley niece, taken from the front, the rear, and both
sides. With each specimen Debby delivered a de-
scriptive lecture.

" You see that house? " she asked. " Well, 'tain't

much of a one to look at, but it's got the most interestin' story tagged on to it. I made Eva, that's my
niece, take a picture of it just on that account. The
woman that lives there's had the hardest time. Her
fust name's Desire, and that kind of made me take an
interest in her right off, 'cause I had an Aunt Desire
once, and it's a name you don't hear very often. Afterwards I got to know her real well. She was a
widder woman, like me, only she didn't have as much
sense as I've got, and went and married a second
time. 'Twas 'long in 1886 she done it. This man
Higgins, he went to work for her on her place, and
pretty soon he married her. They lived together,
principally on her fust husband's insurance money, I
cal'late, until a year or so ago. Then the insurance
money give out, and Mr. Higgins he says: ' Old
woman,' he says—*I'd* never let a husband of mine
call me ' old woman,' but Desire didn't seem to
mind—' Old woman,' he says, ' I'm goin' over to
Phœnix '—that's another city in Arizona—' to look
for a job.' And he went, and she ain't heard hide—
I mean seen hide nor heard hair—What *does* ail me?
She ain't seen nor heard of him since. And she ad-
vertised in the weekly paper, and I don't know what
all. She thinks he was murdered, you know; that's
what makes it so sort of creepy and interestin'.
Everybody was awful kind to her, and we got to
be real good friends. Why, I——"

This was but the beginning. It was evident that

Mrs. Beasley had thoroughly enjoyed herself in Blazeton, and that the sorrows of the bereaved Desire Higgins had been one of the principal sources of that enjoyment. The schoolmistress endeavored to turn the subject, but it was useless.

"I fetched home a whole pile of them newspapers," continued Debby. "They was awful interestin'; full of pictures of Blazeton buildin's and leadin' folks and all. And in some of the back numbers was the advertisement about Mr. Higgins. I do wish I could show 'em to you, but I lent 'em to Mrs. Atwood up to the Center. If 'twan't such a ways I'd go and fetch 'em. Mrs. Atwood's been awful nice to me. She took care of my trunks and things when I went West—yes, and afore that when I went to Bayport to keep house for that miser'ble Cap'n Whittaker. I ain't told you about that, but I will by and by. Them trunks had lots of things in 'em that I didn't want to lose nor have anybody see. My diaries—I've kept a diary since 1850—and——"

"Diaries?" interrupted Phœbe, grasping at straws. "Did you keep a diary while you were at the Thayers?"

"Yes. Now, why didn't I think of that afore? More'n likely there'd be somethin' in that to help you with that geographical tree. I used to put down everything that happened, and—— Where you goin'?"

# DEBBY BEASLEY TO THE RESCUE

Miss Dawes had risen and was peering out of the window.

"I was looking to see if my driver was anywhere about," she replied. "I thought perhaps he would drive over to Mrs. Atwood's and get the diary for you. But I don't see him."

Just then, from around the corner of the house, peeped an agitated face; an agitated forefinger beckoned. Debby stepped to the window beside her visitor, and the face and finger went out of sight as if pulled by a string.

Miss Phœbe smiled.

"I think I'll go out and look for him," she said. "He must be near here. I'll be right back, Mrs. Beasley."

Without stopping to put on her jacket, she hurried through the dining room, out of the door, and around the corner. There she found Mr. Bangs in a highly nervous state.

"Why didn't you tell me 'twas Debby Beasley you was comin' to see?" he demanded. "If you'd mentioned that deef image's name you'd never got *me* to drive you, I tell you that!"

"Yes," answered the teacher sweetly. "I imagined that. That's why I didn't tell you, Mr. Bangs. Now I want you to do me a favor. Will you drive over to Trumet Center, and deliver a note and get a package for me? Then you can come back here, and I shall be ready to start for home."

"Drive! Drive nothin'! The blacksmith's out, and won't be back for another hour. His boy's there, but he's a big enough lunkhead to try bailin' out a dory with a fork, and that buggy axle is bent so it's simply got to be fixed. I'd no more go home to Ketury with that buggy as 'tis than I'd— Oh! my land of love!"

The ejaculation was almost a groan. There at the corner, ear trumpet adjusted, and spectacles glistening, stood Debby Beasley. Bailey appeared to wilt under her gaze as if the spectacles were twin suns. Miss Dawes looked as if she very much wanted to laugh. The widow stared in silence.

"How—how d'ye do, Mrs. Beasley?" faltered Mr. Bangs, not forgetting to raise his voice. "I hope you're lookin' as well as you feel. I mean, I hope you're smart."

Mrs. Beasley nodded decisively.

"Yes," she answered. "I'm pretty toler'ble, thank you. What was the matter, Mr. Bangs? Why didn't you come in? Do you usually make your calls round the corner?"

The gentleman addressed seemed unable to reply. The schoolmistress came to the rescue.

"You mustn't blame Mr. Bangs, Mrs. Beasley," she explained. "He wasn't responsible for what happened at Captain Whittaker's. He is the gentleman who drove me over here. I was going to send him to Mrs. Atwood's for the diary."

"Who said I was blamin' him?" queried the widow. "If 'twas that little Tidditt thing I might feel different. But, considerin' that I got this horn from Mr. Bangs, I'm willin' to let bygones be past. It helps my hearin' a lot. Them ear-fixin's was good while they lasted, but they got out of kilter quick. *I* shan't bother Mr. Bangs. If he can square his own conscience, I'm satisfied."

Bailey's conscience was not troubling him greatly, and he seemed relieved. Phœbe told of the damaged buggy.

"Humph!" grunted the widow. "The horse didn't get bent, too, did he?"

Mr. Bangs indignantly declared that the horse was all right.

"Um—hum. Well, then, I guess I can supply a carriage. My fust cousin Ezra that died used to be doctor here, and he give me his sulky when he got a new one. It's out in the barn. Go fetch your horse, and harness him in. I'll be ready time the harnessin's done."

"You?" gasped the teacher. "You don't need to go, Mrs. Beasley. I wouldn't think of giving you that trouble."

"No trouble at all. I wouldn't trust nobody else with them trunks. And besides, I always do enjoy ridin'. You could go, too, Miss Dorcas, but the sulky seat's too narrer for three. You can set in the settin' room till we get back. 'Twon't take us long. Don't say another word; I'm *a-goin'*."

# CHAPTER XVI

### A REMARKABLE DRIVE AND WHAT FOLLOWED

THE number of reasons given by Mr. Bangs
one after the other, to prove that it would
be quite impossible for him to be Mrs.
Beasley's charioteer was a credit to the resources of
his invention. The blacksmith might be back any
minute; it was dinner time, and he was hungry;
Henry, the horse, was tired; it wasn't a nice day for
riding, and he would come over some other time and
take the widow out; he— But Debby had a conclusive answer for each protest.

"You said yourself the blacksmith wouldn't be
back for an hour," she observed. "And you can
leave word with the boy what he's to do when he
does come. As for dinner, I'll be real glad to give
you and Miss Dorcas a snack soon's we get back. I
don't mind if it ain't a pleasant day; a little fresh
air 'll do me good. I been shut up here houseclean-
in' ever since I got back from out West. Now, hurry
right along, and fetch your horse. I'll unlock the
barn."

"But, Mrs. Beasley," put in the schoolmistress,

292

" why couldn't you give us a note to Mrs. Atwood and let us stop for the diary on our way home? I could return it to you by mail. Or you might get it yourself some other day and mail it to me."

" No, no! Never put off till to-morrer what you can do to-day. My husband was a great hand to put off and put off. For the last eight years of his life I was at him to buy a new go-to-meetin' suit of clothes. The one he had was blue to start with, but it faded to a brown, and, toward the last of it, I declare if it didn't commence to turn green. Nothin' I could say would make him heave it away even then. Seemed to think more of it than ever. Said he wanted to hang to it a spell and see what 'twould turn next. But he died and was laid out in that same suit, and I was so mortified at the funeral I couldn't think of nothin' else. No, I'll go after them papers and the diary while they're fresh in my mind. And besides, do you s'pose I'd let Sarah Ann Atwood rummage through my trunks? I guess not! "

Phœbe began to be sorry she had thought of sending for the diary, particularly as the chance of its containing valuable information was so remote. Mrs. Beasley went into the house to dress for the ride. The schoolmistress went with her as far as the sitting room. The perturbed Bailey stalked off, muttering, to the blacksmith's.

In a little while he returned, leading Henry by the bridle. Debby, adorned with the beflowered bonnet

293

she had worn when she arrived at the Cy Whittaker
place, and with a black cloth cape over her lean
shoulders, was waiting for him by the open door of
the barn. The cape had a fur collar—"cat fur,"
so Mr. Bangs said afterwards in describing it.

"Pull the sulky right out," commanded the widow.

Bailey stared into the black interior of the barn.

"Which is it?" he shouted.

Mrs. Beasley pointed with her ear trumpet.

"Why, that one there, of course. 'Tother's a
truck cart. You wouldn't expect me to ride in that,
would you?"

Mr. Bangs entered the barn, seized the vehicle indicated by the shafts, and drew it out into the yard.
He inspected it deliberately, and then sat weakly
down on the chopping block near by. Apparently he
was overcome by emotion.

The "sulky" bequeathed by the late doctor had
been built to order for its former owner. It was of
the "carryall" variety, except that it had but a
single narrow seat. Its top was square and was curtained, the curtains being tightly buttoned down.
Altogether it was something of a curiosity. Miss
Dawes, who had come out to see the start, looked
at the "sulky," then at Mr. Bangs's face, and turned
her back. Her shoulders shook:

"It used to be a real nice carriage when Ezra had
it," commented the widow admiringly. "It needs
ilin' and sprucin' up now, but I guess 'twill do.

Come!" to Bailey, who had not risen from the chopping block. "Hurry up and harness or we'll never get started. Thought you wanted to get back for dinner?"

Mr. Bangs stood up and heaved a sigh.

"I did," he answered slowly, "but," with a glance at the sulky, "somethin' seems to have took away my appetite. Teacher, do you mean to——"

But Miss Dawes had withdrawn to the corner of the house, from which viewpoint she seemed to be inspecting the surrounding landscape. Bailey seized Henry by the bridle and backed him into the shafts.

"Back up!" he roared. "Back up, I tell you! You needn't look at me that way," he added, in a lower tone. "*I* can't help it. You ain't any worse ashamed than I am. There! the ark's off the ways. All aboard!"

Turning to the expectant widow, he "boosted" her, not too tenderly, up to the narrow seat. Then he climbed in himself. Two on that seat made a tight fit. Bailey took up the reins. Debby leaned forward and peered around the edge of the curtains.

"You!" she shouted. "You, Miss What's-your-name—Dorcas! Come here a minute. I want to tell you somethin'."

The schoolmistress, her face red and her eyes moist, approached.

"I just wanted to say," explained Debby, "that I ain't real sure as that diary's there. I burnt up a lot of my old letters and things a spell ago, and seems to me I burnt some old diaries, too, but maybe that wan't one of 'em. Anyhow, I can get them Arizona papers, and I do want you to see 'em. They're the most *interestin'* things. Now," she added, turning to her companion on the seat, "you can git dap just as soon as you want to."

Whether or not Mr. Bangs wanted to "git dap" is a doubtful question. But at all events he did. Before the astonished Miss Dawes could think of an answer to the observation concerning the diary, the carriage, its long unused axles shrieking protests, moved out of the yard. The schoolmistress watched it go. Then she returned to the sitting room and collapsed in a rocking chair.

Once out from the shelter of the house and on the open road, the sulky received the full force of the wind. The first gust that howled in from the bay struck its curtained side with a sudden burst of power that caused Mrs. Beasley to clutch her driver's arm.

"Good land of mercy!' she screamed. "It blows real hard, don't it?"

Mr. Bangs's answer was in the form of delicate sarcasm, bellowed into the ear trumpet.

"Sho!" he exclaimed. "I want to know! You don't say! Now you mention it, seems as if I had noticed a little air stirrin'."

Another gust tilted the carriage top. Debby clutched the arm still tighter.

"Why, it blows awful hard!" she cried. "I'd no idee it blew like this."

"Want to 'bout ship and go home again?" whooped Bailey, hopefully. But the widow didn't intend to give up the rare luxury of a "ride" which a kind Providence had cast in her way.

"No, no!" she answered. "I guess if you folks come all the way from Bayport I can stand it as fur's the Center. But hurry all you can, won't you? I'm kind of 'fraid of the springs."

"Springs? What springs? Let go my arm, will you? It's goin' to sleep."

Mrs. Beasley let go of the arm momentarily.

"I mean the springs on this carriage," she explained. "Last time I lent it to anybody—Solon Davis, 'twas—he said the bolts underneath was pretty nigh rusted out, and about all that held the wagon part on was its own weight. So we'll have to be kind of careful."

"Well—I—swan—to—man!" was Mr. Bangs's sole comment on the amazing disclosure; however, as an expression of concentrated and profound disgust it was quite sufficient. He spoke but once during the remainder of the trip to the "Center." Then, when his passenger begged to know if "that Whittaker man" had been well since she left, he shouted: "Yes—ever since," and relapsed into his former gloomy silence.

The widow's stop at the Atwood house, which was

in the immediate rear of the Atwood store, was of a half hour's duration. Bailey refused to leave the seat of the sulky and sat there, speaking to no one; not even replying to the questions of a group of loungers who gathered to inspect the ancient vehicle, and professed to be in doubt as to whether it had been washed in with the tide or been "left" to him in a will.

At last Debby made her appearance, her arms filled with newspapers. The latter she piled under the carriage seat, and then climbed to her former place beside the driver. Henry, in response to a slap from the reins, got under way once more. The axles squeaked and screamed.

"Gee!" cried one youngster, from the steps of the store. "It's the steam calliope. When's the rest of the show comin'?"

"Hi!" yelled another. "See how close they're hugged up together. Ain't they lovin'! It's a weddin'!"

"Shut up!" roared the tortured Bailey, whose hat had blown back into the body of the sulky, leaving his bald head exposed to the cutting wind.

The audience begged him to give them a lock of his hair, and added other remarks of a personal nature concerning the youth and beauty of the bridal couple and their chariot. Mr. Bangs was in a state of dumb frenzy. Debby, who, without her trumpet, had heard nothing of all this, was smiling and garrulous.

# A DRIVE AND WHAT FOLLOWED

" I found all the papers," she said. " They're right under the seat. I'm goin' to look 'em over so's to have the interestin' parts all ready to show Miss Dorcas when we get home. Ain't it nice I found 'em? "

In spite of her driver's remonstrances, unheard because of the nonadjustment of the trumpet, she reached under the seat and brought out the pile of Blazeton weeklies. With her feet upon the pile to keep it from blowing away, she proceeded to unfold one of the papers. It crackled and snapped in the wind like a loose mainsail.

" Keep that dratted thing out of my face, won't you? " shrieked the agonized Bailey. " How'm I goin' to see to steer with that smackin' me between the eyes every other second? "

" Hey? Did you speak to me? " asked the widow sweetly.

" Did I *speak*? No, I screeched! What in tunket——"

" I want you to see this picture of the mayor's house in Blazeton. Eva, my husband's niece, lives right acrost the road from him. Many's the time I've set on their piazza and seen him come out and go to the City Hall."

" Keep it out of my face, I tell you! Reef it! Furl it, you—you woman! I wish to thunder the piazza had caved in on you! I never see such an old fool in my born days. *Take it away!* "

Mrs. Beasley removed the paper, but only to substitute another.

" Here's Eva's brother-in-law," she screamed. " He's one of the prominent business men out there, so they put him in the paper. Ain't he nice-lookin'? "

Bailey's comments on the prominent business man's appearance were anything but flattering. Debby continued to reach for more papers, carefully replacing those she had inspected in the pile beneath her feet. The wind blew as hard as ever; even harder, for it was now almost dead ahead. Henry plodded along. They were in the hollow at the foot of the last long hill, that from which the blacksmith shop had first been sighted.

" I know what I'll do," declared the passenger. " I'll hunt for that missin' husband advertisement of Desire Higgins's. Let's see now! 'Twill be down at the bottom of the pile, 'cause the paper it's in is a last year one."

She bobbed down behind the high dashboard. Mr. Bangs stood up in order that her gymnastics might interfere, to a lesser degree, with his driving. The equipage began to move up the slope of the hill, bouncing and twisting in the frozen ruts.

" Here 'tis! " exclaimed Debby. " I remember it's in this number, 'cause there's a picture of the Palace Hotel on the front page. Let's see—' Dog lost '—no, that ain't it. ' Corner lot for sale '—wish

I had money enough to buy it; I'd like nothin' better than to live out there. 'Information wanted of my husband '—Here 'tis! Um—hum! "

She straightened up and eagerly began reading the advertisement. The hill was very steep just at its top, and the sulky slanted backward at a sharp angle. A terrific burst of wind tore around the corner of the bluff. It eddied through the sulky between the dashboard and the curtained sides. The widow, in her excitement at finding the advertisement, had inadvertently removed her feet from the pile of papers. In an instant the air was filled with whirling copies of the *Blazeton Weekly Courier.*

Henry, the horse, was a sober animal who had long ago reached the age of discretion. But to have his old ears and eyes suddenly blanketed with a flapping white thing swooping apparently from nowhere was too much even for his sedate nerves. He jumped sidewise. The reins were jerked from the driver's hands and fell in the road.

"Mercy on us! " shrieked Debby, clutching her companion about the waist. "What——"

"Let go of me! " howled Bailey, pushing her violently aside. "Whoa! Stand still! "

But Henry refused to stand still. The flapping paper still clung to his agitated head. He reared and pranced, jerking the sulky back and forth, its wheels still wedged in the ruts. Bailey sprang to the ground to pick up the reins. He seized them, but fell as he did so. The tug at his bits turned Henry's head, literally and figuratively. He reared and whirled about. The sulky rose on two wheels. The screaming Mrs. Beasley collapsed against its downward side. Another moment, and the whole upper half of the sulky—body, seat, curtains, and Debby—tilted over the lower wheels, and, the rusted bolts failing to hold, slid with a thump to the frozen road. The wind, catching it underneath as it slid, tipped it backward. Then Henry ran away.

Miss Dawes, left alone in the house at the foot of the hill, had amused herself for a time with the Beasley library, which partially filled a shelf in the sitting room. But "The Book of Martyrs" and "A Believer's Thoughts on Death" were not cheering literature, particularly as the author of the latter volume "thought" so dismally concerning the future of all who did not believe precisely as he did. So the teacher laid down the book, with a shudder, and wandered about the room, inspecting the late Mr. Beasley's portrait, the photographs in splintwork frames, the "alum basket" on the mantel, the blue castles, blue trees, and blue people pictured on the window shades, and other works of art in the apartment. She even peeped into the parlor, but the musty, shut-up smell of that dusky tomb was too much for her, and she sat down by the sitting-room window, under the empty bird cage, to look up the

"Sprawled across the rear axle and still clinging to the reins,
hung an individual by the name of Bangs."

road and watch for the return of the sulky and its occupants.

Sitting there, she was a witness of the alarming catastrophe on the hilltop, and reached the front gate just in time to see Henry go galloping by, dragging the four wheels and springs of the sulky, while, sprawled across the rear axle and still clinging to the reins, hung a familiar, howling, and most wickedly profane individual by the name of Bangs.

The runaway dashed on toward the blacksmith shop. Phœbe, bareheaded and coatless, ran up the hill. Before she reached the crest, she was aware of muffled screams, which sounded as if the screamer was shut up in a trunk.

"O-o-oh!" screamed Mrs. Beasley. "O-o-oh! Ow! Let me out! Help! I'm stuck! My back's broke! He-e-lp!"

The upper part of the sulky, with its boxlike curtained top, lay on its side in the road. From somewhere within the box came the groans and screams. The gale swept the hilltop, and, for a quarter mile to leeward, the scenery was animated by soaring, fluttering copies of the *Blazeton Courier*, that swooped and ducked like mammoth white butterflies.

The panting and alarmed teacher stooped and peered into the dark shadow between the dashboard and the back curtain. All she could make out at first were a pair of thin ankles and "Congress" shoes in agitated motion. These bobbed up and down behind the overturned seat and its displaced cushion.

"O Mrs. Beasley!" screamed Phœbe. "Are you hurt?"

Debby, of course, did not hear the question. She continued to groan and scream for help. Her lungs were not injured, at all events. The schoolmistress, dropping on her knees, reached into the sulky top and tugged at the seat. It was rather tightly wedged, but she managed to loosen it and pull it toward her.

The widow raised herself on an elbow and looked out between the flowers of her smashed bonnet.

"Who is it?" she demanded. "Oh, is that you, Miss Dorcas? Oh, my soul and body! Oh, my stars! Oh, my goodness me!"

"Are you hurt?" shrieked Phœbe.

"Hey? I don't know! I don't know *what* I be! I don't know nothin'!"

"Can you help yourself? Can you get up?"

"Hey? I don't know. Maybe I can if you haul that everlastin' seat out of the way. Oh, my sakes alive!"

Her rescuer pulled the seat forward, and, with an effort, tumbled it clear of the curtains. Debby raised herself still higher.

"Oh!" she groaned. "Talk about— Land sakes! who's comin'? Men, ain't it? Let me out of here quick! *quick!*"

She scrambled out of her prison on hands and

knees, and jumped to her feet with reassuring alac-
rity. Her fur-collared cape was draped in a roll
about her neck, and her bonnet hung jauntily over her
left eye.

"I'm a sight, ain't I?" she asked. "Haul this
bunnet straight, quick's ever you can. Hurt? No,
no! I ain't hurt none but my feelin's. Hurry *up*!
S'pose I want them men folks to see me with everything all hind side to?"

Miss Dawes, relieved to find that the accident had
had no serious consequences, and trying her hardest
not to laugh, assisted the widow to rearrange her
wearing apparel. The blacksmith and his helper
came running up the hill.

"Hello, Debby!" hailed the former. "What's
the matter? Hurt, be you?"

Mrs. Beasley, whether she heard or not, did not
deign to reply.

"Get my horn out of that carriage," she ordered.
"Don't stand there gapin'. Get it."

The ear trumpet was resurrected from the interior of the vehicle. The widow adjusted it with
dignity.

"Had a spill, didn't you, Debby?" inquired the
blacksmith. "Upset, didn't you?"

Debby glared at him.

"No," she replied with sarcasm. "Course I
didn't upset! Just thought I'd roll round in the
road for the fun of it. Smart question, that is!

Where's that Bailey Bangs gone to with the rest of my carriage?"

The blacksmith pointed to his shop in the hollow. Before it stood Mr. Bangs, holding Henry by the bridle, and staring in their direction.

"He's all right," volunteered the "helper." "The horse stopped runnin' soon's he got to the foot of the next hill."

Mrs. Beasley was not, apparently, overjoyed at the news.

"Humph!" she grunted. "I 'most wish he'd broke his neck! Pesky, careless thing! gettin' us run away with and upset. Who's goin' to pay for fixin' my sulky, I want to know?"

"Mr. Bangs will pay for it, I'm sure," said Phœbe soothingly. "If he doesn't, I will. Oh, Mrs. Beasley! did you find the diary?"

"Diary? No, no! I told you I was afraid I'd burnt it up. Well, I had, and a whole lot more of them old ones. But I did get all them Arizona papers, and took the trouble to tote 'em all the way here so's you could look at 'em. And now"—she shook with indignation and waved her hand toward a section of horizon where little white dots indicated the whereabouts of the *Couriers*—"now look where they be! Blowed from Dan to Beersheby! Come on to the house and let me set down. I been standin' on my head till I'm tired. Here, Jabez," to the blacksmith, "you tend to that carriage, will you?"

# A DRIVE AND WHAT FOLLOWED

She stalked off down the hill. The schoolmistress turning to follow her, caught a glimpse of the "helper" doubled up with silent laughter, and the blacksmith grinning broadly as he stooped toward the capsized sulky.

Phœbe was downcast and disappointed. She was convinced, in her own mind, that the Honorable Atkins had some hidden motive for his espousal of the Thomas cause. Asaph's fruitless quest in Orham had not shaken her faith. Captain Cy had refused to seek Debby Beasley for information concerning the Thayers, and so she, on her own responsibility, had done so. And this was the ridiculous ending of her journey. The diary had been a forlorn hope; now that was burned. Poor Bos'n! and poor—some one else!

Debby marching down the hill, continued to sputter about the lost weeklies.

"It's an everlastin' shame!" she declared. "I'd just found the one with that advertisement in it and was readin' it. I remember the part I read, plain as could be. While we're eatin' dinner I'll tell you about it."

But Miss Dawes did not care for dinner. Like Mr. Tiditt and the captain, she had had about all the Debby Beasley she wanted.

"Yes, yes, you will stop, too," affirmed the widow. "I want to tell you more about Blazeton. I can see that advertisement this minute, right afore my eyes—'Information wanted of my husband, Edward Higgins. Five foot eight inches tall, sandy complected, brown hair, and yellowish mustache; not lame, but has a peculiar slight limp with his left foot——' "

"What?" asked the schoolmistress, stopping short.

"Hey? 'Has a peculiar limp with his left foot.' I remember how Desire used to talk about that limp. She said 'twas almost as if he stuttered with his leg. He hurt it when he was up in Montana, and——"

"Oh!" cried Miss Dawes. The color had left her face.

"Yes. You see he used to be a miner or somethin' up there. He'd never say much about his younger days, but one time he did tell that. I'd just got as far as that limp when the sulky upset. Talk about bein' surprised! I never was so surprised in my life as when that horse critter rared up and——"

Phœbe interrupted. Her color had come back, and her eyes were shining.

"Mrs. Beasley," she cried, "I think I shall change my mind. I believe I will stay to dinner after all. I'm *ever* so much interested in Arizona."

Bailey and the teacher began their long drive home about four o'clock. The buggy axle had been fixed, and the wind was less violent. Mr. Bangs was glum and moody. He seemed to be thinking.

" Say, teacher," he said at length, " I'd like to ask a favor of you. If it ain't necessary, I wish you wouldn't say nothin' about that upsettin' business to the folks to home. It does sound so dum foolish! I'll never hear the last of it."

Miss Dawes, who had been in high spirits, now took a moment for reflection.

" All right! " she said, nodding vigorously. " We won't mention it, then. We won't tell a soul. You can say that I called at the Atwoods', if you want to; that will be true, because I did. And we'll have Mrs. Beasley for our secret—yours and mine—until we decide to tell. It's a bargain, Mr. Bangs. We must shake hands on it."

They shook hands, and Bailey, looking in her face, thought he never saw her look so well or as young. She was pretty, he decided. Then he thought of his own choice of a wife, and—well, if he had any regrets, he hasn't mentioned them, not even to his fellow-member of the Board of Strategy.

## CHAPTER XVII

### THE CAPTAIN REMEMBERS HIS AGE

DECEMBER was nearly over. Christmas had come. Bos'n had hung up her stocking by the base-burner stove, and found it warty and dropsical the next morning, with a generous overflow of gifts piled on the floor beneath it. The Board of Strategy sent presents; so did Miss Dawes and Georgianna. As for Captain Cy he spent many evening hours, after the rest of his household was in bed, poring over catalogues of toys and books, and the orders he sent to the big shops in Boston were lengthy and costly. The little girl's eyes opened wide when she saw the stocking and the treasures heaped on the floor. She sat in her " nighty " amidst the wonders, books, and playthings in a circle about her, and the biggest doll of all hugged close in her arms. Captain Cy, who had arisen at half past five in order to be with her on the great occasion, was at least as happy as she.

" Like 'em, do you? " he asked, smiling.

" *Like* 'em! O Uncle Cy! What makes everybody so good to me? "

"I don't know. Strange thing, ain't it—considerin' what a hard little ticket you are."

Bos'n laughed. She understood her "Uncle Cy," and didn't mind being called a "hard ticket" by him.

"I—I—didn't believe anybody *could* have such a nice Christmas. I never saw so many nice things."

"Humph! What do you like best?"

The answer was a question, and was characteristic.

"Which did you give me?" asked Bos'n.

The captain would have dodged, but she wouldn't let him. So one by one the presents he had given were indicated and put by themselves. The remainder were but few, but she insisted that the givers of these should be named. When the sorting was over she sat silently hugging her doll and, apparently, thinking.

"Well?" inquired the amused captain. "Made up your mind yet? Which do you like best?"

The child nodded.

"Why, these, of course," she declared with emphasis, pointing with her dollie's slippered foot at Captain Cy's pile.

"So? Do, hey? Didn't know I could pick so well. All right; the first prize is mine. Who takes the second?"

This time Bos'n deliberated before answering. At last, however, she bent forward and touched the teacher's gifts.

"These," she said. "I like these next best."

Captain Cy was surprised.

"Sho!" he exclaimed. "You don't say!"

"Yes. I think I like teacher next to you. I like Georgianna and Mr. Tidditt and Mr. Bangs, of course, but I like her a little better. Don't you, Uncle Cyrus?"

The captain changed the subject. He asked her what she should name her doll.

The Board of Strategy came in during the forenoon, and the presents had to be shown to them. While the exhibition was in progress Miss Dawes called. And before she left Gabe Lumley drove up in the depot wagon bearing a big express package addressed to "Miss Emily Thomas, Bayport."

"Humph!" exclaimed Captain Cy. "Somethin' more for Bos'n, hey! Who in the world sent it, do you s'pose?"

Asaph and Bailey made various inane suggestions as to the sender. Phœbe said nothing. There was a frown on her face as she watched the captain get to work on the box with chisel and hammer. It contained a beautiful doll, fully and expensively dressed, and pinned to the dress was a card—"To dear little Emmie, from her lonesome Papa."

The Board of Strategy looked at the doll in wonder and astonishment. Captain Cy strode away to the window.

"Well!" exclaimed Mr. Bangs. "I didn't believe

312

he had that much heart inside of him. I bet you
that cost four or five dollars; ain't that so, Cy?"

The captain did not answer.

"Don't you think so, teacher?" repeated Bailey,
turning to Phœbe. "What ails you? You don't
seem surprised."

"I'm not," replied the lady. "I expected something of that sort."

Captain Cy wheeled from the window.

"You *did*?" he asked.

"Yes. Miss Phinney said the other day she had
heard that that man was going to give his daughter
a beautiful present. She was very enthusiastic about
his generosity and self-sacrifice. I asked who told
her and she said Mr. Simpson."

"Oh! Tad? Is that so!" The captain looked
at her.

"Yes. And I think there is no doubt that Simpson had orders to make the 'generosity' known to
as many townspeople as possible."

"Hum! I see. You figure that Thomas cal'lates
'twill help his popularity and make his case stronger;
is that it?"

"Not exactly. I doubt if he ever thought of such
a thing himself. But some one thought for him—
and some one must have supplied the money."

"Well, they say he's to work up in Boston."

"I know. But no one can tell where he works.
Captain Whittaker, this is Mr. Atkins's doing—you

know it. Now, *why* does he, a busy man, take such an interest in getting this child away from you?"

Captain Cy shook his head and smiled.

"Teacher," he said, "you're dead set on taggin' Heman with a mystery, ain't you?"

"Miss Dawes," asked the forgetful Bailey, "when you and me went drivin' t'other day did you find out anything from——"

Phœbe interrupted quickly.

"Mr. Bangs," she said, "at what time do we distribute Christmas presents at your boarding house? I suppose you must have many Christmas secrets to keep. You keep a secret *so* well."

Mr. Bangs turned red. The hint concerning secret keeping was not wasted. He did not mention the drive again.

A little later Captain Cy found Bos'n busily playing with the doll he had given her. The other, her father's gift, was nowhere in sight.

"I put her back in the box," said the child in reply to his question. "She was awful pretty, but I think I'm goin' to love this one best."

The remark seems a foolish thing to give comfort to a grown man, but Captain Cy found comfort in it, and comfort was what he needed.

He needed it more as time went on. In January the court gave its decision. The captain's appointment as guardian was revoked. With the father alive, and professedly anxious to provide for the child's support, nothing else was to be expected, so Mr. Peabody said. The latter entered an appeal which would delay matters for a time, two or three months perhaps; meanwhile Captain Cy was to retain custody of Bos'n.

But the court's action, expected though it was, made the captain very blue and downcast. He could see no hope. He felt certain that he should lose the little girl in the end, in spite of the long succession of appeals which his lawyer contemplated. And what would become of her then? What sort of training would she be likely to have? Who would her associates be, under the authority of a father such as hers? And what would he do, alone in the old house, when she had gone for good? He could not bear to think of it, and yet he thought of little else.

The evenings, after Bos'n had gone to bed, were the worst. During the day he tried his best to be busy at something or other. The doll house was finished, and he had begun to fashion a full-rigged ship in miniature. In reality Emily, being a normal little girl, was not greatly interested in ships, but, because Uncle Cy was making it, she pretended to be vastly concerned about this one. On Saturdays and after school hours she sat on a box in the wood shed, where the captain had put up a small stove, and watched him work. The taboo which so many of our righteous and Atkins-worshiping townspeople had put upon the Whittaker place and its occupants included her, and a number of children had been forbidden to play with her. This, however, did not prevent their tormenting her about her father and her disreputable guardian.

But the captain's evenings were miserable. He no longer went to Simmons's. He didn't care for the crowd there, and knew they were all " down " on him. Josiah Dimick called occasionally, and the Board of Strategy often, but their conversation was rather tiresome. There were times when Captain Cy hated Bayport, the house he had " fixed up " with such interest and pride, and the old sitting room in particular. The mental picture of comfort and contentment which had been his dream through so many years of struggle and wandering, looked farther off than ever. Sometimes he was tempted to run away, taking Bos'n with him. But the captain had never run away from a fight yet; he had never abandoned a ship while there was a chance of keeping her afloat. And, besides, there was another reason.

Phœbe Dawes had come to be his chief reliance. He saw a great deal of her. Often when she walked home from school, she found him hanging over the front gate, and they talked of various things—of Bos'n's progress with her studies, of the school work, and similar topics. He called her by her first name now, although in this there was nothing unusual— after a few weeks' acquaintance we Bayporters almost invariably address people by their "front" names. Sometimes she came to the house with Emily. Then the three sat by the stove in the sitting room, and the apartment became really cheerful, in the captain's eyes.

Phœbe was in good spirits. She was as hopeful as Captain Cy was despondent. She seemed to have little fear of the outcome of the legal proceedings, the appeals and the rest. In fact, she now appeared desirous of evading the subject, and there was about her an air of suppressed excitement. Her optimism was the best sort of bracer for the captain's failing courage. Her advice was always good, and a talk with her left him with shoulders squared, mentally, and almost happy.

One cold, rainy afternoon, early in February, she came in with Bos'n, who had availed herself of the shelter of the teacher's umbrella. Georgianna was in the kitchen baking, and Emily had been promised a "saucer pie"—so the child went out to superintend the construction of that treat.

"Set down, teacher," said Captain Cy, pushing forward a rocker. "My! but I'm glad to see you. 'Twas bluer'n a whetstone 'round here to-day. What's the news—anything?"

"Why, no," replied Phœbe, accepting the rocker and throwing open her wet jacket; "there's no news in particular. But I wanted to ask if you had seen the *Breeze*?"

" Um—hum," was the listless answer. " I presume likely you mean the news about the appropriation, and the editorial dig at yours truly? Yes, I've seen it. They don't bother me much. I've got more important things on my mind just now."

Congressman Atkins's pledge in his farewell speech, concerning the mighty effort he was to make toward securing the appropriation for Bayport harbor, was in process of fulfillment—so he had written to the local paper. But, alas! the mighty effort was likely to prove unavailing. In spite of the Honorable Heman's battle for his constituents' rights it seemed certain that the bill would not provide the thirty thousand dollars for Bayport; at least, not this year's bill. Other and more powerful interests would win out and, instead, another section of the coast be improved at the public expense. The congressman was deeply sorry, almost broken-hearted. He had battled hard for his beloved town, he had worked night and day. But, to be perfectly frank, there was little or no hope.

Few of us blamed Heman Atkins. The majority considered his letter " noble " and " so feeling." But some one must be blamed for a community disappointment like this, and the scapegoat was on the premises. How about that " committee of one " self-appointed at town meeting? How about the blatant person who had declared *he* could have gotten the appropriation? What had the " committee " done? Nothing! nothing at all! He had not even written to the Capital—so far as anyone could find out—much less gone there.

So, at Simmons's and the sewing circle, and after meeting on Sunday, Cy Whittaker was again discussed and derided. And this week's *Breeze*, out that morning, contained a sarcastic editorial which mentioned no names, but hinted at "a certain now notorious person" who had boasted loudly, but who had again "been weighed in the balance of public opinion and found wanting."

Miss Dawes did not seem pleased with the captain's nonchalant attitude toward the *Breeze* and its editorial. She tapped the braided mat with her foot.

"Captain Cyrus," she said, "if you intended doing nothing toward securing that appropriation why did you accept the responsibility for it at the meeting?"

Captain Cy looked up. Her tone reminded him of their first meeting, when she had reproved him for going to sleep and leaving Bos'n to the mercy of the Cahoon cow.

"Well," he said, "afore this Thomas business happened, to knock all my plans on their beam ends, I'd done consider'ble thinkin' about that appropriation. It seemed to me that there must be some reason for Heman's comin' about so sudden. He was sartin sure of the thirty thousand for a spell; then, all to once, he begun to take in sail and go on t'other

319

tack. I don't know much about politics, but I know *he* knows all the politics there is. And it seemed to me that if a live man, one with eyes in his head, went to Washington and looked around he might find the reason. And, if he did find it, maybe Heman could be coaxed into changin' his mind again. Anyhow, I was willin' to take the risk of tryin'; and, besides, Tad and Abe Leonard had me on the griddle at that meetin', and I spoke up sharp—too sharp, maybe."

"But you still believe that you *might* help if you went to Washington?"

"Yes. I guess I do. Anyhow, I'd ask some pretty p'inted questions. You see, I ain't lived here in Bayport all my life, and I don't swaller *all* the bait Heman heaves overboard."

"Then why don't you go?"

"Hey? Why don't I go? And leave Bos'n and——"

"Emily would be all right and perfectly safe. Georgianna thinks the world of her. And, Captain Whittaker, I don't like to hear these people talk of you as they do. I don't like to read such things in the paper, that you were only bragging in order to be popular, and meant to shirk when the time came for action. I know they're not true. I *know* it!"

Captain Cy was gratified, and his gratification showed in his voice.

"Thank you, Phœbe," he said. "I am much

obliged to you. But, you see, I don't take any interest in such things any more. When I realize that pretty soon I've got to give up that little girl for good I can't bear to be away from her a minute hardly. I don't like to leave her here alone with Georgianna and——"

"I will keep an eye on her. You trust me, don't you?"

"Trust *you*? By the big dipper, you're about the only one I *can* trust these days. I don't know how I'd have pulled through this if you hadn't helped. You're diff'rent from Ase and Bailey and their kind—not meanin' anything against them, either. But you're broad-minded and cool-headed and—and— Do you know, if I'd had a woman like you to advise me all these years and keep me from goin' off the course, I might have been somebody by now."

"I think you're somebody as it is."

"Don't talk that way. I own up I like to hear you, but I'm 'fraid it ain't true. You say I amount to somethin'. Well, what? I come back home here, with some money in my pocket, thinkin' that was about all was necessary to make me a good deal of a feller. The old Cy Whittaker place, I said to myself, was goin' to be a real Cy Whittaker place again. And I'd be a real Whittaker, a man who should stand for somethin', as my dad and grand-dad did afore me. The town should respect me, and

I'd do things to help it along. And what's it all come to? Why, every young one on the street is told to be good for fear he'll grow up like me. Ain't that so? Course it's so! I'm——"

"You *shall* not speak so! Do you imagine that you're not respected by everyone whose respect counts for anything? Yes, and by others, too. Don't you suppose Mr. Atkins respects you, down in his heart —if he has one? Doesn't your housekeeper, who sees you every day, respect and like you? And little Emily—doesn't she love you more than she does all the rest of us together?"

"Well, I guess Bos'n does care for the old man some, that's a fact. She says she likes you next best, though. Did you know that?"

But Miss Dawes was indignant.

"Captain Whittaker," she declared, "one would think you were a hundred years old to hear you. You are always calling yourself an old man. Does Mr. Atkins call himself old? And he is older than you."

"Well, I'm over fifty, Phœbe." In spite of the habit for which he had just been reproached, the captain found this a difficult statement to make.

"I know. But you're younger than most of us at thirty-five. You see, I'm confessing, too," she added with a laugh and a little blush.

Captain Cy made a mental calculation.

"Twenty years," he said musingly. "Twenty

years is a long time. No, I'm old. And worse than that, I'm an old fool, I guess. If I hadn't been I'd have stayed in South America instead of comin' here to be hooted out of the town I was born in."

The teacher stamped her foot.

"Oh, what *shall* I do with you!" she exclaimed. "It is wicked for you to say such things. Do you suppose that Mr. Atkins would find it necessary to work as he is doing to beat a fool? And, besides, you're not complimentary to me. Should I, do you think, take such an interest in one who was an imbecile?"

"Well, 'tis mighty good of you. Your comin' here so to help Bos'n's fight along is——"

"How do you know it is Bos'n altogether? I——" She stopped suddenly, and the color rushed to her face. She rose from the rocker. "I—really, I don't see how we came to be discussing such nonsense," she said. "Our ages and that sort of thing! Captain Cyrus, I wish you would go to Washington. I think you ought to go."

But the captain's thoughts were far from Washington at that moment. His own face was alight, and his eyes shone.

"Phœbe," he faltered unbelievingly, "what was you goin' to say? Do you mean that—that——"

The side door of the house opened. The next instant Mr. Tidditt, a dripping umbrella in his hand, entered the sitting room.

"Hello, Whit!" he hailed. "Just run in for a minute to say howdy." Then he noticed the schoolmistress, and his expression changed. "Oh! how be you, Miss Dawes?" he said. "I didn't see you fust off. Don't run away on my account."

"I was just going," said Phœbe, buttoning her jacket. Captain Cy accompanied her to the door.

"Good-by," she said. "There was something else I meant to say, but I think it is best to wait. I hope to have some good news for you soon. Something that will send you to Washington with a light heart. Perhaps I shall hear to-morrow. If so, I will call after school and tell you."

"Yes, do," urged the captain eagerly. "You'll find me here waitin'. Good news or not, do come. I—I ain't said all I wanted to, myself."

He returned to the sitting room. The town clerk was standing by the stove. He looked troubled.

"What's the row, Ase?" asked Cy cheerily. He was overflowing with good nature.

"Oh, nothin' special," replied Mr. Tidditt. "You look joyful enough for two of us. Had good company, ain't you?"

"Why, yes; 'bout as good as there is. What makes you look so glum?"

Asaph hesitated.

"Phœbe was here yesterday, too, wan't she?" he asked.

"Yup. What of it?"

324

" And the day afore that? "

" No, not for three days afore that. But what
*of* it, I ask you? "

" Well, now, Cy, you mustn't get mad. I'm a
friend of yours, and friends ought to be able to say
'most anything to each other. If—if I was you, I
wouldn't let Phœbe come so often—not here, you
know, at your house. Course, I know she comes with
Bos'n and all, but——"

" Out with it! " The captain's tone was ominous.
" What are you drivin' at? "

The caller fidgeted.

" Well, Whit," he stammered, " there's consider'ble talkin' goin' on, that's all."

" Talkin'? What kind of talkin'? "

" Well, you know the kind. This town does a
good deal of it, 'specially after church and prayer
meetin'. Seem's if they thought 'twas a sort of
proper place. *I* don't myself; I kind of like to keep
my charity and brotherly love spread out through the
week, but——"

" Ase, are the folks in this town sayin' a word
against Phœbe Dawes because she comes here to
see—Bos'n? "

" Don't—don't get mad, Whit. Don't look at
me like that. *I* ain't said nothin'. Why, a spell
ago, at the boardin' house, I——"

He told of the meal at the perfect boarding
house where Miss Dawes championed his friend's

"'Don't—don't get mad, Whit. I ain't said nothin'.'"

cause. Also of the conversation which followed, and his own part in it. Captain Cy paced the floor.

"I wouldn't have her come so often, Cy," pleaded

Asaph. " Honest, I wouldn't. Course, you and me
know they're mean, miser'ble liars, but it's her I'm
thinkin' of. She's a young woman and single. And
you're a good many years older'n she is. And so,
of course, you and she ain't ever goin' to get married. And have you thought what effect it might
have on her keepin' her teacher's place? The committee's a majority against her as 'tis. And—you
know *I* don't think so, but a good many folks do—
you ain't got the best name just now. Darn it all!
I ain't puttin' this the way I'd ought to, but *you* know
what I mean, don't you, Cy? "

Captain Cy was leaning against the window frame,
his head upon his arm. He was not looking out,
because the shade was drawn. Tidditt waited anxiously for him to answer. At last he turned.

" Ase," he said, " I'm much obliged to you. You've
pounded it in pretty hard, but I cal'late I'd ought
to have had it done to me. I'm a fool—an *old*
fool, just as I said a while back—and nothin' nor
*nobody* ought to have made me forget it. For a
minute or so I—but there! don't you fret. That
young woman shan't risk her job nor her reputation
on account of me—nor of Bos'n, either. I'll see to
that. And see here," he added fiercely, " I can't stop
women's tongues, even when they're as bad as some
of the tongues in this town, *but* if you hear a *man*
say one word against Phœbe Dawes, only one word,
you tell me his name. You hear, Ase? You tell me

his name. Now run along, will you? I ain't safe company just now."

Asaph, frightened at the effect of his words, hurriedly departed. Captain Cy paced the room for the next fifteen minutes. Then he opened the kitchen door.

"Bos'n," he called, "come in and set in my lap a while; don't you want to? I'm—I'm sort of lonesome, little girl."

The next afternoon, when the schoolmistress, who had been delayed by the inevitable examination papers, stopped at the Cy Whittaker place, she was met by Georgianna; Emily, who stood behind the housekeeper in the doorway, was crying.

"Cap'n Cy has gone away—to Washin'ton," declared Georgianna. "Though what he's gone there for's more'n I know. He said he'd send his hotel address soon's he got there. He went on the three o'clock train."

Phœbe was astonished.

"Gone?" she repeated. "So soon! Why, he told me he should certainly be here to hear some news I expected to-day. Didn't he leave any message for me?"

The housekeeper turned red.

"Miss Phœbe," she said, "he told me to tell you somethin', and it's so dreadful I don't hardly dast to say it. I think his troubles have driven him crazy. He said to tell you that you'd better not come to this house any more."

# CHAPTER XVIII

## CONGRESSMAN EVERDEAN

IN the old days, the great days of sailing ships and merchant fleets, Bayport was a community of travelers. Every ambitious man went to sea, and eventually, if he lived, became a captain. Then he took his wife, and in most cases his children, with him on long voyages. To the stay-at-homes came letters with odd, foreign stamps and postmarks. Our what-nots and parlor mantels were filled with carved bits of ivory, gorgeous shells, alabaster candlesticks, and plaster miniatures of the Leaning Tower at Pisa or the Coliseum at Rome. We usually began a conversation with "When my husband and I were at Hong Kong the last time—" or "I remember at Mauritius they always—" New Orleans or 'Frisco were the nearest domestic ports the mention of which was considered worth while.

But this is so no longer. A trip to Boston is, of course, no novelty to the most of us; but when we visit New York we take care to advertise it beforehand. And the few who avail themselves of the spring "cut rates" and go on excursions to Washington, plan definite programmes for each day at the Capital, and discuss them with envious friends for weeks in advance. And if the prearranged programme is not scrupulously carried out, we feel that we have been defrauded. It was the regret of Aunt Sophronia Hallett's life that, on her Washington excursion, she had not seen the "Diplomatic Corpse." She saw the President and the Monument and Congress and "the relics in the Smithsonian Institute," but the "Corpse" was not on view; Aunt Sophronia never quite got over the disappointment.

Probably no other Bayporter, in recent years, has started for Washington on such short notice or with so ill-defined a programme as Captain Cy. He went because he felt that he must go somewhere. After the conversation with Asaph, he simply could not remain at home. If Phœbe Dawes called, he knew that he must see her, and if he saw her, what should he say to her? He could not tell her that she must not visit the Cy Whittaker place again. If he did, she would insist upon the reason. If he told her of the "town talk," he felt sure, knowing her, that she would indignantly refuse to heed the malicious gossip. And he was firmly resolved not to permit her to compromise her life and her future by friendship with a social outcast like himself. As for anything deeper and more sacred than friendship, that was ridiculous. If, for a moment, a remark of hers had led him to dream of such a thing, it was because he was, as he had so often declared, an " old fool."

So Captain Cy had resolved upon flight, and he fled to Washington because the business of the " committee of one " offered a legitimate excuse for going there. The blunt message he had intrusted to Georgianna would, he believed, arouse Phœbe's indignation. She would not call again. And when he returned to Bos'n, it would be to take up the child's fight alone. If he lost that fight, or *when* he lost it, he would close the Cy Whittaker place, and leave Bayport for good.

He had been in Washington once before, years ago, when he was first mate of a ship and had a few weeks' shore leave. Then he went there on a pleasure trip with some seagoing friends, and had a jolly time. But there was precious little jollity in the present visit. He had never felt so thoroughly miserable. In order to forget, he made up his mind to work his hardest to discover why the harbor appropriation was not to be given to Bayport.

The city had changed greatly. He would scarcely have known it. He went to the hotel where he had stayed before, and found a big, modern building in its place. The clerk was inclined to be rather curt and perfunctory at first, but when he learned that the captain was not anxious concerning the price of accommodations, but merely wanted a " comf'table berth somewheres on the saloon deck," and appeared to have plenty of money, he grew polite. Captain

Cy was shown to his room, where he left his valise.
Then he went down to dinner.

After the meal was over, he seated himself in one
of the big leather chairs in the hotel lobby, smoked
and thought. In the summer, before Bos'n came,
and before her father had arisen to upset every calculation and wreck all his plans, the captain had given
serious thought to what he should do if Congressman
Atkins failed, as even then he seemed likely to do, in
securing that appropriation. The obvious thing, of
course, would have been to hunt up Mr. Atkins and
question him. But this was altogether too obvious.
In the first place, the strained relations between them
would make the interview uncomfortable; and, in
the second, if there was anything underhand in Heman's backsliding on the appropriation, Atkins was
too wary a bird to be snared with questions.

But Captain Cy had another acquaintance in the
city, the son of a still older acquaintance, who had
been a wealthy shipping merchant and mine owner
in California. The son was also a congressman, from
a coast State, and the captain had read of him in the
papers. A sketch of his life had been printed, and
this made his identity absolutely certain. Captain
Cy's original idea had been to write to this congressman. Now he determined to find and interview him.

He inquired concerning him of the hotel clerk,
who, like all Washington clerks, was a walking edi-
tion of " Who's Who at the Capital."

# CONGRESSMAN EVERDEAN

" Congressman Everdean? " repeated the all-knowing young gentleman. " Yes. He's in town. Has rooms at the Gloria; second hotel on the right as you go up the avenue. Only a short walk. What can I do for you, sir? "

The Gloria was an even bigger hotel than the one where the captain had his " berth." An inquiry at the desk, of another important clerk, was answered with a brisk:

" Mr. Everdean? Yes, he rooms here. Don't know whether he's in or not. Evening, judge. Nice winter weather we're having."

The judge, who was a ponderous person vaguely suggesting the great Heman, admitted that the weather was fine, patronizing it as he did so. The clerk continued the conversation. Captain Cy waited. At length he spoke.

" Excuse me, commodore," he said; " I don't like to break in until you've settled whether you have it snow or not, but I'm here to see Congressman Everdean. Hadn't you better order one of your fo'mast hands to hunt him up? "

The judge condescended to smile, as did several other men who stood near. The clerk reddened.

" Do you want to see Mr. Everdean? " he snapped.

" Why, yes, I did. But I can't see him from here without strainin' my eyesight."

The clerk sharply demanded one of the captain's

333

visiting cards. He didn't get one, for the very good reason that there was none in existence.

"Tell him an old friend of his dad's is here on the main deck waitin' for him," said Captain Cy. "That'll do first rate. Thank you, admiral."

Word came that the congressman would be down in a few moments. The captain beguiled the interval by leaning on the rail and regarding the clerk with an awed curiosity that annoyed its object exceedingly. The inspection was still on when a tall man, of an age somewhere in the early thirties, walked briskly up to the desk.

"Who is it that wants to see me?" he asked.

The clerk waved a deprecatory hand in Captain Cy's direction. The newcomer turned.

"My name is Everdean," he said. "Are you— hey?—Great Scott! Is it possible this is Captain Whittaker?"

The captain was immensely pleased.

"Well, I declare, Ed!" he exclaimed. "I didn't believe you'd remember me after all these years. You was nothin' but a boy when I saw you out in 'Frisco. Well! well! No wonder you're in Congress. A man that can remember faces like that ought to be President."

Everdean laughed as they shook hands.

"Don't suppose I'd forget the chap who used to dine with us and tell me those sea stories, do you?" he said. "I'm mighty glad to see you. What are

334

you doing here? The last father and I heard of you, you were in South America. Given up the sea, they said, and getting rich fast."

Captain Cy chuckled.

"It's a good thing I learned long ago not to believe all I hear," he answered, "else I'd have been so sure I was rich that I'd have spent all I had, and been permanent boarder at the poorhouse by now. No, thanks; I've had dinner. Why, yes, I'll smoke, if you'll help along. How's your father? Smart, is he?"

The congressman insisted that they should adjourn to his rooms. An unmarried man, he kept bachelor's hall at the hotel during his stay in Washington. There, in comfortable chairs, they spoke of old times, when the captain was seafaring and the Everdean home had been his while his ship was in port at 'Frisco. He told of his return to Bayport, and the renovation of the old house. Of Bos'n he said nothing. At last Everdean asked what had brought him to Washington.

"Well," said Captain Cy, "I'll tell you. I'm like the feller in court without a lawyer; he said he couldn't tell whether he was guilty or not 'count of havin' no professional advice. That's what I've come to you for, Ed—professional advice."

He told the harbor appropriation story. At the incident of the "committee of one" his friend laughed heartily.

"Rather put your foot in it that time, Captain, didn't you?" he said.

"Yup. Then I got t'other one stuck tryin' to get the first clear. How's it look to you? All straight, do you think? or is there a nigger in the wood pile?"

Mr. Everdean seemed to reflect.

"Well, Captain," he said, "I can't tell. You're asking delicate questions. Politicians are like doctors, they usually back up each other's opinions. Still, you're at least as good a friend of mine as Atkins is. Queer *he* should bob up in this matter! Why, he—but never mind that now. I tell you, Captain Whittaker, you come around and have dinner with me to-morrow night. In the meantime I'll see the chairman of the committee on that bill—one of the so-called 'pork' bills it is. Possibly from him and some other acquaintances of mine I may learn something. At any rate, you come to dinner."

So the invitation was accepted, and Captain Cy went back to his own hotel and his room. He slept but little, although it was not worry over the appropriation question which kept him awake. Next morning he wrote a note to Georgianna, giving his Washington address. With it he enclosed a long letter to Bos'n, telling her he should be home pretty soon, and that she must be a good girl and "boss the ship" during his absence. He sent his regards to Asaph and Bailey, but Phœbe's name he did not mention. Then he put in a miserable day wandering

about the city. At eight that evening he and his
Western friend sat down at a corner table in the
big dining room of the Gloria.

The captain began to ask questions as soon as the
soup was served, but Everdean refused to answer.

" No, no," he said, " pleasure first and business
afterwards; that's a congressional motto. I can't
talk Atkins with my dinner and enjoy it."

" Can't, hey? You wouldn't be popular at our perfect boarding house back home. There they serve
Heman hot for breakfast and dinner, and warm him
over for supper. All right, I can wait."

The conversation wandered from Buenos Ayres
to 'Frisco and back again until the cigars and coffee
were reached. Then the congressman blew a fragrant
ring into the air and, from behind it, looked quiz-
zically at his companion.

" Well," he observed, " so far as that appropriation of yours is concerned——"

He paused and blew a second ring. Captain Cy
stroked his beard.

" Um—yes," he drawled, " now that you mention
it, seems to me there was some talk of an appropriation."

Mr. Everdean laughed.

" I've been making inquiries," he said. " I saw
the chairman of the committee on the pork bill. I
know him well. He's a good fellow, but——"

" Yes, I know. I've seen lots of politicians like

that; they're all good fellers, but— If I was in politics I'd make a law to cut 'But' out of the dictionary."

"Well, this chap really is a good fellow. I asked about the thirty thousand dollars for your town. He asked me why I didn't go to the congressman from that district, and not bother him about it. I said perhaps I would go to the congressman later, but I came to him first."

"Sartin. Same as the feller with a sick mother-in-law stopped in at the undertaker's on his way to call the doctor. All right; heave ahead."

"Well, we had a rather long conversation. I discovered that the Bayport item was originally included in the bill, but recently had been stricken out."

"Yes, I see. Uncle Sam had to economize, hey? Save somethin' for a rainy day."

"Well, possibly. Still the bill is just as heavy. Now, Captain Whittaker, I don't *know* anything about this affair, and it's not my business. But I've been about to-day, and I asked questions, and—I'm going to tell you a fairy tale. It isn't as interesting as your sea yarns, but— Do you like fairy stories?"

"Land, yes! Tell a few myself when it's necessary. Sometimes I almost believe 'em. Well?"

"Of course, you must remember this *is* a fairy story. Let's suppose that once on a time—that's the way they always begin—once on a time there was a great man, great in his own country, who was sent

338

abroad by his people to represent them among the rulers of the land. So, in order to typically represent them, he dressed in glad and expensive raiment, went about in dignity, and——"

"And whiskers. Don't leave out the whiskers!"

"All right—and whiskers. And it came to pass that the people whom he represented wished to—to —er—bring about a certain needed improvement in their—their beautiful and enterprising community."

"Sho! sho! how natural that sounds! You must be a mind reader."

"No. But I have to make speeches in my own community occasionally. Well, the people asked their great man to get the money needed for this improvement from the rulers of the land aforementioned. And he was at first all enthusiasm and upon the—the parchment scroll where such matters are inscribed was written the name of the beautiful and enterprising community, and the sum of money it asked for. And the deal was as good as made. Excuse the modern phraseology; my fairy lingo got mixed there."

"Never mind. I can get the drift just as well— maybe better."

"And the deal was as good as made. But before the vote was taken another chap came to the great man and said: 'Look here! I want to get an appropriation of, say, fifty thousand dollars, to deepen and improve a river down in my State '—a Southern

State we'll say. ' I've been to the chairman of the pork bill committee, and he says it's impossible. The bill simply can't be loaded any further. But I find that you have an item in there for deepening and improving a harbor back in your own district. Why don't you cut that item out—shove it over until next year? You can easily find a satisfactory explanation for your constituents. *And* you want to remember this: the improvement of this river means that the—the— well, a certain sugar-growing company—can get their stuff to market at a figure which will send its stock up and up. And you are said to own a considerable amount of that stock. So why not drop the harbor item and substitute my river slice? Then—' Well, I guess that's the end of the tale."

He paused and relit his cigar. Captain Cy thoughtfully marked with his fork on the table-cloth.

"Hum!" he grunted. "That's a very interestin' yarn. Yes, yes! don't know's I ever heard a more interestin' one. I presume likely there ain't a mite of proof that it's true?"

"Not an atom. I told you it was a fairy tale. And I mustn't be quoted in the matter. Honestly, the most of it is guess work, at that. But perhaps a 'committee of one,' dropping a hint at home, might at least arouse some uncomfortable questioning of a certain great man. That's about all, though. Proof is quite another thing."

# CONGRESSMAN EVERDEAN

The captain pondered. He was fully aware that the unpopularity of the " committee " would nullify whatever good its hinting might do.

" Humph! " he grunted again. " It's one thing to smell a rat and another to nail its tail to the floor. But I'm mighty obliged to you, all the same. And I'll think it over hard. Say! I can see one thing —you don't take a very big shine to Heman yourself."

" Not too big—no. Do you? "

" Well, I don't wake up nights and cry for him." Everdean laughed.

" That's characteristic," he said. " You have your own way of putting things, Captain, and it's hard to be improved on. Atkins has never done anything to me. I just—I just don't like him, that's all. Father never liked him, either, in the old days; and yet—and it's odd, too—he was the means of the old gentleman's making the most of his money."

" He? Who? Not Heman? "

" Yes, Heman Atkins. But, so far as that goes, father started him toward wealth, I suppose. At least, he was poor enough before the mine was sold."

" What are you talkin' about? Heman got his start tradin' over in the South Seas. Sellin' the Kanakas glass beads and calico for pearls and copra —two cupfuls of pearls for every bead. Anyhow, that's the way the yarn goes."

" I can't help that. He was just a common sailor

who had run away from his ship and was gold mining in California. And when he and his partner struck it rich father borrowed money, headed a company, and bought them out. That mine was the Excelsior, and it's just as productive to-day as it ever was. I rather think Atkins must be very sorry he sold. I suppose, by right, I should be very grateful to your distinguished representative."

"Well, I do declare! Sho, sho! Ain't that funny now? He's never said a word about it at home. I don't believe there's a soul in Bayport knows that. We all thought 'twas South Sea tradin' that boosted Heman. And your own dad! I declare, this is a small world!"

"It's odd father never told you about it. It's one of the old gentleman's pet stories. He came West in 1850, and was running a little shipping store in 'Frisco. He met Atkins and the other young sailor, his partner, before they left their ship. They were in the store, buying various things, and father got to know them pretty well. Then they ran away to the diggings—you simply couldn't keep a crew in those times—and he didn't see them again for a good while. Then they came in one day and showed him specimens from a claim they had back in the mountains. They were mighty good specimens, and what they said about the claim convinced father that they had a valuable property. So he went to see a few well-to-do friends of his, and the outcome was that a party was made up to go and inspect. The young fellows were willing to sell out, for it was a quartz working and they hadn't the money to carry it on.

"The inspection showed that the claim was likely to be even better than they thought, so, after some bargaining, the deal was completed. They sold out for seventy-five thousand dollars, and it was the best trade father ever made. He's so proud of his judgment and foresight in making it that I wonder he never told you the story."

"He never did. When was this?"

"In '54. What?"

"I didn't speak. The date seemed kind of familiar to me, that's all. Seem's as if I heard it recent, but I can't remember when. Seventy-five thousand, hey? Well, that wan't so bad, was it? With that for a nest egg, no wonder Heman's managed to hatch a pretty respectable brood of dollars."

"Oh, the whole seventy-five wasn't his, of course. Half belonged to his partner. But the poor devil didn't live to enjoy it. After the articles were signed and before the money was paid over, he was taken sick with a fever and died."

"Hey? He died? With a *fever*?"

"Yes. But he left a pretty good legacy to his heirs, didn't he. For a common sailor—or second mate; I believe that's what he was—thirty-seven

· 343

thousand five hundred is doing well. It must have come as a big surprise to them. The whole sum was paid to Atkins, who— What's the matter with you?"

Captain Cy was leaning back in his chair. He was as white as the tablecloth.

"Are you ill?" asked the congressman anxiously. "Take some water. Shall I call——"

The captain waved his hand.

"No, no!" he stammered. "No! I'm all right. Do you—for the Lord's sake tell me this! What was the name of this partner that died?"

Mr. Everdean looked curiously at his friend before he answered.

"Sure you're not sick?" he asked. "Well, all right. The partner's name? Why, I've heard it often enough. It's on the deed of sale that father has framed in his room at home. The old gentleman is as proud of that as anything in the house. The name was—was——"

"For God sakes," cried Captain Cy, "don't say 'twas John Thayer! 'Cause if you do I shan't believe it."

"That's what it was—John Thayer. How did you guess? Did you know him? I remember now that he was another Down Easter, like Atkins."

The captain did not answer. He clasped his forehead with both hands and leaned his elbows on the table. Everdean was plainly alarmed.

344

"'Set still!' he ordered. 'Set still, I tell you!'"

"I'm going to call a doctor," he began, rising. But Captain Cy waved him back again.

"Set still!" he ordered. "Set still, I tell you! You say the whole seventy-five thousand was paid to Heman, but that John Thayer signed the bill of sale afore he died, as half partner? And your dad's got the original deed and—and—he remembers the whole business?"

"Yes, he's got the deed—framed. It's on record, too, of course. Remembers? I should say he did! He'll talk for a week on that subject, if you give him a chance."

The captain sprang to his feet. His chair tipped backward and fell to the floor. An obsequious waiter ran to right it, but Captain Cy paid no attention to him.

"Where's my coat?" he demanded. "Where's my coat and hat?"

"What ails you?" asked Everdean. "Are you going crazy?"

"Goin' *crazy*? No, no! I'm goin' to California. When's the next train?"

# CHAPTER XIX

### THE TOPPLING OF A MONUMENT

THE Honorable Heman Atkins sat in the library of his Washington home, before a snapping log fire, reading a letter. Mr. Atkins had, as he would have expressed it, " served his people " in Congress for so many years that he had long since passed the hotel stage of living at the Capital. He rented a furnished house on an eminently respectable street, and the polished doorplate bore his name in uncompromising characters.

The library furniture was solid and dignified. Its businesslike appearance impressed the stray excursionist from the Atkins district, when he or she visited the great man in whose affairs we felt such a personal interest. Particularly impressive and significant was a map of the district hanging over the congressman's desk, and an oil painting of the Atkins mansion at Bayport, which, with the iron dogs and urns conspicuous in its foreground, occupied the middle of the largest wall space.

The cheery fire was very comforting on a night like this, for the sleet was driving against the win-

346

dowpanes, the sidewalks were ankle deep in slush, and the wet, cold wind from the Potomac was whistling down the street. Somewhere about the house an unfastened shutter slammed in the gusts. Mr. Atkins should have been extremely comfortable as he sat there by the fire. He had spent many comfortable winters in that room. But now there was a frown on his face as he read the letter in his hand. It was from Simpson, and stated, among other things, that Cyrus Whittaker had been absent from Bayport for over two weeks, and that no one seemed to know where he had gone. "The idea seems to be that he started for Washington," wrote Tad; "but if that is so, it is queer you haven't seen him. I am suspicious that he is up to something about that harbor business. I should keep my eye peeled if I was you."

Alicia, the Atkins hopeful, rustled into the room.

"Papa," she said, "I've come to kiss you good night."

Her father performed the ceremony in a perfunctory way.

"All right, all right," he said. "Now run along to bed and don't bother me, there's a good girl. I wish," he added testily to the housekeeper who had followed Alicia into the room, "I wish you'd see to that loose blind. It makes me nervous. Such things as that should be attended to without specific orders from me."

The housekeeper promised to attend to the blind. She and the girl left the library. Heman reread the Simpson letter. Then he dropped it in his lap and sat thinking and twirling his eyeglasses at the end of their black cord. His thoughts seemed to be not of the pleasantest. The lines about his mouth had deepened during the last few months. He looked older.

The telephone bell rang sharply. Mr. Atkins came out of his reverie with a start, arose and walked across the room to the wall where the instrument hung. It was before the days of the convenient desk 'phone. He took the receiver from its hook and spoke into the transmitter.

"Hello!" he said. "Hello! Yes, yes! stop ringing. What is it?"

The wire buzzed and purred in the storm. "Hello!" said a voice. "Hello, there! Is this Mr. Atkins's house?"

"Yes; it is. What do you want?"

"Hey? Is this where the Honorable Heman Atkins lives?"

"Yes, yes, I tell you! This is Mr. Atkins speaking. What do you want?"

"Oh! is that you, Heman? This is Whittaker— Cy Whittaker. Understand?"

Mr. Atkins understood. Yet for an instant he did not reply. He had been thinking, as he sat by the fire, of certain persons and certain ugly, though remote, possibilities. Now, from a mysterious somewhere, one of those persons was speaking to him. The hand holding the receiver shook momentarily.

"Hello! I say, Heman, do you understand? This is Whittaker talkin'."

"I—er—understand," said the congressman, slowly. "Well, sir?"

"I'm here in Washin'ton."

"I have been informed that you were in the city. Well, sir?"

"Oh! knew I was here, did you? Is that so? Who told you? Tad wrote, I suppose, hey?"

The congressman did not reply immediately. This man, whom he disliked more than anyone else in the world, had an irritating faculty of putting his finger on the truth. And the flippancy in the tone was maddening. Mr. Atkins was not used to flippancy.

"I believe I am not called upon to disclose my source of information," he said with chilling dignity. "It appears to have been trustworthy. I presume you have 'phoned me concerning the appropriation matter. I do not recognize your right to intrude in that affair, and I shall decline to discuss it. Yes, sir. To my people, to those who have a right to question, I am and shall always be willing to explain my position. Good night."

"Wait! Hello! Hold on a minute. Don't get

mad, Heman. I only wanted to say just a word. You'll let me say a word, won't you?"

This was more like it. This was more nearly the tone in which Mr. Atkins was wont to be addressed. It was possible that the man, recognizing the uselessness of further opposition, desired to surrender.

"I cannot," declared the Honorable, "understand why you should wish to speak with me. We have very little in common, very little, I'm thankful to say. However, I will hear you briefly. Go on."

"Much obliged. Well, Heman, I only wanted to say that I thought maybe you'd better have a little talk with me. I'm here at the hotel, the Regent. You know where 'tis, I presume likely. I guess you'd better come right down and see me."

Heman gasped, actually gasped, with astonishment.

"*I* had better come and see *you*? I—! Well, sir! *well*! I am not accustomed——"

"I know, but I think you'd better. It's dirty weather, and I've got cold somehow or other. I ain't feelin' quite up to the mark, so I cal'late I'll stay in port much as I can. You come right down. I'll be in my room, and the hotel folks 'll tell you where 'tis. I'll be waitin' for you."

Mr. Atkins breathed hard. In his present frame of mind he would have liked to deliver a blast into that transmitter which would cause the person at the other end of the line to shrivel under its heat. But he was a politician of long training, and he knew that such blasts were sometimes expensive treats. It might be well to hear what his enemy had to say. But as to going to see him—that was out of the question.

"I do not," he thundered, "I do not care to continue this conversation. If—if you wish to see me, after what has taken place between us, I am willing, in spite of personal repugnance, to grant you a brief interview. My servants will admit you here at nine o'clock to-morrow morning. But I tell you now, that your interference with this appropriation matter is as useless as it is ridiculous and impudent. It is of a piece with the rest of your conduct."

"All right, Heman, all right," was the calm answer. "I don't say you've got to come. I only say I guess you'd better. I'm goin' back to Bayport to-morrer, early. And if I was you I'd come and see me to-night."

"I have no wish to see you. Nor do I care to talk with you further. That appropriation——"

"Maybe it ain't all appropriation."

"Then I cannot understand——"

"I know, but *I* understand. I've come to understand consider'ble many things in the last fortni't. There! I can't holler into this machine any longer. I've been clear out to 'Frisco and back in eleven days, and I got cold in those blessed sleepin' cars. I——"

# CY WHITTAKER'S PLACE

The receiver fell from the congressman's hand. It was a difficult object to pick up again. Heman groped for it in a blind, strangely inadequate way. Yet he wished to recover it very much.

"Wait! wait!" he shouted anxiously. "I—I—I dropped the— Are you there, Whittaker? Are you— Oh! yes! I didn't— Did you say—er— 'Frisco?"

"Yes, San Francisco, California. I've been West on a little cruise. Had an interestin' time. It's an interestin' place; don't you think so? Well, I'm sorry you can't come. Good night."

"Wait!" faltered the great man. "I—I—let me think, Cyrus. I do not wish to seem—er—arrogant in this matter. It is not usual for me to visit my constituents, but—but—I have no engagement this evening, and you are not well, and— Hello! are you there? Hello! Why, under the circumstances, I think— Yes, I will come. I'll come—er —at once."

The telephone enables one to procure a cab in a short time. Yet, to Heman Atkins, that cab was years in coming. He paced the library floor, his hand to his forehead and his brain whirling. It couldn't be! It must be a coincidence! He had been an idiot to display his agitation and surrender so weakly. And yet—and yet——

The ride through the storm to the Regent Hotel gave him opportunity for more thought. But he

"The receiver fell from the congressman's hand."

gained little comfort from thinking. If it was a coincidence, well and good. If not——

A bell boy conducted him to the Whittaker room " on the saloon deck." It was a small room, very different from the Atkins library, and Captain Cy, in a cane-seated chair, was huddled close to the steam radiator. He looked far from well.

" Evenin', Heman," he said as the congressman entered. " Pretty dirty night, ain't it? What we'd call a gray no'theaster back home. Sit down. Don't mind my not gettin' up. This heatin' arrangement feels mighty comf'table just now. If I get too far away from it I shiver my deck planks loose. Take off your things."

Mr. Atkins did not remove his overcoat. His hat he tossed on the bed. He glanced fearfully at his companion. The latter's greeting had been so casual and everyday that he took courage. And the captain looked anything but formidable as he hugged the radiator. Perhaps things were not so bad as he had feared. He resolved not to seem alarmed, at all events.

" Have a cigar, Heman?" said Captain Cy. " No? Well, all right; I will, if you don't mind."

He lit the cigar. The congressman cleared his throat.

" Cyrus," he said, " I am not accustomed to run at the beck and call of my—er—acquaintances, but, even though we have disagreed of late, even though to me your conduct seems quite unjustifiable, still, for the sake of our boyhood friendship, and, because you are not well, I—er—came."

Captain Cy coughed spasmodically, a cough that seemed to be tearing him to pieces. He looked at his cigar regretfully, and laid it on the top of the radiator.

"Too bad," he observed. "Tobacco gen'rally iles up my talkin' machinery, but just now it seems to make me bark like a ship's dog shut up in the hold. Why, yes, Heman, I see you've come. Much obliged to you."

This politeness was still more encouraging. Atkins leaned back in his chair and crossed his legs.

"I presume," he said, "that you wish to ask concerning the appropriation. I regret——"

"You needn't. I guess we'll get the appropriation."

Heman's condescension vanished. He leaned forward and uncrossed his legs.

"Indeed?" he said slowly, his eyes fixed on the captain's placid face.

"Yes—indeed."

"Whittaker, what are you talking about? Do you suppose that I have been the representative of my people in Congress all these years without knowing whereof I speak? They left the matter in my hands, and your interference——"

"I ain't goin' to interfere. *I'm* goin' to leave it

354

in your hands, too. And I cal'late you'll be able to find a way to get it. Um—hum, I guess likely you will."

The visitor rose to his feet. The time had come for another blast from Olympus. He raised the mighty right arm. But Captain Cy spoke first.

"Sit down, Heman," said the captain quietly. "Sit down. This ain't town meetin'. Never mind the appropriation now. There's other matters to be talked about first. Sit down, I tell you."

Mr. Atkins was purple in the face, but he sat down. The captain coughed again.

"Heman," he began when the spasm was over, "I asked you to come here to-night for—well, blessed if I know exactly. It didn't make much difference to me whether you came or not."

"Then, sir, I must say that, of all the impudent——"

"S-s-h-h! for the land sakes! Speechmakin' must be as bad as the rum habit, when a feller's got it chronic as you have. No, it didn't make much difference to me whether you came or not. But, honest, you've got to be a kind of Bunker Hill monument to the folks back home. They kneel down at your foundations and look up at you, and tell each other how many foot high you are, and what it cost to build you, and how you stand for patriotism and purity, till—well, *I* couldn't see you tumble down

355

without givin' you a chance. I couldn't; 'twould be like blowin' up a church."

The purple had left the Atkins face, but the speechmaking habit is not likely to be broken.

"Cyrus Whittaker," he stammered, "have you been drinking? Your language to me is abominable. Why I permit myself to remain here and listen to such——"

"If you'll keep still I'll tell you why. And, if I was you, I wouldn't be too anxious to find out. This everlastin' cold don't make me over 'n' above good-tempered, and when I think of what you've done to that little girl, or what you tried to do, I have to hold myself down tight, *tight,* and don't you forget it! Now, you keep quiet and listen. It'll be best for you, Heman. Your cards ain't under the table any longer. I've seen your hand, and I know why you've been playin' it. I know the whole game. I've been West, and Everdean and I have had a talk."

Mr. Atkins had again risen from the chair. Now he fell heavily back into it. His lips moved as if he meant to speak, but he did not. At the mention of the Everdean name he made a queer, choking sound in his throat.

"I know the whole business, Heman," went on the captain. "I know why you was so knocked over when you learned who Bos'n was, the night of the party. I know why you took up with that blackguard, Thomas, and why you've spent your good money hirin' lawyers for him. I know about the mine. I know the whole thing from first to last. Shall I tell you? Do you want to hear it?"

The great man did not answer. A drop of perspiration shone on his high forehead, and the veins of his big, white hands stood out as he clutched the arms of his chair. The monument was tottering on its base.

"It's a dirty mess, the whole of it," continued Captain Cy. "And yet, I can see—I suppose I can see some excuse for you at the beginnin'. When old man Everdean and his crowd bought you and John Thayer out, 'way back there in '54, after John died, and all the money was put into your hands, I cal'late you was honest then. I wouldn't wonder if you *meant* to hand over the thirty-seven thousand five hundred dollars to your partner's widow. But 'twas harder and more risky to send money East in them days than 'tis now, and so you waited, thinkin' maybe that you'd fetch it to Emily when you come yourself. But you didn't come home for some years; you went tradin' down along the Feejees and around that way. That's how I reasoned it out these last few days on the train. I give you credit for bein' honest first along.

"But never mind whether you was or not, you haven't been since. You never paid over a cent of that poor feller's money—honest money, that belonged to his heirs, and belongs to 'em now. You've hung onto it, stole it, used it for yours. And Emily worked and scratched for a livin' and died poor. And Mary, she died, after bein' abused and deserted by that cussed husband of hers. And you thought you was safe, I cal'late. And then Bos'n turns up right in your own town, right acrost the road from you! By the big dipper! it's enough to make a feller believe that the Almighty does take a hand in straightenin' out such things, when us humans bungle 'em—it is so!

"Course I ain't sure, Heman, what you meant to do when you found that the child you'd stole that money from was goin' to be under your face and eyes till you or she died. I cal'late you was afraid I'd find somethin' out, wan't you? I presume likely you thought that I, not havin' quite the reverence for you that the rest of the Bayporters have, might be sharp enough or lucky enough to smell a rat. Perhaps you suspicioned that I knew the Everdeans. Anyhow, you wanted to get the child as fur out of your sight and out of my hands as you could—ain't that so? And when her dad turned up, you thought you saw your chance. Heman, you answer me this: Ain't it part of your bargain with Thomas that when he gets his little girl, he shall take her and clear out, away off somewheres, for good? Ain't it, now—what?"

The monument was swaying, was swinging from

side to side, but it did not quite fall—not then. The congressman's cheeks hung flabby, his forehead was wet, and he shook from head to foot; but he clenched his jaws and made one last attempt at defiance.

"I—I don't know what you mean," he declared. "You—you seem to be accusing me of something. Of stealing, I believe. Do you understand who I am? I have some influence and reputation, and it is dangerous to—to try to frighten me. Proofs are required in law, and——"

"S-s-h-h! You know I've got the proofs. They were easy enough to get, once I happened on the track of 'em. Lord sakes, Heman, I ain't a fool! What's the use of your pretendin' to be one? There's the deed out in 'Frisco, with yours and John's name on it. There's the records to prove the sale. There's the receipt for the seventy-five thousand signed by you, on behalf of yourself and your partner's widow. There's old man Everdean alive and competent to testify. There's John Thayer's will on file over to Orham. Proofs! Why, you *thief*! if it's proofs you want, I've got enough to send you to state's prison for the rest of your life. Don't you dare say 'proofs' to me again! Heman Atkins, you owe me, as Bos'n's guardian, thirty-seven thousand five hundred dollars, with interest since 1854. What you goin' to do about it?"

Here was one ray, a feeble ray, of light.

"You're not her guardian," cried Atkins. "The courts have thrown you out. And your appeal won't stand, either. If any money is due, it belongs to her father. She isn't of age! No, sir! her father——"

Captain Cy's patience had been giving way. Now he lost it altogether. He strode across the room and shook his forefinger in his victim's face.

"So!" he cried. "That's your tack, is it? By the big dipper! You *go* to her father—just you go to him and tell him! Just hint to him that you owe his daughter thirty-odd thousand dollars, and see what he'll do. Good heavens above! he was ready to sell her out to me for fifty dollars' wuth of sand bank in Orham. Almost ready, he was, till you offered a higher price to him to fight. Why, he'll have your hide nailed up on the barn door! If you don't pay him every red copper, down on the nail, he'll wring you dry. And then he'll blackmail you forever and ever, amen! Unless, of course, *I* go home and stop the blackmail by printing my story in the *Breeze*. I've a precious good mind to do it. By the Almighty, I *will* do it! unless you come off that high horse of yours and talk like a man."

And then the monument fell, fell prostrate, with a sickly, pitiful crash. If we of Bayport could have seen our congressman then! The great man, great no longer, broke down completely. He cried like a baby. It was all true—all true. He had not

meant to steal, at first. He had been led into using
the money in his business. Then he had meant to
send it to the heirs, but he didn't know their whereabouts. Captain Cy smiled at this excuse. And
now he couldn't pay—he *couldn't*. He had hardly
that sum in the world. He had lost money in stocks;
his property in the South had gone to the bad! He
would be ruined. He would have to go to prison.
He was getting to be an old man. And there was
Alicia, his daughter! Think of her! Think of
the disgrace! And so on, over and over, with the
one recurring burden—what was the captain going
to do? what was he going to do? It was a miserable, dreadful exhibition, and Captain Cy could feel
no pride in his triumph.

"There! there!" he said at last. "Stop it, man;
stop it, for goodness sakes! Pull yourself together.
I guess we can fix it up somehow. I ain't goin' to
be too hard on you. If it wan't for your meanness
in bein' willin' to let Bos'n suffer her life long with
that drunken beast of a dad of hers, I'd feel almost
like tellin' you to get up and forget it. But *that's*
got to be stopped. Now, you listen to me."

Heman listened. He was on his knees beside the
bed, his face buried in his arms, and his gray hair,
the leonine Atkins hair, which he was wont to toss
backward in the heated periods of his eloquence,
tumbled and draggled. Captain Cy looked down at
him.

"This whole business about Bos'n must be stopped," he said, "and stopped right off. You tell your lawyers to drop the case. Her dad is only hangin' around because you pay him to. He don't want her; he don't care what becomes of her. If you pay him enough, he'll go, won't he? and not come back?"

The congressman raised his head.

"Why, yes," he faltered; "I think he will. Yes, I think I could arrange that. But, Cyrus——"

The captain held up his hand.

"I intend to look out for Bos'n," he said. "She cares for me more'n anyone else in the world. She's as much to me as my own child ever could be, and I'll see that she is happy and provided for. I'm religious enough to believe she was sent to me, and I intend to stick to my trust. As for the money——"

"Yes, yes! The money?"

"Well, I won't be too hard on you that way, either. We'll talk that over later on. Maybe we can arrange for you to pay it a little at a time. You can sign a paper showin' that you owe it, and we'll fix the payin' to suit all hands. 'Tain't as if the child was in want. I've got some money of my own, and what's mine's hers. I think we needn't worry about the money part."

"God bless you, Cyrus! I——"

"Yes, all right. I'm sure your askin' for the blessin' 'll be a great help. Now, you do your part,

"He was on his knees beside the bed, his face buried in his arms."

and I'll do mine. No one knows of this business but me. I didn't tell Everdean a word. He don't know why I hustled out there and back, nor why I asked so many questions. And he ain't the kind to pry into what don't concern him. So you're pretty safe, I cal'late. Now, if you don't mind, I wish you'd run along home. I'm—I'm used up, sort of."

Mr. Atkins arose from his knees. Even then, broken as he was—he looked ten years older than when he entered the room—he could hardly believe what he had just heard.

"You mean," he faltered, "Cyrus, do you mean that—that you're not going to reveal this—this——"

"That I'm not goin' to tell on you? Yup; that's what I mean. You get rid of Thomas and squelch that law case, and I'll keep mum. You can trust me for that."

"But—but, Cyrus, the people at home? Your story in the *Breeze*? You're not——"

"No, they needn't know, either. It'll be between you and me."

"God bless you! I'll never forget——"

"That's right. You mustn't. Forgettin' is the one thing you mustn't do. And, see here, you're boss of the political fleet in Bayport; you steer the school committee now. Phœbe Dawes ain't too popular with that committee; I'd see that she was popularized."

"Yes, yes; she shall be. She shall not be disturbed. Is there anything else I can do?"

"Why, yes, I guess there is. Speakin' of popularity made me think of it. That harbor appropriation had better go through."

A very faint tinge of color came into the congressman's chalky face. He hesitated in his reply.

"I—I don't know about that, Cyrus," he said. "The bill will probably be voted on in a few days. It is made up and——"

"Then I'd strain a p'int and make it over. I'd work real hard on it. I'm sorry about that sugar river, but I cal'late Bayport 'll have to come first. Yes, it'll have to, Heman; it sartin will."

The reference to the "sugar river" was the final straw. Evidently this man knew everything.

"I—I'll try my best," affirmed Heman. "Thank you, Cyrus. You have been more merciful than I had a right to expect."

"Yes, I guess I have. Why do I do it?" He smiled and shook his head. "Well, I don't know. For two reasons, maybe. First, I'd hate to be responsible for tippin' over such a sky-towerin' idol as you've been to make ruins for Angie Phinney and the other blackbirds to peck at and caw over. And second—well, it does sound presumin', don't it, but I kind of pity you. Say, Heman," he added with a chuckle, "that's a kind of distinction, in a way, ain't it? A good many folks have hurrahed over you and worshipped you—some of 'em, I guess likely, have envied you; but, by the big dipper! I do believe I'm the only one in this round world that ever *pitied* you. Good-by. The elevator's right down the hall."

It required some resolution for the Honorable Atkins to walk down that corridor and press the elevator button. But he did it, somehow. A guest came out of one of the rooms and approached him as he stood there. It was a man he knew. Heman squared his shoulders and set every nerve and muscle.

"Good evening, Mr. Atkins," said the man. "A miserable night, isn't it?"

"Miserable, indeed," replied the congressman. The strength in his voice surprised him. The man passed on. Heman descended in the elevator, walked steadily through the crowded lobby and out to the curb where his cab was waiting. The driver noticed nothing strange in his fare's appearance. He noticed nothing strange when the Atkins residence was reached and its tenant mounted the stone steps and opened the door with his latchkey. But, if he had seen the dignified form collapse in a library chair and moan and rock back and forth until the morning hours, he would have wondered very much indeed.

Meanwhile Captain Cy, coughing and shivering by the radiator, had been summoned from that warm haven by a knock at his door. A bell boy stood at the threshold, holding a brown envelope in his hand.

"The clerk sent this up to you, sir," he said. "It came a week ago. When you went away, you didn't leave any address, and whatever letters came for you were sent back to Bayport, Massachusetts. The clerk says you registered from there, sir. But he kept this telegram. It was in your box, and the day clerk forgot to give it to you this afternoon."

The captain tore open the envelope. The telegram was from his lawyer, Mr. Peabody. It was dated a week before, and read as follows:

"Come home at once. Important."

# CHAPTER XX

## DIVIDED HONORS

THE blizzard began that night. Bayport has a generous allowance of storms and gales during a winter, although, as a usual thing, there is more rain than snow and more wind than either. But we can count with certainty on at least one blizzard between November and April, and about the time when Captain Cy, feverish and ill, the delayed telegram in his pocket and a great fear in his heart, boarded the sleeper of the East-bound train at Washington, snow was beginning to fall in our village.

Next morning, when Georgianna came downstairs to prepare Bos'n's breakfast—the housekeeper had ceased to " go home nights " since the captain's absence—the world outside was a tumbled, driving whirl of white. The woodshed and barn, dimly seen through the smother, were but gray shapes, emerging now and then only to be wiped from the vision as by a great flapping cloth wielded by the mighty hand of the wind. The old house shook in the blasts, the windowpanes rattled as if handfuls of small shot were being thrown against them, and the carpet on the floor of the dining room puffed up in miniature billows.

School was out of the question, and Bos'n, her breakfast eaten, prepared to put in a cozy day with her dolls and Christmas playthings.

"When *do* you s'pose Uncle Cyrus will get home?" she asked of the housekeeper. She had asked the same thing at least three times a day during the fortnight, and Georgianna's answer was always just as unsatisfactory:

"I don't know, dearie, I'm sure. He'll be here pretty soon, though, don't you fret."

"Oh, I ain't going to fret. I know he'll come. He said he would, and Uncle Cy always does what he says he will."

About twelve Asaph made his appearance, a white statue.

"Godfrey scissors!" he panted, shaking his snow-plastered cap over the coal hod. "Say, this is one of 'em, ain't it? Don't know's I ever see more of a one. Drift out by the front fence pretty nigh up to my waist. This 'll be a nasty night along the Orham beach. The lifesavers'll have their hands full. Whew! I'm about tuckered out."

"Been to the post office?" asked Georgianna in a low tone.

"Yup. I been there. Mornin' mail just this minute sorted. Train's two hours late. Gabe says more'n likely the evenin' train won't be able to get through at all, if this keeps up."

"Was there anything from———"

Mr. Tidditt glanced at Bos'n and shook his head.

"Not a word," he said. "Funny, ain't it? It don't seem a bit like him. And he can't be to Washin'ton, because all them letters came back. I—I swan to man, I'm beginnin' to get worried."

"Worried? I'm pretty nigh crazy! What does Phœbe Dawes say?"

"She don't say much. It's pretty tough, when everything else is workin' out so fine, thanks to her, to have this happen. No, she don't say much, but she acts pretty solemn."

"Say, Mr. Tidditt?"

"Yes, what is it?"

"You don't s'pose anything that happened betwixt her and Cap'n Whittaker that afternoon is responsible for—for his stayin' away so, do you? You know what he told me to tell her—about her not comin' here?"

Asaph fidgeted with the wet cap.

"Aw, that ain't nothin'," he stammered. "That is, I hope it ain't. I did say somethin' to him that —but Phœbe understands. She's a smart woman."

"You haven't told them boardin' house tattle-tales about the—Emmie, you go fetch me a card of matches from the kitchen, won't you—of what's been found out about that Thomas thing?"

" Course I ain't. Didn't Peabody say not to tell a soul till we was sure? S'pose I'd tell Keturah and Angie? Might's well paint it on a sign and be done with it. No, no! I've kept mum and you do the same. Well, I must be goin'. Hope to goodness we hear some good news from Whit by to-morrer."

But when to-morrow came news of any kind was unobtainable. No trains could get through, and the telephone and telegraph wires were out of commission, owing to the great storm. Bayport was buried under a white coverlet, three feet thick on a level, which shone in the winter sun as if powdered with diamond dust. The street-shoveling brigade, meaning most of the active male citizens, was busy with plows and shovels. Simmons's was deserted in the evenings, for most of the regular *habitués* went to bed after supper, tired out.

Two days of this. Then Gabe Lumley, his depot wagon replaced by a sleigh, drove the panting Daniel into the yard of the Cy Whittaker place. Gabe was much excited. He had news of importance to communicate and was puffed up in consequence.

" The wire's all right again, Georgianna," he said to the housekeeper, who had hurried to the door to meet him. " Fust message just come through. Guess who it's for?"

" Stop your foolishness, Gabe Lumley!" ordered Miss Taylor. " Hand over that telegram this minute. Don't you stop to talk! Hand it over!"

# DIVIDED HONORS

Gabe didn't intend to be "corked" thus peremptorily.

"It's pretty important news, Georiganna," he declared. "Kind of bad news, too. I think I'd ought to prepare you for it, sort of. When Cap'n Obed Pepper died, I——"

"*Died!* For the land sakes! *What* are you sayin'? Give me that, you foolhead! Give it to me!"

She snatched the telegram from him and tore it open. It was not as bad as might have been, but it was bad enough. Lawyer Peabody wired that Captain Cyrus Whittaker was at his home in Ostable, sick in bed, and threatened with pneumonia.

Captain Cy, hurrying homeward in response to the attorney's former telegram, had reached Boston the day of the blizzard. He had taken the train for Bayport that afternoon. The train had reached Ostable after nine o'clock that night, but could get no farther. The captain, burning with fever and torn by chills, had wallowed through the drifts to his lawyer's home and collapsed on his doorstep. Now he was very ill and, at times, delirious.

For two weeks he lay, fighting off the threatened attack of pneumonia. But he won the fight, and, at last, word came to the anxious ones at Bayport that he was past the danger point and would pull through. There was rejoicing at the Cy Whittaker place. The Board of Strategy came and performed

371

an impromptu war dance around the dining-room table.

"Whe-e-e!" shouted Bailey Bangs, tossing Bos'n above his head. "Your Uncle Cy's weathered the Horn and is bound for clear water now. Three cheers for our side! Won't we give him a reception when we get him back here!"

"Won't we?" crowed Asaph. "Well, I just guess we will! You ought to hear Angie and the rest of 'em chant hymns of glory about him. A body'd think they always knew he was the salt of the earth. Maybe I don't rub it in a little, hey? Oh, no, maybe not!"

"And Heman!" chimed in Mr. Bangs. "And Heman! Would you ever believe *he'd* change so all of a sudden? Bully old Whit! I can mention his name now without Ketury's landin' onto me like a snowslide. Whee! I say, wh-e-e-e!"

He continued to say it; and Georgianna and Asaph said what amounted to the same thing. A change had come over our Bayport social atmosphere, a marvelous change. And at Simmons's and —more wonderful still—at Tad Simpson's barber shop, plans were being made and perfected for proceedings in which Cyrus Whittaker was to play the most prominent part.

Meanwhile the convalescence went on at a rapid rate. As soon as he was permitted to talk, Captain Cy began to question his lawyer. How about the appeal? Had Atkins done anything further? The answers were satisfactory. The case had been dropped: the Honorable Heman had announced its withdrawal. He had said that he had changed his mind and should not continue to espouse the Thomas cause. In fact, he seemed to have whirled completely about on his pedestal and, like a compass, now pointed only in one direction—toward his "boyhood friend" and present neighbor, Cyrus Whittaker.

"It's perfectly astounding," commented Peabody. "What in the world, captain, did you do to him while you were in Washington?"

"Oh! nothin' much," was the rather disinterested answer. "Him and me had a talk, and he saw the error of his ways, I cal'late. How's Bos'n to-day? Did you give her my love when you 'phoned?"

"So far as the case is concerned," went on the lawyer, "I think we should have won that, anyway. It's a curious thing. Thomas has disappeared. How he got word, or who he got it from, *I* don't know; but he must have, and he's gone somewhere, no one knows where. And yet I'm not certain that we were on the right trail. It seemed certain a week ago, but now——"

The captain had not been listening. He was thinking. Thomas had gone, had he! Good! Heman was living up to his promises. And Bos'n, God bless her, was free from that danger.

" Have you heard from Emmie, I asked you? " he repeated.

He would not listen to anything further concerning Thomas, either then or later. He was sick of the whole business, he declared, and now that everything was all right, didn't wish to talk about it again. He asked nothing about the appropriation, and the lawyer, acting under strict orders, did not mention it.

Only once did Captain Cy inquire concerning a person in his home town who was not a member of his household.

" How is—er—how's the teacher? " he inquired one morning.

" How's who? "

" Why—Phœbe Dawes, the school-teacher. Smart, is she? "

" Yes, indeed! Why, she has been the most——"

The doctor came in just then and the interview terminated. It was not resumed, because that afternoon Mr. Peabody started for Boston on a business trip, to be gone some time.

And at last came the great day, the day when Captain Cy was to be taken home. He was up and about, had been out for several short walks, and was very nearly his own self again. He was in good spirits, too, at times, but had fits of seeming depression which, under the circumstances, were unexplainable. The doctor thought they were due to his recent illness and forbade questioning.

# DIVIDED HONORS

The original plan had been for the captain to go to Bayport in the train, but the morning set for his departure was such a beautiful one that Mr. Peabody, who had the day before returned from the city, suggested driving over. So the open carriage, drawn by the Peabody "span," was brought around to the front steps, and the captain, bundled up until, as he said, he felt like a wharf rat inside a cotton bale, emerged from the house which had sheltered him for a weary month and climbed to the back seat. The attorney got in beside him.

"All ashore that's goin' ashore," observed Captain Cy. Then to the driver, who stood by the horses' heads, he added: "Stand by to get ship under way, commodore. I'm homeward bound, and there's a little messmate of mine waitin' on the dock already, I wouldn't wonder. So don't hang around these waters no longer'n you can help."

But Mr. Peabody smiled and laid a hand on his shoulder.

"Just a minute, captain," he said. "We've got another passenger. She came to the house last evening, but Dr. Cole thought this would be an exciting day for you, and you must sleep in preparation for it. So we kept her in the background. It was something of a job but— Hurrah! here she is!"

Mrs. Peabody, the lawyer's wife, opened the front door. She was laughing. The next moment a small

375

figure shot past her, down the steps, and into the carriage like a red-hooded bombshell.

"Uncle Cyrus!" she screamed joyously. "Uncle Cyrus, it's me! Here I am!"

And Captain Cy, springing up and shedding wraps and robes, received the bombshell with open arms and hugged it tight.

"Bos'n!" he shouted. "By the big dipper! *Bos'n!* Why, you little—you—you——"

That was a wonderful ride. Emily sat in the captain's lap—he positively refused to let her sit beside him on the seat, although Peabody urged it, fearing the child might tire him—and her tongue rattled like a sewing machine. She had a thousand things to tell, about her school, about Georgianna, about her dolls, about Lonesome, the cat, and how many mice he had caught, about the big snowstorm.

"Georgianna wanted me to stay at home and wait for you, Uncle Cy," she said, "but I teased and teased and finally they said I could come over. I came yesterday on the train. Mr. Tidditt went with me to the depot. Mrs. Peabody let me peek into your room last night and I saw you eating supper. You didn't know I was there, did you?"

"You bet I didn't! There'd have been a mutiny right then if I'd caught sight of you. You little sculpin! Playin' it on your Uncle Cy, was you? I didn't know you could keep a secret so well."

"Oh, yes I can! Why, I know an ever so much

376

bigger secret, too. It is— Why! I 'most forgot. You just wait."

The captain laughingly begged her to divulge the big secret, but she shook her small head and refused. The horses trotted on at a lively pace, and the miles separating Ostable and Bayport were subtracted one by one. It was magnificent winter weather. The snow had disappeared from the road, except in widely separated spots, but the big drifts still heaped the fields and shone and sparkled in the sunshine. Against their whiteness the pitch pines and cedars stood darkly green and the skeleton scrub oaks and bushes cast delicate blue-penciled shadows. The bay, seen over the flooded, frozen salt meadows and distant dunes, was in its winter dress of the deepest sapphire, trimmed with whitecaps and fringed with stranded ice cakes. There was a snap and tang in the breeze which braced one like a tonic. The party in the carriage was a gay one.

" Getting tired, captain?" asked Peabody.

" Who? Me? Well, I guess not. 'Most home, Bos'n. There's the salt works ahead there."

They passed the abandoned salt works, the crumbling ruins of a dead industry, and the boundary stone, now half hidden in a drift, marking the beginning of Bayport township. Then, from the pine grove at the curve farther on, appeared two capped and coated figures, performing a crazy fandango.

" Who's them two lunatics," inquired Captain

377

Cy, " whoopin' and carryin' on in the middle of the road? Has anybody up this way had a jug come by express or— Hey! *What?* Why, you old idiots you! *Come* here and let me get a hold of you!"

The Board of Strategy swooped down upon the carriage like Trumet mosquitoes on a summer boarder. They swarmed into the vehicle, Bailey on the front seat and Asaph in the rear, where, somehow or other, they made room for him. There were handshakings and thumps on the back.

"What you doin' 'way up here in the west end of nowhere?" demanded Captain Cy. "By the big dipper, I'm glad to see you! How'd you get here?"

"Walked," cackled Bailey. "Frogged it all the way. Soon's Mrs. Peabody wired you was goin' to ride, me and Ase started to meet you. Wan't you surprised?"

"We wanted to be the fust to say howdy, old man," explained Asaph. "Wanted to welcome you back, you know."

The captain was immensely pleased.

"Well, I'm glad I've got so much popularity, anyhow," he said. "Guess 'twill be different when I get down street, hey? Don't cal'late Tad and Angie 'll shed the joyous tear over me. Never mind; long's my friends are glad I don't care about the rest."

The Board looked at each other.

# DIVIDED HONORS

"Tad?" repeated Bailey. "And Angie? What you talkin' about? Why, they— Ugh!"

The last exclamation was the result of a tremendous dig in the ribs from the Tidditt fist. Asaph, who had leaned forward to administer it, was frowning and shaking his head. Mr. Bangs relapsed into a grinning silence.

West Bayport seemed to be deserted. At one or two houses, however, feminine heads appeared at the windows. One old lady shook a calico apron at the carriage. A child beside her cried: "Hurrah!"

"Aunt Hepsy h'istin' colors by mistake," laughed the captain. "She ain't got her specs, I guess, and thinks I'm Heman. That comes of ridin' astern of a span, Peabody."

But as they drew near the Center flags were flying from front-yard poles. Some of the houses were decorated.

"What in the world—" began Captain Cy. "Land sakes! look at the schoolhouse. And Simmons's! And—and Simpson's!"

The schoolhouse flag was flapping in the wind. The scarred wooden pillars of its portico were hidden with bunting. Simmons's front displayed a row of little banners, each bearing a letter—the letters spelled "Welcome Home." Tad's barber shop was more or less artistically wreathed in colored tissue paper. There, too, a flag was draped over the front door. Yet not a single person was in sight.

"For goodness' sake!" cried the bewildered captain. "What's all this mean? And where is everybody. Have all hands——"

He stopped in the middle of the sentence. They were at the foot of Whittaker's Hill. Its top, between the Atkins's gate and the Whittaker fence, was black with people. Children pranced about the outskirts of the crowd. A shout came down the wind. The horses, not in the least fatigued by their long canter, trotted up the slope. The shouting grew louder. A wave of youngsters came racing to meet the equipage.

"What—what in time?" gasped Captain Cy. "What's up? I——"

And then the town clerk seized him by the arm. Peabody shook his other hand. Bos'n threw her arms about his neck. Bailey stood up and waved his hat.

"It's you, you old critter!" whooped Asaph. "It's *you*, d'you understand?"

"The appropriation has gone through," explained the lawyer, "and this is the celebration in consequence. And you are the star attraction because, you see, everyone knows you are responsible for it."

"That's what!" howled the excited Bangs. "And we're goin' to show you what we think of you for doin' it. We've been plannin' this for over a fortni't."

# DIVIDED HONORS

"And I knew it all the time," squealed Bos'n, "and I didn't tell a word, did I?"

"Three cheers for Captain Whittaker!" bellowed a person in the crowd. This person—wonder of wonders!—was Tad Simpson.

The cheering was, considering the size of the crowd, tremendous. Bewildered and amazed, Captain Cy was assisted from the carriage and escorted to his front door. Amidst the handkerchief-waving, applauding people he saw Keturah Bangs and Alpheus Smalley and Angeline Phinney and Captain Salters—even Alonzo Snow, his recent opponent in town meeting. Josiah Dimick was there, too, apparently having a fit.

On the doorstep stood Georgianna and—and— yes, it was true—beside her, grandly extending a welcoming hand, the majestic form of the Honorable Heman Atkins. Some one else was there also, some one who hurriedly slipped back into the crowd as the owner of the Cy Whittaker place came up the path between the hedges.

Mr. Atkins shook the captain's hand and then, turning toward the people, held up his own for silence. To all outward appearance, he was still the great Heman, our district idol, philanthropist, and leader. His silk hat glistened as of old, his chest swelled in the old manner, his whiskers were just as dignified and awe-inspiring. For an instant, as he met the captain's eye, his own faltered and fell, and

381

there was a pleading expression in his face, the lines of which had deepened just a little. But only for an instant; then he began to speak.

"Cyrus," he said, "it is my pleasant duty, on behalf of your neighbors and friends here assembled, to welcome you to your—er—ancestral home after your trying illness. I do it heartily, sincerely, gladly. And it is the more pleasing to me to perform this duty, because, as I have explained publicly to my fellow-townspeople, all disagreement between us is ended. I was wrong—again I publicly admit it. A scheming blackleg, posing in the guise of a loving father, imposed upon me. I am sorry for the trouble I have caused you. Of you and of the little girl with you I ask pardon—I entreat forgiveness."

He paused. Captain Cy, the shadow of a smile at the corner of his mouth, nodded, and said briefly:

"All right, Heman. I forgive you." Few heard him: the majority were applauding the congressman. Sylvanus Cahoon, whispering in the ear of "Uncle Bedny," expressed as his opinion that "that was about as magnaminious a thing as ever I heard said. Yes, sir! mag-na-min-ious—that's what *I* call it."

"But," continued the great Atkins, "I have said all this to you before. What I have to say now— what I left my duties in Washington expressly to come here and say—is that Bayport thanks you, *I* thank you, for your tremendous assistance in obtaining the appropriation which is to make our harbor

382

"'Cyrus,' he said, 'it is my pleasant duty . . . to welcome you to your—er—ancestral home.'"

a busy port where our gallant fishing fleet may ride
at anchor and unload its catch, instead of transfer-
ring it in dories as heretofore. Friends, I have already told you how this man "—laying a hand on
the captain's shoulder—" came to the Capital and
used his influence among his acquaintances in high
places, with the result that the thirty thousand dollars, which I had despaired of getting, was added
to the bill. I had the pleasure of voting for that
bill. It passed. I am proud of that vote."

Tremendous applause. Then some one called for
three cheers for Mr. Atkins. They were given. But
the recipient merely bowed.

"No, no," he said deprecatingly. "No, no! not
for me, my friends, much as I appreciate your gratitude. My days of public service are nearly at an
end. As I have intimated to some of you already,
I am seriously considering retiring from political
life in the near future. But that is irrelevant; it is
not material at present. To-day we meet, not to
say farewell to the setting, but to greet the rising
sun. *I* call for three cheers for our committee of
one—Captain Cyrus Whittaker."

When the uproar had at last subsided, there were
demands for a speech from Captain Cy. But the
captain, facing them, his arms about the delighted
Bos'n, positively declined to orate.

"I—I'm ever so much obliged to you, folks," he
stammered. "I am so. But you'll have to excuse

me from speechmaking. They—they didn't teach it afore the mast, where I went to college. Thank you, just the same. And do come and see me, everybody. Me and this little girl," drawing Emily nearer to him, " will be real glad to have you."

After the handshaking and congratulating were over, the crowd dispersed. It was a great occasion; all agreed to that, but the majority considered it a divided triumph. The captain had done a lot for the town, of course, but the Honorable Atkins had made another splendid impression by his address of welcome. Most people thought it as fine as his memorable effort at town meeting. Unlike that one, however, in this instance it is safe to say that none, not even the adoring and praise-chanting Miss Phinney, derived quite the enjoyment from the congressman's speech that Captain Cy did. It tickled his sense of humor.

" Ase," he observed irrelevantly when the five— Tidditt, Georgianna, Bailey, Bos'n, and himself were at last alone again in the sitting room, " it *don't* pay to tip over a monument, does it—not out in public, I mean. You wouldn't want to see me blow up Bunker Hill, would you? "

" Blow up Bunker Hill! " repeated Asaph in alarmed amazement. " Godfrey scissors! I believe you're goin' loony. This day's been too much for you. What are you talkin' about? "

" Oh, nothin'," with a quiet chuckle. " I was

thinkin' out loud, that's all. Did you ever notice them imitation stone pillars on Heman's house? They're holler inside, but you'd never guess it. And, long as you do know they're holler, you can keep a watch on 'em. And there's one thing sure," he added, " they *are* ornamental."

# CHAPTER XXI

### CAPTAIN CY'S "PICTURE"

W ONDER where Phœbe went to," remarked Mr. Tidditt, a little later. "I
thought I saw her with Heman and
Georgianna on the front steps when we drove up."

"She was there," affirmed the housekeeper.
"She'd been helpin' me trim up the rooms here.
What do you think of 'em, Cap'n Cyrus? Ain't they
pretty?"

The sitting room and dining room were gay with
evergreens and old-fashioned flowers. Our living
room windows in the winter time are usually filled
with carefully tended potted plants, and the neighbors had loaned their geraniums and fuchsias and
heliotrope and begonias to brighten the Whittaker
house for its owner's return. Captain Cy, who was
sitting in the rocker, with Bos'n on his knee, looked
about him. Now that the first burst of excitement
was over, he seemed grave and preoccupied.

"They look mighty pretty, Georgianna," he said.
"Fine enough. But what was that you just said?
Did——"

386

# CAPTAIN CY'S "PICTURE"

"Yup," interrupted Miss Taylor, who had scarcely ceased talking since breakfast that morning. "Yes, 'twas teacher that helped fix 'em. Not that I wouldn't have got along without her, but I had more to do than a little, cleanin' and scrubbin' up. So Phœbe she come in, and— Oh! yes, as I was sayin', she was out front with me, but the minute your carriage drove up with that lovely span— *Ain't* that a fine span! I cal'late they're——"

"What become of teacher?" broke in Bailey.

"Why, she run off somewheres. I didn't see where she went to; I was too busy hollerin' at Cap'n Whittaker and noticin' that span. I bet you they made Angie Phinney's eyes stick out. I guess she realizes that we in this house are some punkins now. If I don't lord it over her when I run acrost her these days, then I miss my guess. I——"

"Belay!" ordered Captain Cy, his gravity more pronounced than ever. "How does it happen that you— See here, Georgianna, did you tell Ph—er— Miss Dawes what I told you to tell her when I went away?"

"Why, yes, I told her. I hated to, dreadful, but I done it. She was awful set back at fust, but I guess she asked Mr. Tidditt— Where you goin', Mr. Tidditt?"

The town clerk, his face red, was on his way to the door.

"Asked Ase?" repeated the captain. "Ase, come here! Did you tell her anything?"

Asaph was very much embarrassed.

"Well," he stammered, "I didn't mean to, Cy, but she got to askin' me questions, and somehow or 'nother I did tell her about our confab, yours and mine. I told her that I knew folks was talkin', and I felt 'twas my duty to tell you so. That's why I done it, and I told her you said—well, you know what you said yourself, Cy."

Captain Cy was evidently much disturbed. He put Bos'n down, and rose to his feet.

"Well," he asked sharply, "what did she say?"

"Oh! she was white and still for a minute or two. Then she kind of stamped her foot and went off and left me. But next time she met me she was nice as pie. She's been pretty frosty to Angie and the rest of 'em, but she's been always nice to Bailey and me. Why, when I asked her pardon, she said not at all, she was very glad to know the truth; it helped her to understand things. And you could see she meant it, too. She——"

"So she has been comin' here ever since. And the gossip has been goin' on, I s'pose. Well, by the big dipper, it'll stop now! I'll see to that."

The Board of Strategy and the housekeeper were amazed.

"Gossip!" repeated Bailey. "Well, I guess there ain't nothin' said against her now—not in *this* town,

there ain't! Why, all hands can't praise her enough
for her smartness in findin' out about that
Thomas. If it wan't for her, he'd be botherin'
you yet, Cy. You know it. What are you talkin'
about?"

Captain Cy passed his hand over his forehead.

"Bos'n," he said slowly, "you run and help
Georgianna in the kitchen a spell. She's got her
dinner to look out for, I guess likely. Georgianna,"
to the housekeeper, who looked anything but eager,
"you better see to your dinner right off, and take
Emmie with you."

Miss Taylor reluctantly departed, leading Bos'n
by the hand. The child was loath to leave her uncle,
but he told her he wouldn't give a cent for his first
dinner at home if she didn't help in preparing it.
So she went out happy.

"Now, then," demanded the captain, "what's
this about Phœbe and Thomas? I want to know.
Stop! Don't ask another question. Answer me
first."

So the Board of Strategy, by turns and in concert,
told of the drive to Trumet and the call on Debby
Beasley. Asaph would have narrated the story of
the upset sulky, but Bailey shut him up in short
order.

"Never mind that foolishness," he snapped.
"You see, Cy, Debby had just been out to Arizona
visitin' old Beasley's niece. And she'd fell in with

389

a woman out there whose husband had run off and left her. And Debby, she read the advertisement about him in the Arizona paper, and it said he had the spring halt in his off hind leg, or somethin' similar. Now, Thomas, he had that, too, and there was other things that reminded Phœbe of him. So she don't say nothin' to nobody, but she writes to this woman askin' for more partic'lars and a photograph of the missin' one. The partic'lars come, but the photograph didn't; the wife didn't have none, I b'lieve. But there was enough to send Phœbe hotfoot to Mr. Peabody. And Peabody he writes to his lawyer friend in Butte, Montana. And the Butte man he——"

"Well, the long and short of it is," cut in Tidditt, "that it looked safe and sartin that Thomas *had* married the Arizona woman while his real wife, Bos'n's ma, was livin', and had run off and left her same as he did Mary. And the funny part of it is——"

"The funny part of it is," declared Bangs, drowning his friend's voice by raising his own, "that somebody out there, some scalawag friend of this Thomas, must have got wind of what was up, and sent word to him. 'Cause, when they went to hunt for him in Boston, he'd gone, skipped, cut stick. And they ain't seen him since. He was afraid of bein' took up for bigamist, you see—for bein' a bigamy, I mean. Well, you know what I'm tryin' to say. Anyhow, if it hadn't been for me and Phœbe——"

"*You* and Phœbe!" snorted Asaph. "You had a whole lot to do with it, didn't you? You and Aunt Debby 'll do to go together. I understand she's cruisin' round makin' proclamations that *she* was responsible for the whole thing. No, sir-ree! it's Phœbe Dawes that the credit belongs to, and this town ain't done nothin' but praise her since it come out. You never see such a quick come-about in your life—unless 'twas Heman's. But you knew all this afore, Whit. Peabody must have told you."

Captain Cy had listened to his friends' story with a face expressive of the most blank astonishment. As he learned of the trip to Trumet and its results, his eyes and mouth opened, and he repeatedly rubbed his forehead and muttered exclamations. Now, at the mention of his lawyer's name, he seemed to awaken.

"Hold on!" he interrupted, waving his hand. "Hold on! By the big dipper! this is—is— Where *is* Peabody? I want to see him."

"Here I am, captain," said the attorney. He had been out to the barn to superintend the stabling of the span, but for the past five minutes had been standing, unnoticed by his client, on the threshold of the dining room.

"See here," demanded Captain Cy, "see here,

Peabody; is this yarn true? *Is* it, now? this about
—about Phœbe and all?"

"Certainly it's true. I supposed you knew it.
You didn't seem surprised when I told you the case
was settled."

"Surprised? Why, no! I thought Heman had—
Never mind that. Land of love! *She* did it.
She!"

He sat weakly down. The lawyer looked anxious.

"Mr. Tidditt," he whispered, "I think perhaps
he had better be left alone for the present. He's
just up from a sick bed, and this has been a trying
forenoon. Come in again this afternoon. I shall
try to persuade him to take a nap."

The Board of Strategy, its curiosity unsatisfied,
departed reluctantly. When Mr. Peabody returned
to the sitting room he found that naps were far, indeed, from the captain's thoughts. The latter was
pacing the sitting-room floor.

"Where is she?" he demanded. "She was standin' on the steps with Heman. Have you seen her
since?"

His friend was troubled.

"Why, yes, I've seen her," he said. "I have
been talking with her. She has gone away."

"Gone *away!* Where? What do you mean?
She ain't—ain't left Bayport?"

"No, no. What in the world should she leave
Bayport for? She has gone to her boarding house,

I guess; at all events, she was headed in that direction."

"Why didn't she shake hands with me? What made her go off and not say a word? Oh, well, I guess likely I know the why!" He sighed despondently. "I told her never to come here again."

"You did? What in the world——"

"Well, for what I thought was good reasons; all on her account they was. And yet she did come back, and kept comin', even after Ase blabbed the whole thing. However, I s'pose that was just to help Georgianna. Oh, hum! I *am* an old fool."

The lawyer inspected him seriously.

"Well, captain," he said slowly, "if it is any comfort for you to know that your reason isn't the correct one for Miss Dawes's going away, I can assure you on that point. I think she went because she was greatly disappointed, and didn't wish to see you just now."

"Disappointed? What do you mean?"

"Humph! I didn't mean to tell you yet, but I judge that I'd better. No one knows it here but Miss Dawes and I, and probably no one but us three need ever know it. You see, the fact is that the Arizona woman, Desire Higgins, isn't Mrs. Thomas at all. He isn't her missing husband."

"What?"

"Yes, it's so. Really, it was too much of a coincidence to be possible, and yet it certainly did seem that it would prove true. This Higgins woman was, apparently, so anxious to find her missing man that she was ready to recognize almost any description; and the slight lameness and the fact of his having been in Montana helped along. If we could have gotten a photograph sooner, the question would have been settled. Only last week, while I was in Boston, I got word from the detective agency that a photo had been received. I went to see it immediately. There was some resemblance, but not enough. Henry Thomas was never Mr. Higgins."

"But—but—they say Thomas has skipped out."

"Yes, he has. That's the queer part of it. At the place where he boarded we learned that he got a letter from Arizona—trust the average landlady to look at postmarks—that he seemed greatly agitated all that day, and left that night. No one has seen him since. Why he went is a puzzle. Where, we don't care. So long as he keeps out of our way, that's enough."

Captain Cy did not care, either. He surmised that Mr. Atkins might probably explain the disappearance. And yet, oddly enough, this explanation was not the true one. The Honorable Heman solemnly assured the captain that he had not communicated with Emily's father. He intended to do so, as a part of the compact agreed upon at the hotel, but the man had fled. And the mystery is still unsolved. The supposition is that there really was a wife somewhere in the West. Who or where she was no Bayporter knows. Henry Thomas has never come back to explain.

"I told Miss Dawes of the photograph and what it proved," went on Peabody. "She was dreadfully disappointed. She could hardly speak when she left me. I urged her to come in and see you, but she wouldn't. Evidently she had set her heart on helping you and the child. It is too bad, because, practically speaking, we owe everything to her. There is little doubt that the inquiry set on foot by her scared the Thomas fellow into flight. And she has worked night and day to aid us. She is a very clever woman, Captain Whittaker, and a good one. You can't thank her enough. Here! what are you about?"

Captain Cy strode past him into the dining room. The hat rack hung on the wall by the side door. He snatched his cap from the peg, and was struggling into his overcoat.

"Where are you going?" demanded the lawyer. "You mustn't attempt to walk now. You need rest."

"Rest! I'll rest by and by. Just now I've got business to attend to. Let go of that pea-jacket."

"But——"

"No buts about it. I'll see you later. So long."

He threw open the door and hurried down the walk. The lawyer watched him in amazement. Then a slow smile overspread his face.

"Captain," he called. "Captain Whittaker."

Captain Cy looked back over his shoulder. "What do you want?" he asked.

Mr. Peabody's face was now intensely solemn, but there was a twinkle in his eye.

"I think she's at the boarding house," he said demurely. "I'm pretty certain you'll find her there."

All the regulars at the perfect boarding house had, of course, attended the reception at the Cy Whittaker place. None of them, with the exception of the schoolmistress, had as yet returned. Dinner had been forgotten in the excitement of the great day, and Keturah and Angeline and Mrs. Tripp had stopped in at various dwellings along the main road, to compare notes on the captain's appearance and the Atkins address. Asaph and Bailey and Alpheus Smalley were at Simmons's.

Captain Cy knew better than to attempt his hurried trip by way of the road. He had no desire to be held up and congratulated. He went across lots, in the rear of barns and orchards, wading through drifts and climbing fences as no sane convalescent should. But the captain at that moment was suffering from the form of insanity known as the fixed idea. She had done all this for him—for *him*. And his last message to her had been an insult.

He approached the Bangs property by the stable lane. No one locks doors in our village, and those

"'I don't think I'd ought to let you shake hands with me,
Phoebe.'"

of the perfect boarding house were unfastened. He entered by way of the side porch, just as he had done when Gabe Lumley's depot wagon first deposited him in that yard. But now he entered on tiptoe. The dining room was empty. He peeped into the sitting room. There, by the center table, sat Phœbe Dawes, her elbow on the arm of her chair, and her head resting on her hand.

"Ahem! Phœbe!" said Captain Cy.

She started, turned, and saw him standing there. Her eyes were wet, and there was a handkerchief in her lap.

"Phœbe," said the captain anxiously, "have you been cryin'?"

She rose on the instant. A great wave of red swept over her face. The handkerchief fell to the floor, and she stooped and picked it up.

"Crying?" she repeated confusedly. "Why, no, of course—of course not! I—How do you do, Captain Whittaker? I'm—we're all very glad to see you home again—and well."

She extended her hand. Captain Cy reached forward to take it; then he hesitated.

"I don't think I'd ought to let you shake hands with me, Phœbe," he said. "Not until I beg your pardon."

"Beg my pardon? Why?"

He absently took the hand and held it.

"For the word I sent to you when I went away.

397

'Twas an awful thing to say, but I meant it for your sake, you know. Honest, I did."

She laughed nervously.

"Oh! that," she said. "Well, I did think you were rather particular as to your visitors. But Mr. Tidditt explained, and then— You needn't beg my pardon. I appreciate your thoughtfulness. I knew you meant to be kind to me."

"That's what I did. But you didn't obey orders. You kept comin'. Now, why——"

"Why? Did you suppose that *I* cared for the malicious gossip of—such people? I came because you were in trouble, and I hoped to help you. And —and I thought I had helped, until a few minutes ago."

Her lip quivered. That quiver went to the captain's heart.

"Helped?" he faltered. "Helped? Why, you've done so much that I can't ever thank you. You've been the only real helper I've had in all this miserable business. You've stood by me all through."

"But it was all wrong. He isn't the man at all. Didn't Mr. Peabody tell you?"

"Yes, yes, he told me. What difference does that make? Peabody be hanged! He ain't in this. It's you and me—don't you see? What made you do all this for me?"

She looked at the floor and not at him as she answered.

398

## CAPTAIN CY'S "PICTURE"

"Why, because I wanted to help you," she said.
"I've been alone in the world ever since mother died,
years ago. I've had few real friends. Your friendship had come to mean a great deal to me. The
splendid fight you were making for that little girl
proved what a man you were. And you fought so
bravely when almost everyone was against you, I
couldn't help wanting to do something for you.
How could I? And now it has come to nothing—
my part of it. I'm so sorry."

"It ain't, neither. It's come to everything.
Phœbe, I didn't mean to say very much more than
to beg your pardon when I headed for here. But
I've got to—I've simply got to. This can't go
on. I can't have you keep comin' to see me—and
Bos'n. I can't keep meetin' you every day. I
*can't.*"

She looked up, as if to speak, but something, possibly the expression in his face, caused her to look
quickly down again. She did not answer.

"I can't do it," continued the captain desperately. "'Tain't for what folks might say. They
wouldn't say much when I was around, I tell you. It
ain't that. It's because I can't bear to have you
just a friend. Either you must be more'n that, or—
or I'll have to go somewheres else. I realized that
when I was in Washin'ton and cruisin' to California
and back. I've either got to take Bos'n and go
away for good, or—or——"

She would not help him. She would not speak.

"You see?" he groaned. "You see, Phœbe, what an old fool I am. I can't ask you to marry me, me fifty-five, and rough from knockin' round the world, and you, young and educated, and a lady. I ain't fool enough to ask such a thing as that. And yet, I couldn't stay here and meet you every day, and by and by see you marry somebody else. By the big dipper, I couldn't do it! So that's why I can't shake hands with you to-day—nor any more, except when I say good-by for keeps."

Then she looked up. The color was still bright in her face, and her eyes were moist, but she was smiling.

"Can't shake hands with me?" she said. "Please, what have you been doing for the last five minutes?"

Captain Cy dropped her hand as if his own had been struck with paralysis.

"Good land!" he stammered. "I didn't know I did it; honest truth, I didn't."

Phœbe's smile was still there, faint, but very sweet.

"Why did you stop?" she queried. "I didn't ask you to."

"Why did I stop? Why, because I—I—I declare I'm ashamed——"

She took his hand and clasped it with both her own.

"I'm not," she said bravely, her eyes brightening

as the wonder and incredulous joy grew in his. "I'm very proud. And very, very happy."

There was to be a big supper at the Cy Whittaker place that night. It was an impromptu affair, arranged on the spur of the moment by Captain Cy, who, in spite of the lawyer's protests and anxiety concerning his health, went serenely up and down the main road, inviting everybody he met or could think of. The captain's face was as radiant as a spring sunrise. His smile, as Asaph said, " pretty nigh cut the upper half of his head off." People who had other engagements, and would, under ordinary circumstances, have refused the invitation, couldn't say no to his hearty, " Can't come? Course you'll come! Man alive! I *want* you."

"Invalid, is he?" observed Josiah Dimick, after receiving and accepting his own invitation. "Well, I wish to thunder I could be took down with the same kind of disease. I'd be willin' to linger along with it quite a spell if it pumped me as full of joy as Whit seems to be. Don't give laughin' gas to keep off pneumonia, do they? No? Well, I'd like to know the name of his medicine, that's all."

Supper was to be ready at six. Georgianna, assisted by Keturah Bangs, Mrs. Sylvanus Cahoon, and other volunteers, was gloriously busy in the kitchen. The table in the dining room reached from one end of the big apartment to the other. Guests would begin to arrive shortly. Wily Mr. Peabody, guessing that Captain Cy might prefer to be alone, had taken the Board of Strategy out riding behind the span.

In the sitting room, around the baseburner stove, were three persons—Captain Cy, Bos'n, and Phœbe. Miss Dawes had " come early," at the captain's urgent appeal. Now she was sitting in the rocker, at one side of the stove, gazing dreamily at the ruddy light behind the isinglass panes. She looked quietly, blissfully contented and happy. At her feet, on the braided mat, sat Bos'n, playing with Lonesome, who purred lazily. The little girl was happy, too, for was not her beloved Uncle Cyrus at home again, with all danger of their separation ended forever-more?

As for Captain Cy himself, the radiant expression was still on his face, brighter than ever. He looked across at Phœbe, who smiled back at him. Then he glanced down at Bos'n. And all at once he realized that this was the fulfillment of his dream. Here was his " picture "; the sitting room was now as he had always loved to think of it—as it used to be. He was in his father's chair, Phœbe in the one his mother used to occupy, and between them—just where he had sat so often when a boy—the child. The Cy Whittaker place had again, and at last, come into its own.

He drew a long breath, and looked about the

room; at the stove, the lamp, the old, familiar furniture, at his grandfather's portrait over the mantel. Then, in a flash of memory, his father's words came back to him, and he said, laughing aloud from pure happiness:

"Bos'n, run down cellar and get me a pitcher of cider, won't you?—there's a good feller."

**THE END**